THE WORLD'S CLASSICS

JACK LONDON

The Sea

Edited with an Introduction by
JOHN SUTHERLAND

Oxford   New York
OXFORD UNIVERSITY PRESS

Oxford University Press, Walton Street, Oxford OX2 6DP

Oxford New York Toronto
Delhi Bombay Calcutta Madras Karachi
Kuala Lumpur Singapore Hong Kong Tokyo
Nairobi Dar es Salaam Cape Town
Melbourne Auckland Madrid

and associated companies in
Berlin Ibadan

Oxford is a trade mark of Oxford University Press

Editorial matter © John Sutherland 1992

The Sea-Wolf first published 1904
First issued as a World's Classics paperback 1992

British Library Cataloguing in Publication Data
Data available

Library of Congress Cataloging in Publication Data
London, Jack, 1876–1916.
The Sea-Wolf / Jack London: edited with an introduction by
John Sutherland.
p.   cm. – (The World's classics)
Includes bibliographical references (p.
First published 1904. – T.p. verso.
Bibliography: p.
I. Sutherland, John, 1938-   .   II. Title.   III. Series.
PS3523.O4655   1992   91–45705
ISBN 0-19-282931-9

3 5 7 9 10 8 6 4

Printed in Great Britain by
BPC Paperbacks Ltd
Aylesbury, Bucks

CONTENTS

CONTENTS

thing than he lets on in his autobiographical accounts. Even if the life of a professional sailor was not to be his main "adventure path" through life, Jack never outgrew his passion for the romance of the sea. His library abounded with volumes of sea travel, manuals of seaman-

INTRODUCTION

IN June 1894 Jack London, then an 18-year-old hobo, was arrested near Niagara Falls on a charge of vagrancy. He gave his occupation to the authorities as "sailor". Twenty years later, now a wealthy rancher, London had as one of his many current projects an autobiography to be called "Sailor on Horseback". Few men have packed so much living into such a short lifetime—just thirty-nine years. Jack London was, at different times, factory worker, oyster pirate, coastguard, politician, bum, gold prospector, farmer, and (by some assessments) the best-selling author in America. But the core of himself he always took to be "Jack London, sailor". It was in his transactions with the sea that he was most himself.

Given the tang of brine that plays over his life it is a surprise to discover that London's experiences as a deep-sea sailor were limited. In 1893, at the age of seventeen, he enlisted as an able-bodied seaman and boat-puller on a sealing vessel, the *Sophia Sutherland*, a three-masted schooner. The subsequent voyage to the north Pacific, which lasted seven months, directly inspired *The Sea-Wolf* (1904). Once he returned to San Francisco, Jack effectively ran away to land. He gave up the sea and went to work in a jute mill for a wretched ten cents an hour. The reason he gives in his "alcoholic memoirs", *John Barleycorn*, is that his family—more particularly his mother—wanted him to do something less perilous. (Casualties among the sealing fleet were fearsomely high.) Jack had fallen seriously ill with shingles on the return voyage. He was, it tran-spired, something less than able-bodied. Some biographers surmise that his rough and ready fellow sailors may have given the young man (scarcely more than a boy) a harder time than he lets on in his autobiographical accounts.[1]

Even if the life of a professional sailor was not to be
his main "adventure path" through life, Jack never outgrew his passion for messing about in boats. His library
abounded with volumes of sea travel, manuals of seamanship, and navigational aids. Since buying a skiff at the
age of fourteen, he had loved to sail along the northern
California coast, in the maze of waterways that form the
San Francisco Bay system. Just before writing *The Sea-
Wolf* he had bought himself a 30-foot sloop, the *Spray*,
with part of the $2,000 Macmillan paid for the copyright
of *The Call of the Wild* in 1902. It was partly on the *Spray*,
and while enthusiastically fitting the craft out, that he
wrote *The Sea-Wolf*. (With some heroic exaggeration, his
efforts are projected on to Humphrey Van Weyden's single-
handed remasting of the *Ghost*, which makes up the last
third of the novel.)

The *Spray* had a cabin which could sleep two, and a
galley. But for all Jack's pride of ownership it was a coastal
craft, a hobby-boat—a newly rich man's toy. In 1906, two
years after publishing *The Sea-Wolf*—and still basking in
the wealth and fame it brought him—Jack built himself
a proper ocean-going yacht, the *Snark*. His intention was
to sail around the world with his new wife, Charmian (in
heroic emulation of Humphrey and Maud's solo voyage
from Endeavor Island to Japan, at the end of *The Sea-
Wolf*). The voyage, which lasted from April 1907 to summer 1909, was a disaster. Jack was eventually invalided
back by tramp steamer from Australia, at death's door
from a variety of tropical illnesses. Given the press attention which the enterprise had attracted it was something
of a humiliation for him.

Jack's last deep-sea voyage took place in 1912. He and
Charmian enlisted as crew on a four-masted barque, the

---

[1] See Appendix 1 "Jack London and the *Sophia Sutherland*."

Dirigo, and made a five-month trip around Cape Horn. In
reality the Londons were passengers—their sailor status
was a ruse to circumvent marine regulations. Jack's main
personal motive in embarking on the ship was to recover
his precarious health and refresh his writing energies. Although it was enjoyable, the *Dirigo* voyage did not, in fact,
much help. Four years later he was dead.

Despite the mystique with which he invested it, Jack
London's career as an ocean-going sailor was neither
extensive nor glorious. "Jack London, sailor" is a lot
less impressive than "Jack London, writer", or "Jack
London, socialist", or even "Jack London, rancher".[2]
Although Humphrey Van Weyden and Maud Brewster
discover their latent strength of body and spirit at sea—
and attain a bounding good health from the hardships they
endure—Jack's most ambitious voyages were all attended
by disabling sickness and a degree of disappointment.
Here, as elsewhere (his experiences as a miner in the
Yukon, for instance), one has to separate myth and fact in
the London biography. None the less, it is clear that the
open sea was a vital element in Jack's version of himself.
His experiences at sea—particularly his seven months
on the *Sophia Sutherland*—were a theatre in which he
could picture himself melodramatically combatting the
extremities of life. Here, as in the frozen snows of the
north, was where civilization ended and a man might
discover his kinship with the wolf, that animal which is
social, uxorious, yet ruthlessly savage. It was the wolf (and
the caveman) that London took to be the perfect analogue
of the human being living at his fullest.

Jack London's seven months at sea in 1893 played a
critical part in forming his politics. Despite striking physical similarities, the *Sophia Sutherland* was nothing like

[2] London's "Valley of the Moon" estate in northern California survives as a State Historic Park, and as a winery still in
the ownership of the author's descendants.

the "hell ship", the *Ghost*. Nor was its superannuated
and eminently respectable master, Captain Sutherland, at
all like the "Blond Beast", Wolf Larsen. None the less
Jack's experiences on the *Sophia Sutherland* were both
shocking and educative. It was in the north Pacific that he
learned the nature of exploitation—a necessary lesson for
any socialist. The ruthless harvesting of gravid seals at the
end of the nineteenth century was the ecological equivalent
of a gold rush. It virtually exterminated a species. Between
1886 and 1911 the northern Pacific fur seals went the same
way as the American passenger pigeon and the bison. The
herd was reduced from some two million to a few thousand. And for what? Because seal fur (like ostrich feathers
and whalebone stays) was temporarily fashionable with
middle-class women in Europe—a fad for which they were
willing to pay high prices. Sailors like the 17-year-old Jack
London lived "an obscure and sordid existence", and risked
their lives (one of his best friends on the *Sophia Sutherland*
died on his next voyage) for some $40 a month and board.
The most horrifying scenes in *The Sea-Wolf* are not those
describing Wolf Larsen's psychopathic violence, but the
very business-like paragraphs in Chapter 17 describing the
skinning of the seals, many of them pregnant, who have
been shotgunned or clubbed to death ("humane" killing
with a rifle would cause them to sink before they could be
dragged on board):

It was wanton slaughter, and all for woman's sake. No man
ate of the seal meat or the oil. After a good day's killing I
have seen our decks covered with hides and bodies, slippery
with fat and blood, the scuppers running red; masts, ropes,
and rails spattered with the sanguinary color; and the men,
like butchers, plying their trade, naked and red of arm and
hand, hard at work with ripping and flensing-knives, removing
the skins from the pretty sea-creatures they had killed.

London had nothing against hunting, whether for sport,
for the table, or even for a working man's livelihood.

Humphrey and Maud are fully justified in killing seals
on Endeavor Island to furnish themselves with shelter
from the elements, oil for lighting, and meat for the long
winter ahead of them. But what was happening with the
pelagic hunting fleets in the 1890s and early 1900s was the
wholesale extermination of a species (and a lot of seamen
as well) "for the satisfaction of woman's vanity and love
of decoration".

The writing of *The Sea-Wolf* occurs at a significant juncture in Jack London's life and career. He was 27 years
old and had "made" himself against all the odds. He had
been born with no social advantages. His childhood was
chronically deprived, nor did it seem that he was destined
for anything other than a life of petty crime and probable
early death. His first sixteen years were singularly inauspi-
cious. As he approached 17 and the crisis of his adolescence
Jack evidently touched bottom. He was drinking heavily
and living among the rascals who inhabited the Benicia
wharves. After one particularly drunken evening he fell
into the Bay, and allowed himself to be swept out to what
he expected would be certain death. He wanted to die—or
at least had no overwhelming interest in living any more.
But after four hours in the water, he was picked up by
Greek fishermen. He would, after all, live. (This brush
with watery death clearly inspires the opening scenes of
The Sea-Wolf.) Soon after, on the morning of 23 January
1893 (the same day that Humphrey Van Weyden is fished
out from San Francisco Bay by the *Ghost*), Jack embarked
as a sailor on the sealer *Sophia Sutherland*. He was a few
days past the legal age of 17.

On his return from the northern seas in August Jack
published his first piece of writing, for a competition in
the *San Francisco Morning Call*. Entitled "Typhoon off
the Coast of Japan" it described an exciting episode on
the *Sophia Sutherland*. (London uses it again in Chapter
17 of *The Sea-Wolf*.) But he was not yet ready for full-

time authorship. He tried another spell of dollar-a-day factory work and loathed it. The industrial depression was at its height (it was now April 1894) and he joined Jacob Coxey's "army of the unemployed" in its protest march on Washington. Halfway across the country Jack—who was never one to be regimented—deserted and took off on his own, as a hobo. (His experiences were later written up in *The Road*, 1907.) On his return to California, in 1895, Jack returned to high school, and became a card-carrying socialist. He went on to attend the University of California at Berkeley for a semester before dropping out in 1897 to join the Klondike gold rush. He returned in July 1898— with some $4 worth of gold dust and a million dollars' worth of ideas. He settled down to writing for his living. His stories and books were increasingly successful and his fourth book—*The Call of the Wild* (1903)—outstandingly so.

It was in this context—the success of *The Call of the Wild*—that Jack London embarked on *The Sea-Wolf* in spring 1903. He had made it. The sky was the limit. But success, welcome as it certainly was, had its uneasy aspect. The still-young man evidently feared that as "Jack London, author" he was in danger of losing the manhood which he had laboriously earned by sweat, danger, and struggle. It is clear from various remarks he made that Jack identified both with Wolf Larsen, the male "brute", and with "Sissy" Van Weyden, the sexless and bloodless "scholar and a dilettante". *The Sea-Wolf* dramatizes Jack London's fear that, like Humphrey, he might with literary fame turn into a "bookworm". He might end up like the literary grandee Charley Furuseth "lounging in a dressing gown on the be-pillowed window couch and delivering himself of oracular and pessimistic epigrams". Furuseth— who never appears but is frequently mentioned—is apparently an amalgam of the professional cynic Ambrose Bierce, Jack's poetic friend George Sterling, and others

of "The Crowd": a set of bohemian *littérateurs* that Jack
had fallen in with in San Francisco. He was both attracted
by their sophistication and disgusted by their effeteness.
Literary success might, Jack London feared, spoil him by
robbing him of his hard-won masculinity. How to be a man
of letters *and* a man of action? That is the question posed
by *The Sea-Wolf*.

The answer is given in the progress of the bookworm
hero-narrator, Humphrey. *The Sea-Wolf* is an allegory of
manhood discovered first as crude, reflexive instinct for
survival, then as a set of manly skills, finally as tran-
scendent heroism. The novel opens brilliantly, with one
of the finest scenes in Jack London's work—the fog-bound
ferry boat *Martinez* hooting its way across the Bay, in an
atmosphere shrouded in gloomy foreboding. The exactly
middle-aged man of letters (Jack London himself had considerably less than Humphrey's Dantean 35 years in 1903)
is pleased with himself—more particularly he is pleased
with his literary reputation and power. He idly observes
one of his fellow passengers, a man with no legs who walks
on artificial limbs. Humphrey Van Weyden does not as yet
perceive the allegory in this. Later, in one of their painful
tutorials on the meaning of life, Wolf Larsen will tell him:
"You stand on dead men's legs. You've never had any of
your own. You couldn't walk alone between two sunrises
and hustle the meat for your belly for three meals." As
the story progresses, Humphrey will gradually get his "sea
legs". And in a metaphorical sense, he will learn how to
stand on his own two feet. (Wolf Larsen congratulates him
on this achievement, in their last epic struggle on Endeavor
Island).

During Humphrey's complacent reverie the *Martinez*
collides with another vessel, is holed, and rapidly sinks.
So "civilized" is Humphrey that at first he simply watches
the spectacle as a disinterested observer. It surely cannot
affect *him*—the "Dean of American Letters the Second"?

Why are these women squealing like "pigs"? He is too
refined even to struggle for his life—at least initially. (He
reacts rather more energetically when he feels the sting
of the cold Bay water). At the point of drowning, that
mystical moment when the whole of one's life is supposed
to flash in front of the eyes, Humphrey is plucked from his
doom by a god-like Larsen. As Humphrey drifts into final
oblivion and certain death, the *Ghost* sweeps silently past
(it is sail driven—unlike the noisy steam-powered vessels
which collided). Humphrey glimpses a man on the boat's
bridge, "who seemed to be doing little else than smoke a
cigar. I saw the smoke issuing from his lips as he slowly
turned his head and glanced out over the water in my
direction. It was a careless, unpremeditated glance . . .
His face wore an absent expression, as if of deep thought,
and I became afraid that if his eyes did light upon me he
would nevertheless not see me."

Wolf Larsen nevertheless does "see" Humphrey and
brings the *Ghost* about to save the nearly drowned man.
Why? As later events in the story show, Larsen is quite
capable of watching people drown—indeed the spectacle
rather pleases him. Why, having saved Humphrey, does
he spurn the $1,000 which the rich author offers to be
allowed to board a passing pilot boat? It would only delay
Larsen a minute or two and the sum far exceeds any
possible value he can extract from an effete landlubber.
Wolf Larsen's only explanation for first saving Humphrey
and then kidnapping him is that it is his humour, or
"whim". The story implies it is the two men's destiny
to come together, to struggle, and finally—in a mystical
way—to join in one body, "Wolf Van Weyden"—the "Sea
Wolf" of the title as we finally understand.

Once hauled to the deck of the *Ghost*, Humphrey is
brought round from an ecstatic vision of nirvana, to a
world of pain and humiliation. He is reborn like a baby,
naked and slapped into breathing again by the horny

hands of the Swede, Johnson. Under protest, Humphrey
is promptly pressed into service as cabin boy and cook's
assistant. Not only are these the lowest positions in the
crew, they mark Humphrey as something less than a man.
He—at 35—will do boy's work, and woman's work. He is
given the sexually suggestive nickname "Hump". (Luckily,
his new ship-mates do not know that his literary friends
call him "Sissy Van Weyden". It is, of course, 1893 and
the cult of Oscar is still strong in literary circles.) Later,
on Endeavor Island, Maud Brewster "demands" to do the
cooking, and with her sweet little "boy's cap" does the
menial tasks (making beds, serving meals, emptying slop)
that Hump is obliged to carry out for the "men" as cabin
boy on the *Ghost*. It is natural that she should do it,
unnatural for him.

London is careful to insist that Humphrey is no "in-
vert". He has simply let his manly powers fall into disuse:
"The doctors had always said that I had a remarkable
constitution, but I had never developed it or my body
through exercise. My muscles were small and soft, like a
woman's, or so the doctors had said time and again in
the course of their attempts to persuade me to go in for
physical-culture fads." This may well be so. But there is
none the less something at least latently homosexual in
Humphrey's relationship with Wolf Larsen, particularly
in the middle stages of his new life on board the *Ghost*,
when he has to carry out a variety of personal services
for the captain. On first sight Humphrey was, if anything,
repelled by Wolf Larsen's physique which he dismissively
described as being "of the enlarged gorilla order". Re-
pulsion gradually changes into something less clear cut.
A number of commentators have drawn attention to the
scene in which Humphrey tends Larsen, after the captain
has been wounded while putting down the mutinous scum
of the *Ghost*'s forecastle. In the privacy of his cabin, Wolf
strips. It is the first time Humphrey has seen him naked:

The sight of his body quite took my breath away . . . I was
fascinated by the perfect lines of Wolf Larsen's figure, and by
what I may term the terrible beauty of it. I had noted the
men in the forecastle. Powerfully muscled though some of them
were, there had been something wrong with all of them, an
insufficient development here, an undue development there, a
twist or a crook that destroyed symmetry, legs too short or too
long, or too much sinew or bone exposed, or too little. . . .
But Wolf Larsen was the man-type, the masculine, and almost
a god in his perfectness. As he moved about or raised his arms
the great muscles leapt and moved under the satiny skin. I
have forgotten to say that the bronze ended with his face. His
body, thanks to his Scandinavian stock, was fair as the fairest
woman's. I remember his putting his hand up to feel of the
wound on his head, and my watching the biceps move like a
living thing under its white sheath.

Observing Humphrey's admiration, Wolf Larsen invites
Humphrey to "feel them" (i.e., his arm muscles). They
are flexed "hard as iron" under Humphrey's fingers. One
of the early discarded titles for *The Sea-Wolf* was "The
Triumph of the Spirit". Humphrey has recently been
reading Nietzsche, and his remarks here recall the eulogy
of the "Blond Beast" in *A Genealogy of Morals*. With
these echoes in mind, it is tempting to blend the image
of Larsen's "satiny" white musculature with that of Leni
Riefenstahl's fascist–erotic discus thrower in the opening
frames of *Triumph of the Will*.

There are other provocatively sexual aspects in the two
men's relationship. Take, for instance, Wolf's appointing
Hump his "mate". Hump desperately does not want the
promotion, even if it will mean his being called "sir" and
"Mr Van Weyden" again. "I won't be mate on this hell-
ship", Humphrey cries, "defiantly". But then he "weakly"
submits, when he sees the "merciless glitter" in Larsen's
eyes. "Mate" is, of course, a highly loaded word in the Jack
London lexicon. This is the term Humphrey will use later
on, to describe his consummated relationship with Maud
Brewster: "Truly she was my woman, my mate-woman,

fighting with me [i.e. on my side] and for me as the mate of a caveman would have fought." In the scene that prompts this reflection Maud Brewster shows herself willing to club the semi-paralysed Wolf as he attempts to hug Humphrey to death (itself an interestingly sexual form of murder). It is a climactic moment. Maud and Humphrey embrace for the first time, a hug of life not death. Wolf Larsen's mate has found a mate of his own.

Wolf Larsen is a fascinating paradox. He is a murderer, a rapist, a ravager of the marine environment. But in all his crimes Wolf Larsen is motivated less by psychopathic sadism, revenge, or greed, than by pure philosophy. He is not even angry at the world he destroys and plunders. His features, as a wondering Humphrey observes, display "no evil stamp. There seemed nothing vicious in them. True, there were lines, but they were lines of decision and firmness. It seemed, rather, a frank and open countenance." There is no question but that Wolf Larsen is a mouthpiece for Jack London—or at least a part of Jack London. Echoes of the Wolfish philosophy can be found word-forword in the novelist's letters of the period. Two years after finishing *The Sea Wolf* Jack London told his friend Caroline Sterling, "You will remember . . . the black moods that used to come upon me at that time [i.e., 1903] and the black philosophy that I worked out at that time, and afterwards put into Wolf Larsen's mouth."[3]

In fact, Wolf Larsen's philosophy is less "worked out" than cobbled together from Jack's current reading. Nietzsche and Schopenhauer—names prominently dropped in the second sentence of *The Sea-Wolf*—were recent finds. London noted, although he did not entirely swallow, their pessimism, and their misogyny ("Always take a stick when you talk to a woman"). Other parts of the Germans' phi-

[3] *The Letters of Jack London*, ed. Earle Labor, Robert C. Leitz III, and I. Milo Shepard (Stanford: Stanford University Press, 1988), I, 520.

losophy were more to his taste. In the crisis of the typhoon, Wolf is pictured as a Nietzschean superman, opposing his "will" against the elements, and conquering. There is, of course, a strong element of Darwin in Wolf's philosophy. *The Origin of Species* is the subject of one of the debates between Larsen and Humphrey (in Chapter 6). Both men are Darwinists, but of a different stamp. Wolf has been steeped in the thinking of Ernest Haeckel—a now forgotten philosopher whose *Riddle of the Universe* made a huge impression on Jack London when he read it in 1901. Haeckel inspired Wolf's "materialistic monism", his conviction that human history is merely "an eternity of piggishness". The truth of existence (what Haeckel called "the law of substance") is invariably to be found in life's lowest forms or "monera" (i.e., the "yeast" about which Larsen goes on rather tiresomely). Wolf's arguments reflect a strand in Jack's own thinking. On 6 January 1902, for instance, he declared to Cloudesley Johns: "But after all, what squirming, anywhere, damned or otherwise, means anything? That's the question I am always prone to put: What's this chemical ferment called life all about? . . . I have at last discovered what I am. I am a materialistic monist." (*Letters*, I, 270. See Wolf Larsen's nearly identical comments on page 61 of *The Sea-Wolf*.)

For his part, Humphrey Van Weyden espouses a different brand of Darwinism. He is a disciple of the popularizer of Darwin, Herbert Spencer. Spencer's optimistic "Social-Darwinism"—the theory that unbridled competition will produce desirable social progress—is pitted against Wolf Larsen's more tragic vision of the survival of the fittest individual, that is to say the cruellest. Similarly Spencer's opinion that altruism was a necessary component in social evolution is pitted against Larsen's ruthless creed of egoism. In less pessimistic periods than 1903 (when Jack's domestic world was crashing round his ears) Spencer was probably the stronger influence on his thinking. To this extent the doctrines of Wolf Larsen represent an aberration in the current of his thought. This aberrant pessimism was to reach a climax in 1904, in the period that Jack called his "long sickness"—the depression precipitated by the break-up of his marriage.

It is significant that Wolf Larsen is by birth a Dane. Hamlet, we are told, is his favourite literary character, and Wolf's everlasting query "as to what it was all about" aligns him strongly with the Prince of Denmark. Several times Wolf seems to echo Hamlet's misanthropic "What a piece of work is man. . . . " But oddly Wolf never reverts—even in the final throes of his illness—to his native language. He dies in English. (His last word, painfully spelled out with his left hand, is "BOSH".)

The most troubling aspect of Wolf Larsen's philosophy for modern readers is its racism. Living when he did, Jack London had no qualms about anatomizing the crew of the *Ghost* in starkly ethnic terms. There is, for instance, the wholly odious cockney Thomas Mugridge. Jack spent six weeks in the East End of London in summer 1902, undertaking research for his book *The People of the Abyss*. ("Thomas Mugridge" was the name of a Cockney he met who was, in fact, rather more amiable than the cook on the *Ghost*.) Jack felt considerable sympathy and class solidarity with the working-class Londoners but his analysis was that they had become hopelessly degenerate. As Anglo-Saxons, they were bred out. Mugridge compares badly with the ox-like Scandinavian-American, Johnson, or the "Kanaka" (i.e. Hawaiian) Oofty-Oofty, with his "almost feminine" physical beauty. The Nova-Scotian Irish Celt, Louis (based closely on one of London's ship-mates on the *Sophia Sutherland*) is fat, lazy, and gifted with second sight. Most admirable of the men is the Irish-American George Leach. Humphrey himself is "of Puritan ancestry"—*Mayflower* stock, a WASP. And presiding over the whole racial mixture is Wolf Larsen, the "Blond Beast". Which of the two—Humphrey or Wolf Larsen—will make the eugenically better mate for Maud Brewster?

With the knowledge of where London's sub-Nietzschean Aryanism would lead in the later twentieth century it is painful to read rhapsodies like the following in Chapter 10 on Wolf's racial glamour:

He is oppressed by the primal melancholy of the race. Knowing him, I review the old Scandinavian myths with clearer understanding. The white-skinned, fair-haired savages who created that terrible pantheon were of the same fibre as he. The frivolity of the Latins is no part of him. When he laughs it is from humor that is nothing else than ferocious. But he laughs rarely. He is too often sad. And it is a sadness as deep-reaching as the roots of the race.

In 1903, as London was writing *The Sea-Wolf*, the eugenics and race debate in America had narrowed on one issue: immigration. As the century turned, there had been an open-door policy. In 1902–3 immigration into the US, driven by the country's insatiable demand for labour, had risen above a million a year. Some nine million immigrants flooded into the country in the first decade of the twentieth century. Larsen would have been one of the more successful. Born in Norway, of poor Danish stock, in the late 1850s, he went to sea as a cabin boy on a Scandinavian coastal craft, aged 10. He drifted into the British merchant marine, where he picked up his flawless English, and learned his craft. At some point—presumably in the 1880s—he came to the West Coast of America, where Norwegian skippers were in great demand. In the early days of the sealing boom Larsen enriched himself—presumably in the service of a land-bound owner. With his bonuses, he bought his own vessel—the *Ghost*. He is now (in 1893) a master in his own right: an American success story. The opposition between Larsen and Van Weyden—new American and *Mayflower* American—was burningly topical, and would have resonated for contemporary readers with the interminable and irreconcilable debates about whether America was being enriched or swamped by the waves of European immigrants surging through Ellis Island.

Over the years many—perhaps most—readers have felt that *The Sea-Wolf* takes a downward turn with the arrival on the scene of Maud Brewster. That America's premier woman poet and her shrewdest critic should meet by accident, as two separate castaways, on the high seas off Japan, strains credulity well past any rational breaking point. But even this coincidence is outdone by some of the subsequent turns of plot (the abandoned *Ghost* washing up on the lovers' doorstep, for instance; or Wolf Larsen having a convenient fit of unconsciousness every time he has Humphrey or Maud at his mercy). There is, none the less, much to enjoy in the Endeavor Island chapters, if one can stomach the general incredibility of it all. The sanguinary comedy of Humphrey learning how to club seals to death (and narrowly escaping death himself at the jaws of an infuriated bull) is, for instance, one of the best pieces of slapstick London wrote.

But what impresses above all in the Endeavor Island chapters is the extraordinarily protracted and densely detailed technical description of Humphrey's stepping the masts on the foundered *Ghost*. In June 1904 London was in two minds whether to shorten this episode for the book version of *The Sea-Wolf* (some readers of the serialized issue of the novel had apparently voiced complaints.) He was right to stick to his original intention and play it out again at full length. The "stepping the mast" saga exercises the same hypnotic fascination over the reader as the protracted description of kindling in London's most famous short story, "To Build a Fire".

As he instructs himself in the arts of shipbuilding, Humphrey discovers his body and his hands (but not—

thanks to the susceptibilities of the American reading
public—his sexual organs). He becomes a physical man.
Meanwhile, with the inexorable growth of his brain tu-
mour, Wolf Larsen retreats into pure mind, voyaging like
Newton "through strange seas of Thought, alone". By
the end of *The Sea-Wolf* the two heroes have exchanged
roles. Humphrey is now *homo faber*, the doer; Wolf is the
thinker, *homo sapiens*.[4] And by the last chapter Humphrey
is master of the *Ghost*; Wolf Larsen has been consigned
as a corpse to the waves (from which Humphrey was
plucked out, a virtual corpse, nine months earlier). They
have battled, exchanged ideas, and finally changed places.
By the end of the novel the hero can effectively build
his own vessel, his own house, kill his own meat and
still pronounce expertly on literature. No more division
of labour for Humphrey Van Weyden. And what kind
of literature will the erstwhile author of "The Necessity
for Freedom: a Plea for the Artist" himself write after
his transforming experiences on the *Ghost* and Endeavor
Island? We do not directly know, but as he sails back to
Japan with the aid of Wolf Larsen's star scale we may
assume that it will be books not unlike *The Sea-Wolf*, and
that Humphrey Van Weyden will be reintroduced to his
readers as a writer not unlike Jack London.

Like *Othello*, *The Sea-Wolf* has two irreconcilable time
schemes. As Humphrey's conversation with Johansen in
Chapter 14 makes clear the primary historical setting is
1893 (see note to page 117.) References to the state of the
pelagic seal fishing industry also predicate 1893. But later
in the novel Maud and Humphrey quote from a variety
of books which were published in the period 1897–9. Pre-

---

[4] The two men have also, at the end of the narrative, become
personifications of their respective philosophies. Humphrey's
refitting the *Ghost* with the assistance of Maud is an illustration
of Spencerian "altruism" at work. The paralytic Larsen has re-
verted to the condition of one of Haeckel's protozoic "monera".

sumably the second time scheme of *The Sea* or less contemporary with the composition 1902–3.

These two settings, a decade apart, mark ̲ ̲ in London's career. In 1893 he pulled himself together ̲ ̲ the brink of dissolution and made something of his life. His going to sea affirmed that he wanted to live and that henceforth he would dedicate himself to a harder, more purifying ideal. In 1903 he was contemplating a departure no less formative. In the early part of that year (as he wrote the first part of *The Sea-Wolf*) he discovered the overwhelming extent of his love for Charmian Kittredge. In June 1903 (with half the novel still to write) he consummated his adulterous affair with her. The following month he resolved to leave his wife of three years, Bess Maddern London, and his two little daughters, and live with Charmian.

By conventional standards it was a dastardly act. Jack London was consigning three helpless females who depended on him utterly to a wretched existence. He knew that abandoning his family would invite scandal and criticism. It was in the light of this knowledge, and with his momentous decision fresh in his mind, that he wrote the Endeavor Island chapters. These chapters were conceived as an offering to Charmian. (It was she, incidentally, who marked the proofs—something that must have mystified London's publisher). Large sections are mere love letters to the woman he had suddenly discovered he must live with, whatever the cost. Passages like the opening of Chapter 34 echo with coy laughter and the cooing of the two lovers—miraculously free from the tattling tongues of society in their island idyll.

Not everyone likes this turtle-doving. Ambrose Bierce told Jack's closest friend, George Sterling, in February 1905 that "the 'love' element, with its absurd suppressions and impossible proprieties, is awful". Other commentators e been equally unkind about the lovers' separate little huts. One almost warms to Larsen's biting sarcasm on being washed up at their doorstep: "Where's Maud?—I beg your pardon, Miss Brewster—or should I say, 'Mrs Van Weyden'?" What Jack London does in this last section of *The Sea-Wolf* is to invent a wholly fantastic universe in which she is the only girl in the world and he is the only boy. In this fantasy world, all sorts of caveman and Edenic idylls can be played out. Humphrey is Tarzan, Adam, and Robinson Crusoe, all in one. Maud is Jane, Eve, and a girl Friday who does all the housework. The fact that the relationship is ostentatiously sexless (it is noted as a big thing when the lovers go so far as to use their first names with each other) may be attributed to the susceptibilities of the "American prude"—as Jack called the generic reader of the *Century* magazine. Its editor, R. W. Gilder, was comically nervous of the Endeavor Island episodes. (There is a moment of sublime absurdity in which Humphrey is actually described knocking on the door of Maud's little hut, after a chaste night in his own little hut, in which one has to wonder if Jack London is not having a private joke at his editor's expense.)

This delicacy, or timidity, may well reflect London's own nervousness about what the world would think of his adulteries when they read about them in the gutter press. Such things are always obscure. But it seems that he held off any actual sexual activity with Charmian until June 1903, well into their relationship. The holding back cannot have been easy. And all the while he was on tenterhooks lest the affair should make the newspapers. He hoped against hope that his divorce could be finalized without Charmian's name being drawn into it. At this period all that was required as "proof" of adultery was evidence that London and Charmian had shared the same room overnight. The behaviour of the lovers and their separate huts on Endeavor Island is indeed strained and unnatural. But it is no less so than the behaviour of middle-class, turn-of-the-century Americans caught in the toils of their marriage laws.

For those that want it there is plenty of sexual violence and frankness lurking in the crevices of *The Sea-Wolf*. Take, for example, the description by Louis in Chapter 6 of the Japanese ladies Wolf casually abducted on an earlier voyage:

"An' wasn't there the Governor of Kura Island, an' the Chief iv Police, Japanese gentlemen, sir, an' didn't they come aboard the *Ghost* as his guests, abringin' their wives along—wee an' pretty little bits of things like you see 'em painted on fans. An' as he was a-gettin' under way, didn't the fond husbands get left astern-like in their sampan, as it might be by accident? An' wasn't it a week later that the poor little ladies was put ashore on the other side of the island, with nothin' before 'em but to walk home acrost the mountains on their weeny-teeny little straw sandals which wouldn't hang together a mile? Don't I know? 'Tis the beast he is, this Wolf Larsen—the great big beast mentioned iv in Revelation."

There is no need to ask what Wolf Larsen and his crew did with these unfortunate women. They were raped until the men tired of them then they were thrown away as casually as fish offal. Nor is there anything particularly reticent in the description of Wolf Larsen's attempt to rape Maud in Chapter 26. And, if one digs for it, there is sexual innuendo in the lavishly phallic description of the lovers setting the *Ghost*'s mast. (The passage was written, if one cares to calculate, at exactly the time that Jack and Charmian made love for the first time.) "It's not over the hole", Maud tells Humphrey. They jiggle with the apparatus, until finally the climax is reached:

Slowly the butt descended the several intervening inches, at the same time slightly twisting again. Again Maud rectified the twist with the watch-tackle, and again she lowered away from the windlass. Square fitted into square. The mast was stepped.
  I raised a shout, and she ran down to see. In the yellow

lantern light we peered at what we had accomplished. We looked at each other, and our hands felt their way and clasped. The eyes of both of us, I think, were moist with the joy of success.

The Sea-Wolf is far from being a perfect work. It is certainly patchy: melodrama, philosophic debate, travelogue, and love story do not, finally, mix entirely smoothly. But for all its unevenness *The Sea-Wolf* has in abundance the zest, vitality, and intellectual energy that enriches Jack London's best writing. It has always been the most popular of his fictions with two-legged heroes. Although as he advanced in his career he wrote better-constructed works, he never wrote a novel that was livelier, more enjoyable, or more self-revealing.

NOTE ON THE TEXT

Evidently George P. Brett, of the Macmillan publishing company, suggested some sea stories to Jack London in early 1902. On 16 April of that year, the author wrote back: "As for sea novels, I am waiting to make a lucky strike some time, when I can devote a few months to them. You see, though once a sailor myself, I have gone stale on sea men and sea atmosphere, and I have control enough not to attempt such work until I have refreshed myself. My plan is, when I can see expenses clear for half a dozen months, to take passage on a sailing vessel almost anywhere, and with typewriter and paper along, to do my work in the thick of it" (*Letters*, I, 289).

The embryo of *The Sea-Wolf* is subsequently found in a very salesmanlike letter of London's to Brett dated 21 November 1902 in which the novelist made a bulk offer of six books to Macmillan. Beside other works, London told Brett,

for which I have been gathering material a long while, I have three books which I should like to write as soon as I can get at them. The third book, with which I shall bid for a popularity such as Bellamy received [for the utopian romance, *Looking Backward*, 1888] I shall write last, in the meantime preparing for it while I write the other two. The first of these two I have thought of calling *The Flight of the Duchess*. It will be in the Here and Now, and though situated in California, it will not be peculiarly local, but will be really a world-story which might take place anywhere in the *civilized* world. It will end happily. The second is a sea story, or, better, a sea study. I have thought of calling it *The Mercy of the Sea*, though I am not altogether satisfied with the title—it will be almost literally a narrative of things that happened on a seven-months' voyage I once made as a sailor. The oftener I have thought upon the things that happened that trip, the more remarkable they appear to me.

Looking back, they hardly seem real. I can no more say that this story will end happily than can I say that it will end unhappily. It is, in fact, a sea-tragedy, and not to end it as it did end would be a distinct disappointment to the reader. (*Letters*, I, 318).

"I guarantee to have in your hands *The Flight of the Duchess* and *The Mercy of the Sea* by December 1st., 1903", London added (*Letters*, I, 319). Brett was keen to exploit London's fame—which had been boosted by *The Call of the Wild*—and a contract was signed in early December.

The first of the six projected novels—the Bellamy-like story—eventually became *The Iron Heel* (1908). The second ("The Flight of the Duchess") was never written, although some notes for it survive. The sea story became *The Sea-Wolf*. But "The Mercy of the Sea" evidently differed in conception from the novel which we have here. The central figure of "The Mercy of the Sea" was to be a landlubber, a Missourian called the "Bricklayer", who "never caught the rhythm of the sea" and who came to an unhappy end. In truncated form, this idea was eventually written up as the ghost story "That Dead Men Rise Up Never" in *The Human Drift* (1917; see Appendix 1, for the original of the "Bricklayer" on the *Sophia Sutherland*).

The formative next stage in the evolution of *The Sea-Wolf* came with London's reading of Albert Sonnichsen's *Deep Sea Vagabonds*, a fictionalized account of various ocean voyages. London's copy of this work was published in 1903, and presumably he read it early in that year. As David Mike Hamilton records in his account of the novelist's personal library,

his interest in this book centred on a number of sea chanties, a description of a deep sea tyrant, the sailing ship *Calcutta*, the tale of a common sailor who educated himself with a trunk full of books, the sailor's spirit of unrest, striking sailors, and a cockney accent. At the end of the book, London wrote: "40–

learning in fo'k'sle. reference to Wolf Larsen [.] 139—chanty—
'on the Banks of the Sacramento[.]' 146-7—chanties[.] 171—
chanty[.] 320—to get the best of a captain without mutiny"
(*The Tools of my Trade*, pp. 254-5).

It would seem that after—or while—reading this book
London conceived of the character of the master of the
Ghost and its seethingly mutinous crew.

London outlined his newly conceived sea story to Brett
in a letter of 20 January 1903:

Concerning the first novel I write, I have made up my mind that
it shall be a sea story. But it shall not be *The Mercy of the Sea*,
which same is a tragedy, unrelieved by love, comradeship, or
anything else. I am on the track of a sea story, however, which
shall have adventure, storm, struggle, tragedy, and love. The
love-element will run throughout, as the man and woman will
occupy the center of the stage pretty much of all the time.
Also, it will end happily. The *motif*, however, the human motif
underlying all, will be what I may call *mastery*. My idea is
to take a cultured, refined, super-civilized man and woman,
(whom the subtleties of artificial, civilized life have blinded to
the real facts of life), and throw them into a primitive sea-
environment where all is stress and struggle and life expresses
itself, simply, in terms of food and shelter; and make this man
and woman rise to the situation and come out of it with flying
colors. (*Letters*, I, 337-8).

This is substantially *The Sea-Wolf*.

In this same letter of 20 January Jack London declares
himself "on the track of this story, and it is slowly taking
shape. By the first or tenth of February [1903], if I do not
hear otherwise from you, I expect to have it well enough in
hand to begin the first chapter" (*Letters*, I, 338). He seems
none the less not to have got to grips with the novel for a
while. He was, evidently, still preoccupied with *The Call of
the Wild*. London wrote to Cloudesley Johns (currently in
New York) on 21 February 1903: "Do, by all means, stop
over and see us. I hope, by May, to have a sloop on the Bay
and be writing a sea novel!" (*Letters*, I, 344). The sloop

Spray was bought in early March and London made his maiden cruise in her a month later. He took no less than fifteen people out on 4 May. The day after, he jubilantly informed Johns, "Have started the sea novel, and expect to swing along 5000 word per week till it is completed." On 29 May, he told the same correspondent that he had "finished 30,000 words of sea story". The first sections of the novel were thus written in the excitement of London's sailing his own craft.

There were other excitements. In early June 1903 Jack London's affair with Charmian Kittredge reached its climax. According to Clarice Stasz it was in that month, "amid a redwood grove while on an outing" that the lovers had "their first sexual encounter." By early July, Jack London had determined that they would "live life together" (*Letters*, I, 372). He steeled himself to what must be an unpleasant divorce from a wife to whom he had been married for only three years, who was devoted to him, and who had borne him two children. But Jack did not make his divorce intention entirely clear to Bess Maddern London, who continued over the early summer to believe that their marriage was reparable.

The final break apparently came on 24 July. London left his home in Piedmont, and moved in with a friend (Frank Atherton) in Oakland. All this while, he was conducting a passionate but still highly secret affair with Charmian. Neither his wife nor many of his close friends knew about her place in his affections (Bess suspected that the other woman was Jack's previous collaborator, Anna Strunsky). London's sense of fulfilment and of having found a new "mate-woman" colour the Endeavor Island sections of the novel, which he began to write in the fall of 1903.

On 24 July—amidst all this psychic and personal upheaval—London told Brett "I have the sea novel about half-done". It would, he said, "be utterly different in theme and treatment from the stereotyped sea novel" (*Letters*,

I, 376). On 10 August he expressed himself not sure that "the sea novel" would lend itself to serialization. Its length, he guessed, would be between 90,000 and 100,000 words (in fact, it came out at 105,000). In September, serialization was arranged with Richard W. Gilder of the *Century Magazine.* Gilder paid $4,000 for serial rights. Magazine editors were anxious not to offend their "family" readership, and Gilder voiced doubts about the "sickening brutality" of the first half of the novel. Jack London refused to soften anything for what he called "American prudes" and "Mrs Grundy". But the susceptibilities of the magazine reader may well account for the increasingly sentimental and soft nature of the second half of the novel.

Gilder remained chronically nervous about Humphrey and Maud being all alone on Endeavor Island. Again London refused to alter his conception, although in a letter to Brett on 2 September 1903 he gave Gilder permission "to blue pencil all he wishes". The magazine version of *The Sea-Wolf* is, in fact, quite heavily amended—all of London's bad language and some of Larsen's atheism is removed. For example, Larsen's sarcastic and sexually offensive comments to "George Leach" (on page 24 of this edition) are toned down as follows in the *Century*:

"Not an Irish name," the captain snapped sharply. "O'Toole or McCarthy would suit your mug a damn sight better. Unless, very likely, there's an Irishman in your mother's woodpile."
    I saw the young fellow's hands clench at the insult, and the blood crawl scarlet up his neck.
    "But let that go," Wolf Larsen continued.

"Not an Irish name," the captain snapped sharply. "O'Toole or McCarthy would suit your mug a — sight better"
    "But let that go," he continued.

The magazine editors also tidied up the changes from past to present tense in Humphrey's narrative from the sixth to the fourteenth chapter.

In the same letter to Brett of 2 September, London indicated his intention of "taking plenty of time on the book. . . . In fact, because of the changes in my life which have just been occurring, yesterday morning is the first actual work on the book I have done in a month" (*Letters*, I, 383). These changes refer, of course, to his new attachment to Charmian, which colours the latter ecstatically romantic chapters of *The Sea-Wolf*. He would have the whole narrative finished by the first of December, London told Brett. The title of the "sea novel" was still unfixed. A week later, Brett suggested "The Triumph of the Spirit". London preferred "The Sea Wolf" or "The Sea Wolves". *The Sea-Wolf* (hyphenated) was eventually settled on. London sent the first half of the novel to his friend Cloudesley Johns for comments in late September (Johns read carefully, and found at least one major error in the novel, see the note to page 96 of this edition). On October 13, he reported himself to be working hard on the *Spray*, and he told Johns "I simply *have* to get this sea novel done." At the same time, he was becoming impatient to marry Charmian. Originally the lovers had intended to wait a year, in deference to "Mrs Grundy's dictates". Bess was meanwhile feeling increasingly injured by Jack's behaviour and was making public and misguided accusations against Anna Strunsky. Charmian was still working at her job in a shipping office and Jack hoped to keep her name out of the now inevitable divorce proceedings.

On 20 December, London told Brett that if he came to visit on 2 January "praise the Lord, I'll have the *Sea Wolf* finished". The manuscript was in fact sent off by post on 7 January 1904, just before Jack went to Korea to report on the Russo-Japanese war. The book form of the novel was published by Macmillan in the first week of October, with some of the half-tone illustrations by W. J. Aylward which had accompanied the story in the *Century*. The magazine issue ran from January to November 1904, giving London time to revise the book version of *The Sea-Wolf*. The eleven instalments (each with one illustration) were made up as follows: January, chapters 1–3; February, 4–6; March, 7–11; April, 12–15; May, 16–18; June, 19–21; July, 22–25; August, 26–27; September, 28–31; October, 32–35; November, 36–39. London had mixed feelings about the serialization. He wrote to Brett, from Wiju, on 24 April 1904 that "Much that the *Century* cut out I should like in the book; and on other hand, many *Century* alterations I should like to retain" (*Letters*, I, 427). He left it to Charmian to do the final merging of texts and to correct the Macmillan proofs which were ready at the end of July.

There are three texts of *The Sea-Wolf*, as London explained in a letter of 7 October 1913 (a period in which he was worried about his ownership of the copyright):

there were three (3) versions of *The Sea-Wolf*: My original Manuscript constituted one version that was published in paper covers by The Macmillan Co. in order to get copyright in England and the United States. The second version was copyrighted by the Century Co., and published in *The Century Magazine*, and was a revision, with many radical changes, of my Manuscript. The third version of *The Sea-Wolf* was that which was brought out in the original regular edition [in which I made] so many changes from my manuscript-version that I had to pay the cost of making the changes in the plate proofs. (*Letters*, III, 1250).

This edition follows the third of these versions, the October 1904 "regular" edition brought out by Macmillan. Those interested in the important variations in *The Sea-Wolf*'s texts are referred to the expert discussion and description in Matthew Bruccoli's 1964 *Riverside* edition of the novel. I am glad also to acknowledge the guidance of the magnificent "Library of America" two-volume selection of London's works, edited by Donald Pizer.

Ideally an edition of *The Sea-Wolf* should have some reference to and description of the manuscript of the novel, more so since on London's own testimony it is significantly different from what was eventually published. This is not possible. What survives of London's manuscript is held at the Huntington Library, in California (call mark JL 1191). The library notes regretfully that "This manuscript was burned in the San Francisco earthquake and fire of 1906. The charred cinders cannot be used under any circumstances, and may be viewed only with staff approval and assistance." No working materials seem to have survived for the novel, although the Huntington has two sets of notes for the earlier-conceived "The Mercy of the Sea" (JL 941–2).

The Sea-Wolf enjoyed a great success in 1904, and buoyed Jack London's reputation even higher than The Call of the Wild had done the year before. Macmillan quickly sold something over 63,000 copies of their one-volume version (sales were helped when the Ladies' Home Journal bought several thousand copies as premiums for their subscribers: they apparently were less worried than Gilder about the sexual implications of Endeavor Island). In a letter of 1 June 1905 Jack London estimated that The Sea-Wolf "made me about $15,000". As Russ Kingman points out, The Sea-Wolf and The Call of the Wild were the only works of Jack London's to make first place on the newly-devised American bestseller list. Kingman also notes that "the majority of the reviews were favourable but, as usual, there were a few who saw the book as no better than the average 'dime novel'." This judgment is contradicted by John Perry in his hostile monograph Jack London, an American Myth (1981). As part of a general denunciation of Jack London and all he represents Perry claims that "most reviews criticized The Sea-Wolf's contrived plot, flat characterization, and hideous exhibition of violence." It seems that like most innovative novels The Sea-Wolf received its share of both good and bad notices.

SELECT BIBLIOGRAPHY

THE best collection of Jack London's works is the two-volume "Library of America" set (1982), edited and annotated by Donald Pizer. The previously standard *Letters from Jack London* (1965), edited by King Hendricks and Irving Shepard has been superseded by the three-volume *The Letters of Jack London*, edited by Earle Labor, Robert C. Leitz III, and I. Milo Shepard and published by Stanford University Press in 1988. Among various bibliographies, most useful are: Dale L. Walker and James E. Sisson III's *The Fiction of Jack London; a Chronological Bibliography* (1972) and *Jack London, A Bibliography* (1966, revised 1973) by Hensley C. Woodbridge, John London, and George H. Tweney.

There are numerous critical biographies, many with their individual biases. The wife Charmian London's *The Book of Jack London* (1921) is very close to its subject, but also very protective of his reputation. The daughter Joan London's *Jack London and his Times* (1939) is, by contrast, very frank. The same author's *Jack London and his Daughters* (1990) is more affectionate in tone. Irving Stone's *Sailor on Horseback* (1938) ushered in a new era of unrestrained London biography and is dismissed by the editors of the recent *Letters* as a "biographical novel". Joseph Noel's *Footloose in Arcadia* (1940) is anecdotal, spiteful and not trustworthy. Richard O'Connor's *Jack London, a Biography* (1964) provides a clear narrative, although it is not always sympathetic to Jack. Franklin Walker's *Jack London and the Klondike* (1972) is amazingly informative and detailed, although it only covers in depth a year of the writer's diverse life. Andrew Sinclair's *Jack* (1977) is an influential modern critical biography which has provoked some controversy. Earle Labor's *Jack London* (1974), a volume in Twayne's "United States Authors" series, usefully combines biography with extended critical discussion. Robert Barltrop's *Jack London, the Man, the Writer, the Rebel* (1976) offers more of the political background to the writing. Clarice Stasz's *American Dreamers* (1988) is a biographical study of the Charmian Kittredge and Jack London relationship which began at the time he was writing *The Sea-Wolf*. David Mike Hamilton's *The Tools of my*

Trade (1986) is an invaluable exposition of London's thought, as reflected by annotations in his vast personal library. Russ Kingman's *A Pictorial Life of Jack London* (1979) vividly reconstructs the author's life and career around a photograph narrative.

There are four modern editions of *The Sea-Wolf* which the student may wish to consult. The "Riverside" edition, prepared by Matthew Bruccoli in 1964, and the "Library of America" edition, prepared by Donald Pizer in 1982, both have excellent critical apparatus and annotation to London's text. The "Penguin" edition, prepared by Andrew Sinclair in 1989, has a stimulating introductory essay about the author. The New American Library's "Signet Classic" edition (1964, repr. 1981) has a brief but most informative "Afterword" by Franklin Walker.

Readers may wish to follow up on some of London's sources for *The Sea-Wolf*. The general theme—the effete intellectual toughened into manhood by his experience at sea—derives from Richard Henry Dana's *Two Years before the Mast* (first published in 1840, republished with changes in 1869). Dana's sadistic Captain Thompson may also have inspired something of Wolf Larsen's personality. The plot of *The Sea-Wolf* owes much to Frank Norris's *Moran of the Lady Letty*, which London read and enjoyed shortly after it first came out in 1898. The first chapter, in which Humphrey Van Weyden is rescued from drowning, strongly recalls the opening of Kipling's "Story of the Grand Banks", *Captains Courageous* (1897). The arrival of the beautiful heroine in a lifeboat is very reminiscent of W. Clark Russell's *The Wreck of the Grosvenor* (1877). The small boat experiences of Humphrey and Maud recall Conrad's *Youth* (a work which captivated London in 1903) and Stephen Crane's long short-story *The Open Boat* (1898). The lovers' idyll on Endeavor Island strongly recalls Charles Reade's *Foul Play* (1868). According to Joseph Noel, the character of Wolf Larsen was based (at Noel's suggestion) on a brutal sailor in a story called "The South Sea Pearler" which I have been unable to identify.

A CHRONOLOGY OF JACK LONDON

1876 Born John Griffith Chaney 12 January in San Francisco; the son of Flora Wellman and her common-law husband (1874–75), William Henry Chaney, "a footloose astrologer". On 7 September 1876, Wellman marries John London, whose name the young Jack adopts.

1878 The London family moves to Oakland, where John London runs a grocery store.

1881 John London's grocery business fails and the family leases a 20-acre "ranch" in Alameda, where in 1882 Jack first attends grade school.

1882 The London family moves down the San Francisco peninsula to a 75-acre ranch, between Pedro Point and Moss Beach.

1884 The London family moves to another farm near Livermore, where John London builds ambitious facilities for rearing chickens. This fails.

1886 The London family returns to Oakland, where Flora runs an unsuccessful boarding house. Jack works as a newspaper delivery boy and at other odd jobs. He also uses the Oakland Public Library extensively under the tutelage of Ina Coolbrith.

1891 Jack graduates from Cole Grammar School (eighth grade). In the summer he works at a local cannery. Some months later with a borrowed $300 he buys the sloop *Razzle Dazzle* and sets up as an oyster pirate in San Francisco Bay.

1892 Jack serves as an deputy officer in the Fish Patrol in Benicia for the best part of a year.

1893 On his seventeenth birthday, Jack enlists as a boat-puller on the sealing schooner *Sophia Sutherland*, and spends seven months at sea in northern waters off Japan. On his return in August, during an industrial depression, he works in a jute mill for 10 cents an hour. His essay "Typhoon off the Coast of Japan" wins a prize for young writers run by the *San Francisco Morning Call.*

1894 Early in the year Jack works shovelling coal at the power plant of the Oakland, San Leandro and Haywards Electric Railway. In April, Jack joins C. T. Kelly's division of Jacob Coxey's Army of the Unemployed, which intends to march on Washington. In May, in Hannibal, Missouri, Jack deserts the bedraggled remnants of Kelly's Army and strikes out for himself across the eastern USA. In late June, he is sentenced to thirty days in Erie County Penitentiary, for vagrancy at the Niagara Falls. He works his passage back to Oakland, via Vancouver, as a coal stoker on the SS *Umatilla.* Out of this experience, Jack was later to write *The Road* (1907).

1895 Jack returns to Oakland High School. The school paper, the *Aegis,* publishes some of his fiction. Falls in love with Mabel Applegarth (the Ruth Morse of *Martin Eden*) who encourages his ambition to enter the University of California.

1896 Joins the Socialist Labor Party. Briefly attends a cramming academy at Alameda. Helped to study by his future wife, Bessie (Mae) Maddern. He takes his university entrance exams in August and passes. Meanwhile London has been attacked in the newspapers as Oakland's "boy socialist".

1897 In February leaves the University of California at Berkeley after only one semester. Begins to write seriously. Works for some time as an assistant in the Belmont Academy steam laundry. In July 1897, Jack persuades his stepsister Eliza to finance his expedition to the Yukon, to mine for gold.

1898 In July, Jack returns from the Yukon, still poor and sick with scurvy. Takes up serious writing again at his mother's encouragement. John London having died in October 1897, Jack is now the family breadwinner.

1899 In January, Jack sells his first story, "To the Man on Trail" to the *Overland Monthly* for $5. During the course of the year he publishes some twenty-four stories and essays. In winter meets Anna Strunsky, with whom he falls in love.

1900 In April, Houghton Mifflin publishes Jack's first volume of short stories, *The Son of the Wolf*. In the same month, he marries Bessie Mae Maddern. They set up home in Oakland, initially with Jack's mother and nephew.

1901 In January the Londons' first daughter, Joan, is born. In July, Jack stands unsuccessfully as Social Democrat mayor of Oakland. Publishes *The God of his Fathers*.

1902 In the summer, Jack travels to the East End of London, where he undertakes six weeks' investigation into social conditions. Later publishes *The People of the Abyss* (1903) from the experience. In October, the Londons have a second daughter, Becky. Jack publishes his first novel, *A Daughter of the Snows* and *The Cruise of the Dazzler*.

1903 *The Call of the Wild* published by Macmillan. Becomes a bestseller. Jack separates from his wife, having fallen in love with Charmian Kittredge. Buys a sloop, the *Spray*. Publishes *The Kempton-Wace Letters* with Anna Strunsky.

1904 From January to June Jack is in Korea as a war correspondent for Hearst newspapers. *The Sea-Wolf* published in October and is another bestseller. Bessie sues for divorce in June on grounds of desertion, naming Anna Strunsky. Publishes *The Faith of Men*.

1905 Jack again stands unsuccessfully as Social Democrat mayor of Oakland. He marries Charmian Kittredge in November. Honeymoons in the West Indies. Buys property and 129 acres in the Sonoma Valley which later becomes a portion of the larger Beauty Ranch. Lectures at American universities and publishes his sociological essays, *War of the Classes*, *Tales of the Fish Patrol* and the novel *The Game*.

1906 London lectures extensively on political topics in January and February. Begins building the 45-foot yacht, the *Snark*. Publishes *White Fang*, *Scorn of Women* and *Moon-Face and*

Other Stories. Writes on the San Francisco earthquake for *Collier's Magazine.*

1907 In April, Jack and Charmian set out from San Francisco in the *Snark* for a voyage through the South Seas. By late December, they are in Tahiti. *Before Adam, Love of Life* and *The Road* published.

1908 The Londons travel to the Samoan Islands (May), Fiji (June) and on to Australia by November. Jack treated in Sydney for multiple ailments. He makes further purchases of land around the Glen Ellen area, in Sonoma County. *The Iron Heel* published.

1909 The Londons return in early summer by tramp steamer to New Orleans. Arrive home in Glen Ellen in August. Jack still recuperating from illnesses contracted on the *Snark* voyage in late October. *Martin Eden* published.

1910 Establishes himself and his family at the Beauty Ranch, now almost 1,000 acres in extent. Charmian's newborn daughter dies. Publishes *Revolution, Lost Face, Theft* and *Burning Daylight.* Plans construction of Wolf House.

1911 Jack and Charmian take a sailing trip in San Francisco Bay in April and a four-horse driving trip through northern California and Oregon, from June to September. Publishes *South Sea Tales, The Cruise of the Snark, Adventure* and *When God Laughs.*

1912 Over January–February, Jack and Charmian are in New York, on vacation. In early March, they leave Baltimore on the *Dirigo,* a four-masted barque, for a voyage round the Horn. In late July they arrive in Seattle, and return to Beauty Ranch in early August. On 12 August, Charmian has a miscarriage. Jack has planned *John Barleycorn* on the sea trip and begins writing it in November. Publishes *A Son of the Sun, Smoke Bellew* and *The House of Pride.* Jack is now earning $70,000 a year.

1913 Publishes *John Barleycorn* in the *Saturday Evening Post,*

March–May. Wolf House burns down on 22 August. Publishes *The Abysmal Brute, Valley of the Moon* and *The Night-Born*.

1914 From April to June, Jack covers the Mexican Revolution for *Collier's Magazine*. Assignment cut short by attack of dysentery, complicating his already chronic ill health. Publishes *The Mutiny of the Elsinore, The Strength of the Strong*.

1915 Travels to Hawaii, February–July. Publishes *The Scarlet Plague, The Star Rover*.

1916 Spends the first half of the year as a semi-invalid in Hawaii. Resigns from the Socialist Party in March. Dies 22 November, either from kidney failure or from a self-administered overdose (possibly accidental) of morphine. *The Acorn-Planter, The Little Lady of the Big House* and *The Turtles of Tasman* published in 1916; *The Human Drift, Jerry of the Islands, Michael Brother of Jerry, On the Makaloa Mat* and *The Red One* published in 1917; *Hearts of Three* published in 1920; *Dutch Courage* published in 1922; *The Assassination Bureau* published in 1963.

March–May: Wolf House burns down on 22 August. Publishes The Abysmal Brute, Valley of the Moon and The Night Born.

1914 From April to June, Jack covers the Mexican Revolution for Collier's Magazine. Assignment cut short; he took of dysentery, complicating his already chronic ill health. Publishes The Mutiny of the Elsinore, The Strength of the Strong.

1915 Travels to Hawaii, February–July. Publishes The Scarlet Plague, The Star Rover.

1916 Spends the first half of the year as a semi-invalid in Hawaii. Resigns from the Socialist Party in March. Dies 22 November, either from kidney failure or from a self-administered overdose (possibly accidental) of morphine. The Acorn Planter, The Little Lady of the Big House and The Turtles of Tasman published in 1916. The Human Drift, Jerry of the Islands, Michael, Brother of Jerry. On the Makaloa Mat and The Red One published in 1919. Hearts of Three published in 1920. Dutch Courage published in 1922. The Assassination Bureau published in 1963.

THE SEA-WOLF

CHAPTER ONE

I SCARCELY know where to begin, though I sometimes
facetiously place the cause of it all to Charley Furuseth's
credit. He kept a summer cottage in Mill Valley,* under the
shadow of Mount Tamalpais, and never occupied it except
when he loafed through the winter months and read Nietzsche and Schopenhauer* to rest his brain. When summer
came on, he elected to sweat out a hot and dusty existence
in the city and to toil incessantly. Had it not been my
custom to run up to see him every Saturday afternoon and
to stop over till Monday morning, this particular January
Monday morning* would not have found me afloat on San
Francisco Bay.

Not but that I was afloat in a safe craft, for the *Martinez*
was a new ferry-steamer, making her fourth or fifth trip
on the run between Sausalito and San Francisco.* The
danger lay in the heavy fog which blanketed the bay, and
of which, as a landsman, I had little apprehension. In fact,
I remember the placid exaltation with which I took up my
position on the forward upper deck, directly beneath the
pilot-house, and allowed the mystery of the fog to lay hold
of my imagination. A fresh breeze was blowing, and for a
time I was alone in the moist obscurity—yet not alone, for
I was dimly conscious of the presence of the pilot, and of
what I took to be the captain, in the glass house above my
head.

I remember thinking how comfortable it was, this division of labor which made it unnecessary for me to study
fogs, winds, tides, and navigation, in order to visit my
friend who lived across an arm of the sea. It was good that
men should be specialists, I mused. The peculiar knowledge of the pilot and captain sufficed for many thousands

of people who knew no more of the sea and navigation than I knew. On the other hand, instead of having to devote my energy to the learning of a multitude of things, I concentrated it upon a few particular things, such as, for instance, the analysis of Poe's place in American literature—an essay of mine, by the way, in the current *Atlantic.** Coming aboard, as I passed through the cabin, I had noticed with greedy eyes a stout gentleman reading the *Atlantic*, which was open at my very essay. And there it was again, the division of labor, the special knowledge of the pilot and captain which permitted the stout gentleman to read my special knowledge on Poe while they carried him safely from Sausalito to San Francisco.

A red-faced man, slamming the cabin door behind him and stumping out on the deck, interrupted my reflections, though I made a mental note of the topic for use in a projected essay which I had thought of calling "The Necessity for Freedom: A Plea for the Artist."* The red-faced man shot a glance up at the pilot-house, gazed around at the fog, stumped across the deck and back (he evidently had artificial legs), and stood still by my side, legs wide apart, and with an expression of keen enjoyment on his face. I was not wrong when I decided that his days had been spent on the sea.

"It's nasty weather like this here that turns heads gray before their time," he said, with a nod toward the pilot-house.

"I had not thought there was any particular strain," I answered. "It seems as simple as A, B, C. They know the direction by compass, the distance, and the speed. I should not call it anything more than mathematical certainty."

"Strain!" he snorted. "Simple as A, B, C! Mathematical certainty!"

He seemed to brace himself up and lean backward against the air as he stared at me. "How about this here tide that's rushin' out through the Golden Gate?" he demanded, or

bellowed, rather. "How fast is she ebbin'? What's the drift, eh? Listen to that, will you? A bell-buoy, and we're a-top of it! See 'em alterin' the course!"

From out of the fog came the mournful tolling of a bell, and I could see the pilot turning the wheel with great rapidity. The bell, which had seemed straight ahead, was now sounding from the side. Our own whistle was blowing hoarsely, and from time to time the sound of other whistles came to us from out of the fog.

"That's a ferry-boat of some sort," the newcomer said, indicating a whistle off to the right. "And there! D'ye hear that? Blown by mouth. Some scow schooner, most likely. Better watch out, Mr. Schooner-man. Ah, I thought so. Now hell's a-poppin' for somebody!"

The unseen ferry-boat was blowing blast after blast, and the mouth-blown horn was tooting in terror-stricken fashion.

"And now they're payin' their respects to each other and tryin' to get clear," the red-faced man went on, as the hurried whistling ceased.

His face was shining, his eyes flashing with excitement, as he translated into articulate language the speech of the horns and sirens. "That's a steam siren a-goin' it over there to the left. And you hear that fellow with a frog in his throat—a steam schooner as near as I can judge, crawlin' in from the Heads* against the tide."

A shrill little whistle, piping as if gone mad, came from directly ahead and from very near at hand. Gongs sounded on the *Martinez*. Our paddle-wheels stopped, their pulsing beat died away, and then they started again. The shrill little whistle, like the chirping of a cricket amid the cries of great beasts, shot through the fog from more to the side and swiftly grew faint and fainter. I looked to my companion for enlightenment.

"One of them dare-devil launches," he said. "I almost wish we'd sunk him, the little rip! They're the cause of

more trouble. And what good are they? Any jackass gets
aboard one and runs it from hell to breakfast, blowin' his
whistle to beat the band and tellin' the rest of the world
to look out for him, because he's comin' and can't look
out for himself! Because he's comin'! And you've got to
look out, too! Right of way! Common decency! They don't
know the meanin' of it!"

I felt quite amused at his unwarranted choler, and while
he stumped indignantly up and down I fell to dwelling
upon the romance of the fog. And romantic it certainly
was—the fog, like the gray shadow of infinite mystery,
brooding over the whirling speck of earth; and men, mere
motes of light and sparkle, cursed with an insane relish
for work, riding their steeds of wood and steel through the
heart of the mystery, groping their way blindly through the
Unseen, and clamoring and clanging in confident speech
the while their hearts are heavy with incertitude and fear.

The voice of my companion brought me back to myself
with a laugh. I too had been groping and floundering, the
while I thought I rode clear-eyed through the mystery.

"Hello; somebody comin' our way," he was saying. "And
d'ye hear that? He's comin' fast. Walking right along.
Guess he don't hear us yet. Wind's in wrong direction."

The fresh breeze was blowing right down upon us, and
I could hear the whistle plainly, off to one side and a little
ahead.

"Ferry-boat?" I asked.

He nodded, then added, "Or he wouldn't be keepin' up
such a clip." He gave a short chuckle. "They're gettin'
anxious up there."

I glanced up. The captain had thrust his head and shoulders out of the pilot-house, and was staring intently into
the fog as though by sheer force of will he could penetrate
it. His face was anxious, as was the face of my companion,
who had stumped over to the rail and was gazing with a
like intentness in the direction of the invisible danger.

Then everything happened, and with inconceivable rapidity. The fog seemed to break away as though split by a wedge, and the bow of a steamboat emerged, trailing fog-wreaths on either side like seaweed on the snout of Leviathan. I could see the pilot-house and a white-bearded man leaning partly out of it, on his elbows. He was clad in a blue uniform, and I remember noting how trim and quiet he was. His quietness, under the circumstances, was terrible. He accepted Destiny, marched hand in hand with it, and coolly measured the stroke. As he leaned there, he ran a calm and speculative eye over us, as though to determine the precise point of the collision, and took no notice whatever when our pilot, white with rage, shouted, "Now you've done it!"

On looking back, I realize that the remark was too obvious to make rejoinder necessary.

"Grab hold of something and hang on," the red-faced man said to me. All his bluster had gone, and he seemed to have caught the contagion of preternatural calm. "And listen to the women scream," he said grimly—almost bitterly, I thought, as though he had been through the experience before.

The vessels came together before I could follow his advice. We must have been struck squarely amidships, for I saw nothing, the strange steamboat having passed beyond my line of vision. The *Martinez* heeled over, sharply, and there was a crashing and rending of timber.* I was thrown flat on the wet deck, and before I could scramble to my feet I heard the scream of the women. This it was, I am certain,—the most indescribable of blood-curdling sounds,—that threw me into a panic. I remembered the life-preservers stored in the cabin, but was met at the door and swept backward by a wild rush of men and women. What happened in the next few minutes I do not recollect, though I have a clear remembrance of pulling down life-preservers from the overhead racks, while the red-faced

man fastened them about the bodies of an hysterical group
of women. This memory is as distinct and sharp as that
of any picture I have seen. It is a picture, and I can see
it now,—the jagged edges of the hole in the side of the
cabin, through which the gray fog swirled and eddied; the
empty upholstered seats, littered with all the evidences of
sudden flight, such as packages, hand satchels, umbrellas,
and wraps; the stout gentleman who had been reading my
essay, encased in cork and canvas, the magazine still in
his hand, and asking me with monotonous insistence if I
thought there was any danger; the red-faced man, stumping gallantly around on his artificial legs and buckling life-
preservers on all comers; and finally, the screaming bedlam
of women.

This it was, the screaming of the women, that most tried
my nerves. It must have tried, too, the nerves of the red-
faced man, for I have another picture which will never
fade from my mind. The stout gentleman is stuffing the
magazine into his overcoat pocket and looking on curiously. A tangled mass of women, with drawn, white faces
and open mouths, is shrieking like a chorus of lost souls;
and the red-faced man, his face now purplish with wrath,
and with arms extended overhead as in the act of hurling
thunderbolts, is shouting, "Shut up! Oh, shut up!"

I remember the scene impelled me to sudden laughter,
and in the next instant I realized I was becoming hysterical
myself; for these were women of my own kind, like my
mother and sisters, with the fear of death upon them
and unwilling to die. And I remember that the sounds
they made reminded me of the squealing of pigs under
the knife of the butcher, and I was struck with horror at
the vividness of the analogy. These women, capable of the
most sublime emotions, of the tenderest sympathies, were
open-mouthed and screaming. They wanted to live, they
were helpless, like rats in a trap, and they screamed.

The horror of it drove me out on deck. I was feeling

sick and squeamish, and sat down on a bench. In a hazy
way I saw and heard men rushing and shouting as they
strove to lower the boats. It was just as I had read de-
scriptions of such scenes in books. The tackles jammed.
Nothing worked. One boat lowered away with the plugs
out, filled with women and children and then with water,
and capsized. Another boat had been lowered by one end,
and still hung in the tackle by the other end, where it had
been abandoned. Nothing was to be seen of the strange
steamboat which had caused the disaster, though I heard
men saying that she would undoubtedly send boats to our
assistance.

I descended to the lower deck. The *Martinez* was sinking
fast, for the water was very near. Numbers of the passengers were leaping overboard. Others, in the water, were
clamoring to be taken aboard again. No one heeded them.
A cry arose that we were sinking. I was seized by the
consequent panic, and went over the side in a surge of
bodies. How I went over I do not know, though I did know,
and instantly, why those in the water were so desirous of
getting back on the steamer. The water was cold—so cold
that it was painful. The pang, as I plunged into it, was
as quick and sharp as that of fire. It bit to the marrow.
It was like the grip of death. I gasped with the anguish
and shock of it, filling my lungs before the life-preserver
popped me to the surface. The taste of the salt was strong
in my mouth, and I was strangling with the acrid stuff in
my throat and lungs.

But it was the cold that was most distressing. I felt that
I could survive but a few minutes. People were struggling
and floundering in the water about me. I could hear them
crying out to one another. And I heard, also, the sound
of oars. Evidently the strange steamboat had lowered its
boats. As the time went by I marvelled that I was still
alive. I had no sensation whatever in my lower limbs, while
a chilling numbness was wrapping about my heart and

creeping into it. Small waves, with spiteful foaming crests, continually broke over me and into my mouth, sending me off into more strangling paroxysms.

The noises grew indistinct, though I heard a final and despairing chorus of screams in the distance and knew that the *Martinez* had gone down. Later,—how much later I have no knowledge,—I came to myself with a start of fear. I was alone. I could hear no calls or cries—only the sound of the waves, made weirdly hollow and reverberant by the fog. A panic in a crowd, which partakes of a sort of community of interest, is not so terrible as a panic when one is by oneself; and such a panic I now suffered. Whither was I drifting? The red-faced man had said that the tide was ebbing through the Golden Gate. Was I, then, being carried out to sea? And the life-preserver in which I floated? Was it not liable to go to pieces at any moment? I had heard of such things being made of paper and hollow rushes which quickly became saturated and lost all buoyancy. And I could not swim a stroke. And I was alone, floating, apparently, in the midst of a gray primordial vastness. I confess that a madness seized me, that I shrieked aloud as the women had shrieked, and beat the water with my numb hands.

How long this lasted I have no conception, for a blankness intervened, of which I remember no more than one remembers of troubled and painful sleep. When I aroused, it was as after centuries of time; and I saw, almost above me and emerging from the fog, the bow of a vessel, and three triangular sails, each shrewdly lapping the other and filled with wind. Where the bow cut the water there was a great foaming and gurgling, and I seemed directly in its path. I tried to cry out, but was too exhausted. The bow plunged down, just missing me and sending a swash of water clear over my head. Then the long, black side of the vessel began slipping past, so near that I could have touched it with my hands. I tried to reach it, in a mad resolve to claw into the wood with my nails, but my arms were heavy and lifeless. Again I strove to call out, but made no sound.

The stern of the vessel shot by, dropping, as it did so, into a hollow between the waves; and I caught a glimpse of a man standing at the wheel, and of another man who seemed to be doing little else than smoke a cigar. I saw the smoke issuing from his lips as he slowly turned his head and glanced out over the water in my direction. It was a careless, unpremeditated glance, one of those haphazard things men do when they have no immediate call to do anything in particular, but act because they are alive and must do something.

But life and death were in that glance. I could see the vessel being swallowed up in the fog; I saw the back of the man at the wheel, and the head of the other man turning, slowly turning, as his gaze struck the water and casually lifted along it toward me. His face wore an absent expression, as of deep thought, and I became afraid that if his eyes did light upon me he would nevertheless not see me. But his eyes did light upon me, and looked squarely into mine; and he did see me, for he sprang to the wheel, thrusting the other man aside, and whirled it round and round, hand over hand, at the same time shouting orders of some sort. The vessel seemed to go off at a tangent to its former course and leapt almost instantly from view into the fog.

I felt myself slipping into unconsciousness, and tried with all the power of my will to fight above the suffocating blankness and darkness that was rising around me. A little later I heard the stroke of oars, growing nearer and nearer, and the calls of a man. When he was very near I heard him crying, in vexed fashion, "Why in hell don't you sing out?" This meant me, I thought, and then the blankness and darkness rose over me.

CHAPTER TWO

I SEEMED swinging in a mighty rhythm through orbit vastness. Sparkling points of light spluttered and shot past me. They were stars, I knew, and flaring comets, that peopled my flight among the suns. As I reached the limit of my swing and prepared to rush back on the counter swing, a great gong struck and thundered. For an immeasurable period, lapped in the rippling of placid centuries, I enjoyed and pondered my tremendous flight.*

But a change came over the face of the dream, for a dream I told myself it must be. My rhythm grew shorter and shorter. I was jerked from swing to counter swing with irritating haste. I could scarcely catch my breath, so fiercely was I impelled through the heavens. The gong thundered more frequently and more furiously. I grew to await it with a nameless dread. Then it seemed as though I were being dragged over rasping sands, white and hot in the sun. This gave place to a sense of intolerable anguish. My skin was scorching in the torment of fire. The gong clanged and knelled. The sparkling points of light flashed past me in an interminable stream, as though the whole sidereal system were dropping into the void. I gasped, caught my breath painfully, and opened my eyes. Two men were kneeling beside me, working over me. My mighty rhythm was the lift and forward plunge of a ship on the sea. The terrific gong was a frying-pan, hanging on the wall, that rattled and clattered with each leap of the ship. The rasping, scorching sands were a man's hard hands chafing my naked chest. I squirmed under the pain of it, and half lifted my head. My chest was raw and red, and I could see tiny blood globules starting through the torn and inflamed cuticle.

"That'll do, Yonson," one of the men said. "Carn't yer see you've bloomin' well rubbed all the gent's skin orf?"

The man addressed as Yonson, a man of the heavy Scandinavian type, ceased chafing me, and arose awkwardly to his feet. The man who had spoken to him was clearly a Cockney, with the clean lines and weakly pretty, almost effeminate, face of the man who has absorbed the sound of Bow Bells with his mother's milk.* A draggled muslin cap on his head and a dirty gunny-sack about his slim hips proclaimed him cook of the decidedly dirty ship's galley in which I found myself.

"An' 'ow yer feelin' now, sir?" he asked, with the subservient smirk which comes only of generations of tip-seeking ancestors.

For reply, I twisted weakly into a sitting posture, and was helped by Yonson to my feet. The rattle and bang of the frying-pan was grating horribly on my nerves. I could not collect my thoughts. Clutching the woodwork of the galley for support,—and I confess the grease with which it was scummed put my teeth on edge,—I reached across a hot cooking-range to the offending utensil, unhooked it, and wedged it securely into the coal-box.

The cook grinned at my exhibition of nerves, and thrust into my hand a steaming mug with an "'Ere, this'll do yer good." It was a nauseous mess,—ship's coffee,—but the heat of it was revivifying. Between gulps of the molten stuff I glanced down at my raw and bleeding chest and turned to the Scandinavian.

"Thank you, Mr. Yonson," I said; "but don't you think your measures were rather heroic?"

It was because he understood the reproof of my action, rather than of my words, that he held up his palm for inspection. It was remarkably calloused. I passed my hand over the horny projections, and my teeth went on edge once more from the horrible rasping sensation produced.

"My name is Johnson, not Yonson," he said, in very

good, though slow, English, with no more than a shade of
accent to it.

There was mild protest in his pale blue eyes, and withal
a timid frankness and manliness that quite won me to him.

"Thank you, Mr. Johnson," I corrected, and reached out
my hand for his.

He hesitated, awkward and bashful, shifted his weight
from one leg to the other, then blunderingly gripped my
hand in a hearty shake.

"Have you any dry clothes I may put on?" I asked the
cook.

"Yes, sir," he answered, with cheerful alacrity. "I'll run
down an' tyke a look over my kit, if you've no objections,
sir, to wearin' my things."

He dived out of the galley door, or glided rather, with a
swiftness and smoothness of gait that struck me as being
not so much cat-like as oily. In fact, this oiliness, or greasi-
ness, as I was later to learn, was probably the most salient
expression of his personality.

"And where am I?" I asked Johnson, whom I took, and
rightly, to be one of the sailors. "What vessel is this, and
where is she bound?"

"Off the Farallones,* heading about sou'west," he answered, slowly and methodically, as though groping for his
best English, and rigidly observing the order of my queries.
"The schooner *Ghost*, bound seal-hunting to Japan."*

"And who is the captain? I must see him as soon as I
am dressed."

Johnson looked puzzled and embarrassed. He hesitated
while he groped in his vocabulary and framed a complete
answer. "The cap'n is Wolf Larsen, or so men call him.
I never heard his other name. But you better speak soft
with him. He is mad this morning. The mate—"

But he did not finish. The cook had glided in.

"Better sling yer 'ook* out of 'ere, Yonson," he said.
"The old man'll be wantin' yer on deck, an' this ayn't no

d'y to fall foul of 'im.' "

Johnson turned obediently to the door, at the same time, over the cook's shoulder, favoring me with an amazingly solemn and portentous wink, as though to emphasize his interrupted remark and the need for me to be soft-spoken with the captain.

Hanging over the cook's arm was a loose and crumpled array of evil-looking and sour-smelling garments.

"They was put aw'y wet, sir," he vouchsafed explanation. "But you'll 'ave to make them do till I dry yours out by the fire."

Clinging to the woodwork, staggering with the roll of the ship, and aided by the cook, I managed to slip into a rough woollen undershirt. On the instant my flesh was creeping and crawling from the harsh contact. He noticed my involuntary twitching and grimacing, and smirked:

"I only 'ope yer don't ever 'ave to get used to such as that in this life, 'cos you've got a bloomin' soft skin, that you 'ave, more like a lydy's than any I know of. I was bloomin' well sure you was a gentleman as soon as I set eyes on yer."

I had taken a dislike to him at first, and as he helped to dress me this dislike increased. There was something repulsive about his touch. I shrank from his hand; my flesh revolted. And between this and the smells arising from various pots and bubbling on the galley fire, I was in haste to get out into the fresh air. Further, there was the need of seeing the captain about what arrangements could be made for getting me ashore.

A cheap cotton shirt, with frayed collar and a bosom discolored with what I took to be ancient blood-stains, was put on me amid a running and apologetic fire of comment. A pair of workman's brogans* encased my feet, and for trousers I was furnished with a pair of pale blue, washed-out overalls, one leg of which was fully ten inches shorter than the other. The abbreviated leg looked as though the devil had there clutched for the Cockney's soul and missed the shadow for the substance.

"And whom have I to thank for this kindness?" I asked, when I stood completely arrayed, a tiny boy's cap on my head, and for coat a dirty, striped cotton jacket which ended at the small of my back and the sleeves of which reached just below my elbows.

The cook drew himself up in a smugly humble fashion, a deprecating smirk on his face. Out of my experience with stewards on the Atlantic liners at the end of the voyage, I could have sworn he was waiting for his tip. From my fuller knowledge of the creature I now know that the posture was unconscious. An hereditary servility, no doubt, was responsible.

"Mugridge, sir," he fawned, his effeminate features running into a greasy smile. "Thomas Mugridge,* sir, an' at yer service."

"All right, Thomas," I said. "I shall not forget you—when my clothes are dry."

A soft life suffused his face and his eyes glistened, as though somewhere in the deeps of his being his ancestors had quickened and stirred with dim memories of tips received in former lives.

"Thank you, sir," he said, very gratefully and very humbly indeed.

Precisely in the way that the door slid back, he slid aside, and I stepped out on deck. I was still weak from my prolonged immersion. A puff of wind caught me, and I staggered across the moving deck to a corner of the cabin, to which I clung for support. The schooner, heeled over far out from the perpendicular, was bowing and plunging into the long Pacific roll. If she were heading southwest as Johnson had said, the wind, then, I calculated, was blowing nearly from the south. The fog was gone, and in its place the sun sparkled crisply on the surface of the water. I turned to the east, where I knew California must lie, but could see nothing save low-lying fog-banks—the same fog, doubtless, that had brought about the disaster to the *Martinez* and placed me in my present situation. To the north, and not far away, a group of naked rocks thrust above the sea, on one of which I could distinguish a lighthouse. In the southwest, and almost in our course, I saw the pyramidal loom of some vessel's sails.

Having completed my survey of the horizon, I turned to my more immediate surroundings. My first thought was that a man who had come through a collision and rubbed shoulders with death merited more attention than I received. Beyond a sailor at the wheel who stared curiously across the top of the cabin, I attracted no notice whatever.

Everybody seemed interested in what was going on amidships. There, on a hatch, a large man was lying on his back. He was fully clothed, though his shirt was ripped open in front. Nothing was to be seen of his chest, however, for it was covered with a mass of black hair, in appearance like the furry coat of a dog. His face and neck were hidden beneath a black beard, intershot with gray, which would have been stiff and bushy had it not been limp and draggled and dripping with water. His eyes were closed, and he was apparently unconscious; but his mouth was wide open, his breast heaving as though from suffocation as he labored noisily for breath. A sailor, from time to time and quite methodically, as a matter of routine, dropped a canvas bucket into the ocean at the end of a rope, hauled it in hand under hand, and sluiced its contents over the prostrate man.

Pacing back and forth the length of the hatchway, and savagely chewing the end of cigar, was the man whose casual glance had rescued me from the sea. His height was probably five feet ten inches, or ten and a half; but my first impression, or feel of the man, was not of this, but of his strength. And yet, while he was of massive build, with broad shoulders and deep chest, I could not characterize his strength as massive. It was what might be termed a sinewy, knotty strength, of the kind we ascribe to lean and wiry men, but which, in him, because of his heavy build, partook more of the enlarged gorilla order. Not that in appearance he seemed in the least gorilla-like. What I am striving to express is this strength itself, more as a thing apart from his physical semblance. It was a strength we are wont to associate with things primitive, with wild animals, and the creatures we imagine our tree-dwelling prototypes to have been—a strength savage, ferocious, alive in itself, the essence of life in that it is the potency of motion, the elemental stuff itself out of which the many forms of life have been molded; in short, that which writhes in the body of a snake when the head is cut off, and the snake, as a snake, is dead, or which lingers in a shapeless lump of turtle-meat and recoils and quivers from the prod of a finger.

Such was the impression of strength I gathered from this man who paced up and down. He was firmly planted on his legs; his feet struck the deck squarely and with surety; every movement of a muscle, from the heave of the shoulders to the tightening of the lips about the cigar, was decisive, and seemed to come out of a strength that was excessive and overwhelming. In fact, though this strength pervaded every action of his, it seemed but the advertisement of a greater strength that lurked within, that lay dormant and no more than stirred from time to time, but which might arouse, at any moment, terrible and compelling, like the rage of a lion or the wrath of a storm.

The cook stuck his head out of the galley door and grinned encouragingly at me, at the same time jerking his thumb in a the direction of the man who paced up and down by the hatchway. Thus I was given to understand that he was the captain, the "Old Man," in the cook's vernacular, the individual whom I must interview and put to the trouble of somehow getting me ashore. I had half

started forward, to get over with what I was certain would
be a stormy five minutes, when a more violent suffocating
paroxysm seized the unfortunate person who was lying on
his back. He wrenched and writhed about convulsively.
The chin, with the damp black beard, pointed higher in
the air as the back muscles stiffened and the chest swelled
in an unconscious and instinctive effort to get more air.
Under the whiskers, and all unseen, I knew that the skin
was taking on a purplish hue.

The captain, or Wolf Larsen, as men called him, ceased
pacing and gazed down at the dying man. So fierce had
this final struggle become that the sailor paused in the
act of flinging more water over him and stared curiously,
the canvas bucket partly tilted and dripping its contents
to the deck. The dying man beat a tattoo on the hatch
with his heels, straightened out his legs, and stiffened in
one great tense effort, and rolled his head from side to
side. Then the muscles relaxed, the head stopped rolling,
and a sigh, as of profound relief, floated upward from his
lips. The jaw dropped, the upper lip lifted, and two rows
of tobacco-discolored teeth appeared. It seemed as though
his features had frozen into a diabolical grin at the world
he had left and outwitted.

Then a most surprising thing occurred. The captain
broke loose upon the dead man like a thunderclap. Oaths
rolled from his lips in a continuous stream. And they were
not namby-pamby oaths, or mere expressions of indecency.
Each word was a blasphemy, and there were many words.
They crisped and crackled like electric sparks. I had never
heard anything like it in my life, nor could I have conceived
it possible. With a turn for literary expression myself, and
a penchant for forcible figures and phrases, I appreciated,
as no other listener, I dare say, the peculiar vividness and
strength and absolute blasphemy of his metaphors. The
cause of it all, as near as I could make out, was that
the man, who was mate, had gone on a debauch before

leaving San Francisco, and then had the poor taste to die
at the beginning of the voyage and leave Wolf Larsen short-
handed.

It should be unnecessary to state, at least to my friends,
that I was shocked. Oaths and vile language of any sort
had always been repellent to me. I felt a wilting sensation, a sinking at the heart, and, I might just as well
say, a giddiness. To me, death had always been invested
with solemnity and dignity. It had been peaceful in its
occurrence, sacred in its ceremonial. But death in its more
sordid and terrible aspects was a thing with which I had
been unacquainted till now. As I say, while I appreciated
the power of the terrific denunciation that swept out of
Wolf Larsen's mouth, I was inexpressibly shocked. The
scorching torrent was enough to wither the face of the
corpse. I should not have been surprised if the wet black
beard had frizzled and curled and flared up in smoke and
flame. But the dead man was unconcerned. He continued
to grin with a sardonic humor, with a cynical mockery and
defiance. He was master of the situation.

CHAPTER THREE

WOLF LARSEN ceased swearing as suddenly as he had begun. He relighted his cigar and glanced around. His eyes chanced upon the cook.

"Well, Cooky?" he began, with a suaveness that was cold and of the temper of steel.

"Yes, sir," the cook eagerly interpolated, with appeasing and apologetic servility.

"Don't you think you've stretched that neck of yours just about enough? It's unhealthy, you know. The mate's gone, so I can't afford to lose you too. You must be very, very careful of your health, Cooky. Understand?"

His last word, in striking contrast with the smoothness of his previous utterance, snapped like the lash of a whip. The cook quailed under it.

"Yes, sir," was the meek reply, as the offending head disappeared into the galley.

At this sweeping rebuke, which the cook had only pointed, the rest of the crew became uninterested and fell to work at one task or another. A number of men, however, who were lounging about a companionway between the galley and the hatch, and who did not seem to be sailors, continued talking in low tones with one another. These, I afterward learned, were the hunters, the men who shot the seals, and a very superior breed to common sailor-folk.*

"Johansen!" Wolf Larsen called out. A sailor stepped forward obediently. "Get your palm* and needle and sew the beggar up. You'll find some old canvas in the sail-locker. Make it do."

"What'll I put on his feet, sir?" the man asked, after the customary "Ay, ay, sir."

"We'll see to that," Wolf Larsen answered, and elevated his voice in a call of "Cooky!"

Thomas Mugridge popped out of his galley like a jack-in-the-box.

"Go below and fill a sack with coal."

"Any of you fellows got a Bible or prayer-book?" was the captain's next demand, this time of the hunters lounging about the companionway.

They shook their heads, and some one made a jocular remark which I did not catch, but which raised a general laugh.

Wolf Larsen made the same demand of the sailors. Bibles and prayer-books seemed scarce articles, but one of the men volunteered to pursue the quest amongst the watch below, returning in a minute with the information that there was none.

The captain shrugged his shoulders. "Then we'll drop him over without any palavering, unless our clerical looking cast-away has the burial service at sea by heart."

By this time he had swung fully around and was facing me.

"You're a preacher, aren't you?" he asked.

The hunters,—there were six of them,—to a man, turned and regarded me. I was painfully aware of my likeness to a scarecrow. A laugh went up at my appearance,—a laugh that was not lessened or softened by the dead man stretched and grinning on the deck before us; a laugh that was as rough and harsh and frank as the sea itself; that arose out of coarse feelings and blunted sensibilities, from natures that knew neither courtesy nor gentleness.

Wolf Larsen did not laugh, though his gray eyes lighted with a slight glint of amusement; and in that moment, having stepped forward quite close to him, I received my first impression of the man himself, of the man as apart from his body and from the torrent of blasphemy I had heard him spew forth. The face, with large features and strong lines, of the square order, yet well filled out, was apparently massive at first sight; but again, as with the body, the massiveness seemed to vanish and a conviction to grow of a tremendous and excessive mental or spiritual strength that lay behind, sleeping in the deeps of his being. The jaw, the chin, the brow rising to a goodly height and swelling heavily above the eyes,—these, while strong in themselves, unusually strong, seemed to speak an immense vigor or virility of spirit that lay behind and beyond and out of sight. There was no sounding such a spirit, no measuring, no determining of metes and bounds, nor neatly classifying in some pigeonhole with others of similar type.

The eyes—and it was my destiny to know them well— were large and handsome, wide apart as the true artist's are wide, sheltering under a heavy brow and arched over by thick black eyebrows. The eyes themselves were of that baffling protean gray which is never twice the same; which runs through many shades and colorings like intershot silk in sunshine; which is gray, dark and light, and greenish gray, and sometimes of the clear azure of the deep sea. They were eyes that masked the soul with a thousand guises, and that sometimes opened, at rare moments, and allowed it to rush up as though it were about to fare forth nakedly into the world on some wonderful adventure,— eyes that could brook with the hopeless sombreness of leaden skies; that could snap and crackle points of fire like those which sparkle from a whirling sword; that could grow chill as an arctic landscape, and yet again, that could warm and soften and be all a-dance with love-lights, intense and masculine, luring and compelling, which at the same time fascinate and dominate women till they surrender in a gladness of joy and of relief and sacrifice.

But to return. I told him that, unhappily for the burial service, I was not a preacher, when he sharply demanded:

"What do you do for a living?"

I confess I had never had such a question asked me

before, nor had I ever canvassed it. I was quite taken aback, and before I could find myself had sillily stammered, "I—I am a gentleman."

His lip curled in a swift sneer.

"I have worked, I do work," I cried impetuously, as though he were my judge and I required vindication, and at the same time very much aware of my arrant idiocy in discussing the subject at all.

"For your living?"

There was something so imperative and masterful about him that I was quite beside myself—"rattled," as Furuseth would have termed it, like a quaking child before a stern schoolmaster.

"Who feeds you?" was his next question.

"I have an income," I answered stoutly, and could have bitten my tongue the next instant. "All of which, you will pardon my observing, has nothing whatsoever to do with what I wish to see you about."

But he disregarded my protest.

"Who earned it? Eh? I thought so. Your father. You stand on dead men's legs. You've never had any of your own. You couldn't walk alone between two sunrises and hustle the meat for your belly for three meals. Let me see your hand."

His tremendous, dormant strength must have stirred, swiftly and accurately, or I must have slept a moment, for before I knew it he had stepped two paces forward, gripped my right hand in his, and held it up for inspection. I tried to withdraw it, but his fingers tightened, without visible effort, till I thought mine would be crushed. It is hard to maintain one's dignity under such circumstances. I could not squirm or struggle like a schoolboy. Nor could I attack such a creature who had but to twist my arm to break it. Nothing remained but to stand still and accept the indignity. I had time to notice that the pockets of the dead man had been emptied on the deck, and that his body and his grin had been wrapped from view in canvas, the folds of which the sailor, Johansen, was sewing together with coarse white twine, shoving the needle through with a leather contrivance fitted on the palm of his hand.

Wolf Larsen dropped my hand with a flirt of disdain.

"Dead men's hands have kept it soft. Good for little else than dish-washing and scullion work."

"I wish to be put ashore," I said firmly, for I now had myself in control. "I shall pay you whatever you judge your delay and trouble to be worth."

He looked at me curiously. Mockery shone in his eyes.

"I have a counter proposition to make, and for the good of your soul. My mate's gone, and there'll be a lot of promotion. A sailor comes aft to take mate's place, cabin-boy goes for'ard to take sailor's place, and you take the cabin-boy's place, sign the articles for the cruise, twenty dollars per month and found. Now what do you say? And mind you, it's for your own soul's sake. It will be the making of you. You might learn in time to stand on your own legs and perhaps to toddle along a bit."

But I took no notice. The sails of the vessel I had seen off to the southwest had grown larger and plainer. They were of the same schooner-rig as the *Ghost*, though the hull itself, I could see, was smaller. She was a pretty sight, leaping and flying toward us, and evidently bound to pass at close range. The wind had been momentarily increasing, and the sun, after a few angry gleams, had disappeared. The sea had turned a dull leaden gray and grown rougher, and was now tossing foaming whitecaps to the sky. We were travelling faster and heeled farther over. Once, in a gust, the rail dipped under the sea, and the decks on that side were for the moment awash with water that made a couple of the hunters hastily lift their feet.

"That vessel will soon be passing us," I said, after a moment's pause. "As she is going in the opposite direction, she is very probably bound for San Francisco."

"Very probably," was Wolf Larsen's answer, as he turned partly away from me and cried out, "Cooky! Oh, Cooky!"

The Cockney popped out of the galley.

"Where's that boy? Tell him I want him."

"Yes, sir;" and Thomas Mugridge fled swiftly aft and disappeared down another companionway near the wheel. A moment later he emerged, a heavy-set young fellow of eighteen or nineteen, with a glowering, villanous countenance, trailing at his heels.

"'Ere 'e is, sir," the cook said.

But Wolf Larsen ignored that worthy, turning at once to the cabin-boy.

"What's your name, boy?"

"George Leach, sir," came the sullen answer, and the boy's bearing showed clearly that he divined the reason for which he had been summoned.

"Not an Irish name," the captain snapped sharply.* "O'Toole or McCarthy would suit your mug a damn sight better. Unless, very likely, there's an Irishman in your mother's woodpile."

I saw the young fellow's hands clench at the insult, and the blood crawl scarlet up his neck.

"But let that go," Wolf Larsen continued. "You may have very good reasons for forgetting your name, and I'll like you none the worse for it as long as you toe the mark. Telegraph Hill,* of course, is your port of entry. It sticks out all over your mug. Tough as they make them and twice as nasty. I know the kind. Well, you can make up your mind to have it taken out of you on this craft. Understand? Who shipped you, anyway?"*

"McCready and Swanson."

"Sir!" Wolf Larsen thundered.

"McCready and Swanson, sir," the boy corrected, his eyes burning with a bitter light.

"Who got the advance money?"

"They did, sir."

"I thought as much. And damned glad you were to let them have it. Couldn't make yourself scarce too quick, with several gentlemen you may have heard of looking for you."

The boy metamorphosed into a savage on the instant. His body bunched together as though for a spring, and his face became as an infuriated beast's as he snarled, "It's a—"

"A what?" Wolf Larsen asked, a peculiar softness in his voice, as though he were overwhelmingly curious to hear the unspoken word.

The boy hesitated, then mastered his temper. "Nothin', sir. I take it back."

"And you have shown me I was right." This with a gratified smile. "How old are you?"

"Just turned sixteen, sir."

"A lie. You'll never see eighteen again.* Big for your age at that, with muscles like a horse. Pack up your kit and go for'ard into the fo'c'sle. You're promoted; see?"

Without waiting for the boy's acceptance, the captain turned to the sailor who had just finished the grewsome task of sewing up the corpse. "Johansen, do you know anything about navigation?"

"No, sir."

"Well, never mind; you're mate just the same. Get your traps aft into the mate's berth."

"Ay, ay, sir," was the cheery response, as Johansen started forward.

In the meantime the erstwhile cabin-boy had not moved.

"What are you waiting for?" Wolf Larsen demanded.

"I didn't sign for boat-puller, sir," was the reply. "I signed for cabin-boy. An' I don't want no boat-pullin' in mine."

"Pack up and go for'ard."

This time Wolf Larsen's command was thrillingly imperative. The boy glowered sullenly, but refused to move.

Then came another stirring of Wolf Larsen's tremendous strength. It was utterly unexpected, and it was over and done with between the ticks of two seconds. He had sprung fully six feet across the deck and driven his fist into the other's stomach. At the same moment, as though I had been struck myself, I felt a sickening shock in the pit of my stomach. I instance this to show the sensitiveness of my nervous organization at the time, and how unused I was to spectacles of brutality. The cabin-boy—and he weighed one hundred and sixty-five at the very least—crumpled up. His body wrapped limply about the fist like a wet rag about a stick. He lifted into the air, described a short curve, and struck the deck alongside the corpse on his head and shoulders, where he lay and writhed about in agony.

"Well?" Larsen asked of me. "Have you made up your mind?"

I had glanced occasionally at the approaching schooner, and it was now almost abreast of us and not more than a couple of hundred yards away. It was a very trim and neat little craft. I could see a large, black number on one of its sails, and I had seen pictures of pilot-boats.*

"What vessel is that?" I asked.

"The pilot-boat *Lady Mine*," Wolf Larsen answered grimly. "Got rid of her pilots and running into San Francisco. She'll be there in five or six hours with this wind."

"Will you please signal it, then, so that I may be put ashore."

"Sorry, but I've lost the signal book overboard," he remarked, and the group of hunters grinned.

I debated a moment, looking him squarely in the eyes. I had seen the frightful treatment of the cabin-boy, and knew that I should very probably receive the same, if not worse. As I say, I debated with myself, and then I did what I consider the bravest act of my life. I ran to the side, waving my arms and shouting:

"*Lady Mine* ahoy! Take me ashore! A thousand dollars if you take me ashore!"

I waited, watching two men who stood by the wheel, one of them steering. The other was lifting a megaphone to his lips. I did not turn my head, though I expected every moment a killing blow from the human brute behind me. At last, after what seemed centuries, unable longer to stand the strain, I looked around. He had not moved. He was standing in the same position, swaying easily to the roll of the ship and lighting a fresh cigar.

"What is the matter? Anything wrong?"

This was the cry from the *Lady Mine*.

"Yes!" I shouted, at the top of my lungs. "Life or death! One thousand dollars if you take me ashore!"

"Too much 'Frisco tanglefoot* for the health of my crew!" Wolf Larsen shouted after. "This one,"—indicating me with his thumb,—"fancies sea-serpents and monkeys just now!"

The man on the *Lady Mine* laughed back through the megaphone. The pilot-boat plunged past.

"Give him hell for me!" came a final cry, and the two men waved their arms in farewell.

I leaned despairingly over the rail, watching the trim little schooner swiftly increasing the bleak sweep of ocean between us. And she would probably be in San Francisco in five or six hours! My head seemed bursting. There was an ache in my throat as though my heart were up in it. A curling wave struck the side and splashed salt spray on my lips. The wind puffed strongly, and the *Ghost* heeled far over, burying her lee rail. I could hear the water rushing down upon the deck.

When I turned around, a moment later, I saw the cabin-boy staggering to his feet. His face was ghastly white, twitching with suppressed pain. He looked very sick.

"Well, Leach, are you going for'ard?" Wolf Larsen asked.

"Yes, sir," came the answer of a spirit cowed.

"And you?" I was asked.

"I'll give you a thousand—" I began, but was interrupted.

"Stow that! Are you going to take up your duties as cabin-boy? Or do I have to take you in hand?"

What was I to do? To be brutally beaten, to be killed perhaps, would not help my case. I looked steadily into the cruel gray eyes. They might have been granite for all the light and warmth of a human soul they contained. One may see the soul stir in some men's eyes, but his were bleak, and cold, and gray as the sea itself.

"Well?"

"Yes," I said.

"Say 'yes, sir.' "

"Yes, sir," I corrected.

"What is your name?"

"Van Weyden, sir."

"First name?"

"Humphrey, sir; Humphrey Van Weyden."

"Age?"

"Thirty-five, sir."

"That'll do. Go to the cook and learn your duties."

And thus it was that I passed into a state of involuntary servitude to Wolf Larsen. He was stronger than I, that was all. But it was very unreal at the time. It is no less unreal now that I look back upon it. It will always be to me a monstrous, inconceivable thing, a horrible nightmare.

"Hold on, don't go yet."

I stopped obediently in my walk toward the galley.

"Johansen, call all hands. Now that we've everything cleaned up, we'll have the funeral and get the decks cleared of useless lumber."

While Johansen was summoning the watch below, a couple of sailors, under the captain's direction, laid the canvas-swathed corpse upon a hatch-cover. On either side the deck, against the rail and bottoms up, were lashed a

number of small boats. Several men picked up the hatch-
cover with its ghastly freight, carried it to the lee side,
and rested it on the boats, the feet pointing overboard. To
the feet was attached the sack of coal which the cook had
fetched.

I had always conceived a burial at sea to be a very
solemn and awe-inspiring event, but I was quickly disil-
lusioned, by this burial at any rate.* One of the hunters,
a little dark-eyed man whom his mates called "Smoke,"
was telling stories, liberally intersprinkled with oaths and
obscenities; and every minute or so the group of hunters
gave mouth to a laughter that sounded to me like a wolf-
chorus or the barking of hell-hounds. The sailors trooped
noisily aft, some of the watch below rubbing the sleep from
their eyes, and talked in low tones together. There was
an ominous and worried expression on their faces. It was
evident that they did not like the outlook of a voyage under
such a captain and begun so inauspiciously. From time to
time they stole glances at Wolf Larsen, and I could see
that they were apprehensive of the man.

He stepped up to the hatch-cover, and all caps came off.
I ran my eyes over them—twenty men all told, twenty-
two including the man at the wheel and myself. I was
pardonably curious in my survey, for it appeared my fate
to be pent up with them on this miniature floating world
for I knew not how many weeks or months. The sailors,
in the main, were English and Scandinavian, and their
faces seemed of the heavy, stolid order. The hunters, on
the other hand, had stronger and more diversified faces,
with hard lines and the marks of the free play of passions.
Strange to say, and I noted it at once, Wolf Larsen's features showed no such evil stamp. There seemed nothing
vicious in them. True, there were lines, but they were the
lines of decision and firmness. It seemed, rather, a frank
and open countenance, which frankness or openness was
enhanced by the fact that he was smooth-shaven. I could

hardly believe,—until the next incident occurred,—that it
was the face of a man who could behave as he had behaved
to the cabin-boy.

At this moment, as he opened his mouth to speak, puff
after puff struck the schooner and pressed her side under.
The wind shrieked a wild song through the rigging. Some of
the hunters glanced anxiously aloft. The lee rail, where the
dead man lay, was buried in the sea, and as the schooner
lifted and righted the water swept across the deck, wetting
us above our shoe-tops. A shower of rain drove down upon
us, each drop stinging like a hailstone. As it passed, Wolf
Larsen began to speak, the bare-headed men swaying in
unison to the heave and lunge of the deck.

"I only remember one part of the service," he said, "and
that is, 'And the body shall be cast into the sea.' So cast
it in."

He ceased speaking. The men holding the hatch-cover
seemed perplexed, puzzled no doubt by the briefness of
the ceremony. He burst upon them in a fury.

"Lift up that end there, damn you! What the hell's the
matter with you?"

They elevated the end of the hatch-cover with pitiful
haste, and, like a dog flung overside, the dead man slid
feet first into the sea. The coal at his feet dragged him
down. He was gone.

"Johansen," Wolf Larsen said briskly to the new mate,
"keep all hands on deck now they're here. Get in the
topsails and jibs and make a good job of it. We're in for
a sou'easter. Better reef the jib and mainsail, too, while
you're about it."

In a moment the decks were in commotion, Johansen
bellowing orders and the men pulling or letting go ropes of
various sorts—all naturally confusing to a landsman such
as myself. But it was the heartlessness of it that especially
struck me. The dead man was an episode that was past,
an incident that was dropped, in a canvas covering with a

"Look sharp or you'll get doused," was Mr. Mugridge's parting injunction, as I left the galley with a big tea-pot in one hand, and in the hollow of the other arm several loaves of fresh-baked bread. One of the hunters, a tall, loose-jointed chap named Henderson, was going aft at the time from the steerage, (the name the hunters facetiously gave their midships sleeping quarters), to the cabin. Wolf Larsen was on the poop, smoking his ever-lasting cigar.

"'Ere she comes. Sling yer 'ook!" the cook cried.

I stopped, for I did not know what was coming, and saw the galley door slide shut with a bang. Then I saw Henderson leaping like a madman for the main rigging, up which he shot, on the inside, till he was many feet higher than my head. Also I saw a great wave, curling and foaming, poised far above the rail. I was directly under it. My mind did not work quickly, everything was so new and strange. I grasped that I was in danger, but that was all. I stood still, in trepidation. Then Wolf Larsen shouted from the poop:—

"Grab hold of something, you—you Hump!"

But it was too late. I sprang toward the rigging, to which I might have clung, and was met by the descending wall of water. What happened after that was very confusing. I was beneath the water, suffocating and drowning. My feet were out from under me, and I was turning over and over and being swept along I knew not where. Several times I collided against hard objects, once striking my right knee a terrible blow. Then the flood seemed suddenly to subside and I was breathing the good air again. I had been swept against the galley and around the steerage companionway from the weather side into the lee scuppers. The pain from my hurt knee was agonizing.* I could not put my weight on it, or, at least, I thought I could not put my weight on it; and I felt sure the leg was broken. But the cook was after me, shouting through the lee galley door:

"'Ere, you! Don't tyke all night about it! Where's the

pot? Lost overboard? Serve you bloody well right if yer neck was broke!"

I managed to struggle to my feet. The great tea-pot was still in my hand. I limped to the galley and handed it to him. But he was consumed with indignation, real or feigned.

"Gawd blime me* if you ayn't a slob. Wot're you good for anyw'y, I'd like to know? Eh? Wot're you good for anyw'y? Cawn't even carry a bit of tea aft without losin' it. Now I'll 'ave to boil some more."

"An' wot're you snifflin' about?" he burst out at me, with renewed rage. "'Cos you've 'urt yer pore little leg, pore little mamma's darlin'."

I was not sniffling, though my face might well have been drawn and twitching from the pain. But I called up all my resolution, set my teeth, and hobbled back and forth from galley to cabin and cabin to galley without further mishap. Two things I had acquired by my accident: an injured kneecap that went undressed and from which I suffered for weary months, and the name of "Hump," which Wolf Larsen had called me from the poop. Thereafter, fore and aft, I was known by no other name, until the term became a part of my thought-processes and I identified it with myself, thought of myself as Hump, as though Hump were I and had always been I.

It was no easy task, waiting on the cabin table, where sat Wolf Larsen, Johansen, and the six hunters. The cabin was small, to begin with, and to move around, as I was compelled to, was not made easier by the schooner's violent pitching and wallowing. But what struck me most forcibly was the total lack of sympathy on the part of the men whom I served. I could feel my knee through my clothes, swelling, and swelling, and I was sick and faint from the pain of it. I could catch glimpses of my face, white and ghastly, distorted with pain, in the cabin mirror. All the men must have seen my condition, but not one spoke or took notice of me, till I was almost grateful to Wolf Larsen, later on, (I was washing the dishes), when he said:

"Don't let a little thing like that bother you. You'll get used to such things in time. It may cripple you some, but all the same you'll be learning to walk."

"That's what you call a paradox, isn't it?" he added.

He seemed pleased when I nodded my head with the customary, "Yes, sir."

"I suppose you know a bit about literary things? Eh? Good. I'll have some talks with you sometime."

And then, taking no further account of me, he turned his back and went up on deck.

That night, when I had finished an endless amount of work, I was sent to sleep in the steerage, where I made up a spare bunk. I was glad to get out of the detestable presence of the cook and to be off my feet. To my surprise, my clothes had dried on me and there seemed no indications of catching cold, either from the last soaking or from the prolonged soaking from the foundering of the *Martinez*. Under ordinary circumstances, after all that I had undergone, I should have been fit for bed and a trained nurse.

But my knee was bothering me terribly. As well as I could make out, the kneecap seemed turned up on edge in the midst of the swelling. As I sat in my bunk examining it, (the six hunters were all in the steerage, smoking and talking in loud voices), Henderson took a passing glance at it.

"Looks nasty," he commented. "Tie a rag around it and it'll be all right."

That was all; and on the land I would have been lying on the broad of my back, with a surgeon attending on me, and with strict injunctions to do nothing but rest. But I must do these men justice. Callous as they were to my suffering, they were equally callous to their own when anything befell them. And this was due, I believe, first, to habit; and second, to the fact that they were less sensitively organized. I really believe that a finely organized, high-strung man would suffer twice and thrice as much as they from a like injury.

Tired as I was,—exhausted, in fact,—I was prevented from sleeping by the pain in my knee. It was all I could do to keep from groaning aloud. At home I should un-doubtedly have given vent to my anguish; but this new and elemental environment seemed to call for a savage repression. Like the savage, the attitude of these men was stoical in great things, childish in little things. I remember, later in the voyage, seeing Kerfoot, another of the hunters, lose a finger by having it smashed to a jelly; and he did not even murmur or change the expression on his face. Yet I have seen the same man, time and again, fly into the most outrageous passion over a trifle.

He was doing it now, vociferating, bellowing, waving his arms, and cursing like a fiend, and all because of a disagree-ment with another hunter as to whether a seal pup knew instinctively how to swim. He held that it did, that it could swim the moment it was born. The other hunter, Latimer, a lean, Yankee-looking fellow with shrewd, narrow-slitted eyes, held otherwise, held that the seal pup was born on the land for no other reason than that it could not swim, that its mother was compelled to teach it to swim as birds were compelled to teach their nestlings how to fly.

For the most part, the remaining four hunters leaned on the table or lay in their bunks and left the discussion to the two antagonists. But they were supremely inter-ested, for every little while they ardently took sides, and sometimes all were talking at once, till their voices surged back and forth in waves of sound like mimic thunder-rolls in the confined space. Childish and immaterial as the topic was, the quality of their reasoning was still more childish and immaterial. In truth, there was very little reasoning or none at all. Their method was one of as-

sertion, assumption, and denunciation. They proved that
a seal pup could swim or not swim at birth by stating
the proposition very bellicosely and then following it up
with an attack on the opposing man's judgment, common
sense, nationality, or past history. Rebuttal was precisely
similar. I have related this in order to show the mental
caliber of the men with whom I was thrown in contact.
Intellectually they were children, inhabiting the physical
forms of men.

And they smoked, incessantly smoked, using a coarse,
cheap, and offensive-smelling tobacco. The air was thick
and murky with the smoke of it; and this, combined with
the violent movement of the ship as she struggled through
the storm, would surely have made me seasick had I been
a victim to that malady. As it was, it made me quite
squeamish, though this nausea might have been due to
the pain of my leg and exhaustion.

As I lay there thinking, I naturally dwelt upon myself
and my situation. It was unparalleled, undreamed-of, that
I, Humphrey Van Weyden, a scholar and a dilettante, if
you please, in things artistic and literary, should be lying here on a Bering Sea seal-hunting schooner. Cabin-
boy! I had never done any hard manual labor, or scullion labor, in my life. I had lived a placid, uneventful,
sedentary existence all my days—the life of a scholar and
a recluse on an assured and comfortable income. Violent
life and athletic sports had never appealed to me. I had
always been a book-worm; so my sisters and father had
called me during my childhood. I had gone camping but
once in my life, and then I left the party almost at its
start and returned to the comforts and conveniences of
a roof. And here I was, with dreary and endless vistas
before me of table-setting, potato-peeling, and dishwash-
ing. And I was not strong. The doctors had always said
that I had a remarkable constitution, but I had never
developed it or my body through exercise. My muscles

were small and soft, like a woman's, or so the doctors
had said time and again in the course of their attempts
to persuade me to go in for physical-culture fads. But
I had preferred to use my head, rather than my body;
and here I was, in no fit condition for the rough life in
prospect.

These are merely a few of the things that went through
my mind, and are related for the sake of vindicating myself
in advance in the weak and helpless rôle I was destined to
play. But I thought, also, of my mother and sisters, and
pictured their grief. I was among the missing dead of the
Martinez disaster, an unrecovered body. I could see the
headlines in the papers; the fellows at the University Club
and the Bibelot* shaking their heads and saying, "Poor
chap!" And I could see Charley Furuseth, as I had said
good-bye to him that morning, lounging in a dressing-gown
on the be-pillowed window couch and delivering himself of
oracular and pessimistic epigrams.

And all the while, rolling, plunging, climbing the
moving mountains and falling and wallowing in the
foaming valleys, the schooner *Ghost* was fighting her
way farther and farther into the heart of the Pacific—
and I was on her. I could hear the wind above. It
came to my ears as a muffled roar. Now and again
feet stamped overhead. An endless creaking was going on all about me, the woodwork and the fittings
groaning and squeaking and complaining in a thousand
keys. The hunters were still arguing and roaring like
some semi-human amphibious breed. The air was filled
with oaths and indecent expressions. I could see their
faces, flushed and angry, the brutality distorted and
emphasized by the sickly yellow of the sea-lamps which
rocked back and forth with the ship. Through the dim
smoke-haze the bunks looked like the sleeping dens of
animals in a menagerie. Oilskins and sea-boots were
hanging from the walls, and here and there rifles and

shotguns rested securely in the racks. It was a sea-
fitting for the buccaneers and pirates of bygone years.
My imagination ran riot, and still I could not sleep.
And it was a long, long night, weary and dreary and
long.

CHAPTER FIVE

BUT my first night in the hunters' steerage was also my
last. Next day Johansen, the new mate, was routed from
the cabin by Wolf Larsen, and sent into the steerage to
sleep thereafter, while I took possession of the tiny cabin
stateroom, which, on the first day of the voyage, had already had two occupants. The reason for this change was
quickly learned by the hunters, and became the cause of a
deal of grumbling on their part. It seemed that Johansen,
in his sleep, lived over each night the events of the day.
His incessant talking and shouting and bellowing of orders
had been too much for Wolf Larsen, who had accordingly
foisted the nuisance upon his hunters.

After a sleepless night, I arose weak and in agony, to
hobble through my second day on the *Ghost*. Thomas
Mugridge routed me out at half-past five, much in the
fashion that Bill Sykes must have routed out his dog;* but
Mr. Mugridge's brutality to me was paid back in kind and
with interest. The unnecessary noise he made, (I had lain
wide-eyed the whole night), must have awakened one of
the hunters; for a heavy shoe whizzed through the semi-
darkness, and Mr. Mugridge, with a sharp howl of pain,
humbly begged everybody's pardon. Later on, in the galley,
I noticed that his ear was bruised and swollen. It never
went entirely back to its normal shape, and was called a
"cauliflower ear" by the sailors.

The day was filled with miserable variety. I had taken my
dried clothes down from the galley the night before, and
the first thing I did was to exchange the cook's garments
for them. I looked for my purse. In addition to some small
change, (and I have a good memory for such things), it
had contained one hundred and eighty-five dollars in gold

and paper.* The purse I found, but its contents, with the exception of the small silver, had been abstracted. I spoke to the cook about it, when I went on deck to take up my duties in the galley, and though I had looked forward to a surly answer, I had not expected the belligerent harangue that I received.

"Look 'ere, 'Ump," he began, a malicious light in his eyes and a snarl in his throat; "d'ye want yer nose punched? If you think I'm a thief, just keep it to yerself, or you'll find 'ow bloody well mistyken you are. Strike me blind if this ayn't gratitude for yer! 'Ere you come, a pore mis'rable specimen of 'uman scum, an' I tykes yer into my galley an' treats yer 'ansom, an' this is wot I get for it. Nex' time you can go to 'ell, say I, an' I've a good mind to give you what-for anyw'y."

So saying, he put up his fists and started for me. To my shame be it, I cowered away from the blow and ran out the galley door. What else was I to do? Force, nothing but force, obtained on this brute-ship. Moral suasion was a thing unknown. Picture it to yourself: a man of ordinary stature, slender of build, and with weak, undeveloped muscles, who has lived a peaceful, placid life, and is unused to violence of any sort—what could such a man possibly do? There was no more reason that I should stand and face these human beasts than that I should stand and face an infuriated bull.

So I thought it out at the time, feeling the need for vindication and desiring to be at peace with my conscience. But this vindication did not satisfy. Nor to this day can I permit my manhood to look back upon those events and feel entirely exonerated. The situation was something that really exceeded rational formulas for conduct and demanded more than the cold conclusions of reason. When viewed in the light of formal logic, there is not one thing of which to be ashamed; but nevertheless a shame rises within me at the recollection, and in the pride of my manhood

I feel that my manhood has in unaccountable ways been smirched and sullied.

All of which is neither here nor there. The speed with which I ran from the galley caused excruciating pain in my knee, and I sank down helplessly at the break of the poop. But the Cockney had not pursued me.

"Look at 'im run! Look at 'im run!" I could hear him crying. "An' with a gyme leg at that! Come on back, you pore little mamma's darling. I won't 'it yer; no, I won't."

I came back and went on with my work; and here the episode ended for the time, though further developments were yet to take place. I set the breakfast-table in the cabin, and at seven o'clock waited on the hunters and officers. The storm had evidently broken during the night, though a huge sea was still running and a stiff wind blowing. Sail had been made in the early watches, so that the *Ghost* was racing along under every-thing except the two topsails and the flying jib. These three sails, I gathered from the conversation, were to be set immediately after breakfast. I learned, also, that Wolf Larsen was anxious to make the most of the storm, which was driving him to the southwest into that portion of the sea where he expected to pick up with the northeast trades. It was before this steady wind that he hoped to make the major portion of the run to Japan, curving south into the tropics and north again as he approached the coast of Asia.

After breakfast I had another unenviable experience. When I had finished washing the dishes, I cleaned the cabin stove and carried the ashes up on deck to empty them. Wolf Larsen and Henderson were standing near the wheel, deep in conversation. The sailor, Johnson, was steering. As I started toward the weather side I saw him make a sudden motion with his head, which I mistook for a token of recognition and good morning. In reality, he was attempting to warn me to throw my ashes over the lee side. Unconscious of my blunder, I passed by Wolf Larsen and

the hunter and flung the ashes over the side to windward.
The wind drove them back, and not only over me, but
over Henderson and Wolf Larsen. The next instant the
latter kicked me, violently, as a cur is kicked. I had not
realized there could be so much pain in a kick. I reeled
away from him and leaned against the cabin in a half-
fainting condition. Everything was swimming before my
eyes, and I turned sick. The nausea overpowered me, and
I managed to crawl to the side of the vessel. But Wolf
Larsen did not follow me up. Brushing the ashes from his
clothes, he had resumed his conversation with Henderson.
Johansen, who had seen the affair from the break of the
poop, sent a couple of sailors aft to clean up the mess.

Later in the morning I received a surprise of a totally
different sort. Following the cook's instructions, I had gone
into Wolf Larsen's state-room to put it to rights and make
the bed. Against the wall, near the head of the bunk, was
a rack filled with books. I glanced over them, noting with
astonishment such names as Shakespeare, Tennyson, Poe,
and De Quincey.* There were scientific works, too, among
which were represented men such as Tyndall, Proctor, and
Darwin. Astronomy and physics were represented, and I
remarked Bulfinch's "Age of Fable," Shaw's "History of
English and American Literature," and Johnson's "Natural History" in two large volumes. Then there were a
number of grammars, such as Metcalf's, and Reed and
Kellogg's; and I smiled as I saw a copy of "The Dean's
English."*

I could not reconcile these books with the man from
what I had seen of him, and I wondered if he could possibly
read them. But when I came to make the bed I found,
between the blankets, dropped apparently as he had sunk
off to sleep, a complete Browning, the Cambridge Edition.
It was open at "In a Balcony,"* and I noticed, here and
there, passages underlined in pencil. Further, letting drop
the volume during a lurch of the ship, a sheet of paper fell

out. It was scrawled over with geometrical diagrams and calculations of some sort.

It was patent that this terrible man was no ignorant clod, such as one would inevitably suppose him to be from his exhibitions of brutality. At once he became an enigma. One side or the other of his nature was perfectly comprehensible; but both sides together were bewildering. I had already remarked that his language was excellent, marred with an occasional slight inaccuracy. Of course, in common speech with the sailors and hunters, it sometimes fairly bristled with errors, which was due to the vernacular itself; but in the few words he had held with me it had been clear and correct.

This glimpse I had caught of his other side must have emboldened me, for I resolved to speak to him about the money I had lost.

"I have been robbed," I said to him, a little later, when I found him pacing up and down the poop alone.

"Sir," he corrected, not harshly, but sternly.

"I have been robbed, sir," I amended.

"How did it happen?" he asked.

Then I told him the whole circumstance, how my clothes had been left to dry in the galley, and how, later, I was nearly beaten by the cook when I mentioned the matter.

He smiled at my recital. "Pickings," he concluded; "Cooky's pickings. And don't you think your miserable life worth the price? Besides, consider it a lesson. You'll learn in time how to take care of your money for yourself. I suppose, up to now, your lawyer has done it for you, or your business agent."

I could feel the quiet sneer through his words, but demanded, "How can I get it back again?"

"That's your lookout. You haven't any lawyer or business agent now, so you'll have to depend on yourself. When you get a dollar, hang on to it. A man who leaves his money lying around, the way you did, deserves to lose it. Besides, you have sinned. You have no right to put temptation in the way of your fellow-creatures. You tempted Cooky, and he fell. You have placed his immortal soul in jeopardy. By the way, do you believe in the immortal soul?"

His lids lifted lazily as he asked the question, and it seemed that the deeps were opening to me and that I was gazing into his soul. But it was an illusion. Far as it might have seemed, no man has ever seen very far into Wolf Larsen's soul, or seen it at all,—of this I am convinced. It was a very lonely soul, I was to learn, that never unmasked, though at rare moments it played at doing so.

"I read immortality in your eyes,"* I answered, dropping the "sir,"—an experiment, for I thought the intimacy of the conversation warranted it.

He took no notice. "By that, I take it, you see something that is alive, but that necessarily does not have to live forever."

"I read more than that," I continued boldly.

"Then you read consciousness. You read the consciousness of life that it is alive; but still no further away, no endlessness of life."

How clearly he thought, and how well he expressed what he thought! From regarding me curiously, he turned his head and glanced out over the leaden sea to windward. A bleakness came into his eyes, and the lines of his mouth grew severe and harsh. He was evidently in a pessimistic mood.

"Then to what end?" he demanded abruptly, turning back to me. "If I am immortal—why?"

I halted. How could I explain my idealism* to this man? How could I put into speech a something felt, a something like the strains of music heard in sleep, a something that convinced yet transcended utterance?

"What do you believe, then?" I countered.

"I believe that life is a mess," he answered promptly. "It is like yeast, a ferment, a thing that moves and may move for a minute, an hour, a year, or a hundred years, but that in the end will cease to move. The big eat the little that they may continue to move, the strong eat the weak that they may retain their strength. The lucky eat the most and move the longest, that is all. What do you make of those things?"

He swept his arm in an impatient gesture toward a number of the sailors who were working on some kind of rope stuff amidships.

"They move; so does the jellyfish move.* They move in order to eat in order that they may keep moving. There you have it. They live for their belly's sake, and the belly is for their sake. It's a circle; you get nowhere. Neither do they. In the end they come to a standstill. They move no more. They are dead."

"They have dreams," I interrupted, "radiant, flashing dreams—"

"Of grub," he concluded sententiously.

"And of more—"

"Grub. Of a larger appetite and more luck in satisfying it." His voice sounded harsh. There was no levity in it. "For look you, they dream of making lucky voyages which will bring them more money, of becoming the mates of ships, of finding fortunes—in short, of being in a better position for preying on their fellows, of having all night in, good grub, and somebody else to do the dirty work. You and I are just like them. There is no difference, except that we have eaten more and better. I am eating them now, and you, too. But in the past you have eaten more than I have. You have slept in soft beds, and worn fine clothes, and eaten good meals. Who made those beds? and those clothes? and those meals? Not you. You never made anything in your own sweat. You live on an income which your father earned. You are like a frigate bird* swooping down upon the boobies and robbing them of the fish they have caught. You are one with a crowd of men who have made what they call a government, who are masters of all the other men, and who eat the food the other men get and would like to eat themselves. You wear the warm clothes. They made the clothes, but they shiver in rags and ask you, the lawyer, or business agent who handles your money, for a job."

"But that is beside the matter," I cried.

"Not at all." He was speaking rapidly, now, and his eyes were flashing. "It is piggishness, and it is life. Of what use or sense is an immortality of piggishness? What is the end? What is it all about? You have made no food. Yet the food you have eaten or wasted might have saved the lives of a score of wretches who made the food but did not eat it. What immortal end did you serve? Or did they? Consider yourself and me. What does your boasted immortality amount to when your life runs foul of mine? You would like to go back to the land, which is a favorable place for your kind of piggishness. It is a whim of mine to keep you aboard this ship, where my piggishness flourishes. And keep you I will. I can make or break you. You may die today, this week, or next month. I could kill you now, with a blow of my fist, for you are a miserable weakling. But if we are immortal, what is the reason for this? To be piggish as you and I have been all our lives does not seem to be just the thing for immortals to be doing. Again, what's it all about? Why have I kept you here?—"

"Because you are stronger," I managed to blurt out.

"But why stronger?" he went on at once with his perpetual queries. "Because I am a bigger bit of the ferment than you? Don't you see? Don't you see?"

"But the hopelessness of it," I protested.

"I agree with you," he answered. "Then why move at all, since moving is living? Without moving and being part of the yeast there would be no hopelessness. But, —and there it is,—we want to live and move, though we have no reason to, because it happens that it is the nature of life to live and move, to want to live and move. If it were not for this, life would be dead. It is because of this life that is in you that you dream of your immortality. The life that is in you is alive and wants to go on being alive forever. Bah! An eternity of piggishness!"

He abruptly turned on his heel and started forward. He stopped at the break of the poop and called me to him.

"By the way, how much was it that Cooky got away with?" he asked.

"One hundred and eighty-five dollars, sir," I answered.

He nodded his head. A moment later, as I started down the companionway stairs to lay the table for dinner, I heard him loudly cursing some men amidships.

CHAPTER SIX

BY the following morning the storm had blown itself quite out and the *Ghost* was rolling slightly on a calm sea without a breath of wind. Occasional light airs were felt, however, and Wolf Larsen patrolled the poop constantly, his eyes ever searching the sea to the northeastward, from which direction the great trade-wind must blow.

The men were all on deck and busy preparing their various boats for the season's hunting. There are seven boats aboard, the captain's dingey, and the six which the hunters will use. Three, a hunter, a boat-puller, and a boat-steerer, compose a boat's crew. On board the schooner the boat-pullers and steerers are the crew. The hunters, too, are supposed to be in command of the watches, subject, always, to the orders of Wolf Larsen.

All this, and more, I have learned. The *Ghost* is considered the fastest schooner in both the San Francisco and Victoria fleets.* In fact, she was once a private yacht, and was built for speed. Her lines and fittings—though I know nothing about such things—speak for themselves. Johnson was telling me about her in a short chat I had with him during yesterday's second dog-watch. He spoke enthusiastically, with the love for a fine craft such as some men feel for horses. He is greatly disgusted with the outlook, and I am given to understand that Wolf Larsen bears a very unsavory reputation among the sealing captains. It was the *Ghost* herself that lured Johnson into signing for the voyage, but he is already beginning to repent.

As he told me, the *Ghost* is an eighty-ton schooner of a remarkably fine model. Her beam, or width, is twenty-three feet, and her length a little over ninety feet. A lead keel of fabulous but unknown weight makes her very stable, while

she carries an immense spread of canvas. From the deck to
the truck of the maintopmast is something over a hundred
feet, while the foremast with its topmast is eight or ten
feet shorter. I am giving these details so that the size of
this little floating world which holds twenty-two men may
be appreciated. It is a very little world, a mote, a speck,
and I marvel that men should dare to venture the sea on
a contrivance so small and fragile.

Wolf Larsen has, also, a reputation for reckless carrying on of sail. I overheard Henderson and another of the
hunters, Standish, a Californian, talking about it. Two
years ago he dismasted the *Ghost* in a gale on Bering
Sea,* whereupon the present masts were put in, which
are stronger and heavier in every way. He is said to have
remarked, when he put them in, that he preferred turning
her over to losing the sticks.

Every man aboard, with the exception of Johansen, who
is rather overcome by his promotion, seems to have an excuse for having sailed on the *Ghost*. Half the men forward
are deep-water sailors, and their excuse is that they did not
know anything about her or her captain. And those who do
know, whisper that the hunters, while excellent shots, were
so notorious for their quarrelsome and rascally proclivities
that they could not sign on any decent schooner.

I have made the acquaintance of another one of the
crew,—Louis he is called, a rotund and jovial-faced Nova
Scotia Irishman, and a very sociable fellow,* prone to talk
as long as he can find a listener. In the afternoon, while
the cook was below asleep and I was peeling the everlasting
potatoes, Louis dropped into the galley for a "yarn." His
excuse for being aboard was that he was drunk when he
signed. He assured me again and again that it was the last
thing in the world he would dream of doing in a sober
moment. It seems that he has been seal-hunting regularly
each season for a dozen years, and is accounted one of the
two or three very best boat-steerers in both fleets.

"Ah, my boy," he shook his head ominously at me, "'tis the worst schooner ye could iv selected, nor were ye drunk at the time as was I. 'Tis sealin' is the sailor's paradise—on other ships than this. The mate was the first, but mark me words, there'll be more dead men before the trip is done with. Hist, now, between you an' meself and the stanchion there, this Wolf Larsen is a regular devil, an' the *Ghost*'ll be a hellship like she's always ben since he had hold iv her. Don't I know? Don't I know? Don't I remember in Hakodate* two years gone, when he had a row an' shot four iv his men? Wasn't I a-layin' on the *Emma L.*, not three hundred yards away? An' there was a man the same year he killed with a blow iv his fist. Yes, sir, killed 'im dead-oh. His head must iv smashed like an eggshell. An' wasn't there the Governor of Kura Island,* an' the Chief iv Police, Japanese gentlemen, sir, an' didn't they come aboard the *Ghost* as his guests, abringin' their wives along—wee an' pretty little bits of things like you see 'em painted on fans. An' as he was a-gettin' under way, didn't the fond husbands get left astern-like in their sampan, as it might be by accident? An' wasn't it a week later that the poor little ladies was put ashore on the other side of the island, with nothin' before 'em but to walk home acrost the mountains on their weeny-teeny little straw sandals which wouldn't hang together a mile? Don't I know? 'Tis the beast he is, this Wolf Larsen—the great big beast mentioned iv in Revelation;* an' no good end will he ever come to. But I've said nothin' to ye, mind ye. I've whispered never a word; for old fat Louis'll live the voyage out if the last mother's son of yez go to the fishes."

"Wolf Larsen!" he snorted a moment later. "Listen to the word, will ye! Wolf—'tis what he is. He's not black-hearted like some men. 'Tis no heart he has at all. Wolf, just wolf, 'tis what he is. D'ye wonder he's well named?"

"But if he is so well known for what he is," I queried, "how is it that he can get men to ship with him?"

"An' how is it ye can get men to do anything on God's earth an' sea?" Louis demanded with Celtic fire. "How d'ye find me aboard if t'wasn't that I was drunk as a pig when I put me name down? There's them that can't sail with better men, like the hunters, and them that don't know, like the poor devils of wind-jammers for'ard there. But they'll come to it, they'll come to it, an' be sorry the day they was born. I could weep for the poor creatures, did I but forget poor old fat Louis and the troubles before him. But 'tis not a whisper I've dropped, mind ye, not a whisper."

"Them hunters is the wicked boys," he broke forth again, for he suffered from a constitutional plethora of speech. "But wait till they get to cutting up iv jinks and rowin' 'round. He's the boy'll fix 'em. 'Tis him that'll put the fear of God in their rotten black hearts. Look at that hunter iv mine, Horner. 'Jock' Horner they call him, so quiet-like an' easy-goin', soft-spoken as a girl, till ye'd think butter wouldn't melt in the mouth iv him. Didn't he kill his boat-steerer last year? 'Twas called a sad accident, but I met the boat-puller in Yokohama an' the straight iv it was given me. An' there's Smoke, the black little devil—didn't the Roosians have him for three years in the salt mines of Siberia, for poachin' on Copper Island, which is a Roosian preserve?* Shackled he was, hand an' foot, with his mate. An' didn't they have words or a ruction of some kind?—for 'twas the other fellow Smoke sent up in the buckets to the top of the mine; an' a piece at the time he went up, a leg to-day, an' to-morrow an arm, the next day the head, an' so on."

"But you can't mean it!" I cried out, overcome with the horror of it.

"Mean what?" he demanded, quick as a flash. "'Tis nothin' I've said. Deef I am, and dumb, as ye should be for the sake iv your mother; an' never once have I opened me lips but to say fine things iv them an' him, God curse his soul, an' may he rot in purgatory ten thousand years, and then go down to the last an' deepest hell is all!"

Johnson, the man who had chafed me raw when I first came aboard, seemed the least equivocal of the men forward or aft. In fact, there was nothing equivocal about him. One was struck at once by his straightforwardness and manliness, which, in turn, were tempered by a modesty which might be mistaken for timidity. But timid he was not. He seemed, rather, to have the courage of his convictions, the certainty of his manhood. It was this that made him protest, at the commencement of our acquaintance, against being called Yonson. And upon this, and him, Louis passed judgment and prophecy.

"'Tis a fine chap, that squarehead Johnson we've for'ard with us," he said. "The best sailorman in the fo'c'sle. He's my boat-puller. But it's to trouble he'll come with Wolf Larsen, as the sparks fly upward. It's meself that knows. I can see it brewin' an' comin' up like a storm in the sky. I've talked to him like a brother, but it's little he sees in takin' in his lights or flyin' false signals. He grumbles out when things don't go to suit him, and there'll be always some telltale carryin' word iv it aft to the Wolf. The Wolf is strong, and it's the way of a wolf to hate strength, an' strength it is he'll see in Johnson—no knucklin' under, and a 'Yes, sir, thank ye kindly, sir,' for a curse or a blow. Oh, she's a-comin'! She's a-comin'! An' God knows where I'll get another boat-puller! What does the fool up an' say, when the old man calls him Yonson, but 'Me name is Johnson, sir,' an' then spells it out, letter for letter. Ye should iv seen the old man's face! I thought he'd let drive at him on the spot. He didn't but he will, an' he'll break that squarehead's heart, or it's little I know iv the ways iv men on the ships iv the sea."

Thomas Mugridge is becoming unendurable. I am compelled to Mister him and to Sir him with every speech. One reason for this is that Wolf Larsen seems to have taken a fancy to him. It is an unprecedented thing, I take it, for a captain to be chummy with the cook; but this is certainly what Wolf Larsen is doing. Two or three times he put his head into the galley and chaffed Mugridge good-naturedly, and once, this afternoon, he stood by the break of the poop and chatted with him for fully fifteen minutes. When it was over, and Mugridge was back in the galley, he became greasily radiant, and went about his work, humming coster songs* in a nerve-racking and discordant falsetto.

"I always get along with the officers," he remarked to me in a confidential tone. "I know the w'y, I do, to myke myself uppreci-yted. There was my last skipper—w'y I thought nothin' of droppin' down in the cabin for a little chat and a friendly glass. 'Mugridge,' sez 'e to me, 'Mugridge,' sez 'e, 'you've missed yer vokytion.' 'An' 'ow's that?' sez I. 'Yer should 'a been born a gentleman, an' never 'ad to work for yer livin'.' God strike me dead, 'Ump, if that ayn't wot 'e sez, an' me a-sittin' there in 'is own cabin, jolly-like an' comfortable, a smokin' 'is cigars an' drinkin' 'is rum."

This chitter-chatter drove me to distraction. I never heard a voice I hated so. His oily, insinuating tones, his greasy smile, and his monstrous self-conceit grated on my nerves till sometimes I was all in a tremble. Positively, he was the most disgusting and loathsome person I have ever met. The filth of his cooking was indescribable; and, as he cooked everything that was eaten aboard, I was compelled to select what I ate with great circumspection, choosing from the least dirty of his concoctions.

My hands bothered me a great deal, unused as they were to work. The nails were discolored and black, while the skin was already grained with dirt which even a scrubbing-brush could not remove. Then blisters came, in a painful and never-ending procession, and I had a great burn on my forearm, acquired by losing my balance in a roll of the ship and pitching against the galley stove. Nor was my knee any better. The swelling had not gone down, and the cap was still up on edge. Hobbling about on it from morning to night was not helping it any. What I needed was rest, if it were ever to get well.

Rest! I never before knew the meaning of the word. I had been resting all my life and did not know it. But now, could I sit still for one half-hour and do nothing, not even think, it would be the most pleasurable thing in the world. But it is a revelation, on the other hand.* I shall be able to appreciate the lives of the working people hereafter. I did not dream that work was so terrible a thing. From half-past five in the morning till ten o'clock at night I am everybody's slave, with not one moment to myself, except such as I can steal near the end of the second dog-watch. Let me pause for a minute to look out over the sea sparkling in the sun, or to gaze at a sailor going aloft to the gaff-topsails, or running out the bowsprit, and I am sure to hear the hateful voice, "'Ere, you, 'Ump, no sodgerin'.* I've got my peepers on yer."

There are signs of rampant bad temper in the steerage, and the gossip is going around that Smoke and Henderson have had a fight. Henderson seems the best of the hunters, a slow-going fellow, and hard to rouse; but roused he must have been, for Smoke had a bruised and discolored eye, and looked particularly vicious when he came into the cabin for supper.

A cruel thing happened just before supper, indicative of the of the callousness and brutishness of these men. There is one green hand in the crew, Harrison by name, a clumsy-looking country boy, mastered, I imagine, by the spirit of adventure, and making his first voyage.* In the light baffling airs the schooner had been tacking about a great deal, at which times the sails pass from one side to the other and a man is sent aloft to shift over the fore-gaff-topsail. In some way, when Harrison was aloft, the sheet jammed in the block through which it runs at the end of the gaff. As I understood it, there were two ways of getting it cleared,—first, by lowering the foresail, which was comparatively easy and without danger; and second, by climbing out the peak-halyards to the end of the gaff itself, an exceedingly hazardous performance.

Johansen called out to Harrison to go out the halyards. It was patent to everybody that the boy was afraid. And well he might be, eighty feet above the deck, to trust himself on those thin and jerking ropes. Had there been a steady breeze it would not have been so bad, but the *Ghost* was rolling emptily on a long sea, and with each roll the canvas flapped and boomed and the halyards slacked and jerked taut. They were capable of snapping a man off like a fly from a whip-lash.

Harrison heard the order and understood what was demanded of him, but hesitated. It was probably the first time he had been aloft in his life. Johansen, who had caught the contagion of Wolf Larsen's masterfulness, burst out with a volley of abuse and curses.

"That'll do, Johansen," Wolf Larsen said brusquely. "I'll have you know that I do the swearing on this ship. If I need your assistance, I'll call you in."

"Yes, sir," the mate acknowledged submissively.

In the meantime Harrison had started out on the halyards. I was looking up from the galley door, and I could see him trembling, as with ague, in every limb. He proceeded very slowly and cautiously, an inch at a time. Outlined against the clear blue of the sky, he had the appearance of an enormous spider crawling along the tracery of its web.

It was a slight uphill climb, for the foresail peaked high; and the halyards, running through various blocks on the gaff and mast, gave him separate holds for hands and feet. But the trouble lay in that the wind was not strong enough nor steady enough to keep the sail full. When he was halfway out, the *Ghost* took a long roll to windward and back again into the hollow between two seas. Harrison ceased his progress and held on tightly. Eighty feet beneath, I could see the agonized strain of his muscles as he gripped for very life. The sail emptied and the gaff swung amidships. The halyards slackened, and, though it all happened very quickly, I could see them sag beneath the weight of his body. Then the gaff swung to the side with an abrupt swiftness, the great sail boomed like a cannon, and the three rows of reef-points slatted against the canvas like a volley of rifles. Harrison, clinging on, made the giddy rush through the air. This rush ceased abruptly. The halyards became instantly taut. It was the snap of the whip. His clutch was broken. One hand was torn loose from its hold. The other lingered desperately for a moment, and followed. His body pitched out and down, but in some way he managed to save himself with his legs. He was hanging by them, head downward. A quick effort brought his hands up to the halyards again; but he was a long time regaining his former position, where he hung, a pitiable object.

"I'll bet he has no appetite for supper," I heard Wolf Larsen's voice, which came to me from around the corner of the galley. "Stand from under, you, Johansen! Watch out! Here she comes!"

In truth, Harrison was very sick, as a person is seasick; and for a long time he clung to his precarious perch without attempting to move. Johansen, however, continued violently to urge him on to the completion of his task.

"It is a shame," I heard Johnson growling in painfully slow and correct English. He was standing by the main rigging, a few feet away from me. "The boy is willing enough. He will learn if he has a chance. But this is—" He paused awhile, for the word "murder" was his final judgment.

"Hist, will ye!" Louis whispered to him. "For the love iv your mother hold your mouth!"

But Johnson, looking on, still continued his grumbling.

"Look here," the hunter, Standish, spoke to Wolf Larsen, "that's my boat-puller, and I don't want to lose him."

"That's all right, Standish," was the reply. "He's your boat-puller when you've got him in the boat; but he's my sailor when I have him aboard, and I'll do what I damn well please with him."

"But that's no reason—" Standish began in a torrent of speech.

"That'll do, easy as she goes," Wolf Larsen counselled back. "I've told you what's what, and let it stop at that. The man's mine, and I'll make soup of him and eat it if I want to."

There was an angry gleam in the hunter's eye, but he turned on his heel and entered the steerage companionway, where he remained, looking upward. All hands were on deck now, and all eyes were aloft, where a human life was at grapples with death. The callousness of these men, to whom industrial organization gave control of the lives of other men, was appalling. I, who had lived out of the whirl of the world, had never dreamed that its work was carried on in such fashion. Life had always seemed a peculiarly sacred thing, but here it counted for nothing, was a cipher in the arithmetic of commerce. I must say, however, that the sailors themselves were sympathetic, as instance the case of Johnson; but the masters, (the hunters and the captain), were heartlessly indifferent. Even the protest of Standish arose out of the fact that he did not wish to lose his boat-puller. Had it been some other hunter's boat-puller, he, like them, would have been no more than amused.

But to return to Harrison. It took Johansen, insulting and reviling the poor wretch, fully ten minutes to get him started again. A little later he made the end of the gaff, where, astride the spar itself, he had a better chance for holding on. He cleared the sheet, and was free to return, slightly down-hill now, along the halyards to the mast. But he had lost his nerve. Unsafe as was his present position, he was loath to forsake it for the more unsafe position on the halyards.

He looked along the airy path he must traverse, and then down to the deck. His eyes were wide and staring, and he was trembling violently. I had never seen fear so strongly stamped upon a human face. Johansen called vainly for him to come down. At any moment he was liable to be snapped off the gaff, but he was helpless with fright. Wolf Larsen, walking up and down with Smoke and in conversation, took no more notice of him, though he cried sharply, once, to the man at the wheel:—

"You're off your course, my man! Be careful, unless you're looking for trouble!"

"Ay, ay, sir," the helmsman responded, putting a couple of spokes down.

He had been guilty of running the *Ghost* several points off her course in order that what little wind there was should fill the foresail and hold it steady. He had striven to help the unfortunate Harrison at the risk of incurring Wolf Larsen's anger.

The time went by, and the suspense, to me, was terrible. Thomas Mugridge, on the other hand, considered it a laughable affair, and was continually bobbing his head out the galley door to make jocose remarks. How I hated him! And how my hatred for him grew and grew, during that fearful time, to cyclopean dimensions. For the first time in my life I experienced the desire to murder—"saw red," as some of our picturesque writers phrase it. Life in general might still be sacred, but life in the particular case of Thomas Mugridge had become very profane indeed. I was frightened when I became conscious that I was seeing red, and the thought flashed through my mind: was I, too, becoming tainted by the brutality of my environment?— I, who even in the most flagrant crimes had denied the justice and righteousness of capital punishment?

Fully half an hour went by, and then I saw Johnson and

Louis in some sort of altercation. It ended with Johnson
flinging off Louis's detaining arm and starting forward. He
crossed the deck, sprang into the fore rigging, and began
to climb. But the quick eye of Wolf Larsen caught him.

"Here, you, what are you up to?" he cried.

Johnson's ascent was arrested. He looked his captain in
the eyes and replied slowly:—

"I am going to get that boy down."

"You'll get down out of that rigging, and damn lively
about it! D'ye hear? Get down!"

Johnson hesitated, but the long years of obedience to the
masters of ships overpowered him, and he dropped sullenly
to the deck and went on forward.

At half after five I went below to set the cabin table,
but I hardly knew what I did, for my eyes and brain were
filled with the vision of a man, white-faced and trembling,
comically like a bug, clinging to the thrashing gaff. At
six o'clock, when I served supper, going on deck to get
the food from the galley, I saw Harrison, still in the same
position. The conversation at the table was of other things.
Nobody seemed interested in the wantonly imperilled life.
But making an extra trip to the galley a little later, I
was gladdened by the sight of Harrison staggering weakly
from the rigging to the forecastle scuttle. He had finally
summoned the courage to descend.

Before closing this incident, I must give a scrap of conversation I had with Wolf Larsen in the cabin, while I was
washing the dishes.

"You were looking squeamish this afternoon," he began.
"What was the matter?"

I could see that he knew what had made me possibly
as sick as Harrison, that he was trying to draw me, and I
answered, "It was because of the brutal treatment of that
boy."

He gave a short laugh. "Like seasickness, I suppose.
Some men are subject to it, and others are not."

"Not so," I objected.

"Just so," he went on. "The earth is as full of brutality as the sea is full of motion. And some men are made sick by the one, and some by the other. That's the only reason."

"But you, who make a mock of human life, don't you place any value upon it whatever?" I demanded.

"Value? What value?" He looked at me, and though his eyes were steady and motionless, there seemed a cynical smile in them. "What kind of value? How do you measure it? Who values it?"

"I do," I made answer.

"Then what is it worth to you? Another man's life, I mean. Come, now, what is it worth?"

The value of life? How could I put a tangible value upon it? Somehow, I, who have always had expression, lacked expression when with Wolf Larsen. I have since determined that a part of it was due to the man's personality, but that the greater part was due to his totally different outlook. Unlike other materialists I had met and with whom I had something in common to start on, I had nothing in common with him. Perhaps, also, it was the elemental simplicity of his mind that baffled me. He drove so directly to the core of the mater, divesting a question always of all superfluous details, and with such an air of finality, that I seemed to find myself struggling in deep water with no footing under me. Value of life? How could I answer the question on the spur of the moment? The sacredness of life I had accepted as axiomatic. That it was intrinsically valuable was a truism I had never questioned. But when he challenged the truism I was speechless.

"We were talking about this yesterday," he said. "I held that life was a ferment, a yeasty something which devoured life that it might live, and that living was merely successful piggishness. Why, if there is anything in supply and demand, life is the cheapest thing in the world. There is only so much water, so much earth, so much air; but the life that is demanding to be born is limitless. Nature is a spendthrift. Look at the fish and their millions of eggs. For that matter, look at you and me. In our loins are the possibilities of millions of lives. Could we but find time and opportunity and utilize the last bit and every bit of the unborn life that is in us, we could become the fathers of nations and populate continents. Life? Bah! It has no value. Of cheap things it is the cheapest. Everywhere it goes begging. Nature spills it out with a lavish hand. Where there is room for one life, she sows a thousand lives,* and it's life eat life till the strongest and most piggish life is left."

"You have read Darwin," I said. "But you read him misunderstandingly when you conclude that the struggle for existence sanctions your wanton destruction of life."

He shrugged his shoulders. "You know you only mean that in relation to human life, for of the flesh and the fowl and the fish you destroy as much as I or any other man. And human life is in no wise different, though you feel it is and think that you reason why it is. Why should I be parsimonious with this life which is cheap and without value? There are more sailors than there are ships on the sea for them, more workers than there are factories or machines for them. Why, you who live on the land know that you house your poor people in the slums of cities and loose famine and pestilence upon them, and that there still remain more poor people, dying for want of a crust of bread and a bit of meat, (which is life destroyed), than you know what to do with. Have you ever seen the London dockers fighting like wild beasts for a chance to work?"*

He started for the companion stairs, but turned his head for a final word. "Do you know the only value life has is what life puts upon itself? And it is of course overestimated, since it is of necessity prejudiced in its own favor. Take that man I had aloft. He held on as if he were a precious thing, a treasure beyond diamonds or rubies. To

you? No. To me? Not at all. To himself? Yes. But I do
not accept his estimate. He sadly overrates himself. There
is plenty more life demanding to be born. Had he fallen
and dripped his brains upon the deck like honey from the
comb, there would have been no loss to the world. He was
worth nothing to the world. The supply is too large. To
himself only was he of value, and to show how fictitious
even this value was, being dead he is unconscious that he
has lost himself. He alone rated himself beyond diamonds
and rubies. Diamonds and rubies are gone, spread out on
the deck to be washed away by a bucket of sea-water, and
he does not even know that the diamonds and rubies are
gone. He does not lose anything, for with the loss of himself
he loses the knowledge of loss. Don't you see? And what
have you to say?"

"That you are at least consistent," was all I could say,
and I went on washing the dishes.

CHAPTER SEVEN

AT last, after three days of variable winds, we have caught
the northeast trades. I came on deck, after a good night's
rest in spite of my poor knee, to find the *Ghost* foaming
along, wing-and-wing, and every sail drawing except the
jibs, with a fresh breeze astern. Oh, the wonder of the
great trade-wind! All day we sailed, and all night, and
the next day, and the next, day after day, the wind always astern and blowing steadily and strong. The schooner
sailed herself. There was no pulling and hauling on sheets
and tackles, no shifting of topsails, no work at all for the
sailors to do except to steer. At night when the sun went
down, the sheets were slackened; in the morning, when
they yielded up the damp of the dew and relaxed, they
were pulled tight again—and that was all.

Ten knots, twelve knots, eleven knots, varying from time
to time, is the speed we are making. And ever out of the
northeast the brave wind blows, driving us on our course
two hundred and fifty miles between the dawns. It saddens
me and gladdens me, the gait with which we are leaving
San Francisco behind and with which we are foaming down
upon the tropics. Each day grows perceptibly warmer. In
the second dog-watch the sailors come on deck, stripped,
and heave buckets of water upon one another from overside. Flying-fish are beginning to be seen, and during the
night the watch above scrambles over the deck in pursuit of
those that fall aboard. In the morning, Thomas Mugridge
being duly bribed, the galley is pleasantly areek with the
odor of their frying; while dolphin meat is served fore
and aft on such occasions as Johnson catches the blazing
beauties from the bowsprit end.

Johnson seems to spend all his spare time there or aloft

at the crosstrees, watching the *Ghost* cleaving the water under press of sail. There is passion, adoration, in his eyes, and he goes about in a sort of trance, gazing in ecstasy at the swelling sails, the foaming wake, and the heave and the run of her over the liquid mountains that are moving with us in stately procession.

The days and nights are "all a wonder and a wild delight,"* and though I have little time from my dreary work, I steal odd moments to gaze and gaze at the unending glory of what I never dreamed the world possessed. Above, the sky is stainless blue—blue as the sea itself, which under the forefoot is of the color and sheen of azure satin. All around the horizon are pale, fleecy clouds, never changing, never moving, like a silver setting for the flawless turquoise sky.

I do not forget one night, when I should have been asleep, of lying on the forecastle-head and gazing down at the spectral ripple of foam thrust aside by the *Ghost's* forefoot. It sounded like the gurgling of a brook over mossy stones in some quiet dell, and the crooning song of it lured me away and out of myself till I was no longer Hump the cabin-boy, nor Van Weyden, the man who had dreamed away thirty-five years among books. But a voice behind me, the unmistakable voice of Wolf Larsen, strong with the invincible certitude of the man and mellow with appreciation of the words he was quoting, aroused me.

"'O the blazing tropic night, when the wake's a welt of
    light
That holds the hot sky tame,
And the steady forefoot snores through the planet-
    powdered floors
Where the scared whale flukes in flame.
Her plates are scarred by the sun, dear lass,
And her ropes are taut with the dew,
For we're booming down on the old trail, our own trail,

  the out trail,
We're sagging south on the Long Trail—the trail that is
  always new.'"*

"Eh, Hump? How's it strike you?" he asked, after the
due pause which words and setting demanded.

I looked into his face. It was aglow with light, as the sea
itself, and the eyes were flashing in the starshine.

"It strikes me as remarkable, to say the least, that you
should show enthusiasm," I answered coldly.

"Why, man, it's living! it's life!" he cried.

"Which is a cheap thing and without value," I flung his
words at him.

He laughed, and it was the first time I had heard honest
mirth in his voice.

"Ah, I cannot get you to understand, cannot drive it
into your head, what a thing this life is. Of course life is
valueless, except to itself. And I can tell you that my life
is pretty valuable just now—to myself. It is beyond price,
which you will acknowledge is a terrific overrating, but
which I cannot help, for it is the life that is in me that
makes the rating."

He appeared waiting for the words with which to express
the thought that was in him, and finally went on.

"Do you know, I am filled with a strange uplift; I feel as
if all time were echoing through me, as though all powers
were mine. I know truth, divine good from evil, right from
wrong. My vision is clear and far. I could almost believe in
God. But,"—and his voice changed and the light went out
of his face,—"what is this condition in which I find myself?
this joy of living? this exultation of life? this inspiration,
I may well call it? It is what comes when there is nothing
wrong with one's digestion, when his stomach is in trim
and his appetite has an edge, and all goes well. It is the
bribe for living, the champagne of the blood, the effer-
vescence of the ferment—that makes some men think holy

thoughts, and other men to see God or to create him when they cannot see him. That is all, the drunkenness of life, the stirring and crawling of the yeast, the babbling of the life that is insane with consciousness that it is alive. And— bah! To-morrow I shall pay for it as the drunkard pays. And I shall know that I must die, at sea most likely, cease crawling of myself to be all acrawl with the corruption of the sea; to be fed upon, to be carrion, to yield up all the strength and movement of my muscles that it may become strength and movement in fin and scale and the guts of fishes. Bah! And bah! again. The champagne is already flat. The sparkle and bubble has gone out and it is a tasteless drink."

He left me as suddenly as he had come, springing to the deck with the weight and softness of a tiger. The *Ghost* ploughed on her way. I noted the gurgling forefoot was very like a snore, and as I listened to it the effect of Wolf Larsen's swift rush from sublime exultation to despair slowly left me. Then some deep-water sailor, from the waist of the ship, lifted a rich tenor voice in the "Song of the Trade Wind":*

> "Oh, I am the wind the seamen love—
> I am steady, and strong, and true;
> They follow my track by the clouds above,
> O'er the fathomless tropic blue.

> * * * *

> Through daylight and dark I follow the bark,
> I keep like a hound on her trail;
> I'm strongest at noon, yet under the moon,
> I stiffen the bunt of her sail."

CHAPTER EIGHT

SOMETIMES I think Wolf Larsen mad, or half-mad at least, what of his strange moods and vagaries. At other times I take him for a great man, a genius who has never arrived. And, finally, I am convinced that he is the perfect type of the primitive man, born a thousand years or generations too late and an anachronism in this culminating century of civilization.* He is certainly an individualist of the most pronounced type. Not only that, but he is very lonely. There is no congeniality between him and the rest of the men aboard ship. His tremendous virility and mental strength wall him apart. They are more like children to him, even the hunters, and as children he treats them, descending perforce to their level and playing with them as a man plays with puppies. Or else he probes them with the cruel hand of a vivisectionist,* groping about in their mental processes and examining their souls as though to see of what soul-stuff is made.

I have seen him a score of times, at table, insulting this hunter or that, with cool and level eyes and, withal, a certain air of interest, pondering their actions or replies or petty rages with a curiosity almost laughable to me who stood onlooker and who understood. Concerning his own rages, I am convinced that they are not real, that they are sometimes experiments, but that in the main they are the habits of a pose of attitude he has seen fit to take toward his fellow-men. I know, with the possible exception of the incident of the dead mate, that I have not seen him really angry; nor do I wish ever to see him in a genuine rage, when all the force of him is called into play.

While on the question of vagaries, I shall tell what befell Thomas Mugridge in the cabin, and at the same time complete an incident upon which I have already touched once or twice. The twelve o'clock dinner was over, one day, and I had just finished putting the cabin in order, when Wolf Larsen and Thomas Mugridge descended the companion stairs. Though the cook had a cubby-hole of a stateroom opening off from the cabin, in the cabin he had never dared to linger or to be seen, and he flitted to and fro, once or twice a day, like a timid spectre.

"So you know how to play 'Nap',"* Wolf Larsen was saying in a pleased sort of voice. "I might have guessed an Englishman would know. I learned it myself in English ships."

Thomas Mugridge was beside himself, a blithering imbecile, so pleased was he at chumming thus with the captain. The little airs he put on and the painful striving to assume the easy carriage of a man born to a dignified place in life would have been sickening had they not been ludicrous. He quite ignored my presence, though I credited him with being simply unable to see me. His pale, wishy-washy eyes were swimming like lazy summer seas, though what blissful visions they beheld were beyond my imagination.

"Get the cards, Hump," Wolf Larsen ordered, as they took seats at the table. "And bring out the cigars and the whiskey you'll find in my berth."

I returned with the articles in time to hear the Cockney hinting broadly that there was a mystery about him, that he might be a gentleman's son gone wrong or something or other; also, that he was a remittance man* and was paid to keep away from England—"p'yed 'ansomely, sir," was the way he put it; "p'yed 'ansomely to sling my 'ook an' keep slingin' it."

I had brought the customary liquor glasses, but Wolf Larsen frowned, shook his head, and signalled with his hands for me to bring the tumblers. These he filled two-thirds full with undiluted whiskey—"a gentleman's drink," quoth Thomas Mugridge,—and they clinked their glasses to the glorious game of "Nap," lighted cigars, and fell to shuffling and dealing the cards.

They played for money. They increased the amounts of the bets. They drank whiskey, they drank it neat, and I fetched more. I do not know whether Wolf Larsen cheated or not,—a thing he was thoroughly capable of doing,—but he won steadily. The cook made repeated journeys to his bunk for money. Each time he performed the journey with greater swagger, but he never brought more than a few dollars at a time. He grew maudlin, familiar, could hardly see the cards or sit upright. As a preliminary to another journey to his bunk, he hooked Wolf Larsen's buttonhole with a greasy forefinger and vacuously proclaimed and reiterated, "I got money. I got money, I tell yer, an' I'm a gentleman's son."

Wolf Larsen was unaffected by the drink, yet he drank glass for glass, and if anything his glasses were fuller. There was no change in him. He did not appear even amused at the other's antics.

In the end, with loud protestations that he could lose like a gentleman, the cook's last money was staked on the game and lost. Whereupon he leaned his head on his hands and wept. Wolf Larsen looked curiously at him, as though about to probe and vivisect him, then changed his mind, as from the foregone conclusion that there was nothing there to probe.

"Hump," he said to me, elaborately polite, "kindly take Mr. Mugridge's arm and help him up on deck. He is not felling very well."

"And tell Johnson to douse him with a few buckets of salt water," he added, in a lower tone for my ear alone.

I left Mr. Mugridge on deck, in the hands of a couple of grinning sailors who had been told off for the purpose. Mr. Mugridge was sleepily spluttering that he was a gentleman's son. But as I descended the companion stairs to clear the table I heard him shriek as the first bucket of water struck him.

Wolf Larsen was counting his winnings.

"One hundred and eighty-five dollars even," he said aloud. "Just as I thought. The beggar came aboard without a cent."

"And what you have won is mine, sir," I said boldly.

He favored me with a quizzical smile. "Hump, I have studied some grammar in my time, and I think your tenses are tangled. 'Was mine,' you should have said, not 'is mine.'"

"It is a question, not of grammar, but of ethics," I answered.

It was possibly a minute before he spoke.

"D'ye know, Hump," he said, with a slow seriousness which had in it an indefinable strain of sadness, "that this is the first time I have heard the word 'ethics' in the mouth of a man. You and I are the only men on this ship who know its meaning."

"At one time in my life," he continued, after another pause, "I dreamed that I might some day talk with men who used such language, that I might lift myself out of the place in life in which I had been born, and hold conversation and mingle with men who talked about just such things as ethics. And this is the first time I have ever heard the word pronounced. Which is all by the way, for you are wrong. It is a question, neither of grammar nor ethics, but of fact."

"I understand," I said. "The fact is that you have the money."

His face brightened. He seemed pleased at my perspicacity.

"But it is avoiding the real question," I continued, "which is one of right."

"Ah," he remarked, with a wry pucker of his mouth, "I see you still believe in such things as right and wrong."

"But don't you?—at all?" I demanded.

"Not the least bit. Might is right, and that is all there is to it. Weakness is wrong. Which is a very poor way of saying that it is good for oneself to be strong, and evil for oneself to be weak—or better yet, it is pleasurable to be strong, because of the profits; painful to be weak, because of the penalties. Just now the possession of this money is a pleasurable thing. It is good for one to possess it. Being able to possess it, I wrong myself and the life that is in me if I give it to you and forego the pleasure of possessing it."

"But you wrong me by withholding it," I objected.

"Not at all. One man cannot wrong another man. He can only wrong himself. As I see it, I do wrong always when I consider the interests of others. Don't you see? How can two particles of the yeast wrong each other by striving to devour each other? It is their inborn heritage to strive to devour, and to strive not to be devoured. When they depart from this they sin."

"Then you don't believe in altruism?"* I asked.

He received the word as if it had a familiar ring, though he pondered it thoughtfully. "Let me see, it means something about co-operation, doesn't it?"

"Well, in a way there has come to be a sort of connection," I answered, unsurprised by this time at such gaps in his vocabulary, which, like his knowledge, was the acquirement of a self-read, self-educated man, whom no one had directed in his studies, and who had thought much and talked little or not at all. "An altruistic act is an act performed for the welfare of others. It is unselfish, as opposed to an act performed for self, which is selfish."

He nodded his head. "Oh, yes, I remember it now. I ran across it in Spencer."

"Spencer!" I cried. "Have you read him?"

"Not very much," was his confession. "I understood quite a good deal of 'First Principles,' but his 'Biology' took the wind out of my sails, and his 'Psychology' left me butting around in the doldrums for many a day. I honestly could not understand what he was driving at. I put it down to mental deficiency on my part, but since then I have decided that it was for want of preparation. I had no proper basis. Only Spencer and myself know how hard I hammered. But I did get something out of his 'Data of Ethics.'* There's where I ran across 'altruism,' and I remember now how it was used."

I wondered what this man could have got from such a work. Spencer I remembered enough to know that altruism was imperative to his ideal of highest conduct. Wolf Larsen, evidently, had sifted the great philosopher's teachings, rejecting and selecting according to his needs and desires.

"What else did you run across?" I asked.

His brows drew in slightly with the mental effort of suitably phrasing thoughts which he had never before put into speech. I felt an elation of spirit. I was groping into his soul-stuff as he made a practice of groping in the soul-stuff of others. I was exploring virgin territory. A strange, a terribly strange, region was unrolling itself before my eyes.

"In as few words as possible," he began, "Spencer puts it something like this: First, a man must act for his own benefit—to do this is to be moral and good. Next, he must act for the benefit of his children. And third, he must act for the benefit of his race."*

"And the highest, finest, right conduct," I interjected, "is that act which benefits at the same time the man, his children, and his race."

"I wouldn't stand for that," he replied. "Couldn't see the necessity for it, nor the common sense. I cut out the race and the children. I would sacrifice nothing for them. It's just so much slush and sentiment, and you must see it yourself, at least for one who does not believe in eternal life. With immorality before me, altruism would be a paying business proposition. I might elevate my soul to

all kinds of altitudes. But with nothing eternal before me
but death, given for a brief spell this yeasty crawling and
squirming which is called life, why, it would be immoral for
me to perform any act that was a sacrifice. Any sacrifice
that makes me lose one crawl or squirm is foolish,—and not
only foolish, for it is a wrong against myself and a wicked
thing. I must not lose one crawl or squirm if I am to get the
most out of the ferment. Nor will the eternal movelessness
that is coming to me be made easier or harder by the
sacrifices or selfishnesses of the time when I was yeasty
and acrawl."

"Then you are an individualist, a materialist, and, logi-
cally, a hedonist."

"Big words," he smiled. "But what is a hedonist?"*

He nodded agreement when I had given the definition.

"And you are also," I continued "a man one could not
trust in the least thing where it was possible for a selfish
interest to intervene?"

"Now you're beginning to understand," he said, bright-
ening.

"You are a man utterly without what the world calls
morals?"

"That's it."

"A man of whom to be always afraid—"

"That's the way to put it."

"As one is afraid of a snake, or a tiger, or a shark?"

"Now you know me," he said. "And you know me as I
am generally known. Other men call me 'Wolf'."

"You are a sort of monster," I added audaciously, "a
Caliban who has pondered Setebos,* and who acts as you
act, in idle moments, by whim and fancy."

His brow clouded at the allusion. He did not understand,
and I quickly learned that he did not know the poem.

"I'm just reading Browning," he confessed, "and it's
pretty tough. I haven't got very far along, and as it is
I've about lost my bearings."

Not to be tiresome, I shall say that I fetched the book from his state-room and read "Caliban" aloud. He was delighted. It was a primitive mode of reasoning and of looking at things that he understood thoroughly. He interrupted again and again with comment and criticism. When I finished, he had me read it over a second time, and a third. We fell into discussion—philosophy, science, evolution, religion. He betrayed the inaccuracies of the self-read man, and, it must be granted, the sureness and directness of the primitive mind. The very simplicity of his reasoning was its strength, and his materialism was far more compelling than the subtly complex materialism of Charley Furuseth. Not that I,—a confirmed and, as Furuseth phrased it, a temperamental idealist,—was to be compelled; but that Wolf Larsen stormed the last strongholds of my faith with a vigor that received respect, while not accorded conviction.

Time passed. Supper was at hand and the table not laid. I became restless and anxious, and when Thomas Mugridge glared down the companionway, sick and angry of countenance, I prepared to go about my duties. But Wolf Larsen cried out to him:—

"Cooky, you've got to hustle to-night. I'm busy with Hump, and you'll do the best you can without him."

And again the unprecedented was established. That night I sat at table with the captain and the hunters, while Thomas Mugridge waited on us and washed the dishes afterward—a whim, a Caliban-mood of Wolf Larsen's, and one I foresaw would bring me trouble. In the meantime, we talked and talked, much to the disgust of the hunters, who could not understand a word.

CHAPTER NINE

THREE days of rest, three blessed days of rest, are what I had with Wolf Larsen, eating at the cabin table and doing nothing but discuss life, literature, and the universe, the while Thomas Mugridge fumed and raged and did my work as well as his own.

"Watch out for squalls, is all I can say to you," was Louis's warning, given during a spare half-hour on deck while Wolf Larsen was engaged in straightening out a row among the hunters.

"Ye can't tell what'll be happenin'," Louis went on, in response to my query for more definite information. "The man's as contrary as air currents or water currents. You can never guess the ways iv him. 'Tis just as you're thinkin' you know him and are makin' a favorable slant along him, that he whirls around, dead ahead, and comes howlin' down upon you and a-rippin' all iv your fine-weather sails to rags."

So I was not altogether surprised when the squall foretold by Louis smote me. We had been having a heated discussion,—upon life, of course,—and, grown overbold, I was passing stiff strictures upon Wolf Larsen and the life of Wolf Larsen. In fact, I was vivisecting him and turning over his soul-stuff as keenly and thoroughly as it was his custom to do it to others. It may be a weakness of mine that I have an incisive way of speech; but I threw all restraint to the winds and cut and slashed until the whole man of him was snarling. The dark sun-bronze of his face went black with wrath, his eyes were ablaze. There was no clearness or sanity in them—nothing but the terrific rage of a madman. It was the wolf in him that I saw, and a mad wolf at that.

He sprang for me with a half-roar, gripping my arm. I

had steeled myself to brazen it out, though I was trembling inwardly; but the enormous strength of the man was too much for my fortitude. He had gripped me by the biceps with his single hand, and when that grip tightened I wilted and shrieked aloud. My feet went out from under me. I simply could not stand upright and endure the agony. The muscles refused their duty. The pain was too great. My biceps was being crushed to a pulp.

He seemed to recover himself, for a lucid gleam came into his eyes, and he relaxed his hold with a short laugh that was more like a growl. I fell to the floor, feeling very faint, while he sat down, lighted a cigar, and watched me as a cat watches a mouse. As I writhed about I could see in his eyes that curiosity I had so often noted, that wonder and perplexity, that questing, that everlasting query of his as to what it was all about.

I finally crawled to my feet and ascended the companion stairs. Fair weather was over, and there was nothing left but to return to the galley. My left arm was numb, as though paralyzed, and days passed before I could use it, while weeks went by before the last stiffness and pain went out of it. And he had done nothing but put his hand upon my arm and squeeze. There had been no wrenching or jerking. He had just closed his hand with a steady pressure. What he might have done I did not fully realize till next day, when he put his head into the galley, and, as a sign of renewed friendliness, asked me how my arm was getting on.

"It might have been worse," he smiled.

I was peeling potatoes. He picked one up from the pan. It was fair-sized, firm, and unpeeled. He closed his hand upon it, squeezed, and the potato squirted out between his fingers in mushy streams. The pulpy remnant he dropped back into the pan and turned away, and I had a sharp vision of how it might have fared with me had the monster put his real strength upon me.

But the three days' rest was good in spite of it all, for
it had given my knee the very chance it needed. It felt
much better, the swelling had materially decreased, and
the cap seemed descending into its proper place. Also,
the three days' rest brought the trouble I had foreseen.
It was plainly Thomas Mugridge's intention to make me
pay for those three days. He treated me vilely, cursed me
continually, and heaped his own work upon me. He even
ventured to raise his fist to me, but I was becoming animal-
like myself, and I snarled in his face so terribly that it
must have frightened him back. It is no pleasant picture
I can conjure up of myself, Humphrey Van Weyden, in
that noisome ship's galley, crouched in a corner over my
task, my face raised to the face of the creature about to
strike me, my lips lifted and snarling like a dog's, my eyes
gleaming with fear and helplessness and the courage that
comes of fear and helplessness. I do not like the picture. It
reminds me too strongly of a rat in a trap. I do not care
to think of it; but it was effective, for the threatened blow
did not descend.

Thomas Mugridge backed away, glaring as hatefully and
viciously as I glared. A pair of beasts is what we were,
penned together and showing our teeth. He was a coward,
afraid to strike me because I had not quailed sufficiently in
advance; so he chose a new way to intimidate me. There
was only one galley knife that, as a knife, amounted to
anything. This, through many years of service and wear,
had acquired a long, lean blade. It was unusually cruel-
looking, and at first I had shuddered every time I used it.
The cook borrowed a stone from Johansen and proceeded
to sharpen the knife. He did it with great ostentation,
glancing significantly at me the while. He whetted it up
and down all day long. Every odd moment he could find
he had the knife and stone out and was whetting away.
The steel acquired a razor edge. He tried it with the ball
of his thumb or across the nail. He shaved hairs from the

back of his hand, glanced along the edge with microscopic acuteness, and found, or feigned that he found, always, a slight inequality in its edge somewhere. Then he would put it on the stone again and whet, whet, whet, till I could have laughed aloud, it was so very ludicrous.

It was also serious, for I learned that he was capable of using it, that under all his cowardice there was a courage of cowardice, like mine, that would impel him to do the very thing his whole nature protested against doing and was afraid of doing. "Cooky's sharpening his knife for Hump," was being whispered about among the sailors, and some of them twitted him about it. This he took in good part, and was really pleased, nodding his head with direful foreknowledge and mystery, until George Leach, the erstwhile cabin-boy, ventured some rough pleasantry on the subject.

Now it happened that Leach was one of the sailors told off to douse Mugridge after his game of cards with the captain. Leach had evidently done his task with a thoroughness that Mugridge had not forgiven, for words followed and evil names involving smirched ancestries. Mugridge menaced with the knife he was sharpening for me. Leach laughed and hurled more of his Telegraph Hill billingsgate,* and before either he or I knew what had happened, his right arm had been ripped open from elbow to wrist by a quick slash of the knife. The cook backed away, a fiendish expression on his face, the knife held before him in a position of defence. But Leach took it quite calmly, though blood was spouting upon the deck as generously was water from a fountain.

"I'm goin' to get you, Cooky," he said, "and I'll get you hard. And I won't be in no hurry about it. You'll be without that knife when I come for you."

So saying, he turned and walked quietly forward. Mugridge's face was livid with fear at what he had done and at what he might expect sooner or later from the man he had stabbed. But his demeanor toward me was more ferocious than ever. In spite of his fear at the reckoning he must expect to pay for what he had done, he could see that it had been an object-lesson to me, and he became more domineering and exultant. Also there was a lust in him, akin to madness, which had come with sight of the blood he had drawn. He was beginning to see red in whatever direction he looked. The psychology of it is sadly tangled, and yet I could read the workings of his mind as clearly as though it were a printed book.

Several days went by, the *Ghost* still foaming down the trades, and I could swear I saw madness growing in Thomas Mugridge's eyes. And I confess that I became afraid, very much afraid. Whet, whet, whet, it went all day long. The look in his eyes as he felt the keen edge and glared at me was positively carnivorous. I was afraid to turn my shoulder to him, and when I left the galley I went out backwards—to the amusement of the sailors and hunters, who made a point of gathering in groups to witness my exit. The strain was too great. I sometimes thought my mind would give way under it—a meet thing on this ship of madmen and brutes. Every hour, every minute of my existence was in jeopardy. I was a human soul in distress, and yet no soul, fore or aft, betrayed sufficient sympathy to come to my aid. At times I thought of throwing myself on the mercy of Wolf Larsen, but the vision of the mocking devil in his eyes that questioned life and sneered at it would come strong upon me and compel me to refrain. At other times I seriously contemplated suicide, and the whole force of my hopeful philosophy was required to keep me from going over the side in the darkness of night.

Several times Wolf Larsen tried to inveigle me into discussion, but I gave him short answers and eluded him. Finally, he commanded me to resume my seat at the cabin table for a time and let the cook do my work. Then I spoke frankly, telling him what I was enduring from Thomas

Mugridge because of the three days of favoritism which had been shown me. Wolf Larsen regarded me with smiling eyes.

"So you're afraid, eh?" he sneered.

"Yes," I said defiantly and honestly, "I am afraid."

"That's the way with you fellows," he cried, half angrily, "sentimentalizing about your immortal souls and afraid to die. At sight of a sharp knife and a cowardly Cockney the clinging of life to life overcomes all your fond foolishness. Why, my dear fellow, you will live forever. You are a god, and God cannot be killed. Cooky cannot hurt you. You are sure of your resurrection. What's there to be afraid of?

"You have eternal life before you. You are a millionaire in immortality, and a millionnaire whose fortune cannot be lost, whose fortune is less perishable than the stars and as lasting as space or time. It is impossible for you to diminish your principal. Immortality is a thing without beginning or end. Eternity is eternity, and though you die here and now you will go on living somewhere else and hereafter. And it is all very beautiful, this shaking off of the flesh and soaring of the imprisoned spirit. Cooky cannot hurt you. He can only give you a boost on the path you eternally must tread.

"Or, if you do not wish to be boosted just yet, why not boost Cooky? According to your ideas, he, too, must be an immortal millionnaire. You cannot bankrupt him. His paper will always circulate at par. You cannot diminish the length of his living by killing him, for he is without beginning or end. He's bound to go on living, somewhere, somehow. Then boost him. Stick a knife in him and let his spirit free. As it is, it's in a nasty prison, and you'll do him only a kindness by breaking down the door. And who knows?—it may be a very beautiful spirit that will go soaring up into the blue from that ugly carcass. Boost him along, and I'll promote you to his place, and he's getting forty-five dollars a month."

It was plain that I could look for no help or mercy from Wolf Larsen. Whatever was to be done I must do for myself; and out of the courage of fear I evolved the plan of fighting Thomas Mugridge with his own weapons. I borrowed a whetstone from Johansen. Louis, the boat-steerer, had already begged me for condensed milk and sugar. The lazarette, where such delicacies were stored, was situated beneath the cabin floor. Watching my chance, I stole five cans of the milk, and that night, when it was Louis's watch on deck, I traded them with him for a dirk as lean and cruel-looking as Thomas Mugridge's vegetable knife. It was rusty and dull, but I turned the grindstone while Louis gave it an edge. I slept more soundly than usual that night.

Next morning, after breakfast, Thomas Mugridge began his whet, whet, whet. I glanced warily at him, for I was on my knees taking the ashes from the stove. When I returned from throwing them overside, he was talking to Harrison, whose honest yokel's face was filled with fascination and wonder.

"Yes," Mugridge was saying, "an' wot does 'is worship do but give me two years in Reading.* But blimey if I cared. The other mug was fixed plenty. Should 'a seen 'im. Knife just like this. I stuck it in, like into soft butter, an' the w'y 'e squealed was better'n a tu-penny gaff."* He shot a glance in my direction to see if I was taking it in, and went on. " 'I didn't mean it, Tommy,' 'e was sniffin'; 'so 'elp me Gawd, I didn't mean it!' 'I'll fix yer bloody well right,' I sez, an' kept right after 'im. I cut 'im in ribbons, that's wot I did, an' 'e a-squealin' all the time. Once 'e got 'is 'and on the knife an' tried to 'old it. 'Ad 'is fingers around it, but I pulled it through, cuttin' to the bone. O, 'e was a sight, I can tell yer."

A call from the mate interrupted the gory narrative, and Harrison went aft. Mugridge sat down on the raised threshold to the galley and went on with his knife-sharpening. I put the shovel away and calmly sat down on the coal-box facing him. He favored me with a vicious stare. Still calmly, though my heart was going pitapat, I pulled out Louis's dirk and began to whet it on the stone. I had looked for almost any sort of explosion on the Cockney's part, but to my surprise he did not appear aware of what I was doing. He went on whetting his knife. So did I. And for two hours we sat there, face to face, whet, whet, whet, till the news of it spread abroad and half the ship's company was crowding the galley doors to see the sight.

Encouragement and advice were freely tendered, and Jock Horner, the quiet, soft-spoken hunter who looked as though he would not harm a mouse, advised me to leave the ribs alone and to thrust upward for the abdomen, at the same time giving what he called the "Spanish twist" to the blade. Leach, his bandaged arm prominently to the fore, begged me to leave a few remnants of the cook for him; and Wolf Larsen paused once or twice at the break of the poop to glance curiously at what must have been to him a stirring and crawling of the yeasty thing he knew as life.

And I make free to say that for the time being life assumed the same sordid values to me. There was nothing pretty about it, nothing divine—only two cowardly moving things that sat whetting steel upon stone, and a group of other moving things, cowardly and otherwise, that looked on. Half of them, I am sure, were anxious to see us shedding each other's blood. It would have been entertainment. And I do not think there was one who would have interfered had we closed in a death-struggle.

On the other hand, the whole thing was laughable and childish. Whet, whet, whet,—Humphrey Van Weyden sharpening his knife in a ship's galley and trying its edge with his thumb! Of all situations this was the most inconceivable. I know that my own kind could not have believed it possible. I had not been called "Sissy" Van Weyden all my days without reason, and that "Sissy" Van Weyden should be capable of doing this thing was a revelation to Humphrey Van Weyden, who knew not whether to be exultant or ashamed.

But nothing happened. At the end of two hours Thomas Mugridge put away knife and stone and held out his hand.

"Wot's the good of mykin' a 'oly show of ourselves for them mugs?" he demanded. "They don't love us, an' bloody well glad they'd be a-seein' us cuttin' our throats. Yer not 'arf bad, 'Ump! You've got spunk, as you Yanks s'y, an' I like yer in a w'y. So come on an' shyke."

Coward that I might be, I was less a coward than he. It was a distinct victory. I had gained, and I refused to forego any of it by shaking his detestable hand.

"All right," he said pridelessly, "tyke it or leave it, I'll like yer none the less for it." And to save his face he turned fiercely upon the onlookers. "Get outa my galley-doors, you bloomin' swabs!"

This command was reinforced by a steaming kettle of water, and at sight of it the sailors scrambled out of the way. This was a sort of victory for Thomas Mugridge, and enabled him to accept more gracefully the defeat I had given him, though, of course, he was too discreet to attempt to drive the hunters away.

"I see Cooky's finish," I heard Smoke say to Horner.

"You bet," was the reply. "Hump runs the galley from now on, and Cooky pulls in his horns."

Mugridge heard and shot a swift glance at me, but I gave no sign that the conversation had reached me. I had not thought my victory was so far-reaching and complete, but I resolved to let go nothing I had gained. As the days went by, Smoke's prophecy was verified. The Cockney became more humble and slavish to me than even to Wolf Larsen. I mistered him and sirred him no longer, washed no more greasy pots, and peeled no more potatoes. I did my own work, and my own work only, and when and in what fashion I saw fit. Also, I carried the dirk in a sheath at my hip, sailor-fashion, and maintained toward Thomas Mugridge a constant attitude which was composed of equal parts of domineering, insult, and contempt.

CHAPTER TEN

MY intimacy with Wolf Larsen increases—if by intimacy may be denoted those relations which exist between master and man, or, better yet, between king and jester. I am to him no more than a toy, and he values me no more than a child values a toy. My function is to amuse, and so long as I amuse all goes well; but let him become bored, or let him have one of his black moods come upon him, and at once I am relegated from cabin table to galley, while, at the same time, I am fortunate to escape with my life and a whole body.

The loneliness of the man is slowly being borne in upon me. There is not a man aboard but hates or fears him, nor is there a man whom he does not despise. He seems consuming with the tremendous power that is in him and that seems never to have found adequate expression in works. He is as Lucifer would be, were that proud spirit banished to a society of soulless, Tomlinsonian ghosts.*

This loneliness is bad enough in itself, but, to make it worse, he is oppressed by the primal melancholy of the race. Knowing him, I review the old Scandinavian myths with clearer understanding. The white-skinned, fair-haired savages who created that terrible pantheon were of the same fibre as he. The frivolity of the laughter-loving Latins is no part of him. When he laughs it is from a humor that is nothing else than ferocious. But he laughs rarely; he is too often sad. And it is a sadness as deep-reaching as the roots of the race. It is the race heritage, the sadness which has made the race sober-minded, clean-lived, and fanatically moral, and which, in this latter connection, has culminated among the English in the Reformed Church and Mrs. Grundy.*

In point of fact, the chief vent to this primal melancholy has been religion in its more agonizing forms. But the compensations of such religion are denied Wolf Larsen. His brutal materialism will not permit it. So, when his blue moods come on, nothing remains for him but to be devilish. Were he not so terrible a man, I could sometimes feel sorry for him, as instance three mornings ago, when I went into his stateroom to fill his water-bottle and came unexpectedly upon him. He did not see me. His head was buried in his hands, and his shoulders were heaving convulsively as with sobs. He seemed torn by some mighty grief. As I softly withdrew I could hear him groaning, "God! God! God!" Not that he was calling upon god; it was a mere expletive, but it came from his soul.

At dinner he asked the hunters for a remedy for headache, and by evening, strong man that he was, he was half-blind and reeling about the cabin.

"I've never been sick in my life, Hump," he said, as I guided him to his room. "Nor did I ever have a headache except the time my head was healing after having been laid open for six inches by a capstan-bar."

For three days this blinding headache lasted, and he suffered as wild animals suffer, as it seemed the way on ship to suffer, without plaint, without sympathy, utterly alone.

This morning, however, on entering his state-room to make the bed and put things in order, I found him well and hard at work. Table and bunk were littered with designs and calculations. On a large transparent sheet, compass and square in hand, he was copying what appeared to be a scale of some sort or other.

"Hello, Hump," he greeted me genially. "I'm just finishing the finishing touches. Want to see it work?"

"But what is it?" I asked.

"A labor-saving device for mariners, navigation reduced to kindergarten simplicity," he answered gayly. "From today a child will be able to navigate a ship. No more long-winded calculations. All you need is one star in the sky on a dirty night to know instantly where you are. Look. I place the transparent scale on this star-map, revolving the scale on the North Pole. On the scale I've worked out the circles of altitude and the lines of bearing. All I do is to put it on a star, revolve the scale till it is opposite those figures on the map underneath, and presto! there you are, the ship's precise location!"*

There was a ring of triumph in his voice, and his eyes, clear blue this morning as the sea, were sparkling with light.

"You must be well up in mathematics," I said. "Where did you go to school?"

"Never saw the inside of one, worse luck," was the answer. "I had to dig it out for myself."

"And why do you think I have made this thing?" he demanded, abruptly. "Dreaming to leave footprints on the sands of time?"* He laughed one of his horrible mocking laughs. "Not at all. To get it patented, to make money from it, to revel in piggishness with all night in while other men do the work. That's my purpose. Also, I have enjoyed working it out."

"The creative joy," I murmured.

"I guess that's what it ought to be called. Which is another way of expressing the joy of life in that it is alive, the triumph of movement over matter, of the quick over the dead, the pride of the yeast because it is yeast and crawls."

I threw up my hands with helpless disapproval of his inveterate materialism and went about making the bed. He continued copying lines and figures upon the transparent scale. It was a task requiring the utmost nicety and precision, and I could not but admire the way he tempered his strength to the fineness and delicacy of the need.

When I had finished the bed, I caught myself looking

at him in a fascinated sort of way. He was certainly a handsome man—beautiful in the masculine sense. And again, with never-failing wonder, I remarked the total lack of viciousness, or wickedness, or sinfulness, in his face. It was the face, I am convinced, of a man who either did nothing contrary to the dictates of his conscience, or who had no conscience. I am inclined to the latter way of accounting for it. He was a magnificent atavism, a man so purely primitive that he was of the type that came into the world before the development of the moral nature. He was not immoral, but merely unmoral.

As I have said, in the masculine sense his was a beautiful face. Smooth-shaven, every line was distinct, and it was cut as clear and sharp as a cameo; while sea and sun had tanned the naturally fair skin to a dark bronze which bespoke struggle and battle and added both to his savagery and his beauty. The lips were full, yet possessed of the firmness, almost harshness, which is characteristic of thin lips. The set of his mouth, his chin, his jaw, was likewise firm or harsh, with all the fierceness and indomitableness of the male—the nose also. It was the nose of a being born to conquer and command. It just hinted of the eagle beak. It might have been Grecian, it might have been Roman, only it was a shade too massive for the one, a shade too delicate for the other. And while the whole face was the incarnation of fierceness and strength, the primal melancholy from which he suffered seemed to greaten the lines of mouth and eye and brow, seemed to give a largeness and completeness which otherwise the face would have lacked.

And so I caught myself standing idly and studying him. I cannot say how greatly the man had come to interest me. Who was he? What was he? How had he happened to be? All powers seemed his, all potentialities,—why, then, was he no more than the obscure master of a seal-hunting schooner with a reputation for frightful brutality amongst the men who hunted seals?

My curiosity burst from me in a flood of speech.

"Why is it that you have not done great things in this world? With the power that is yours you might have risen to any height. Unpossessed of conscience or moral instinct, you might have mastered the world, broken it to your hand. And yet here you are, at the top of your life, where diminishing and dying begin, living an obscure and sordid existence, hunting sea animals for the satisfaction of woman's vanity and love of decoration, revelling in a piggishness, to use your own words, which is anything and everything except splendid. Why, with all that wonderful strength, have you not done something? There was nothing to stop you, nothing that could stop you. What was wrong? Did you lack ambition? Did you fall under temptation? What was the matter? What was the matter?"

He had lifted his eyes to me at the commencement of my outburst, and followed me complacently until I had done and stood before him breathless and dismayed. He waited a moment, as though seeking where to begin, and then said:

"Hump, do you know the parable of the sower who went forth to sow? If you will remember, some of the seed fell upon stony places, where there was not much earth, and forthwith they sprung up because they had no deepness of earth. And when the sun was up they were scorched, and because they had no root they withered away. And some fell among thorns, and the thorns sprung up and choked them."*

"Well?" I said.

"Well?" he queried, half petulantly. "It was not well. I was one of those seeds."

He dropped his head to the scale and resumed the copying. I finished my work and had opened the door to leave, when he spoke to me.

"Hump, if you will look on the west coast of the map of Norway you will see an indentation called Romsdal Fiord.

I was born within a hundred miles of that stretch of water. But I was not born Norwegian. I am a Dane.* My father and mother were Danes, and how they ever came to that bleak bight of land on the west coast I do not know. I never heard. Outside of that there is nothing mysterious. They were poor people and unlettered. They came of generations of poor unlettered people—peasants of the sea who sowed their sons on the waves as has been their custom since time began. There is no more to tell."

"But there is," I objected. "It is still obscure to me."

"What can I tell you?" he demanded, with a recrude-scence of fierceness. "Of the meagreness of a child's life? of fish diet and coarse living? of going out with the boats from the time I could crawl? of my brothers, who went away one by one to the deep-sea farming and never came back? of myself, unable to read or write, cabin-boy at the mature age of ten on the coastwise, old-country ships? of the rough fare and rougher usage, where kicks and blows were bed and breakfast and took the place of speech, and fear and hatred and pain were my only soul-experiences? I do not care to remember. A madness comes up in my brain even now as I think of it. But there were coastwise skippers I would have returned and killed when a man's strength came to me, only the lines of my life were cast at the time in other places. I did return, not long ago, but unfortunately the skippers were dead, all but one, a mate in the old days, a skipper when I met him, and when I left him a cripple who would never walk again."

"But you who read Spencer and Darwin and have never seen the inside of a school, how did you learn to read and write?" I queried.

"In the English merchant service. Cabin-boy at twelve, ship's boy at fourteen, ordinary seaman at sixteen, able seaman at seventeen, and cock of the fo'c'sle, infinite am-bition and infinite loneliness, receiving neither help nor sympathy, I did it all for myself—navigation, mathematics, science, literature, and what not. And of what use has it been? Master and owner of a ship at the top of my life, as you say, when I am beginning to diminish and die. Paltry, isn't it? And when the sun was up I was scorched, and because I had no root I withered away."

"But history tells of slaves who rose to the purple," I chided.

"And history tells of opportunities that came to the slaves who rose to the purple," he answered grimly. "No man makes opportunity. All the great men ever did was to know it when it came to them. The Corsican* knew. I have dreamed as greatly as the Corsican. I should have known the opportunity, but it never came. The thorns sprung up and choked me. And, Hump, I can tell you that you know more about me than any living man, except my own brother."

"And what is he? And where is he?"

"Master of the steamship *Macedonia*, seal-hunter," was the answer. "We will meet him most probably on the Japan coast. Men call him 'Death' Larsen."

"Death Larsen!" I involuntarily cried. "Is he like you?"

"Hardly. He is a lump of an animal without any head. He has all my—my—"

"Brutishness," I suggested.

"Yes,—thank you for the word,—all my brutishness, but he can scarcely read or write."

"And he has never philosophized on life," I added.

"No," Wolf Larsen answered, with an indescribable air of sadness. "And he is all the happier for leaving life alone. He is too busy living it to think about it. My mistake was in ever opening the books."

CHAPTER ELEVEN

THE *Ghost* has attained the southernmost point of the arc she is describing across the Pacific, and is already beginning to edge away to the west and north toward some lone island, it is rumored, where she will fill her water-casks before proceeding to the season's hunt along the coast of Japan. The hunters have experimented and practised with their rifles and shotguns till they are satisfied, and the boat-pullers and steerers have made their spritsails, bound the oars and rowlocks in leather and sennit so that they will make no noise when creeping on the seals, and put their boats in apple-pie order—to use Leach's homely phrase.

His arm, by the way, has healed nicely, though the scar will remain all his life. Thomas Mugridge lives in mortal fear of him, and is afraid to venture on deck after dark. There are two or three standing quarrels in the forecastle. Louis tells me that the gossip of the sailors finds its way aft, and that two of the telltales have been badly beaten by their mates. He shakes his head dubiously over the outlook for the man Johnson, who is boat-puller in the same boat with him. Johnson, has been guilty of speaking his mind too freely, and has collided two or three times with Wolf Larsen over the pronunciation of his name. Johansen he thrashed on the amidships deck the other night, since which time the mate has called him by his proper name. But of course it is out of the question that Johnson should thrash Wolf Larsen.

Louis has also given me additional information about Death Larsen, which tallies with the captain's brief description. We may expect to meet Death Larsen on the Japan coast. "And look out for squalls," is Louis's prophecy, "for they hate one another like the wolf-whelps they are." Death Larsen is in command of the only sealing-steamer in the fleet, the *Macedonia*, which carries fourteen boats, whereas the rest of the schooners carry only six. There is wild talk of cannon aboard, and of strange raids and expeditions she may make, ranging from opium smuggling into the States and arms smuggling into China, to black-birding* and open piracy. Yet I cannot but believe Louis, for I have never yet caught him in a lie, while he has a cyclopaedic knowledge of sealing and the men of the sealing fleets.

As it is forward and in the galley, so it is in the steerage and aft, on this veritable hell-ship. Men fight and struggle ferociously for one another's lives. The hunters are looking for a shooting scrape at any moment between Smoke and Henderson, whose old quarrel has not healed, while Wolf Larsen says positively that he will kill the survivor of the affair, if such affair comes off. He frankly states that the position he takes is based on no moral grounds, that all the hunters could kill and eat one another so far as he is concerned, were it not that he needs them alive for the hunting. If they will only hold their hands until the season is over, he promises them a royal carnival, when all grudges can be settled and the survivors may toss the non-survivors overboard and arrange a story as to how the missing men were lost at sea. I think even the hunters are appalled at his cold-bloodedness. Wicked men though they be, they are certainly very much afraid of him.

Thomas Mugridge is cur-like in his subjection to me, while I go about in secret dread of him. His is the courage of fear,—a strange thing I know well of myself,—and at any moment it may master the fear and impel him to the taking of my life. My knee is much better, though it often aches for long periods, and the stiffness is gradually leaving the arm which Wolf Larsen squeezed. Otherwise I am in splendid condition, feel that I am in splendid condition.

My muscles are growing harder and increasing in size. My hands, however, are a spectacle for grief. They have a parboiled appearance, are afflicted with hang-nails, while the nails are broken and discolored, and the edges of the quick seem to be assuming a fungoid sort of growth. Also, I am suffering from boils, due to my diet, most likely, for I was never afflicted in this manner before.

I was amused, a couple of evenings back, by seeing Wolf Larsen reading the Bible, a copy of which, after the futile search for one at the beginning of the voyage, had been found in the dead mate's sea-chest. I wondered what Wolf Larsen could get from it, and he read aloud to me from Ecclesiastes. I could imagine he was speaking the thoughts of his own mind as he read to me, and his voice, reverberating deeply and mournfully in the confined cabin, charmed and held me. He may be uneducated, but he certainly knows how to express the significance of the written word. I can hear him now, as I shall always hear him, the primal melancholy vibrant in his voice as he read:

"I gathered me also silver and gold, and the peculiar treasure of kings and of the provinces; I gat me men singers and women singers, and the delights of the sons of men, as musical instruments, and that of all sorts.

"So I was great, and increased more than all that were before me in Jerusalem; also my wisdom remained with me.

"Then I looked on all the works that my hands had wrought and on the labor that I had labored to do; and behold, all was vanity and vexation of spirit, and there was no profit under the sun.

"All things come alike to all; there is one event to the righteous and to the wicked; to the good and to the clean, and to the unclean; to him that sacrificeth, and to him that sacrificeth not; as is the good, so is the sinner; and he that sweareth, as he that feareth an oath.

"This is an evil among all things that are done under the sun, that there is one event unto all; yea, also the heart of the sons of men is full of evil, and madness is in their heart while they live, and after that they go to the dead.

"For to him that is joined to all the living there is hope; for a living dog is better than a dead lion.

"For the living know that they shall die; but the dead know not anything, neither have they any more a reward; for the memory of them is forgotten.

"Also their love, and their hatred, and their envy, is now perished; neither have they any more a portion forever in anything that is done under the sun."*

"There you have it, Hump," he said, closing the book upon his finger and looking up at me. "The Preacher who was king over Israel in Jerusalem thought as I think. You call me a pessimist. Is not this pessimism of the blackest?— 'All is vanity and vexation of spirit,' 'There is no profit under the sun,' 'There is one event unto all,' to the fool and the wise, the clean and the unclean, the sinner and the saint, and that event is death, and an evil thing, he says. For the Preacher loved life, and did not want to die, saying, 'For a living dog is better than a dead lion.' He preferred the vanity and vexation to the silence and unmoveableness of the grave. And so I. To crawl is piggish; but to not crawl, to be as the clod and rock, is loathsome to contemplate. It is loathsome to the life that is in me, the very essence of which is movement, the power of movement, and the consciousness of the power of movement. Life itself is unsatisfaction, but to look ahead to death is greater unsatisfaction."

"You are worse off than Omar," I said. "He, at least, after the customary agonizing of youth, found content and made of his materialism a joyous thing."

"Who was Omar?" Wolf Larsen asked, and I did no more work that day, nor the next, nor the next.

In his random reading he had never chanced upon the Rub'aiy'at, and it was to him like a great find of treasure. Much I remembered, possibly two-thirds of the quatrains, and I managed to piece out the remainder without difficulty. We talked for hours over single stanzas, and I found him reading into them a wail of regret and a rebellion which, for the life of me, I could not discover myself. Possibly I recited with a certain joyous lilt which was my own, for,—his memory was good, and at a second rendering, very often the first, he made a quatrain his own,—he recited the same lines and invested them with an unrest and passionate revolt that was well-nigh convincing.

I was interested as to which quatrain he would like best, and was not surprised when he hit upon the one born of an instant's irritability, and quite at variance with the Persian's complacent philosophy and genial code of life:—

> "What, without asking, hither hurried *Whence*?
> And, without asking, *Whither* hurried hence!
> Oh, many a Cup of this forbidden Wine
> Must drown the memory of that insolence!"*

"Great!" Wolf Larsen cried. "Great! That's the keynote. Insolence! He could not have used a better word."

In vain I objected and denied. He deluged me, overwhelmed me with argument.

"It's not the nature of life to be otherwise. Life, when it knows that it must cease living, will always rebel. It cannot help itself. The Preacher found life and the works of life all a vanity and vexation, an evil thing; but death, the ceasing to be able to be vain and vexed, he found an eviler thing. Through chapter after chapter he is worried by the one event that cometh to all alike. So Omar, so I, so you, even you, for you rebelled against dying when Cooky sharpened a knife for you. You were afraid to die; the life that was in you, that composes you, that is greater than you, did not want to die. You have talked of the instinct of immortality. I talk of the instinct of life, which is to live, and which, when death looms near and large, masters the instinct, so called, of immortality. It mastered it in you (you cannot deny it), because a crazy Cockney cook sharpened a knife.

"You are afraid of him now. You are afraid of me. You cannot deny it. If I should catch you by the throat, thus,"— his hand was about my throat and my breath was shut off,—"and began to press the life out of you, thus, and thus, your instinct of immortality will go glimmering, and your instinct of life, which is longing for life, will flutter up, and you will struggle to save yourself. Eh? I see the fear of death in your eyes. You beat the air with your arms. You exert all your puny strength to struggle to live. Your hand is clutching my arm, lightly it feels as a butterfly resting there. Your chest is heaving, your tongue protruding, your skin turning dark, your eyes swimming. 'To live! To live! To live!' you are crying; and you are crying to live here and now, not hereafter. You doubt your immortality, eh? Ha! Ha! You are not sure of it. You won't chance it. This life only you are certain is real. Ah, it is growing dark and darker. It is the darkness of death, the ceasing to be, the ceasing to feel, the ceasing to move, that is gathering about you, descending upon you, rising around you. Your eyes are becoming set. They are glazing. My voice sounds faint and far. You cannot see my face. And still you struggle in my grip. You kick with your legs. Your body draws itself up in knots like a snake's. Your chest heaves and strains. To live! To live! To live—"

I heard no more. Consciousness was blotted out by the darkness he had so graphically described, and when I came to myself I was lying on the floor and he was smoking a cigar and regarding me thoughtfully with that old familiar light of curiosity in his eyes.

"Well, have I convinced you?" he demanded. "Here, take a drink, of this. I want to ask you some questions."

I rolled my head negatively on the floor. "Your arguments are too—er—forcible," I managed to articulate, at cost of great pain to my aching throat.

"You'll be all right in half an hour," he assured me. "And I promise I won't use any more physical demonstrations. Get up now. You can sit on a chair."

And, toy that I was of this monster, the discussion of Omar and the Preacher was resumed. And half the night we sat up over it.

CHAPTER TWELVE

THE last twenty-four hours have witnessed a carnival of brutality. From cabin to forecastle it seems to have broken out like a contagion. I scarcely know where to begin. Wolf Larsen was really the cause of it. The relations among the men, strained and made tense by feuds, quarrels, and grudges, were in a state of unstable equilibrium, and evil passions flared up in flame like prairie-grass.

Thomas Mugridge is a sneak, a spy, an informer. He has been attempting to curry favor and reinstate himself in the good graces of the captain by carrying tales of the men forward. He it was, I know, that carried some of Johnson's hasty talk to Wolf Larsen. Johnson, it seems, bought a suit of oilskins from the slop-chest and found them to be of greatly inferior quality. Nor was he slow in advertising the fact. The slop-chest is a sort of miniature dry-goods store which is carried by all sealing schooners and which is stocked with articles peculiar to the needs of the sailors. Whatever a sailor purchases is taken from his subsequent earnings on the sealing grounds; for, as it is with the hunters so it is with the boat-pullers and steerers—in the place of wages they receive a "lay," a rate of so much per skin for every skin captured in their particular boat.

But of Johnson's grumbling at the slop-chest I knew nothing, so that what I witnessed came with the shock of sudden surprise. I had just finished sweeping the cabin, and had been inveigled by Wolf Larsen into a discussion of Hamlet, his favorite Shakespearian character, when Johansen descended the companion stairs followed by Johnson. The latter's cap came off after the custom of the sea, and he stood respectfully in the centre of the cabin, swaying heavily and uneasily to the roll of the schooner and facing the captain.

"Shut the doors and draw the slide," Wolf Larsen said to me.

As I obeyed I noticed an anxious light come into Johnson's eyes, but I did not dream of its cause. I did not dream of what was to occur until it did occur, but he knew from the very first what was coming and awaited it bravely. And in his action I found complete refutation of all Wolf Larsen's materialism. The sailor Johnson was swayed by idea, by principle, and truth, and sincerity. He was right, he knew he was right, and he was unafraid. He would die for the right if needs be, he would be true to himself, sincere with his soul. And in this was portrayed the victory of the spirit over the flesh, the indomitability and moral grandeur of the soul that knows no restriction and rises above time and space and matter with a surety and invincibleness born of nothing else than eternity and immortality.

But to return. I noticed the anxious light in Johnson's eyes, but mistook it for the native shyness and embarrassment of the man. The mate, Johansen, stood away several feet to the side of him, and fully three yards in front of him sat Wolf Larsen on one of the pivotal cabin chairs. An appreciable pause fell after I had closed the doors and drawn the slide, a pause that must have lasted fully a minute. It was broken by Wolf Larsen.

"Yonson," he began.

"My name is Johnson, sir," the sailor boldly corrected.

"Well, Johnson, then damn you! Can you guess why I have sent for you?"

"Yes, and no, sir," was the slow reply. "My work is done well. The mate knows that, and you know it, sir. So there cannot be any complaint."

"And is that all?" Wolf Larsen queried, his voice soft, and low, and purring.

"I know you have it in for me," Johnson continued with his unalterable and ponderous slowness. "You do not like me. You—You—"

"Go on," Wolf Larsen prompted. "Don't be afraid of my feelings."

"I am not afraid," the sailor retorted, a slight angry flush rising through his sunburn. "If I speak not fast, it is because I have not been from the old country as long as you. You do not like me because I am too much of a man; that is why, sir."

"You are too much of a man for ship discipline, if that is what you mean, and if you know what I mean," was Wolf Larsen's retort.

"I know English, and I know what you mean, sir" Johnson answered, his flush deepening at the slur on his knowledge of the English language.

"Johnson," Wolf Larsen said, with an air of dismissing all that had gone before as introductory to the main business in hand, "I understand you're not quite satisfied with those oil-skins?"

"No, I am not. They are no good, sir."

"And you've been shooting off your mouth about them."

"I say what I think, sir," the sailor answered courageously, not failing at the same time in ship courtesy, which demanded that "sir" be appended to each speech he made.

It was at this moment that I chanced to glance at Johansen. His big fists were clenching and unclenching, and his face was positively fiendish, so malignantly did he look at Johnson. I noticed a black discoloration, still faintly visible, under Johansen's eye, a mark of the thrashing he had received a few nights before from the sailor. For the first time I began to divine that something terrible was about to be enacted,—what, I could not imagine.

"Do you know what happens to men who say what you've said about my slop-chest and me?" Wolf Larsen was demanding.

"I know, sir," was the answer.

"What?" Wolf Larsen demanded, sharply and imperatively.

"What you and the mate there are going to do to me, sir."

"Look at him, Hump," Wolf Larsen said to me, "look at this bit of animated dust, this aggregation of matter that moves and breathes and defies me and thoroughly believes itself to be compounded of something good; that is impressed with certain human fictions such as righteousness and honesty, and that will live up to them in spite of all personal discomforts and menaces. What do you think of him, Hump? What do you think of him?"

"I think that he is a better man than you are," I answered, impelled, somehow, with a desire to draw upon myself a portion of the wrath I felt was about to break upon his head. "His human fictions, as you choose to call them, make for nobility and manhood. You have no fictions, no dreams, no ideals. You are a pauper."

He nodded his head with a savage pleasantness. "Quite true, Hump, quite true. I have no fictions that make for nobility and manhood. A living dog is better than a dead lion, say I with the preacher. My only doctrine is the doctrine of expediency, and it makes for surviving. This bit of the ferment we call 'Johnson,' when he is no longer a bit of the ferment, only dust and ashes, will have no more nobility than any dust and ashes, while I shall still be alive and roaring."

"Do you know what I am going to do?" he questioned.

I shook my head.

"Well, I am going to exercise my prerogative of roaring and show you how fares nobility. Watch me."

Three yards away from Johnson he was, and sitting down. Nine feet! And yet he left the chair in full leap, without first gaining a standing position. He left the chair, just as he sat in it, squarely, springing from the sitting

posture like a wild animal, a tiger, and like a tiger covered
the intervening space. It was an avalanche of fury that
Johnson strove vainly to fend off. He threw one arm down
to protect the stomach, the other arm up to protect the
head; but Wolf Larsen's fist drove midway between, on
the chest, with a crushing, resounding impact. Johnson's
breath, suddenly expelled, shot from his mouth as suddenly checked, with the forced, audible expiration of a man
wielding an axe. He almost fell backward, and swayed from
side to side in an effort to recover his balance.

I cannot give the further particulars of the horrible scene
that followed. It was too revolting. It turns me sick even
now when I think of it. Johnson fought bravely enough,
but he was no match for Wolf Larsen, much less for Wolf
Larsen and the mate. It was frightful. I had not imagined
a human being could endure so much and still live and
struggle on. And struggle on Johnson did. Of course there
was no hope for him, not the slightest, and he knew it as
well as I, but by the manhood that was in him he could
not cease from fighting for that manhood.

It was too much for me to witness. I felt that I should
lose my mind, and I ran up the companion stairs to open
the doors and escape on deck. But Wolf Larsen, leaving
his victim for the moment, and with one of his tremendous
springs, gained my side and flung me into the far corner
of the cabin.

"The phenomena of life, Hump," he girded at me. "Stay
and watch it. You may gather data on the immortality of
the soul. Besides, you know, we can't hurt Johnson's soul.
It's only the fleeting form we may demolish."

It seemed centuries—possibly it was no more than ten
minutes that the beating continued. Wolf Larsen and Johansen were all about the poor fellow. They struck him
with their fists, kicked him with their heavy shoes, knocked
him down, and dragged him to his feet to knock him down
again. His eyes were blinded so that he could not see, and

the blood running from ears and nose and mouth turned the cabin into a shambles. And when he could no longer rise they still continued to beat and kick him where he lay.

"Easy, Johansen; easy as she goes," Wolf Larsen finally said.

But the beast in the mate was up and rampant, and Wolf Larsen was compelled to brush him away with a backhanded sweep of the arm, gentle enough, apparently, but which hurled Johansen back like a cork, driving his head against the wall with a crash. He fell to the floor, half stunned for the moment, breathing heavily and blinking his eyes in a stupid sort of way.

"Jerk open the doors, Hump," I was commanded.

I obeyed, and the two brutes picked up the senseless man like a sack of rubbish and hove him clear up the companion stairs, through the narrow doorway, and out on deck. The blood from his nose gushed in a scarlet stream over the feet of the helmsman, who was none other than Louis, his boat-mate. But Louis took and gave a spoke and gazed imperturbably into the binnacle.

Not so was the conduct of George Leach, the erstwhile cabin-boy. Fore and aft there was nothing that could have surprised us more than his consequent behavior. He it was that came up on the poop without orders and dragged Johnson forward, where he set about dressing his wounds as well as he could and making him comfortable. Johnson, as Johnson, was unrecognizable; and not only that, for his features, as human features at all, were unrecognizable, so discolored and swollen had they become in the few minutes which had elapsed between the beginning of the beating and the dragging forward of the body.

But of Leach's behavior— By the time I had finished cleansing the cabin he had taken care of Johnson. I had come up on deck for a breath of fresh air and to try to get some repose for my overwrought nerves. Wolf Larsen was smoking a cigar and examining the patent log which the *Ghost* usually towed astern but which had been hauled in for some purpose. Suddenly Leach's voice came to my ears. It was tense and hoarse with an overmastering rage. I turned and saw him standing just beneath the break of the poop on the port side of the galley. His face was convulsed and white, his eyes were flashing, his clenched fists raised overhead.

"May God damn your soul to hell, Wolf Larsen, only hell's too good for you, you coward, you murderer, you pig!" was his opening salutation.

I was thunderstruck. I looked for his instant annihilation. But it was not Wolf Larsen's whim to annihilate him. He sauntered slowly forward to the break of the poop, and, leaning his elbow on the corner of the cabin, gazed down thoughtfully and curiously at the excited boy.

And the boy indicted Wolf Larsen as he had never been indicted before. The sailors assembled in a fearful group just outside the forecastle scuttle and watched and listened. The hunters piled pell-mell out of the steerage, but as Leach's tirade continued I saw that there was no levity in their faces. Even they were frightened, not at the boy's terrible words, but at his terrible audacity. It did not seem possible that any living creature could thus beard Wolf Larsen in his teeth. I know for myself that I was shocked into admiration of the boy, and I saw in him the splendid invincibleness of immortality rising above the flesh and the fears of the flesh, as in the prophets of old, to condemn unrighteousness.

And such condemnation! He haled forth Wolf Larsen's soul naked to the scorn of men. He rained upon it curses from God and High Heaven, and withered it with a heat of invective that savored of a mediaeval excommunication of the Catholic Church. He ran the gamut of denunciation, rising to heights of wrath that were sublime and almost Godlike, and from sheer exhaustion sinking to the vilest and most indecent abuse.

His rage was a madness. His lips were flecked with a soapy froth, and sometimes he choked and gurgled and became inarticulate. And through it all, calm and impassive, leaning on his elbow and gazing down, Wolf Larsen seemed lost in a great curiosity. This wild stirring of yeasty life, this terrific revolt and defiance of matter that moved, perplexed and interested him.

Each moment I looked, and everybody looked, for him to leap upon the boy and destroy him. But it was not his whim. His cigar went out, and he continued to gaze silently and curiously.

Leach had worked himself into an ecstasy of impotent rage.

"Pig! Pig! Pig!" he was reiterating at the top of his lungs. "Why don't you come down and kill me, you murderer? You can do it! I ain't afraid! There's no one to stop you! Damn sight better dead and outa your reach than alive and in your clutches! Come on, you coward! Kill me! Kill me! Kill me!"

It was at this stage that Thomas Mugridge's erratic soul brought him into the scene. He had been listening at the galley door, but he now came out, ostensibly to fling some scraps over the side, but obviously to see the killing he was certain would take place. He smirked greasily up into the face of Wolf Larsen, who seemed not to see him. But the Cockney was unabashed, though mad, stark mad. He turned to Leach, saying:

"Such langwidge! Shockin'!"

Leach's rage was no longer impotent. Here at last was something ready to hand. And for the first time since the stabbing the Cockney had appeared outside the galley without his knife. The words had barely left his mouth when he was knocked down by Leach. Three times he struggled to his feet, striving to gain the galley, and each time was knocked down.

"Oh, Lord!" he cried. "'Elp! 'Elp! Tyke 'im aw'y, can't

yer? Tyke 'im aw'y!"

The hunters laughed from sheer relief. Tragedy had dwindled, the farce had begun. The sailors now crowded boldly aft, grinning and shuffling, to watch the pummelling of the hated Cockney. And even I felt a great joy surge up within me. I confess that I delighted in this beating Leach was giving to Thomas Mugridge, though it was as terrible, almost, as the one Mugridge had caused to be given to Johnson. But the expression of Wolf Larsen's face never changed. He did not change his position either, but continued to gaze down with a great curiosity. For all his pragmatic certitude, it seemed as if he watched the play and movement of life in the hope of discovering something more about it, of discerning in its maddest writhings a something which had hitherto escaped him,—the key to its mystery, as it were, which would make all clear and plain.

But the beating! It was quite similar to the one I had witnessed in the cabin. The Cockney strove in vain to protect himself from the infuriated boy. And in vain he strove to gain the shelter of the cabin. He rolled toward it, grovelled toward it, fell toward it when he was knocked down. But blow followed blow with bewildering rapidity. He was knocked about like a shuttlecock, until, finally, like Johnson, he was beaten and kicked as he lay helpless on the deck. And no one interfered. Leach could have killed him, but, having evidently filled the measure of his vengeance, he drew away from his prostrate foe, who was whimpering and wailing in a puppyish sort of way, and walked forward.

But these two affairs were only the opening events of the day's programme. In the afternoon Smoke and Henderson fell foul of each other, and a fusillade of shots came up from the steerage, followed by a stampede of the other four hunters for the deck. A column of thick, acrid smoke—the kind always made by black powder—was arising through the open companionway, and down through it leaped Wolf

Larsen. The sound of blows and scuffling came to our ears. Both men were wounded, and he was thrashing them both for having disobeyed his orders and crippled themselves in advance of the hunting season. In fact, they were badly wounded, and, having thrashed them, he proceeded to operate upon them in a rough surgical fashion and to dress their wounds. I served as assistant while he probed and cleansed the passages made by the bullets, and I saw the two men endure his crude surgery without anaesthetics and with no more to uphold them than a stiff tumbler of whiskey.

Then, in the first dog-watch, trouble came to a head in the forecastle. It took its rise out of the tittle-tattle and tale-bearing which had been the cause of Johnson's beating, and from the noise we heard, and from the sight of the bruised men next day, it was patent that half the forecastle had soundly drubbed the other half.

The second dog-watch and the day were wound up by a fight between Johansen and the lean, Yankee-looking hunter, Latimer. It was caused by remarks of Latimer's concerning the noises made by the mate in his sleep, and though Johansen was whipped, he kept the steerage awake for the rest of the night while he blissfully slumbered and fought the fight over and over again.

As for myself, I was oppressed with nightmare. The day had been like some horrible dream. Brutality had followed brutality, and flaming passions and cold-blooded cruelty had driven men to seek one another's lives, and to strive to hurt, and maim, and destroy. My nerves were shocked. My mind itself was shocked. All my days had been passed in comparative ignorance of the animality of man. In fact, I had known life only in its intellectual phases. Brutality I had experienced, but it was the brutality of the intellect— the cutting sarcasm of Charley Furuseth, the cruel epigrams and occasional harsh witticisms of the fellows at the Bibelot, and the nasty remarks of some of the professors during my undergraduate days.

That was all. But that men should wreak their anger on others by the bruising of the flesh and the letting of blood was something strangely and fearfully new to me. Not for nothing had I been called "Sissy" Van Weyden, I thought, as I tossed restlessly on my bunk between one nightmare and another. And it seemed to me that my innocence of the realities of life had been complete indeed. I laughed bitterly to myself, and seemed to find in Wolf Larsen's forbidding philosophy a more adequate explanation of life than I found in my own.

And I was frightened when I became conscious of the trend of my thought. The continual brutality around me was degenerative in its effect. It bid fair to destroy for me all that was best and brightest in life. My reason dictated that the beating Thomas Mugridge had received was an ill thing, and yet for the life of me I could not prevent my soul joying in it. And even while I was oppressed by the enormity of my sin,—for sin it was,—I chuckled with an insane delight. I was no longer Humphrey Van Weyden. I was Hump, cabin-boy on the schooner *Ghost*. Wolf Larsen was my captain, Thomas Mugridge and the rest were my companions, and I was receiving repeated impresses from the die which had stamped them all.

CHAPTER THIRTEEN

FOR three days I did my own work and Thomas Mugridge's too; and I flatter myself that I did his work well. I know that it won Wolf Larsen's approval, while the sailors beamed with satisfaction during the brief time my régime lasted.

"The first clean bite since I come aboard," Harrison said to me at the galley door, as he returned the dinner pots and pans from the forecastle. "Somehow Tommy's grub always tastes of grease, stale grease, and I reckon he ain't changed his shirt since he left 'Frisco."

"I know he hasn't," I answered.

"And I'll bet he sleeps in it," Harrison added.

"And you won't lose," I agreed. "The same shirt, and he hasn't had it off once in all this time."

But three days was all Wolf Larsen allowed him in which to recover from the effects of the beating. On the fourth day, lame and sore, scarcely able to see, so closed were his eyes, he was haled from his bunk by the nape of the neck and set to his duty. He sniffled and wept, but Wolf Larsen was pitiless.

"And see that you serve no more slops," was his parting injunction. "No more grease and dirt, mind, and a clean shirt occasionally, or you'll get a tow over the side. Understand?"

Thomas Mugridge crawled weakly across the galley floor, and a short lurch of the *Ghost* sent him staggering. In attempting to recover himself, he reached for the iron railing which surrounded the stove and kept the pots from sliding off; but he missed the railing, and his hand, with his weight behind it, landed squarely on the hot surface. There was a sizzle and odor of burning flesh, and a sharp cry of pain.

"Oh, Gawd, Gawd, wot 'ave I done?" he wailed, sitting down in the coal-box and nursing his new hurt by rocking back and forth. "W'y 'as all this come on me? It mykes me fair sick, it does, an' I try so 'ard to go through life 'armless an' 'urtin' nobody."

The tears were running down his puffed and discolored cheeks, and his face was drawn with pain. A savage expression flitted across it.

"Oh, 'ow I 'ate 'im! 'Ow I 'ate 'im!" he gritted out.

"Whom?" I asked; but the poor wretch was weeping again over his misfortunes. Less difficult it was to guess whom he hated than whom he did not hate. For I had come to see a malignant devil in him which impelled him to hate all the world. I sometimes thought that he hated even himself, so grotesquely had life dealt with him, and so monstrously. At such moments a great sympathy welled up within me, and I felt shame that I had ever joyed in his discomfiture or pain. Life had been unfair to him. It had played him a scurvy trick when it fashioned him into the thing he was, and it had played him scurvy tricks ever since. What chance had he to be anything else than he was? And as though answering my unspoken thought, he wailed:

"I never 'ad no chance, nor 'arf a chance! 'Oo was there to send me to school, or put tommy* in my 'ungry belly, or wipe my bloody nose for me, w'en I was a kiddy? 'Oo ever did anything for me, heh? 'Oo, I s'y?"

"Never mind, Tommy," I said, placing a soothing hand on his shoulder. "Cheer up. It'll all come right in the end. You've long years before you, and you can make anything you please of yourself."

"It's a lie! a bloody lie!" he shouted in my face, flinging off the hand. "It's a lie, and you know it. I'm already myde, an' myde out of leavin's an' scraps. It's all right for you, 'Ump. You was born a gentleman. You never knew wot it was to go 'ungry, to cry yerself asleep with yer little belly gnawin' an' gnawin', like a rat inside yer. It carn't come right. If I was President of the United States to-morrer, 'ow would it fill my belly for one time w'en I was a kiddy and it went empty?

"'Ow could it, I s'y? I was born to sufferin' and sorrer. I've 'ad more cruel sufferin' than any ten men, I 'ave. I've been in 'orspital arf my bleedin' life. I've 'ad the fever in Aspinwall,* in 'Avana, in New Orleans. I near died of the scurvy and was rotten with it six months in Barbadoes. Smallpox in 'Onolulu, two broken legs in Shanghai, pneumonia in Unalaska,* three busted ribs an' my insides all twisted in 'Frisco. An' 'ere I am now. Look at me! Look at me! My ribs kicked loose from my back again. I'll be coughin' blood before eyght bells. 'Ow can it be myde up to me, I arsk? 'Oo's goin' to do it? Gawd? 'Ow Gawd must 'ave 'ated me w'en 'e signed me on for a voyage in this bloomin' world of 'is!"

This tirade against destiny went on for an hour or more, and then he buckled to his work, limping and groaning, and in his eyes a great hatred for all created things. His diagnosis was correct, however, for he was seized with occasional sicknesses, during which he vomited blood and suffered great pain. And as he said, it seemed God hated him too much to let him die, for he ultimately grew better and waxed more malignant than ever.

Several days more passed before Johnson crawled on deck and went about his work in a half-hearted way. He was still a sick man, and I more than once observed him creeping painfully aloft to a topsail, or drooping wearily as he stood at the wheel. But, still worse, it seemed that his spirit was broken. He was abject before Wolf Larsen and almost grovelled to Johansen. Not so was the conduct of Leach. He went about the deck like a tiger cub, glaring his hatred openly at Wolf Larsen and Johansen.

"I'll do for you yet, you slab-footed Swede," I heard him say to Johansen one night on deck.

The mate cursed him in the darkness, and the next moment some missile struck the galley a sharp rap. There was more cursing, and a mocking laugh, and when all was quiet I stole outside and found a heavy knife imbedded over an inch in the solid wood. A few minutes later the mate came fumbling about in search of it, but I returned it privily to Leach next day. He grinned when I handed it over, yet it was a grin that contained more sincere thanks than a multitude of the verbosities of speech common to the members of my own class.

Unlike any one else in the ship's company, I now found myself with no quarrels on my hands and in the good graces of all. The hunters possibly no more than tolerated me, though none of them disliked me; while Smoke and Henderson, convalescent under a deck awning and swinging day and night in their hammocks, assured me that I was better than any hospital nurse and that they would not forget me at the end of the voyage when they were paid off. (As though I stood in need of their money! I, who could have bought them out, bag and baggage, and the schooner and its equipment, a score of times over!) But upon me had devolved the task of tending their wounds, and pulling them through, and I did my best by them.

Wolf Larsen underwent another bad attack of headache which lasted two days. He must have suffered severely, for he called me in, and obeyed my commands like a sick child. But nothing I could do seemed to relieve him. At my suggestion, however, he gave up smoking and drinking; though why such a magnificent animal as he should have headaches at all puzzles me.

"'Tis the hand of god, I'm tellin' you," is the way Louis sees it. "'Tis a visitation for his black-hearted deeds, and there's more behind and comin', or else—"

"Or else," I prompted.

"God is noddin' and not doin' his duty, though it's me as shouldn't say it."

I was mistaken when I said that I was in the good graces of all. Not only does Thomas Mugridge continue to hate me, but he has discovered a new reason for hating me. It took me no little while to puzzle it out, but I finally discovered that it was because I was more luckily born then he—"gentleman born," he put it.

"And still no more dead men," I twitted Louis, when Smoke and Henderson, side by side, in friendly conversation, took their first exercise on deck.

Louis surveyed me with his shrewd gray eyes and shook his head portentously. "She's a-comin', I tell you, and it'll be sheets and halyards, stand by all hands, when she begins to howl. I've had the feel iv it this long time, and I can feel it now as plainly as I feel the rigging iv a dark night. She's close, she's close."

"Who goes first?" I queried.

"Not old fat Louis, I promise you," he laughed. "For 'tis in the bones iv me I know that come this time next year I'll be gazin' in the old mother's eyes, weary with watchin' iv the sea for the five sons she gave to it."

"Wot's 'e been s'yin' to yer?" Thomas Mugridge demanded a moment later.

"That he's going home some day to see his mother," I answered diplomatically.

"I never 'ad none," was the Cockney's comment, as he gazed with lustreless, hopeless eyes into mine.

CHAPTER FOURTEEN

IT has dawned upon me that I have never placed a proper valuation upon womankind. For that matter, though not amative to any considerable degree so far as I have discovered, I was never outside the atmosphere of women until now. My mother and sisters were always about me, and I was always trying to escape them; for they worried me to distraction with their solicitude for my health and with their periodic inroads on my den, when my orderly confusion, upon which I prided myself, was turned into worse confusion and less order, though it looked neat enough to the eye. I never could find anything when they had departed. But now, alas, how welcome would have been the feel of their presence, the frou-frou and swish-swish of their skirts which I had so cordially detested! I am sure, if I ever get home, that I shall never be irritable with them again. They may dose me and doctor me morning, noon, and night, and dust and sweep and put my den to rights every minute of the day, and I shall only lean back and survey it all and be thankful in that I am possessed of a mother and some several sisters.

All of which has set me wondering. Where are the mothers of these twenty and odd men on the *Ghost*? It strikes me as unnatural and unhealthful that men should be totally separated from women and herd through the world by themselves. Coarseness and savagery are the inevitable results. These men about me should have wives, and sisters, and daughters; then would they be capable of softness, and tenderness, and sympathy. As it is, not one of them is married. In years and years not one of them has been in contact with a good woman, or within the influence, or redemption, which irresistibly radiates from such a creature. There is no balance in their lives. Their masculinity, which in itself is of the brute, has been overdeveloped. The other and spiritual side of their natures has been dwarfed—atrophied, in fact.

They are a company of celibates, grinding harshly against one another and growing daily more calloused from the grinding. It seems to me impossible sometimes that they ever had mothers. It would appear that they are a half-brute, half-human species, a race apart, wherein there is no such thing as sex; that they are hatched out by the sun like turtle eggs, or receive life in some similar and sordid fashion; and that all their days they fester in brutality and viciousness and in the end die as unlovely as they have lived.

Rendered curious by this new direction of ideas, I talked with Johansen last night—the first superfluous words with which he has favored me since the voyage began. He left Sweden when he was eighteen, is now thirty-eight, and in all the intervening time has not been home once. He had met a townsman, a couple of years before, in some sailor boarding-house in Chile, so that he knew his mother to be still alive.

"She must be a pretty old woman, now," he said, staring meditatively into the binnacle and then jerking a sharp glance at Harrison, who was steering a point off the course.

"When did you last write to her?"

He performed his mental arithmetic aloud. "Eighty-one; no—eighty-two, eh? no—eighty-three? Yes, eighty-three. Ten years ago.* From some little port in Madagascar. I was trading.

"You see," he went on, as though addressing his neglected mother across half the girth of the earth, "each year I was going home. So what was the good to write? It was only a year. And each year something happened, and I did not go. But I am mate, now, and when I pay off at 'Frisco, maybe with five hundred dollars, I will ship myself on a wind-jammer round the Horn to Liverpool, which will give me more money; and then I will pay my passage from there home. Then she will not do any more work."

"But does she work? now? How old is she?"

"About seventy," he answered. And then, boastingly, "We work from the time we are born until we die, in my country. That's why we live so long. I will live to a hundred."

I shall never forget this conversation. The words were the last I ever heard him utter. Perhaps they were the last he did utter, too. For, going down into the cabin to turn in, I decided that it was too stuffy to sleep below. It was a calm night. We were out of the Trades, and the *Ghost* was forging ahead barely a knot an hour. So I tucked a blanket and pillow under my arm and went up on deck.

As I passed between Harrison and the binnacle, which was built into the top of the cabin, I noticed that he was this time fully three points off. Thinking that he was asleep, and wishing him to escape reprimand or worse, I spoke to him. But he was not asleep. His eyes were wide and staring. He seemed greatly perturbed, unable to reply to me.

"What's the matter?" I asked. "Are you sick?"

He shook his head, and with a deep sigh, as of awakening, caught his breath.

"You'd better get on your course, then," I chided.

He put a few spokes over, and I watched the compass-card swing slowly to N N W and steady itself with slight oscillations.

I took a fresh hold on my bedclothes and was preparing to start on, when some movement caught my eye and I looked astern to the rail. A sinewy hand, dripping with water, was clutching the rail. A second hand took form in the darkness beside it. I watched, fascinated. What visitant from the gloom of the deep was I to behold? Whatever it was, I knew that it was climbing aboard by the log-line.

I saw a head, the hair wet and straight, shape itself, and then the unmistakable eyes and face of Wolf Larsen. His right cheek was red with blood, which flowed from some wound in the head.

He drew himself inboard with a quick effort, and arose to his feet, glancing swiftly, as he did so, at the man at the wheel, as though to assure himself of his identity and that there was nothing to fear from him. The sea-water was streaming from him. It made little audible gurgles which distracted me. As he stepped toward me I shrank back instinctively, for I saw that in his eyes which spelled death.

"All right, Hump," he said in a low voice. "Where's the mate?"

I shook my head.

"Johansen!" he called softly. "Johansen!"

"Where is he?" he demanded of Harrison.

The young fellow seemed to have recovered his composure, for he answered steadily enough, "I don't know, sir. I saw him go for'ard a little while ago."

"So did I go for'ard. But you will observe that I didn't come back the way I went. Can you explain it?"

"You must have been overboard, sir."

"Shall I look for him in the steerage, sir?" I asked.

Wolf Larsen shook his head. "You wouldn't find him, Hump. But you'll do. Come on. Never mind your bedding. Leave it where it is."

I followed at his heels. There was nothing stirring amidships.

"Those cursed hunters," was his comment. "Too damned fat and lazy to stand a four-hour watch."

But on the forecastle-head we found three sailors asleep. He turned them over and looked at their faces. They composed the watch on deck, and it was the ship's custom, in good weather, to let the watch sleep with the exception of the officer, the helmsman, and the look-out.

"Who's look-out?" he demanded.

"Me, sir," answered Holyoak, one of the deep-water sailors, a slight tremor in his voice. "I winked off just this very minute, sir. I'm sorry, sir. It won't happen again."

"Did you hear or see anything on deck?"

"No, sir, I—"

But Wolf Larsen had turned away with a snort of disgust, leaving the sailor rubbing his eyes with surprise at having been let off so easily.

"Softly, now," Wolf Larsen warned me in a whisper, as he doubled his body into the forecastle scuttle and prepared to descend.

I followed with a quaking heart. What was to happen I knew no more than did I know what had happened. But blood had been shed, and it was through no whim of Wolf Larsen that he had gone over the side with his scalp laid open. Besides, Johansen was missing.

It was my first descent into the forecastle, and I shall not soon forget my impression of it, caught as I stood on my feet at the bottom of the ladder. Built directly in the eyes of the schooner, it was the shape of a triangle, along the three sides of which stood the bunks, in double-tier, twelve of them. It was no larger than a hall bedroom in Grub Street, and yet twelve men were herded into it to eat and sleep and carry on all the functions of living. My bedroom at home was not large, yet it could have contained a dozen similar forecastles, and taking into consideration the height of the ceiling, a score at least.

It smelled sour and musty, and by the dim light of the swinging sea-lamp I saw every bit of available wall-space hung deep with sea-boots, oilskins, and garments, clean and dirty, of various sorts. These swung back and forth with every roll of the vessel, giving rise to a brushing sound, as of trees against a roof or wall. Somewhere a boot thumped loudly and at irregular intervals against the wall; and, though it was a mild night on the sea, there was a

continual chorus of the creaking timbers and bulkheads
and of abysmal noises beneath the flooring.

The sleepers did not mind. There were eight of them,—
the two watches below, —and the air was thick with the
warmth and odor of their breathing, and the ear was filled
with the noise of their snoring and of their sighs and half-
groans, tokens plain of the rest of the animal-man. But
were they sleeping? all of them? Or had they been sleeping? This was evidently Wolf Larsen's quest—to find the
men who appeared to be asleep and who were not asleep
or who had not been asleep very recently. And he went
about it in a way that reminded me of a story out of
Boccaccio.*

He took the sea-lamp from its swinging frame and handed it to me. He began at the first bunks forward on the
starboard side. In the top one lay Oofty-Oofty, a Kanaka*
and splendid seaman, so named by his mates. He was
asleep on his back and breathing as placidly as a woman.
One arm was under his head, the other lay on top of
the blankets. Wolf Larsen put thumb and forefinger to
the wrist and counted the pulse. In the midst of it the
Kanaka roused. He awoke as gently as he slept. There
was no movement of the body whatsoever. The eyes, only,
moved. They flashed wide open, big and black, and stared,
unblinking, into our faces. Wolf Larsen put his finger to his
lips as a sign for silence, and the eyes closed again.

In the lower bunk lay Louis, grossly fat and warm and
sweaty, asleep unfeignedly and sleeping laboriously. While
Wolf Larsen held his wrist he stirred uneasily, bowing his
body so that for a moment it rested on shoulders and
heels. His lips moved, and he gave voice to this enigmatic
utterance:

"A shilling's worth a quarter; but keep your lamps out
for thruppenny bits, or the publicans'll shove 'em on you
for sixpence."*

Then he rolled over on his side with a heavy, sobbing

sigh, saying:

"A sixpence is a tanner, and a shilling a bob; but what a pony is I don't know."*

Satisfied with the honesty of his and the Kanaka's sleep, Wolf Larsen passed on to the next two bunks on the starboard side, occupied top and bottom, as we saw in the light of the sea-lamp, by Leach and Johnson.

As Wolf Larsen bent down to the lower bunk to take Johnson's pulse, I, standing erect and holding the lamp, saw Leach's head raise stealthily as he peered over the side of his bunk to see what was going on. He must have divined Wolf Larsen's trick and the sureness of detection, for the light was at once dashed from my hand and the forecastle left in darkness. He must have leaped, also, at the same instant, straight down on Wolf Larsen.

The first sounds were those of a conflict between a bull and a wolf. I heard a great infuriated bellow go up from Wolf Larsen, and from Leach a snarling that was desperate and blood-curdling. Johnson must have joined him immediately, so that his abject and grovelling conduct on deck for the past few days had been no more than planned deception.

I was so terror-stricken by this fight in the dark that I leaned against the ladder, trembling and unable to ascend. And upon me was that old sickness at the pit of the stomach, caused always by the spectacle of physical violence. In this instance I could not see, but I could hear the impact of the blows—the soft crushing sound made by flesh striking forcibly against flesh. Then there was the crashing about of the entwined bodies, the labored breathing, the short, quick gasps of sudden pain.

There must have been more men in the companionway to murder the captain and mate, for by the sounds I knew that Leach and Johnson had been quickly reinforced by some of their mates.

"Get a knife, somebody!" Leach was shouting.

"Pound him on the head! Mash his brains out!" was Johnson's cry.

But after his first bellow, Wolf Larsen made no noise. He was fighting grimly and silently for life. He was sore beset. Down at the very first, he had been unable to gain his feet, and for all of his tremendous strength I felt that there was no hope for him.

The force with which they struggled was vividly impressed on me; for I was knocked down by their surging bodies and badly bruised. But in the confusion I managed to crawl into an empty lower bunk out of the way.

"All hands! We've got him! We've got him!" I could hear Leach crying.

"Who?" demanded those who had been really asleep, and who had awakened to they knew not what.

"It's the bloody mate!" was Leach's crafty answer, strained from him in a smothered sort of way.

This was greeted with whoops of joy, and from then on Wolf Larsen had seven strong men on top of him, Louis, I believe, taking no part in it. The forecastle was like an angry hive of bees aroused by some marauder.

"What ho! below there!" I heard Latimer shout down the scuttle, too cautious to descend into the inferno of passion he could hear raging beneath him in the darkness.

"Won't somebody get a knife? Oh, won't somebody get a knife?" Leach pleaded in the first interval of comparative silence.

The number of the assailants was a cause of confusion. They blocked their own efforts, while Wolf Larsen, with but a single purpose, achieved his. This was to fight his way across the floor to the ladder. Though in total darkness, I followed his progress by its sound. No man less than a giant could have done what he did, once he had gained the foot of the ladder. Step by step, by the might of his arms, the whole pack of men striving to drag him back and down, he drew his body up from the floor till he stood erect. And then, step by step, hand and foot, he slowly struggled up the ladder.

The very last of all, I saw. For Latimer, having finally gone for a lantern, held it so that its light shone down the scuttle. Wolf Larsen was nearly to the top, though I could not see him. All that was visible was the mass of men fastened upon him. It squirmed about, like some huge many-legged spider, and swayed back and forth to the regular roll of the vessel. And still, step by step, with long intervals between, the mass ascended. Once it tottered, about to fall back, but the broken hold was regained and it still went up.

"Who is it?" Latimer cried.

In the rays of the lantern I could see his perplexed face peering down.

"Larsen," I heard a muffled voice from within the mass.

Latimer reached down with his free hand. I saw a hand shoot up to clasp his. Latimer pulled, and the next couple of steps were made with a rush. Then Wolf Larsen's other hand reached up and clutched the edge of the scuttle. The mass swung clear of the ladder, the men still clinging to their escaping foe. They began to drop off, to be brushed off against the sharp edge of the scuttle, to be knocked off by the legs which were now kicking powerfully. Leach was the last to go, falling sheer back from the top of the scuttle and striking on head and shoulders upon his sprawling mates beneath. Wolf Larsen and the lantern disappeared, and we were left in darkness.

CHAPTER FIFTEEN

THERE was a deal of cursing and groaning as the men at the bottom of the ladder crawled to their feet.

"Somebody strike a light, my thumb's out of joint," said one of the men, Parsons, a swarthy, saturnine man, boat-steerer in Standish's boat, in which Harrison was puller.

"You'll find it knockin' about by the bitts," Leach said, sitting down on the edge of the bunk in which I was concealed.

There was a fumbling and a scratching of matches, and the sea-lamp flared up, dim and smoky, and in its weird light bare-legged men moved about, nursing their bruises and caring for their hurts. Oofty-Oofty laid hold of Parson's thumb, pulling it out stoutly and snapping it back into place. I noticed at the same time that the Kanaka's knuckles were laid open clear across and to the bone. He exhibited them, exposing beautiful white teeth in a grin as he did so and explaining that the wounds had come from striking Wolf Larsen in the mouth.

"So it was you, was it, you black beggar?" belligerently demanded one, Kelly, an Irish-American and a longshore-man, making his first trip to sea, and boat-puller for Ker-foot.

As he made the demand he spat out a mouthful of blood and teeth and shoved his pugnacious face close to Oofty-Oofty. The Kanaka leaped backward to his bunk, to return with a second leap, flourishing a long knife.

"Aw, go lay down, you make me tired," Leach interfered. He was evidently, for all of his youth and inexperience, cock of the forecastle. "G'wan, you Kelly. You leave Oofty alone. How in hell did he know it was you in the dark?"

Kelly subsided with some muttering, and the Kanaka

flashed his white teeth in a grateful smile. He was a beautiful creature, almost feminine in the pleasing lines of his
figure, and there was a softness and dreaminess in his large
eyes which seemed to contradict his well-earned reputation
for strife and action.

"How did he get away?" Johnson asked.

He was sitting on the side of his bunk, the whole pose
of his figure indicating utter dejection and hopelessness.
He was still breathing heavily from the exertion he had
made. His shirt had been ripped entirely from him in the
struggle, and blood from a gash in the cheek was flowing
down his naked chest, marking a red path across his white
thigh and dripping to the floor.

"Because he is the devil, as I told you before," was
Leach's answer; and thereat he was on his feet and raging
his disappointment with tears in his eyes.

"And not one of you to get a knife!" was his unceasing
lament.

But the rest of the hands had a lively fear of conse-
quences to come and gave no heed to him.

"How'll he know which was which?" Kelly asked, and
as he went on he looked murderously about him—"unless
one of us peaches."

"He'll know as soon as ever he claps eyes on us," Parsons
replied. "One look at you'd be enough."

"Tell him the deck flopped up and gouged yer teeth
out iv yer jaw," Louis grinned. He was the only man who
was not out of his bunk, and he was jubilant in that he
possessed no bruises to advertise that he had had a hand
in the night's work. "Just wait till he gets a glimpse iv yer
mugs to-morrow, the gang iv ye," he chuckled.

"We'll say we thought it was the mate," said one. And
another, "I know what I'll say—that I heered a row, jump-
ed out of my bunk, got a jolly good crack on the jaw for
my pains and sailed in myself. Couldn't tell who or what
it was in the dark and just hit out."

"An' 'twas me you hit, of course," Kelly seconded, his face brightened for the moment.

Leach and Johnson took no part in the discussion, and it was plain to see that their mates looked upon them as men for whom the worst was inevitable, who were beyond hope and already dead. Leach stood their fears and reproaches for some time. Then he broke out:

"You make me tired! A nice lot of gazabas* you are! If you talked less with yer mouth and did something with yer hands, he'd a-ben done with by now. Why couldn't one of you, just one of you, get me a knife when I sung out? You make me sick! A-beefin' and bellerin' 'round, as though he'd kill you when he gets you! You know damn well he won't. Can't afford to. No shipping masters or beach combers over here, and he wants yer in his business, and he wants yer bad. Who's to pull or steer or sail ship if he loses yer? It's me and Johnson have to face the music. Get into yer bunks, now, and shut yer faces; I want to get some sleep."

"That's all right all right," Parsons spoke up. "Mebbe he won't do for us, but mark my words, hell'll be an icebox to this ship from now on."

All the while I had been apprehensive concerning my own predicament. What would happen to me when these men discovered my presence? I could never fight my way out as Wolf Larsen had done. And at this moment Latimer called down the scuttles:

"Hump! The old man wants you!"

"He ain't down here!" Parsons called back.

"Yes he is," I said, sliding out of the bunk and striving my hardest to keep my voice steady and bold.

The sailors looked at me in consternation. Fear was strong in their faces, and the devilishness which comes of fear.

"I'm coming!" I shouted up to Latimer.

"No, you don't!" Kelly cried, stepping between me and

the ladder, his right hand shaped into a veritable stran-
gler's clutch. "You damn little sneak! I'll shut yer mouth!"

"Let him go," Leach commanded.

"Not on yer life," was the angry retort.

Leach never changed his position on the edge of the
bunk. "Let him go, I say," he repeated; but this time his
voice was gritty and metallic.

The Irishman wavered. I made to step by him, and he
stood aside. When I had gained the ladder, I turned to the
circle of brutal and malignant faces peering at me through
the semi-darkness. A sudden and deep sympathy welled up
in me. I remembered the Cockney's way of putting it. How
God must have hated them that they should be tortured
so!

"I have seen and heard nothing, believe me," I said
quietly.

"I tell yer, he's all right," I could hear Leach saying as
I went up the ladder. "He don't like the old man no more
nor you or me."

I found Wolf Larsen in the cabin, stripped and bloody,
waiting for me. He greeted me with one of his whimsical
smiles.

"Come, get to work, Doctor. The signs are favorable for
an extensive practice this voyage. I don't know what the
Ghost would have been without you, and if I could only
cherish such noble sentiments I would tell you her master
is deeply grateful."

I knew the run of the simple medicine-chest the Ghost
carried, and while I was heating water on the cabin stove
and getting the things ready for dressing his wounds, he
moved about, laughing and chatting, and examining his
hurts with a calculating eye. I had never before seen him
stripped, and the sight of his body quite took my breath
away. It has never been my weakness to exalt the flesh—
far from it; but there is enough of the artist in me to
appreciate its wonder.

I must say that I was fascinated by the perfect lines of Wolf Larsen's figure, and by what I may term the terrible beauty of it. I had noted the men in the forecastle. Powerfully muscled though some of them were, there had been something wrong with all of them, an insufficient development here, an undue development there, a twist or a crook that destroyed symmetry, legs too short or too long, or too much sinew or bone exposed, or too little. Oofty-Oofty had been the only one whose lines were at all pleasing, while, in so far as they pleased, that far had they been what I should call feminine.

But Wolf Larsen was the man-type, the masculine, and almost a god in his perfectness. As he moved about or raised his arms the great muscles leapt and moved under the satiny skin. I had forgotten to say that the bronze ended with his face. His body, thanks to his Scandinavian stock, was fair as the fairest woman's. I remember his putting his hand up to feel of the wound on his head, and my watching the biceps move like a living thing under its white sheath. It was the biceps that had nearly crushed out my life once, that I had seen strike so many killing blows. I could not take my eyes from him. I stood motionless, a roll of antiseptic cotton in my hand unwinding and spilling itself down to the floor.

He noticed me, and I became conscious that I was staring at him.

"God made you well," I said.

"Did he?" he answered. "I have often thought so myself, and wondered why."

"Purpose—" I began.

"Utility," he interrupted. "This body was made for use. These muscles were made to grip, and tear, and destroy living things that get between me and life. But have you thought of the other living things? They, too, have muscles, of one kind and another, made to grip, and tear, and destroy; and when they come between me and life, I out-grip them, out-tear them, out-destroy them. Purpose does not explain that. Utility does."

"It is not beautiful," I protested.

"Life isn't, you mean," he smiled. "Yet you say I was made well. Do you see this?"

He braced his legs and feet, pressing the cabin floor with his toes in a clutching sort of way. Knots and ridges and mounds of muscles writhed and bunched under the skin.

"Feel them," he commanded.

They were hard as iron. And I observed, also, that his whole body had unconsciously drawn itself together, tense and alert; that muscles were softly crawling and shaping about the hips, along the back, and across the shoulders; that the arms were slightly lifted, their muscles contracting, the fingers crooking till the hands were like talons; and that even the eyes had changed expression and into them were coming watchfulness and measurement and a light none other than of battle.

"Stability, equilibrium," he said, relaxing on the instant and sinking his body back into repose. "Feet with which to clutch the ground, legs to stand on and to help withstand, while with arms and hands, teeth and nails, I struggle to kill and to be not killed. Purpose? Utility is the better word."

I did not argue. I had seen the mechanism of the primitive fighting beast, and I was as strongly impressed as if I had seen the engines of a great battleship or Atlantic liner.

I was surprised, considering the fierce struggle in the forecastle, at the superficiality of his hurts, and I pride myself that I dressed them dexterously. With the exception of several bad wounds, the rest were merely severe bruises and lacerations. The blow which he had received before going overboard had laid his scalp open several inches. This, under his direction, I cleansed and sewed together, having first shaved the edges of the wound. Then the calf of his leg was badly lacerated and looked as though it had been mangled by a bulldog. Some sailor, he told me, had laid hold of it by his teeth, at the beginning of the fight, and hung on and been dragged to the top of the forecastle ladder, when he was kicked loose.

"By the way, Hump, as I have remarked, you are a handy man," Wolf Larsen began, when my work was done. "As you know, we're short a mate. Hereafter you shall stand watches, receive seventy-five dollars per month, and be addressed fore and aft as Mr. Van Weyden."

"I—I don't understand navigation, you know," I gasped.

"Not necessary at all."

"I really do not care to sit in the high places," I objected. "I find life precarious enough in my present humble situation. I have no experience. Mediocrity, you see, has its compensations."

He smiled as though it were all settled.

"I won't be mate on this hell-ship!" I cried defiantly.

I saw his face grow hard and the merciless glitter come into his eyes. He walked to the door of his room, saying:

"And now, Mr. Van Weyden, good night."

"Good night, Mr. Larsen," I answered weakly.

CHAPTER SIXTEEN

I CANNOT say that the position of mate carried with it anything more joyful than that there were no more dishes to wash. I was ignorant of the simplest duties of mate, and would have fared badly indeed had the sailors not sympathized with me. I knew nothing of the minutiae of ropes and rigging, of the trimming and setting of sails; but the sailors took pains to put me to rights,—Louis proving an especially good teacher,—and I had little trouble with those under me.

With the hunters it was otherwise. Familiar in varying degree with the sea, they took me as a sort of joke. In truth, it was a joke to me, that I, the veriest landsman, should be filling the office of mate; but to be taken as a joke by others was a different matter. I made no complaint, but Wolf Larsen demanded the most punctilious sea etiquette in my case,—far more than poor Johansen had ever received; and at the expense of several rows, threats, and much grumbling, he brought the hunters to time. I was "Mr. Van Weyden" fore and aft, and it was only unofficially that Wolf Larsen himself ever addressed me as "Hump."

It was amusing. Perhaps the wind would haul a few points while we were at dinner, and as I left the table he would say, "Mr. Van Weyden, will you kindly put about on the port tack." And I would go on deck, beckon Louis to me, and learn from him what was to be done. Then, a few minutes later, having digested his instructions and thoroughly mastered the manoeuvre, I would proceed to issue my orders. I remember an early instance of this kind, when Wolf Larsen appeared on the scene just as I had begun to give orders. He smoked his cigar and looked on quietly till the thing was accomplished, and then paced aft by my side along the weather poop.

"Hump," he said, "I beg pardon, Mr. Van Weyden, I congratulate you. I think you can now fire your father's legs back into the grave to him. You've discovered your own and learned to stand on them. A little rope-work, sail-making, and experience with storms and such things, and by the end of the voyage you could ship on any coasting schooner."

It was during this period, between the death of Johansen and the arrival on the sealing grounds, that I passed my pleasantest hours on the *Ghost*. Wolf Larsen was quite considerate, the sailors helped me, and I was no longer in irritating contact with Thomas Mugridge. And I made free to say, as the days went by, that I found I was taking a certain secret pride in myself. Fantastic as the situation was,—a landlubber second in command,—I was, neverthe-less, carrying it off well; and during that brief time I was proud of myself, and I grew to love the heave and roll of the *Ghost* under my feet as she wallowed north and west through the tropic sea to the islet where we filled our water-casks.

But my happiness was not unalloyed. It was compara-tive, a period of less misery slipped in between a past of great miseries and a future of great miseries. For the *Ghost*, so far as the seamen were concerned, was a hell-ship of the worse description. They never had a moment's rest or peace. Wolf Larsen treasured against them the attempt on his life and the drubbing he had received in the forecastle; and morning, noon, and night, and all night as well, he devoted himself to making life unlivable for them.

He knew well the psychology of the little thing, and it was the little things by which he kept the crew worked up to the verge of madness. I have seen Harrison called from his bunk to put properly away a misplaced paint-brush, and the two watches below haled from their tired sleep to accompany him and see him do it. A little thing, truly, but when multiplied by the thousand ingenious devices of such a mind, the mental state of the men in the forecastle may be slightly comprehended.

Of course much grumbling went on, and little outbursts were continually occurring. Blows were struck, and there were always two or three men nursing injuries at the hands of the human beast who was their master. Concerted action was impossible in face of the heavy arsenal of weapons carried in the steerage and cabin. Leach and Johnson were the two particular victims of Wolf Larsen's diabolic temper, and the look of profound melancholy which had settled on Johnson's face and in his eyes made my heart bleed.

With Leach it was different. There was too much of the fighting beast in him. He seemed possessed by an insatiable fury which gave no time for grief. His lips had become distorted into a permanent snarl, which, at mere sight of Wolf Larsen, broke out in sound, horrible and menacing, and, I do believe, unconsciously. I have seen him follow Wolf Larsen about with his eyes, like an animal its keeper, the while the animal-like snarl sounded deep in his throat and vibrated forth between his teeth.

I remember once, on deck, in bright day, touching him on the shoulder as preliminary to giving an order. His back was toward me, and at the first feel of my hand he leaped upright in the air and away from me, snarling and turning his head as he leaped. He had for the moment mistaken me for the man he hated.

Both he and Johnson would have killed Wolf Larsen at the slightest opportunity, but the opportunity never came. Wolf Larsen was too wise for that, and, besides, they had no adequate weapons. With their fists alone they had no chance whatever. Time and again he fought it out with Leach, who fought back, always, like a wildcat, tooth and nail and fist, until stretched, exhausted or unconscious, on the deck. And he was never averse to another encounter.

All the devil that was in him challenged the devil in Wolf Larsen. They had but to appear on deck at the same time, when they would be at it, cursing, snarling, striking; and I have seen Leach fling himself upon Wolf Larsen without warning or provocation. Once he threw his heavy sheath-knife, missing Wolf Larsen's throat by an inch. Another time he dropped a steel marlinspike from the mizzen crosstree. It was a difficult cast to make on a rolling ship, but the sharp point of the spike, whistling seventy-five feet through the air, barely missed Wolf Larsen's head as he emerged from the cabin companionway and drove its length two inches and over into the solid deck-planking. Still another time, he stole into the steerage, possessed himself of a loaded shot-gun, and was making a rush for the deck with it when caught by Kerfoot and disarmed.

I often wondered why Wolf Larsen did not kill him and make an end of it. But he only laughed and seemed to enjoy it. There seemed a certain spice about it, such as men must feel who take delight in making pets of ferocious animals.

"It gives a thrill to life," he explained to me, "when life is carried in one's hand. Man is a natural gambler, and life is the thrill. Why should I deny myself the joy of exciting Leach's soul to fever-pitch? For that matter, I do him a kindness. The greatness of sensation is mutual. He is living more royally than any man for'ard, though he does not know it. For he has what they have not—purpose, something to do and be done, an all-absorbing end to strive to attain, the desire to kill me, the hope that he may kill me. Really, Hump, he is living deep and high. I doubt that he has ever lived so swiftly and keenly before, and I honestly envy him, sometimes, when I see him raging at the summit of passion and sensibility."

"Ah, but it is cowardly, cowardly!" I cried. "You have all the advantage."

"Of the two of us, you and I, who is the greater coward?" he asked seriously. "If the situation is unpleasing, you compromise with your conscience when you make yourself a party to it. If you were really great, really true to yourself, you would join forces with Leach and Johnson. But you are afraid, you are afraid. You want to live. The life that is in you cries out that it must live, no matter what the cost; so you live ignominiously, untrue to the best you dream of, sinning against your whole pitiful little code, and, if there were a hell, heading your soul straight for it. Bah! I play the braver part. I do no sin, for I am true to the promptings of the life that is in me. I am sincere with my soul at least, and that is what you are not."

There was a sting in what he said. Perhaps, after all, I was playing a cowardly part. And the more I thought about it the more it appeared that my duty to myself lay in doing what he had advised, lay in joining forces with Johnson and Leach and working for his death. Right here, I think, entered the austere conscience of my Puritan ancestry, impelling me toward lurid deeds and sanctioning even murder as right conduct. I dwelt upon the idea. It would be a most moral act to rid the world of such a monster. Humanity would be better and happier for it, life fairer and sweeter.

I pondered it long, lying sleepless in my bunk and reviewing in endless procession the facts of the situation. I talked with Johnson and Leach, during the night watches when Wolf Larsen was below. Both men had lost hope,—Johnson, because of temperamental despondency; Leach, because he had beaten himself out in the vain struggle and was exhausted. But he caught my hand in a passionate grip one night, saying:

"I think yer square, Mr. Van Weyden. But stay where you are and keep yer mouth shut. Say nothin' but saw wood.* We're dead men, I know it; but all the same you might be able to do us a favor some time when we need it damn bad."

It was only next day, when Wainwright Island* loomed

to windward, close abeam, that Wolf Larsen opened his
mouth in prophecy. He had attacked Johnson, been attacked by Leach, and had just finished whipping the pair
of them.

"Leach," he said, "you know I'm going to kill you some
time or other, don't you?"

A snarl was the answer.

"And as for you, Johnson, you'll get so tired of life before
I'm through with you that you'll fling yourself over the
side. See if you don't."

"That's a suggestion," he added, in an aside to me. "I'll
bet you a month's pay he acts upon it."

I had cherished a hope that his victims would find an
opportunity to escape while filling our water-barrels, but
Wolf Larsen had selected his spot well. The *Ghost* lay
half a mile beyond the surf-line of a lonely beach. Here
debouched a deep gorge, with precipitous, volcanic walls
which no man could scale. And here, under his direct
supervision,—for he went ashore himself,—Leach and
Johnson filled the small casks and rolled them down to the
beach. They had no chance to make a break for liberty in
one of the boats.

Harrison and Kelly, however, made such an attempt.
They composed one of the boat's crews, and their task
was to ply between the schooner and the shore, carrying
a single cask each trip. Just before dinner, starting for the
beach with an empty barrel, they altered their course and
bore away to the left to round the promontory which jutted
into the sea between them and liberty. Beyond its foaming
base lay the pretty villages of the Japanese colonists, and
smiling valleys which penetrated deep into the interior.
Once in the fastnesses they promised, and the two men
could defy Wolf Larsen.

I had observed Henderson and Smoke loitering about
the deck all morning, and I now learned why they were
there. Procuring their rifles, they opened fire in a leisurely

manner upon the deserters. It was a cold-blooded exhibition of marksmanship. At first their bullets zipped harmlessly along the surface of the water on either side the boat; but, as the men continued to pull lustily, they struck closer and closer.

"Now watch me take Kelly's right oar," Smoke said, drawing a more careful aim.

I was looking through the glasses, and I saw the oarblade shatter as he shot. Henderson duplicated it, selecting Harrison's right oar. The boat slewed around. The two remaining oars were quickly broken. The men tried to row with the splinters, and had them shot out of their hands. Kelly ripped up a bottom board and began paddling, but dropped it with a cry of pain as its splinters drove into his hands. Then they gave up, letting the boat drift till a second boat, sent from the shore by Wolf Larsen, took them in tow and brought them aboard.

Late that afternoon we hove up anchor and got away. Nothing was before us but the three or four months' hunting on the sealing grounds. The outlook was black indeed, and I went about my work with a heavy heart. An almost funereal gloom seemed to have descended upon the *Ghost.* Wolf Larsen had taken to his bunk with one of his strange, splitting headaches. Harrison stood listlessly at the wheel, half-supporting himself by it, as though wearied by the weight of his flesh. The rest of the men were morose and silent. I came upon Kelly crouching to the lee of the forecastle scuttle, his head on his knees, his arms about his head, in an attitude of unutterable despondency.

Johnson I found lying full length on the forecastle head, staring at the troubled churn of the forefoot, and I remembered with horror the suggestion Wolf Larsen had made. It seemed likely to bear fruit. I tried to break in on the man's morbid thoughts by calling him away, but he smiled sadly at me and refused to obey.

Leach approached me as I returned aft.

"I want to ask a favor, Mr. Van Weyden," he said. "If it's yer luck to ever make 'Frisco once more, will you hunt up Matt McCarthy? He's my old man.* He lives on the Hill, back of the Mayfair bakery, runnin' a cobbler's shop that everybody knows, and you'll have no trouble. Tell him I lived to be sorry for the trouble I brought him and the things I done, and—and just tell him 'God bless him,' for me."

I nodded my head, but said, "We'll all win back to San Francisco, Leach, and you'll be with me when I go to see Matt McCarthy."

"I'd like to believe you," he answered, shaking my hand, "but I can't. Wolf Larsen'll do for me, I know it; and all I can hope is he'll do it quick."

And as he left me I was aware of the same desire at my heart. Since it was to be done, let it be done with despatch. The general gloom had gathered me into its folds. The worst appeared inevitable; and as I paced the deck, hour after hour, I found myself afflicted with Wolf Larsen's repulsive ideas. What was it all about? Where was the grandeur of life that it should permit such wanton destruction of human souls? It was a cheap and sordid thing after all, this life, and the sooner over the better. Over and done with! I, too, leaned upon the rail and gazed longingly into the sea, with the certainty that sooner or later I should be sinking down, down, through the cool green depths of its oblivion.

CHAPTER SEVENTEEN

STRANGE to say, in spite of the general foreboding, nothing of especial moment happened on the *Ghost*. We ran on to the north and west till we raised the coast of Japan and picked up with the great seal herd. Coming from no man knew where in the illimitable Pacific, it was travelling north on its annual migration to the rookeries of Bering Sea. And north we travelled with it, ravaging and destroying, flinging the naked carcasses to the shark and salting down the skins so that they might adorn the fair shoulders of the women of the cities.

It was wanton slaughter, and all for woman's sake. No man ate of the seal meat or the oil. After a good day's killing I have seen our decks covered with hides and bodies, slippery with fat and blood, the scuppers running red; masts, ropes and rails spattered with the sanguinary color; and the men, like butchers plying their trade, naked and red of arm and hand, hard at work with ripping and flensing-knives, removing the skins from the pretty sea-creatures they had killed.

It was my task to tally the pelts as they came aboard from the boats, to oversee the skinning and afterward the cleansing of the decks and bringing things shipshape again. It was not pleasant work. My soul and my stomach revolted at it; and yet, in a way, this handling and directing of many men was good for me. It developed what little executive ability I possessed, and I was aware of a toughening or hardening which I was undergoing and which could not be anything but wholesome for "Sissy" Van Weyden.

One thing I was beginning to feel, and that was that I could never again be quite the same man I had been. While my hope and faith in human life still survived Wolf

Larsen's destructive criticism, he had nonetheless been a cause of change in minor matters. He had opened up for me the world of the real, of which I had known practically nothing and from which I had always shrunk. I had learned to look more closely at life as it was lived, to recognize that there were such things as facts in the world, to emerge from the realm of mind and idea and to place certain values on the concrete and objective phases of existence.

I saw more of Wolf Larsen than ever when we had gained the grounds. For when the weather was fair and we were in the midst of the herd, all hands were away in the boats, and left on board were only he and I, and Thomas Mugridge, who did not count. But there was no play about it. The six boats, spreading out fan-wise from the schooner until the first weather boat and the last lee boat were anywhere from ten to twenty miles apart, cruised along a straight course over the sea till nightfall or bad weather drove them in. It was our duty to sail the *Ghost* well to leeward of the last lee boat, so that all the boats should have fair wind to run for us in case of squalls or threatening weather.

It is no slight matter for two men, particularly when a stiff wind has sprung up, to handle a vessel like the *Ghost*, steering, keeping lookout for the boats, and setting or taking in sail; so it devolved upon me to learn and learn quickly. Steering I picked up easily, but running aloft to the crosstrees and swinging my whole weight by my arms when I left the ratlines and climbed still higher, was more difficult. This, too, I learned, and quickly, for I felt somehow a wild desire to vindicate myself in Wolf Larsen's eyes, to prove my right to live in ways other than of the mind. Nay, the time came when I took joy in the run of the masthead and in the clinging on by my legs at that precarious height while I swept the sea with glasses in search of the boats.

I remember one beautiful day, when the boats left early and the reports of the hunters' guns grew dim and distant and died away as they scattered far and wide over the sea. There was just the faintest wind from the westward; but it breathed its last by the time we managed to get to leeward of the last lee boat. One by one,—I was at the masthead and saw,—the six boats disappeared over the bulge of the earth as they followed the seal into the west. We lay, scarcely rolling on the placid sea, unable to follow. Wolf Larsen was apprehensive. The barometer was down, and the sky to the east did not please him. He studied it with unceasing vigilance.

"If she comes out of there," he said, "hard and snappy, putting us to windward of the boats, it's likely there'll be empty bunks in steerage and fo'c'sle."

By eleven o'clock the sea had become glass. By midday, though we were well up in the northerly latitudes, the heat was sickening. There was no freshness in the air. It was sultry and oppressive, reminding me of what the old Californians term "earthquake weather." There was something ominous about it, and in intangible ways one was made to feel that the worst was about to come. Slowly the whole eastern sky filled with clouds that overtowered us like some black sierra of the infernal regions. So clearly could one see canyon, gorge, and precipice, and the shadows that lie therein, that one looked unconsciously for the white surf-line and bellowing caverns where the sea charges on the land. And still we rocked gently, and there was no wind.

"It's no squall," Wolf Larsen said. "Old Mother Nature's going to get up on her hind legs and howl for all that's in her, and it'll keep us jumping, Hump, to pull through with half our boats. You'd better run up and loosen the topsails."

"But if it is going to howl, and there are only two of us?" I asked, a note of protest in my voice.

"Why, we've got to make the best of the first of it and run down to our boats before our canvas is ripped out of

us. After that I don't give a rap what happens. The sticks'll
stand it, and you and I will have to, though we've plenty
cut out for us."

Still the calm continued. We ate dinner, a hurried and
anxious meal for me with eighteen men abroad on the sea
and beyond the bulge of the earth and with that heaven-
rolling mountain range of clouds moving slowly down upon
us. Wolf Larsen did not seem affected, however; though I
noticed, when we returned to the deck, a slight twitching
of the nostrils, a perceptible quickness of movement. His
face was stern, the lines of it had grown hard, and yet in
his eyes,—blue, clear blue this day,—there was a strange
brilliancy, a bright scintillating light. It struck me that he
was joyous, in a ferocious sort of way; that he was glad
there was an impending struggle; that he was thrilled and
upborne with knowledge that one of the great moments of
living, when the tide of life surges up in flood, was upon
him.

Once, and unwitting that he did so or that I saw, he
laughed aloud, mockingly and defiantly, at the advancing
storm. I see him yet, standing there like a pygmy out of the
"Arabian Nights" before the huge front of some malignant
genie. He was daring destiny, and he was unafraid.

He walked to the galley. "Cooky, by the time you've
finished pots and pans you'll be wanted on deck. Stand
ready for a call."

"Hump," he said, becoming cognizant of the fascinated
gaze I bent upon him, "this beats whiskey, and is where
your Omar misses. I think he only half lived after all."

The western half of the sky had by now grown murky.
The sun had dimmed and faded out of sight. It was two
in the afternoon, and a ghostly twilight, shot through by
wandering purplish lights, had descended upon us. In this
purplish light Wolf Larsen's face glowed and glowed, and
to my excited fancy he appeared encircled by a halo. We
lay in the midst of an unearthly quiet, while all about us

were signs and omens of oncoming sound and movement. The sultry heat had become unendurable. The sweat was standing on my forehead, and I could feel it trickling down my nose. I felt as though I should faint, and reached out to the rail for support.

And then, just then, the faintest possible whisper of air passed by. It was from the east, and like a whisper it came and went. The drooping canvas was not stirred, and yet my face had felt the air and been cooled.

"Cooky," Wolf Larsen called in a low voice. Thomas Mugridge turned a pitiable, scared face. "Let go that fore-boom tackle and pass it across, and when she's willing let go the sheet and come in snug with the tackle. And if you make a mess of it, it will be the last you ever make. Understand?

"Mr. Van Weyden, stand by to pass the head-sails over. Then jump for the topsails and spread them quick as God'll let you—the quicker you do it the easier you'll find it. As for Cooky, if he isn't lively bat him between the eyes."

I was aware of the compliment and pleased, in that no threat had accompanied my instructions. We were lying head to northwest, and it was his intention to jibe over all with the first puff.

"We'll have the breeze on our quarter," he explained to me. "By the last guns the boats were bearing away slightly to the south'ard."

He turned and walked aft to the wheel. I went forward and took my station at the jibs. Another whisper of wind, and another, passed by. The canvas flapped lazily.

"Thank Gawd she's not comin' all of a bunch, Mr. Van Weyden," was the Cockney's fervent ejaculation.

And I was indeed thankful, for I had by this time learned enough to know, with all our canvas spread, what disaster in such event awaited us. The whispers of wind became puffs, the sails filled, the *Ghost* moved. Wolf Larsen put the wheel hard up, to port, and we began to pay off. The wind was now dead astern, muttering and puffing stronger and stronger, and my head-sails were pounding lustily. I did not see what went on elsewhere, though I felt the sudden surge and heel of the schooner as the wind pressures changed to the jibing of the fore- and main-sails. My hands were full with the flying-jib, jib, and staysail; and by the time this part of my task was accomplished the *Ghost* was leaping into the southwest, the wind on her quarter and all her sheets to starboard. Without pausing for breath, though my heart was beating like a trip-hammer from my exertions, I sprang to the topsails, and before the wind had become too strong we had them fairly set and were coiling down. Then I went aft for orders.

Wolf Larsen nodded approval and relinquished the wheel to me. The wind was strengthening steadily and the sea rising. For an hour I steered, each moment becoming more difficult. I had not the experience to steer at the gait we were going on a quartering course.

"Now take a run up with the glasses and raise some of the boats. We've made at least ten knots, and we're going twelve or thirteen now. The old girl knows how to walk."

I contented myself with the fore crosstrees, some seventy feet above the deck. As I searched the vacant stretch of water before me, I comprehended thoroughly the need for haste if we were to recover any of our men. Indeed, as I gazed at the heavy sea through which we were running, I doubted that there was a boat afloat. It did not seem possible that such frail craft could survive such stress of wind and water.

I could not feel the full force of the wind, for we were running with it; but from my lofty perch I looked down as though outside the *Ghost* and apart from her, and saw the shape of her outlined sharply against the foaming sea as she tore along instinct with life. Sometimes she would lift and send across some great wave, burying her starboard rail from view, and covering her deck to the hatches

with the boiling ocean. At such moments, starting from
a windward roll, I would go flying through the air with
dizzying swiftness, as though I clung to the end of a huge,
inverted pendulum, the arc of which, between the greater
rolls, must have been seventy feet or more. Once, the terror
of this giddy sweep overpowered me, and for a while I clung
on, hand and foot, weak and trembling, unable to search
the sea for the missing boats or to behold aught of the sea
but that which roared beneath and strove to overwhelm
the *Ghost*.

But the thought of the men in the midst of it steadied
me, and in my quest for them I forgot myself. For an hour I
saw nothing but the naked, desolate sea. And then, where
a vagrant shaft of sunlight struck the ocean and turned
its surface to wrathful silver, I caught a small black speck
thrust skyward for an instant and swallowed up. I waited
patiently. Again the tiny point of black projected itself
through the wrathful blaze a couple of points off our port-
bow. I did not attempt to shout, but communicated the
news to Wolf Larsen by waving my arm. He changed the
course, and I signalled affirmation when the speck showed
dead ahead.

It grew larger, and so swiftly that for the first time I fully
appreciated the speed of our flight. Wolf Larsen motioned
for me to come down, and when I stood beside him at the
wheel gave me instructions for heaving to.

"Expect all hell to break loose," he cautioned me, "but
don't mind it. Yours is to do your own work and to have
Cooky stand by the fore-sheet."

I managed to make my way forward, but there was little
choice of sides, for the weather-rail seemed buried as often
as the lee. Having instructed Thomas Mugridge as to what
he was to do, I clambered into the fore rigging a few feet.
The boat was now very close, and I could make out plainly
that it was lying head to wind and sea and dragging on
its mast and sail, which had been thrown overboard and

made to serve as a sea-anchor. The three men were bailing. Each rolling mountain whelmed them from view, and I would wait with sickening anxiety, fearing that they would never appear again. Then, and with black suddenness, the boat would shoot clear through the foaming crest, bow pointed to the sky, and the whole length of her bottom showing, wet and dark, till she seemed on end. There would be a fleeting glimpse of the three men flinging water in frantic haste, when she would topple over and fall into the yawning valley, bow down and showing her full inside length to the stern up-reared almost directly above the bow. Each time that she reappeared was a miracle.

The *Ghost* suddenly changed her course, keeping away, and it came to me with a shock that Wolf Larsen was giving up the rescue as impossible. Then I realized that he was preparing to heave to, and dropped to the deck to be in readiness. We were not dead before the wind, the boat far away and abreast of us. I felt an abrupt easing of the schooner, a loss for the moment of all strain and pressure, coupled with a swift acceleration of speed. She was rushing around on her heel into the wind.

As she arrived at right angles to the sea, the full force of the wind, (from which we had hitherto run away), caught us. I was unfortunately and ignorantly facing it. It stood up against me like a wall, filling my lungs with air which I could not expel. And as I choked and strangled, and as the *Ghost* wallowed for an instant, broadside on and rolling straight over and far into the wind, I beheld a huge sea rise far above my head. I turned aside, caught my breath, and looked again. The wave overtopped the *Ghost*, and I gazed sheer up and into it. A shaft of sunlight smote the over-curl, and I caught a glimpse of translucent, rushing green, backed by a milky smother of foam.

Then it descended, pandemonium broke loose, every-thing happened at once. I was struck a crushing, stunning blow, nowhere in particular and yet everywhere. My hold had been broken loose, I was under water, and the thought passed through my mind that this was the terrible thing of which I had heard, the being swept in the trough of the sea. My body struck and pounded as it was dashed helplessly along and turned over and over, and when I could hold my breath no longer, I breathed the stinging salt water into my lungs. But through it all I clung to the one idea—I must get the jib backed over to windward. I had no fear of death. I had no doubt but that I should come through somehow. And as this idea of fulfilling Wolf Larsen's order persisted in my dazed consciousness, I seemed to see him standing at the wheel in the midst of the wild welter, pitting his will against the will of the storm and defying it.

I brought up violently against what I took to be the rail, breathed, and breathed the sweet air again. I tried to rise, but struck my head and was knocked back on hands and knees. By some freak of the waters I had been swept clear under the forecastle-head and into the eyes. As I scrambled out on all fours, I passed over the body of Thomas Mugridge, who lay in a groaning heap. There was no time to investigate. I must get the jib backed over.

When I emerged on deck it seemed that the end of everything had come. On all sides there was a rending and crashing of wood and steel and canvas. The *Ghost* was being wrenched and torn to fragments. The foresail and fore topsail, emptied of the wind by the manoeuvre, and with no one to bring in the sheet in time, were thundering into ribbons, the heavy boom threshing and splintering from rail to rail. The air was thick with flying wreckage, detached ropes and stays were hissing and coiling like snakes, and down through it all crashed the gaff of the foresail.

The spar could not have missed me by many inches, while it spurred me to action. Perhaps the situation was not hopeless. I remembered Wolf Larsen's caution. He had expected all hell to break loose, and here it was. And where was he? I caught sight of him toiling at the main sheet,

heaving it in and flat with his tremendous muscles, the
stern of the schooner lifted high in the air and his body
outlined against a white surge of sea sweeping past. All
this, and more,—a whole world of chaos and wreck,—in
possibly fifteen seconds I had seen and heard and grasped.

I did not stop to see what had become of the small boat,
but sprang to the jib-sheet. The jib itself was beginning to
slap, partially filling and emptying with sharp reports; but
with a turn of the sheet and the application of my whole
strength each time it slapped, I slowly backed it. This I
know: I did my best. I pulled till I burst open the ends of
all my fingers; and while I pulled, the flying-jib and staysail
split their cloths apart and thundered into nothingness.

Still I pulled, holding what I gained each time with a
double turn until the next slap gave me more. Then the
sheet gave with greater ease, and Wolf Larsen was beside
me, heaving in alone while I was busied taking up the slack.

"Make fast!" he shouted. "And come on!"

As I followed him, I noted that in spite of rack and ruin a
rough order obtained. The *Ghost* was hove to. She was still
in working order, and she was still working. Though the
rest of her sails were gone, the jib, backed to windward, and
the mainsail hauled down flat, were themselves holding,
and holding her bow to the furious sea as well.

I looked for the boat, and, while Wolf Larsen cleared
the boat-tackles, saw it lift to leeward on a big sea and
not a score of feet away. And, so nicely had he made his
calculation, we drifted fairly down upon it, so that nothing
remained to do but hook the tackles to either end and hoist
it aboard. But this was not done so easily as it is written.

In the bow was Kerfoot, Oofty-Oofty in the stern, and
Kelly amidships. As we drifted closer, the boat would rise
on a wave while we sank in the trough, till almost straight
above me I could see the heads of the three men craned
overside and looking down. Then, the next moment, we
would lift and soar upward while they sank far down

beneath us. It seemed incredible that the next surge should
not crush the *Ghost* down upon the tiny eggshell.

But, at the right moment, I passed the tackle to the
Kanaka, while Wolf Larsen did the same thing forward
to Kerfoot. Both tackles were hooked in a trice, and the
three men, deftly timing the roll, made a simultaneous leap
aboard the schooner. As the *Ghost* rolled her side out of
water, the boat was lifted snugly against her, and before
the return roll came, we had heaved it in over the side and
turned it bottom up on the deck. I noticed blood spouting
from Kerfoot's left hand. In some way the third finger had
been crushed to a pulp. But he gave no sign of pain, and
with his single right hand helped us lash the boat in its
place.

"Stand by to let that jib over, you Oofty!" Wolf Larsen
commanded, the very second we had finished with the
boat. "Kelly, come aft and slack off the main-sheet! You,
Kerfoot, go for'ard and see what's become of Cooky! Mr.
Van Weyden, run aloft again, and cut away any stray stuff
on your way!"

And having commanded, he went aft with his peculiar
tigerish leaps, to the wheel. While I toiled up the fore-
shrouds the *Ghost* slowly paid off. This time, as we went
into the trough of the sea and were swept, there were
no sails to carry away. And, halfway to the crosstrees
and flattened against the rigging by the full force of the
wind so that it would have been impossible for me to
have fallen, the *Ghost* almost on her beam ends and the
masts parallel with the water, I looked, not down, but at
almost right angles from the perpendicular, to the deck
of the *Ghost*. But I saw, not the deck, but where the
deck should have been, for it was buried beneath a wild
tumbling of water. Out of this water I could see the two
masts rising, and that was all. The *Ghost*, for the moment,
was buried beneath the sea. As she squared off more and
more, escaping from the side pressure, she righted herself

and broke her deck, like a whale's back, through the ocean surface.

Then we raced, and wildly, across the wild sea, the while I hung like a fly in the crosstrees and searched for the other boats. In half an hour I sighted the second one, swamped and bottom up, to which were desperately clinging Jock Horner, fat Louis, and Johnson. This time I remained aloft, and Wolf Larsen succeeded in heaving to without being swept. As before, we drifted down upon it. Tackles were made fast and lines flung to the men, who scrambled aboard like monkeys. The boat itself was crushed and splintered against the schooner's side as it came inboard; but the wreck was securely lashed, for it could be patched and made whole again.

Once more the *Ghost* bore away before the storm, this time so submerging herself that for some seconds I thought she would never reappear. Even the wheel, quite a deal higher than the waist, was covered and swept again and again. At such moments I felt strangely alone with God, alone with him and watching the chaos of his wrath. And then the wheel would reappear, and Wolf Larsen's broad shoulders, his hands gripping the spokes and holding the schooner to the course of his will, himself an earth-god, dominating the storm, flinging its descending waters from him and riding it to his own ends. And oh, the marvel of it! the marvel of it! That tiny men should live and breathe and work, and drive so frail a contrivance of wood and cloth through so tremendous an elemental strife!

As before, the *Ghost* swung out of the trough, lifting her deck again out of the sea, and dashed before the howling blast. It was now half-past five, and half an hour later, when the last of the day lost itself in a dim and furious twilight, I sighted a third boat. It was bottom up, and there was no sign of its crew. Wolf Larsen repeated his manoeuvre, holding off and then rounding up to windward and drifting down upon it. But this time he missed by forty feet, the boat passing astern.

"Number four boat!" Oofty-Oofty cried, his keen eyes reading its number in the one second when it lifted clear of the foam and upside down.

It was Henderson's boat, and with him had been lost Holyoak and Williams, another of the deep-water crowd. Lost they indubitably were; but the boat remained, and Wolf Larsen made one more reckless effort to recover it. I had come down to the deck, and I saw Horner and Kerfoot vainly protest against the attempt.

"By God, I'll not be robbed of my boat by any storm that ever blew out of hell!" he shouted, and though we four stood with our heads together that we might hear, his voice seemed faint and far, as though removed from us an immense distance.

"Mr. Van Weyden!" he cried, and I heard through the tumult as one might hear a whisper. "Stand by that jib with Johnson and Oofty! The rest of you tail aft to the main sheet! Lively now! Or I'll sail you all into Kingdom Come! Understand?"

And when he put the wheel hard over and the *Ghost*'s bow swung off, there was nothing for the hunters to do but obey and make the best of a risky chance. How great the risk I realized when I was once more buried beneath the pounding seas and clinging for life to the pin-rail at the foot of the foremast. My fingers were torn loose, and I swept across to the side and over the side into the sea. I could not swim, but before I could sink I was swept back again. A strong hand gripped me, and when the *Ghost* finally emerged, I found that I owed my life to Johnson. I saw him looking anxiously about him, and noted that Kelly, who had come forward at the last moment, was missing.

This time, having missed the boat and not being in the same position as in the previous instances, Wolf Larsen

was compelled to resort to a different manoeuvre. Running
off before the wind with everything to starboard, he came
about and returned close-hauled on the port tack.

"Grand!" Johnson shouted in my ear, as we successfully came through the attendant deluge, and I knew he
referred, not to Wolf Larsen's seamanship, but to the performance of the *Ghost* herself.

It was now so dark that there was no sign of the boat;
but Wolf Larsen held back through the frightful turmoil as
if guided by unerring instinct. This time, though we were
continually half-buried, there was no trough in which to be
swept, and we drifted squarely down upon the up-turned
boat, badly smashing it as it was heaved inboard.

Two hours of terrible work followed, in which all hands
of us,—two hunters, three sailors, Wolf Larsen, and I,—
reefed, first one and then the other, the jib and mainsail.
Hove to under this short canvas, our decks were comparatively free of water, while the *Ghost* bobbed and ducked
amongst the combers like a cork.

I had burst open the ends of my fingers at the very first,
and during the reefing I had worked with tears of pain
running down my cheeks. And when all was done, I gave
up like a woman and rolled upon the deck in the agony of
exhaustion.

In the meantime Thomas Mugridge, like a drowned rat,
was being dragged out from under the forecastle head
where he had cravenly ensconced himself. I saw him pulled
aft to the cabin and noted with a shock of surprise that
the galley had disappeared. A clean space of deck showed
where it had stood.

In the cabin I found all hands assembled, sailors as well,
and while coffee was being cooked over the small stove
we drank whiskey and crunched hardtack. Never in my
life had food been so welcome. And never had hot coffee
tasted so good. So violently did the *Ghost* pitch and toss
and tumble that it was impossible for even the sailors to

move about without holding on, and several times, after a cry of "Now she takes it!" we were heaped upon the wall of the port cabins as though it had been the deck.

"To hell with a lookout," I heard Wolf Larsen say when we had eaten and drunk our fill. "There's nothing can be done on deck. If anything's going to run us down we couldn't get out of its way. Turn in, all hands, and get some sleep."

The sailors slipped forward, setting the side-lights as they went, while the two hunters remained to sleep in the cabin, it not being deemed advisable to open the slide to the steerage companionway. Wolf Larsen and I, between us, cut off Kerfoot's crushed finger and sewed up the stump. Mugridge, who, during all the time he had been compelled to cook and serve coffee and keep the fire going, had complained of internal pains, now swore that he had a broken rib or two. On examination we found that he had three. But his case was deferred to next day, principally for the reason that I did not know anything about broken ribs and would first have to read it up.

"I don't think it was worth it," I said to Wolf Larsen, "a broken boat for Kelly's life."

"But Kelly didn't amount to much," was the reply. "Good night."

After all that had passed, suffering intolerable anguish in my finger ends, and with three boats missing, to say nothing of the wild capers the *Ghost* was cutting, I should have thought it impossible to sleep. But my eyes must have closed the instant my head touched the pillow, and in utter exhaustion I slept throughout the night, the while the *Ghost*, lonely and undirected, fought her way through the storm.

CHAPTER EIGHTEEN

THE next day, while the storm was blowing itself out, Wolf Larsen and I crammed anatomy and surgery and set Mugridge's ribs. Then, when the storm broke, Wolf Larsen cruised back and forth over that portion of the ocean where we had encountered it, and somewhat more to the westward, while the boats were being repaired and new sails made and bent. Sealing schooner after sealing schooner we sighted and boarded, most of which were in search of lost boats, and most of which were carrying boats and crews they had picked up and which did not belong to them. For the thick of the fleet had been to the westward of us, and the boats, scattered far and wide, had headed in mad flight for the nearest refuge.

Two of our boats, with men all safe, we took off the *Cisco*, and, to Wolf Larsen's huge delight and my own grief, he culled Smoke, with Nilson and Leach, from the *San Diego*. So that, at the end of five days, we found ourselves short but four men,—Henderson, Holyoak, Williams, and Kelly,—and were once more hunting on the flanks of the herd.

As we followed it north we began to encounter the dreaded sea-fogs. Day after day the boats lowered and were swallowed up almost ere they touched the water, while we on board pumped the horn at regular intervals and every fifteen minutes fired the bomb gun. Boats were continually being lost and found, it being the custom for a boat to hunt, on lay, with whatever schooner picked it up, until such time it was recovered by its own schooner. But Wolf Larsen, as was to be expected, being a boat short, took possession of the first stray one and compelled its men to hunt with the *Ghost*, not permitting them to return to

their own schooner when we sighted it. I remember how
he forced the hunter and his two men below, a rifle at their
breasts, when their captain passed by at biscuit-toss* and
hailed us for information.

Thomas Mugridge, so strangely and pertinaciously clinging to life, was soon limping about again and perform-
ing his double duties of cook and cabin-boy. Johnson and
Leach were bullied and beaten as much as ever, and they
looked for their lives to end with the end of the hunting
season; while the rest of the crew lived the lives of dogs and
were worked like dogs by their pitiless master. As for Wolf
Larsen and myself, we got along fairly well; though I could
not quite rid myself of the idea that right conduct, for me,
lay in killing him. He fascinated me immeasurably, and I
feared him immeasurably. And yet, I could not imagine
him lying prone in death. There was an endurance, as of
perpetual youth, about him, which rose up and forbade the
picture. I could see him only as living always, and dominating always, fighting and destroying, himself surviving.

One diversion of his, when we were in the midst of the
herd and the sea was too rough to lower the boats, was
to lower with two boat pullers and a steerer and go out
himself. He was a good shot, too, and brought many a
skin aboard under what the hunters termed impossible
hunting conditions. It seemed the breath of his nostrils,
this carrying his life in his hands and struggling for it
against tremendous odds.

I was learning more and more seamanship; and one clear
day,—a thing we rarely encountered now,—I had the satisfaction of running and handling the *Ghost* and picking up
the boats myself. Wolf Larsen had been smitten with one
of his headaches, and I stood at the wheel from morning
until evening, sailing across the ocean after the last lee
boat and heaving to and picking it and the other five up
without command or suggestion from him.

Gales we encountered now and again, for it was a raw

and stormy region, and, in the middle of June, a typhoon most memorable to me and most important because of the changes wrought through it upon my future. We must have been caught nearly at the centre of this circular storm, and Wolf Larsen ran out of it and to the southward, first under a double-reefed jib, and finally under bare poles. Never had I imagined so great a sea. The seas previously encountered were as ripples compared with these, which ran a half mile from crest to crest and which upreared, I am confident, above our masthead. So great was it that Wolf Larsen himself did not dare heave to, though he was being driven far to the southward and out of the seal herd.

We must have been well in the path of the trans-Pacific steamships* when the typhoon moderated, and here, to the surprise of the hunters, we found ourselves in the midst of seals—a second herd, or sort of rear-guard, they declared, and a most unusual thing. But it was "Boats over!", the boom-boom of guns, and the pitiful slaughter through the long day.

It was at this time that I was approached by Leach. I had just finished tallying the skins of the last boat aboard, when he came to my side, in the darkness, and said in a low tone:

"Can you tell me, Mr. Van Weyden, how far we are off the coast, and what the bearings of Yokohama are?"

My heart leaped with gladness, for I knew what he had in mind, and I gave him the bearings—west-northwest and five hundred miles away.

"Thank you, sir," was all he said as he slipped back into the darkness.

Next morning No. 3 boat and Johnson and Leach were missing. The water-breakers and grub-boxes from all the other boats were likewise missing, as were the beds and sea bags of the two men. Wolf Larsen was furious. He set sail and bore away into the west-northwest, two hunters constantly at the mastheads and sweeping the sea with

glasses, himself pacing the deck like an angry lion. He knew
too well my sympathy for the runaways to send me aloft
as lookout.

The wind was fair but fitful, and it was like looking for
a needle in a haystack to raise that tiny boat out of the
blue immensity. But he put the *Ghost* through her best
paces so as to get between the deserters and the land.
This accomplished, he cruised back and forth across what
he knew must be their course.

On the morning of the third day, shortly after eight bells,
a cry that the boat was sighted came down from Smoke
at the masthead. All hands lined the rail. A snappy breeze
was blowing from the west with the promise of more wind
behind it; and there, to leeward, in the troubled silver of
the rising sun, appeared and disappeared a black speck.

We squared away and ran for it. My heart was as lead.
I felt myself turning sick in anticipation; and as I looked
at the gleam of triumph in Wolf Larsen's eyes, his form
swam before me and I felt almost irresistibly impelled to
fling myself upon him. So unnerved was I by the thought of
impending violence to Leach and Johnson that my reason
must have left me. I know that I slipped down into the
steerage in a daze, and that I was just beginning the ascent
to the deck, a loaded shot-gun in my hands, when I heard
the startled cry:

"There's five men in that boat!"

I supported myself in the companionway, weak and
trembling, while the observation was being verified by the
remarks of the rest of the men. Then my knees gave from
under me and I sank down, myself again, but overcome by
shock at knowledge of what I had so nearly done. Also, I
was very thankful as I put the gun away and slipped back
on deck.

No one had remarked my absence. The boat was near
enough for us to make out that it was larger than any
sealing boat and built on different lines. As we drew closer,

the sail was taken in and the mast unstepped. Oars were shipped, and its occupants waited for us to heave to and take them aboard.

Smoke, who had descended to the deck and was now standing by my side, began to chuckle in a significant way. I looked at him inquiringly.

"Talk of a mess!" he giggled.

"What's wrong!" I demanded.

Again he chuckled.

"Don't you see there, in the stern-sheets, on the bottom. May I never shoot a seal again if that ain't a woman!"

I looked closely, but was not sure until exclamations broke out on all sides. The boat contained four men, and its fifth occupant was certainly a woman. We were agog with excitement, all except Wolf Larsen, who was too evidently disappointed in that it was not his own boat with the two victims of his malice.

We ran down the flying jib, hauled the jib-sheets to windward and the main sheet flat, and came up into the wind. The oars struck the water, and with a few strokes the boat was alongside. I now caught my first fair glimpse of the woman. She was wrapped in a long ulster,* for the morning was raw; and I could see nothing but her face and a mass of light brown hair escaping from under the seaman's cap on her head. The eyes were large and brown and lustrous, the mouth sweet and sensitive, and the face itself a delicate oval, though sun and exposure to briny wind had burnt the face scarlet.

She seemed to me like a being from another world. I was aware of a hungry outreaching for her, as of a starving man for bread. But then, I had not seen a woman for a very long time. I know that I was lost in a great wonder, almost a stupor,—this, then, was a woman?—so that I forgot myself and my mate's duties, and took no part in helping the newcomers aboard. For when one of the sailors lifted her into Wolf Larsen's down-stretched arms, she looked up into our curious faces and smiled amusedly and sweetly, as only a woman can smile, and as I had seen no one smile for so long that I had forgotten such smiles existed.

"Mr. Van Weyden!"

Wolf Larsen's voice brought me sharply back to myself.

"Will you take the lady below and see to her comfort? Make up that spare port cabin. Put Cooky to work on it. And see what you can do for that face. It's burned badly."

He turned brusquely away from us and began to question the new men. The boat was cast adrift, though one of them called it a "bloody shame" with Yokohama so near.

I found myself strangely afraid of this woman I was escorting aft. Also I was awkward. It seemed to me that I was realizing for the first time what a delicate, fragile creature a woman is; and as I caught her arm to help her down the companion stair, I was startled by its smallness and softness. Indeed, she was a slender, delicate woman as women go, but to me she was so ethereally slender and delicate that I was quite prepared for her arm to crumble in my grasp. All this, in frankness, to show my first impression, after long denial, of women in general and of Maud Brewster in particular.

"No need to go to any great trouble for me," she protested, when I had seated her in Wolf Larsen's arm-chair, which I had dragged hastily from his cabin. "The men were looking for land at any moment this morning, and the vessel should be in by night; don't you think so?"

Her simple faith in the immediate future took me aback. How could I explain to her the situation, the strange man who stalked the sea like Destiny, all that it had taken me months to learn? But I answered honestly:

"If it were any other captain except ours, I should say you would be ashore in Yokohama to-morrow. But our captain is a strange man, and I beg of you to be prepared for anything, understand?—for anything."

"I—I confess I hardly do understand," she hesitated, a perturbed but not frightened expression in her eyes. "Or is it a misconception of mine that shipwrecked people are always shown every consideration? This is such a little thing, you know. We are so close to land."

"Candidly, I do not know," I strove to reassure her. "I wished merely to prepare you for the worst, if the worst is to come. This man, this captain, is a brute, a demon, and one can never tell what will be his next fantastic act."

I was growing excited, but she interrupted me with an "Oh, I see," and her voice sounded weary. To think was patently an effort. She was clearly on the verge of physical collapse.

She asked no further questions, and I vouchsafed no remarks, devoting myself to Wolf Larsen's command, which was to make her comfortable. I bustled about in quite housewifely fashion, procuring soothing lotions for her sunburn, raiding Wolf Larsen's private stores for a bottle of port I knew to be there, and directing Thomas Mugridge in the preparation of the spare state-room.

The wind was freshening rapidly, the *Ghost* heeling over more and more, and by the time the state-room was ready she was dashing through the water at a lively clip. I had quite forgotten the existence of Leach and Johnson, when suddenly, like a thunderclap, "Boat ho!" came down the open companionway. It was Smoke's unmistakable voice, crying from the masthead. I shot a glance at the woman, but she was leaning back in the arm-chair, her eyes closed, unutterably tired. I doubted that she had heard, and I resolved to prevent her seeing the brutality I knew would follow the capture of the deserters. She was tired. Very good. She should sleep.

There were swift commands on deck, a stamping of feet and a slapping of reef-points as the *Ghost* shot into the wind and about on the other tack. As she filled away and heeled, the arm-chair began to slide across the cabin floor, and I sprang for it just in time to prevent the rescued woman from being spilled out.

Her eyes were too heavy to suggest more than a hint of the sleepy surprise that perplexed her as she looked up at me, and she half stumbled, half tottered, as I led her to her cabin. Mugridge grinned insinuatingly in my face as I shoved him out and ordered him back to his galley work; and he won his revenge by spreading glowing reports among the hunters as to what an excellent "lydy's myde" I was proving myself to be.

She leaned heavily against me, and I do believe that she had fallen asleep again between the arm-chair and the state-room. This I discovered when she nearly fell into the bunk during a sudden lurch of the schooner. She aroused, smiled drowsily, and was off to sleep again; and asleep I left her, under a heavy pair of sailor's blankets, her head resting on a pillow I had appropriated from Wolf Larsen's bunk.

CHAPTER NINETEEN

I CAME on deck to find the *Ghost* heading up close on the port tack and cutting in to windward of a familiar spritsail close-hauled on the same tack ahead of us. All hands were on deck, for they knew that something was to happen when Leach and Johnson were dragged aboard.

It was four bells. Louis came aft to relieve the wheel. There was a dampness in the air, and I noticed he had on his oilskins.

"What are we going to have?" I asked him.

"A healthy young slip of a gale from the breath iv it, sir," he answered, "with a splatter iv rain just to wet our gills an' no more."

"Too bad we sighted them," I said, as the *Ghost's* bow was flung off a point by a large sea and the boat leaped for a moment past the jibs and into our line of vision.

Louis gave a spoke and temporized. "They'd never iv made the land, sir, I'm thinkin'."

"Think not?" I queried.

"No, sir. Did you feel that?" (A puff had caught the schooner, and he was forced to put the wheel up rapidly to keep her out of the wind.) "'Tis no egg-shell'll float on this sea an hour come, an' it's a stroke iv luck for them we're here to pick 'em up."

Wolf Larsen strode aft from amidships, where he had been talking with the rescued men. The catlike springiness in his tread was a little more pronounced than usual, and his eyes were bright and snappy.

"Three oilers and a fourth engineer," was his greeting. "But we'll make sailors out of them, or boat-pullers at any rate. Now, what of the lady?"

I know not why, but I was aware of a twinge or pang,

like the cut of a knife, when he mentioned her. I thought it a certain silly fastidiousness on my part, but it persisted in spite of me, and I merely shrugged my shoulders in answer.

Wolf Larsen pursed his lips in a long, quizzical whistle.

"What's her name, then?" he demanded.

"I don't know," I replied. "She is asleep. She was very tired. In fact, I am waiting to hear the news from you. What vessel was it?"

"Mail steamer," he answered shortly. "The *City of Tokio*, from 'Frisco, bound for Yokohama. Disabled in that typhoon. Old tub. Opened up top and bottom like a sieve. They were adrift four days. And you don't know who or what she is, eh?—maid, wife, or widow? Well, well."

He shook his head in a bantering way, and regarded me with laughing eyes.

"Are you—" I began. It was on the verge of my tongue to ask if he were going to take the castaways in to Yokohama.

"Am I what?" he asked.

"What do you intend doing with Leach and Johnson?"

He shook his head. "Really, Hump, I don't know. You see, with these additions I've about all the crew I want."

"And they've about all the escaping they want," I said. "Why not give them a change of treatment? Take them aboard, and deal gently with them. Whatever they have done they have been hounded into doing."

"By me?"

"By you," I answered steadily. "And I give you warning, Wolf Larsen, that I may forget love of my own life in the desire to kill you if you go too far in maltreating those poor wretches."

"Bravo!" he cried. "You do me proud, Hump! You've found your legs with a vengeance. You're quite an individual. You were unfortunate in having your life cast in easy places, but you're developing, and I like you the better for it."

His voice and expression changed. His face was serious.

"Do you believe in promises?" he asked. "Are they sacred things?"

"Of course," I answered.

"Then here's a compact," he went on, consummate actor that he was. "If I promise not to lay my hands upon Leach and Johnson, will you promise, in turn, not to attempt to kill me?

"Oh, not that I'm afraid of you, not that I'm afraid of you," he hastened to add.

I could hardly believe my ears. What was coming over the man?

"Is it a go?" he asked impatiently.

"A go," I answered.

His hand went out to mine, and as I shook it heartily I could have sworn I saw the mocking devil shine up for a moment in his eyes.

We strolled across the poop to the lee side. The boat was close at hand now, and in desperate plight. Johnson was steering, Leach bailing. We overhauled them about two feet to their one. Wolf Larsen motioned Louis to keep off slightly, and we dashed abreast of the boat, not a score of feet to windward. The *Ghost* blanketed it. The spritsail flapped emptily and the boat righted to an even keel, causing the two men swiftly to change position. The boat lost headway, and, as we lifted on a huge surge, toppled and fell into the trough.

It was at this moment that Leach and Johnson looked up into the face of their shipmates, who lined the rail amidships. There was no greeting. They were as dead men in their comrades' eyes, and between them was the gulf that parts the living and the dead.

The next instant they were opposite the poop, where stood Wolf Larsen and I. We were falling in the trough, they were rising on the surge. Johnson looked at me, and I could see that his face was worn and haggard. I waved my hand to him, and he answered the greeting, but with a wave that was hopeless and despairing. It was as if he were saying farewell. I did not see into the eyes of Leach, for he was looking at Wolf Larsen, the old and implacable snarl of hatred strong as ever on his face.

Then they were gone astern. The spritsail filled with the wind, suddenly, careening the frail open craft till it seemed it would surely capsize. A whitecap foamed above it and broke across in a snow-white smother. Then the boat emerged, half swamped, Leach flinging the water out and Johnson clinging to the steering-oar, his face white and anxious.

Wolf Larsen barked a short laugh in my ear and strode away to the weather side of the poop. I expected him to give orders for the *Ghost* to heave to, but she kept on her course and he made no sign. Louis stood imperturbably at the wheel, but I noticed the grouped sailors forward turning troubled faces in our direction. Still the *Ghost* tore along, till the boat dwindled to a speck, when Wolf Larsen's voice rang out in command and he went about on the starboard tack.

Back we held, two miles and more to windward of the struggling cockle-shell, when the flying jib was run down and the schooner hove to. The sealing boats are not made for windward work. Their hope lies in keeping a weather position so that they may run before the wind for the schooner when it breezes up. But in all that wild waste there was no refuge for Leach and Johnson save on the *Ghost*, and they resolutely began the windward beat. It was slow work in the heavy sea that was running. At any moment they were liable to be overwhelmed by the hissing combers. Time and again and countless times we watched the boat luff into the big whitecaps, lose headway, and be flung back like a cork.

Johnson was a splendid seaman, and he knew as much about small boats as he did about ships. At the end of an hour and a half he was nearly alongside, standing past our

stern on the last leg out, aiming to fetch us on the next
leg back.

"So you've changed your mind?" I heard Wolf Larsen
mutter, half to himself, half to them as though they could
hear. "You want to come aboard, eh? Well, then, just keep
a-coming."

"Hard up with that helm!" he commanded Oofty-Oofty,
the Kanaka, who had in the meantime relieved Louis at
the wheel.

Command followed command. As the schooner paid off,
the fore and main sheets were slacked away for fair wind.
And before the wind we were, and leaping, when Johnson,
easing his sheet at imminent peril, cut across our wake
a hundred feet away. Again Wolf Larsen laughed, at the
same time beckoning them with his arm to follow. It was
evidently his intention to play with them,—a lesson, I
took it, in lieu of a beating, though a dangerous lesson,
for the frail craft stood in momentary danger of being
overwhelmed.

Johnson squared away promptly and ran after us. There
was nothing else for him to do. Death stalked everywhere,
and it was only a matter of time when some one of those
many huge seas would fall upon the boat, roll over it, and
pass on.

"'Tis the fear iv death at the hearts iv them," Louis
muttered in my ear, as I passed forward to see to taking
in the flying jib and staysail.

"Oh, he'll heave to in a little while and pick them up," I
answered cheerfully. "He's bent upon giving them a lesson,
that's all."

Louis looked at me shrewdly. "Think so?" he asked.

"Surely," I answered. "Don't you?"

"I think nothing but iv my own skin, these days," was his
answer. "An' 'tis with wonder I'm filled as to the workin'
out iv things. A pretty mess that 'Frisco whiskey got me
into, an' a prettier mess that woman's got you into aft

there. Ah, it's myself that knows ye for a blitherin' fool."

"What do you mean?" I demanded; for, having sped his shaft, he was turning away.

"What do I mean?" he cried. "And it's you that asks me! 'Tis not what I mean, but what the Wolf'll mean. The Wolf, I said, the Wolf!"

"If trouble comes, will you stand by?" I asked impulsively, for he had voiced my own fear.

"Stand by? 'Tis old fat Louis I stand by, an' trouble enough it'll be. We're at the beginnin' iv things, I'm tellin' ye, the bare beginnin' iv things."

"I had not thought you so great a coward," I sneered.

He favored me with a contemptuous stare. "If I raised never a hand for that poor fool,"—pointing astern to the tiny sail,—"d'ye think I'm hungerin' for a broken head for a woman I never laid me eyes upon before this day?"

I turned scornfully away and went aft.

"Better get in those topsails, Mr. Van Weyden," Wolf Larsen said, as I came on the poop.

I felt relief, at least as far as the two men were concerned. It was clear he did not wish to run too far away from them. I picked up hope at the thought and put the order swiftly into execution. I had scarcely opened my mouth to issue the necessary commands, when eager men were springing to halyards and downhauls, and others were racing aloft. This eagerness on their part was noted by Wolf Larsen with a grim smile.

Still we increased our lead, and when the boat had dropped astern several miles we hove to and waited. All eyes watched it coming, even Wolf Larsen's; but he was the only unperturbed man aboard. Louis, gazing fixedly, betrayed a trouble in his face he was not quite able to hide.

The boat drew closer and closer, hurling along through the seething green like a thing alive, lifting and sending and uptossing across the huge-backed breakers, or disappearing behind them only to rush into sight again and shoot sky-

ward. It seemed impossible that it could continue to live,
yet with each dizzying sweep it did achieve the impossible.
A rain-squall drove past, and out of the flying wet the boat
emerged, almost upon us.

"Hard up, there!" Wolf Larsen shouted, himself springing to the wheel and whirling it over.

Again the *Ghost* sprang away and raced before the wind,
and for two hours Johnson and Leach pursued us. We hove
to and ran away, hove to and ran away, and ever astern
the struggling patch of sail tossed skyward and fell into
the rushing valleys. It was a quarter of a mile away when
a thick squall of rain veiled it from view. It never emerged.
The wind blew the air clear again, but no patch of sail
broke the troubled surface. I thought I saw, for an instant,
the boat's bottom show black in a breaking crest. At the
best, that was all. For Johnson and Leach the travail of
existence had ceased.

The men remained grouped amidships. No one had gone
below, and no one was speaking. Nor were any looks being
exchanged. Each man seemed stunned—deeply contempla-
tive, as it were, and, not quite sure, trying to realize just
what had taken place. Wolf Larsen gave them little time
for thought. He at once put the *Ghost* upon her course—a
course which meant the seal herd and not Yokohama harbor. But the men were no longer eager as they pulled and
hauled, and I heard curses amongst them, which left their
lips smothered and as heavy and lifeless as were they. Not
so was it with the hunters. Smoke the irrepressible related
a story, and they descended into the steerage, bellowing
with laughter.

As I passed to leeward of the galley on my way aft, I
was approached by the engineer we had rescued. His face
was white, his lips were trembling.

"Good God! sir, what kind of a craft is this?" he cried.

"You have eyes, you have seen," I answered, almost
brutally, what of the pain and fear at my own heart.

"Your promise?" I said to Wolf Larsen.

"I was not thinking of taking them aboard when I made that promise," he answered. "And anyway, you'll agree I've not laid my hands upon them."

"Far from it, far from it," he laughed a moment later.

I made no reply. I was incapable of speaking, my mind was too confused. I must have time to think, I knew. This woman, sleeping even now in the spare cabin, was a responsibility which I must consider, and the only rational thought that flickered through my mind was that I must do nothing hastily if I were to be any help to her at all.

CHAPTER TWENTY

THE remainder of the day passed uneventfully. The young slip of a gale, having wetted our gills, proceeded to moderate. The fourth engineer and the three oilers, after a warm interview with Wolf Larsen, were furnished with outfits from the slop-chests, assigned places under the hunters in the various boats and watches on the vessel, and bundled forward into the forecastle. They went protestingly, but their voices were not loud. They were awed by what they had already seen of Wolf Larsen's character, while the tale of woe they speedily heard in the forecastle took the last bit of rebellion out of them.

Miss Brewster,—we had learned her name from the engineer,—slept on and on. At supper I requested the hunters to lower their voices, so she was not disturbed; and it was not till next morning that she made her appearance. It had been my intention to have her meals served apart, but Wolf Larsen put down his foot. Who was she that she should be too good for cabin table and cabin society? had been his demand.

But her coming to the table had something amusing in it. The hunters fell silent as clams. Jock Horner and Smoke alone were unabashed, stealing stealthy glances at her now and again, and even taking part in the conversation. The other four men glued their eyes on their plates and chewed steadily and with thoughtful precision, their ears moving and wobbling, in time with their jaws, like the ears of so many animals.

Wolf Larsen had little to say at first, doing no more than reply when he was addressed. Not that he was abashed. Far from it. This woman was a new type to him, a different breed from any he had ever known, and he was curious.

He studied her, his eyes rarely leaving her face unless to
follow the movements of her hands or shoulder. I studied
her myself, and though it was I who maintained the conversation, I know that I was a bit shy, not quite self-possessed.
His was the perfect poise, the supreme confidence in self,
which nothing could shake; and he was no more timid of
a woman than he was of storm and battle.

"And when shall we arrive at Yokohama?" she asked,
turning to him and looking him squarely in the eyes.

There it was, the question flat. The jaws stopped working, the ears ceased wobbling, and though eyes remained
glued on plates, each man listened greedily for the answer.

"In four months, possibly three if the season closes
early," Wolf Larsen said.

She caught her breath, and stammered, "I—I thought—
I was given to understand that Yokohama was only a day's
sail away. It—" Here she paused and looked about the
table at the circle of unsympathetic faces staring hard at
the plates. "It is not right," she concluded.

"That is a question you must settle with Mr. Van Weyden there," he replied, nodding to me with a mischievous
twinkle. "Mr. Van Weyden is what you may call an authority on such things as rights. Now I, who am only a sailor,
would look upon the situation somewhat differently. It may
possibly be your misfortune that you have to remain with
us, but it is certainly our good fortune."

He regarded her smilingly. Her eyes fell before his gaze,
but she lifted them again, and defiantly, to mine. I read the
unspoken question there: was it right? But I had decided
that the part I was to play must be a neutral one, so I did
not answer.

"What do you think?" she demanded.

"That it is unfortunate, especially if you have any en-
gagements falling due in the course of the next several
months. But, since you say that you were voyaging to
Japan for your health, I can assure you that it will improve

no better anywhere than aboard the *Ghost.*"

I saw her eyes flash with indignation, and this time it was I who dropped mine, while I felt my face flushing under her gaze. It was cowardly, but what else could I do?

"Mr. Van Weyden speaks with the voice of authority," Wolf Larsen laughed.

I nodded my head, and she, having recovered herself, waited expectantly.

"Not that he is much to speak of now," Wolf Larsen went on, "but he has improved wonderfully. You should have seen him when he came on board. A more scrawny, pitiful specimen of humanity one could hardly conceive. Isn't that so, Kerfoot?"

Kerfoot, thus directly addressed, was startled into dropping his knife on the floor, though he managed to grunt affirmation.

"Developed himself by peeling potatoes and washing dishes. Eh, Kerfoot?"

Again that worthy grunted.

"Look at him now. True, he is not what you would term muscular, but still he has muscles, which is more than he had when he came aboard. Also, he has legs to stand on. You would not think so to look at him, but he was quite unable to stand alone at first."

The hunters were snickering, but she looked at me with a sympathy in her eyes which more than compensated for Wolf Larsen's nastiness. In truth, it had been so long since I had received sympathy that I was softened, and I became then, and gladly, her willing slave. But I was angry with Wolf Larsen. He was challenging my manhood with his slurs, challenging the very legs he claimed to be instrumental in getting for me.

"I may have learned to stand on my own legs," I retorted. "But I have yet to stamp upon others with them."

He looked at me insolently. "Your education is only half completed then," he said dryly, and turned to her.

"We are very hospitable upon the *Ghost*. Mr. Van Weyden has discovered that. We do everything to make our guests feel at home, eh, Mr. Van Weyden?"

"Even to the peeling of potatoes and the washing of dishes," I answered, "to say nothing to wringing their necks out of very fellowship."

"I beg of you not to receive false impressions of us from Mr. Van Weyden," he interposed with mock anxiety. "You will observe, Miss Brewster, that he carries a dirk in his belt, a—ahem—a most unusual thing for a ship's officer to do. While really very estimable, Mr. Van Weyden is sometimes—how shall I say?—er—quarrelsome, and harsh measures are necessary. He is quite reasonable and fair in his calm moments, and as he is calm now he will not deny that only yesterday he threatened my life."

I was well-nigh choking, and my eyes were certainly fiery. He drew attention to me.

"Look at him now. He can scarcely control himself in your presence. He is not accustomed to the presence of ladies, anyway. I shall have to arm myself before I dare go on deck with him."

He shook his head sadly, murmuring, "Too bad, too bad," while the hunters burst into guffaws of laughter.

The deep-sea voices of these men, rumbling and bellowing in the confined space, produced a wild effect. The whole setting was wild, and for the first time, regarding this strange woman and realizing how incongruous she was in it, I was aware of how much a part of it I was myself. I knew these men and their mental processes, was one of them myself, living the seal-hunting life, eating the seal-hunting fare, thinking, largely, the seal-hunting thoughts. There was for me no strangeness to it, to the rough clothes, the coarse faces, the wild laughter, and the lurching cabin walls and swaying sea-lamps.

As I buttered a piece of bread my eyes chanced to rest upon my hand. The knuckles were skinned and inflamed clear across, the fingers swollen, the nails rimmed with black. I felt the mattress-like growth of beard on my neck, knew that the sleeve of my coat was ripped, that a button was missing from the throat of the blue shirt I wore. The dirk mentioned by Wolf Larsen rested in its sheath on my hip. It was very natural that it should be there,—how natural I had not imagined until now, when I looked upon it with her eyes and knew how strange it and all that went with it must appear to her.

But she divined the mockery in Wolf Larsen's words, and again favored me with a sympathetic glance. But there was a look of bewilderment also in her eyes. That it was mockery made the situation more puzzling to her.

"I may be taken off by some passing vessel, perhaps," she suggested.

"There will be no passing vessels, except other sealing schooners," Wolf Larsen made answer.

"I have no clothes, nothing," she objected. "You hardly realize, sir, that I am not a man, or that I am unaccustomed to the vagrant, careless life which you and your men seem to lead."

"The sooner you get accustomed to it, the better," he said.

"I'll furnish you with cloth, needles, and thread," he added. "I hope it will not be too dreadful a hardship for you to make yourself a dress or two."

She made a wry pucker with her mouth, as though to advertise her ignorance of dressmaking. That she was frightened and bewildered, and that she was bravely striving to hide it, was quite plain to me.

"I suppose you're like Mr. Van Weyden there, accustomed to having things done for you. Well, I think doing a few things for yourself will hardly dislocate any joints. By the way, what do you do for a living?"

She regarded him with amazement unconcealed.

"I mean no offence, believe me. People eat, therefore

they must procure the wherewithal. These men here shoot seals in order to live; for the same reason I sail this schooner; and Mr. Van Weyden, for the present at any rate, earns his salty grub by assisting me. Now what do you do?"

She shrugged her shoulders.

"Do you feed yourself? Or does some one else feed you?"

"I'm afraid some one else has fed me most of my life," she laughed, trying bravely to enter into the spirit of his quizzing, though I could see a terror dawning and growing in her eyes as she watched Wolf Larsen.

"And I suppose some one else makes your bed for you?"

"I *have* made beds," she replied.

"Very often?"

She shook her head with mock ruefulness.

"Do you know what they do to poor men in the States, who, like you, do not work for their living?"

"I am very ignorant," she pleaded. "What do they do to the poor men who are like me?"

"They send them to jail. The crime of not earning a living, in their case, is called vagrancy.* If I were Mr. Van Weyden, who harps eternally on questions of right and wrong, I'd ask by what right do you live when you do nothing to deserve living?"

"But as you are not Mr. Van Weyden, I don't have to answer, do I?"

She beamed upon him through her terror-filled eyes, and the pathos of it cut me to the heart. I must in some way break in and lead the conversation into other channels.

"Have you ever earned a dollar by your own labor?" he demanded, certain of her answer, a triumphant vindictiveness in his voice.

"Yes, I have," she answered slowly, and I could have laughed aloud at his crestfallen visage. "I remember my father giving me a dollar once, when I was a little girl, for remaining absolutely quiet for five minutes."

He smiled indulgently.

"But that was long ago," she continued. "And you would scarcely demand a little girl of nine to earn her own living."

"At present, however," she said, after another slight pause, "I earn about eighteen hundred dollars a year."

With one accord, all eyes left the plates and settled on her. A woman who earned eighteen hundred dollars a year was worth looking at. Wolf Larsen was undisguised in his admiration.

"Salary or piece-work?" he asked.

"Piece-work," she answered promptly.

"Eighteen hundred," he calculated. "That's a hundred and fifty dollars a month. Well, Miss Brewster, there is nothing small about the *Ghost*. Consider yourself on salary during the time you remain with us."

She made no acknowledgment. She was too unused as yet to the whims of the man to accept them with equanimity.

"I forgot to inquire," he went on suavely, "as to the nature of your occupation. What commodities do you turn out? What tools and materials do you require?"

"Paper and ink," she laughed. "And, oh! also a type-writer."

"You are Maud Brewster," I said slowly and with certainty, almost as though I were charging her with a crime.

Her eyes lifted curiously to mine. "How do you know?"

"Aren't you?" I demanded.

She acknowledged her identity with a nod. It was Wolf Larsen's turn to be puzzled. The name and its magic signified nothing to him. I was proud that it did mean something to me, and for the first time in a weary while I was convincingly conscious of a superiority over him.

"I remember writing a review of a thin little volume—" I had begun carelessly, when she interrupted me.

"You!" she cried. "You are—"

She was now staring at me in wide-eyed wonder.

I nodded my identity, in turn.

"Humphrey Van Weyden," she concluded; then added with a sigh of relief, and unaware that she had glanced that relief at Wolf Larsen, "I am so glad."

"I remember the review," she went on hastily, becoming aware of the awkwardness of her remark, "that too, too flattering review."

"Not at all," I denied valiantly. "You impeach my sober judgment and make my canons of little worth. Besides, all my brother critics were with me. Didn't Lang include your 'Kiss Endured' among the four supreme sonnets by women in the English language?"*

"But you called me the American Mrs. Meynell!"*

"Was it not true?" I demanded.

"No, not that," she answered. "I was hurt."

"We can measure the unknown only by the known," I replied, in my finest academic manner. "As a critic I was compelled to place you. You have now become a yard-stick yourself. Seven of your thin little volumes are on my shelves; and there are two thicker volumes, the essays, which, you will pardon my saying, and I know not which is flattered more, fully equal your verse. The time is not far distant when some unknown will arise in England and the critics will name her the English Maud Brewster."

"You are very kind, I am sure," she murmured; and the very conventionality of her tones and words, with the host of associations it aroused of the old life on the other side of the world, gave me a quick thrill—rich with remembrance but stinging sharp with homesickness.

"And you are Maud Brewster," I said solemnly, gazing across at her.

"And you are Humphrey Van Weyden," she said, gazing back at me with equal solemnity and awe. "How unusual! I don't understand. We surely are not to expect some wildly romantic sea-story from your sober pen?"

"No, I am not gathering material, I assure you," was my answer. "I have neither aptitude nor inclination for fiction."

"Tell me, why have you always buried yourself in California?" she next asked. "It has not been kind of you. We of the East have seen so very little of you—too little, indeed, of the Dean of American Letters, the Second."*

I bowed to, and disclaimed, the compliment. "I nearly met you, once, in Philadelphia, some Browning affair or other—you were to lecture, you know. My train was four hours late."

And then we quite forgot where we were, leaving Wolf Larsen stranded and silent in the midst of our flood of gossip. The hunters left the table and went on deck, and still we talked. Wolf Larsen alone remained. Suddenly I became aware of him, leaning back from the table and listening curiously to our alien speech of a world he did not know.

I broke short off in the middle of a sentence. The present, with all its perils and anxieties, rushed upon me with stunning force. It smote Miss Brewster likewise, a vague and nameless terror rushing into her eyes as she regarded Wolf Larsen.

He rose to his feet and laughed awkwardly. The sound of it was metallic.

"Oh, don't mind me," he said, with a self-depreciatory wave of his hand. "I don't count. Go on, go on, I pray you."

But the gates of speech were closed, and we, too, rose from the table and laughed awkwardly.

"No, I am not gathering material, I assure you," was
my answer. "I have neither aptitude nor inclination for
fiction."

"Tell me ... "

CHAPTER TWENTY-ONE

THE chagrin Wolf Larsen felt from being ignored by Maud
Brewster and me in the conversation at table had to express itself in some fashion, and it fell to Thomas Mugridge
to be the victim. He had not mended his ways nor his
shirt, though the latter he contended he had changed. The
garment itself did not bear out the assertion, nor did the
accumulations of grease on stove and pot and pan attest
a general cleanliness.

"I've given you warning, Cooky," Wolf Larsen said, "and
now you've got to take your medicine."

Mugridge's face turned white under its sooty veneer,
and when Wolf Larsen called for a rope and a couple of
men, the miserable Cockney fled wildly out of the galley
and dodged and ducked about the deck with the grinning
crew in pursuit. Few things could have been more to their
liking than to give him a tow over the side, for to the
forecastle he had sent messes and concoctions of the vilest
order. Conditions favored the undertaking. The *Ghost* was
slipping through the water at no more than three miles an
hour, and the sea was fairly calm. But Mugridge had little
stomach for a dip in it. Possibly he had seen men towed
before. Besides, the water was frightfully cold, and his was
anything but a rugged constitution.

As usual, the watches below and the hunters turned out
for what promised sport. Mugridge seemed to be in rabid
fear of the water, and he exhibited a nimbleness and speed
we did not dream he possessed. Cornered in the right-angle
of the poop and galley, he sprang like a cat to the top of
the cabin and ran aft. But his pursuers forestalling him, he
doubled back across the cabin, passed over the galley, and
gained the deck by means of the steerage-scuttle. Straight

forward he raced, the boat-puller Harrison at his heels and gaining on him. But Mugridge, leaping suddenly, caught the jib-boom-lift. It happened in an instant. Holding his weight by his arms, and in mid-air doubling his body at the hips, he let fly with both feet. The oncoming Harrison caught the kick squarely in the pit of the stomach, groaned involuntarily, and doubled up and sank backward to the deck.

Hand-clapping and roars of laughter from the hunters greeted the exploit, while Mugridge, eluding half of his pursuers at the foremast, ran aft and through the remainder like a runner on the football field. Straight aft he held, to the poop and along the poop to the stern. So great was his speed that as he curved past the corner of the cabin he slipped and fell. Nilson was standing at the wheel, and the Cockney's hurtling body struck his legs. Both went down together, but Mugridge alone arose. By some freak of pressures, his frail body had snapped the strong man's leg like a pipestem.

Parsons took the wheel, and the pursuit continued. Round and round the decks they went, Mugridge sick with fear, the sailors hallooing and shouting directions to one another, and the hunters bellowing encouragement and laughter. Mugridge went down on the fore-hatch under three men; but he emerged from the mass like an eel, bleeding at the mouth, the offending shirt ripped into tatters, and sprang for the mainrigging. Up he went, clear up, beyond the ratlines, to the very masthead.

Half a dozen sailors swarmed to the crosstrees after him, where they clustered and waited while two of their number, Oofty-Oofty and Black (who was Latimer's boat-steerer), continued up the thin steel stays, lifting their bodies higher and higher by means of their arms.

It was a perilous undertaking, for, at a height of over a hundred feet from the deck, holding on by their hands, they were not in the best of positions to protect themselves from

Mugridge's feet. And Mugridge kicked savagely, till the Kanaka, hanging on with one hand, seized the Cockney's foot with the other. Black duplicated the performance a moment later with the other foot. Then the three writhed together in a swaying tangle, struggling, sliding, and falling into the arms of their mates on the crosstrees.

The aerial battle was over, and Thomas Mugridge, whining and gibbering, his mouth flecked with bloody foam, was brought down to deck. Wolf Larsen rove a bowline in a piece of rope and slipped it under his shoulders. Then he was carried aft and flung into the sea. Forty,—fifty,—sixty feet of line ran out, when Wolf Larsen cried "Belay!" Oofty-Oofty took a turn on a bitt, the rope tautened, and the *Ghost*, lunging onward, jerked the cook to the surface.

It was a pitiful spectacle. Though he could not drown, and was nine-lived in addition, he was suffering all the agonies of half-drowning. The *Ghost* was going very slowly, and when her stern lifted on a wave and she slipped forward she pulled the wretch to the surface and gave him a moment in which to breathe; but between each lift the stern fell, and while the bow lazily climbed the next wave the line slacked and he sank beneath.

I had forgotten the existence of Maud Brewster, and I remembered her with a start as she stepped lightly beside me. It was her first time on deck since she come aboard. A dead silence greeted her appearance.

"What is the cause of the merriment?" she asked.

"Ask Captain Larsen," I answered composedly and coldly, though inwardly my blood was boiling at the thought that she should be witness to such brutality.

She took my advice and was turning to put it into execution, when her eyes lighted on Oofty-Oofty, immediately before her, his body instinct with alertness and grace as he held the turn of the rope.

"Are you fishing?" she asked him.

He made no reply. His eyes, fixed intently on the sea

astern, suddenly flashed.

"Shark ho, sir!" he cried.

"Heave in! Lively! All hands tail on!" Wolf Larsen shouted, springing himself to the rope in advance of the quickest.

Mugridge had heard the Kanaka's warning cry and was screaming madly. I could see a black fin cutting the water and making for him with greater swiftness than he was being pulled aboard. It was an even toss whether the shark or we would get him, and it was a matter of moments. When Mugridge was directly beneath us, the stern descended the slope of a passing wave, thus giving the advantage to the shark. The fin disappeared. The belly flashed white in a swift upward rush. Almost equally swift, but not quite, was Wolf Larsen. He threw his strength into one tremendous jerk. The Cockney's body left the water; so did part of the shark's. He drew up his legs, and the man-eater seemed no more than barely to touch one foot, sinking back into the water with a splash. But at the moment of contact Thomas Mugridge cried out. Then he came in like a fresh-caught fish on a line, clearing the rail generously and striking the deck in a heap, on hands and knees, and rolling over.

But a fountain of blood was gushing forth. The right foot was missing, amputated neatly at the ankle. I looked instantly to Maud Brewster. Her face was white, her eyes dilated with horror. She was gazing, not at Thomas Mugridge, but at Wolf Larsen. And he was aware of it, for he said, with one of his short laughs:

"Man-play, Miss Brewster. Somewhat rougher, I warrant, than what you have been used to, but still—man-play. The shark was not in the reckoning. It—"

But at this juncture, Mugridge, who had lifted his head and ascertained the extent of his loss, floundered over on the deck and buried his teeth in Wolf Larsen's leg. Wolf Larsen stooped, coolly, to the Cockney, and pressed with thumb and finger at the rear of the jaws and below the ears. The jaws opened with reluctance, and Wolf Larsen stepped free.

"As I was saying," he went on, as though nothing unwonted had happened, "the shark was not in the reckoning. It was—ahem—shall we say Providence?"

She gave no sign that she had heard, though the expression of her eyes changed to one of inexpressible loathing as she started to turn away. She no more than started, for she swayed and tottered, and reached her hand weakly out to mine. I caught her in time to save her from falling, and helped her to a seat on the cabin. I thought she must faint outright, but she controlled herself.

"Will you get a tourniquet, Mr. Van Weyden," Wolf Larsen called to me.

I hesitated. Her lips moved, and though they formed no words, she commanded me with her eyes, plainly as speech, to go to the help of the unfortunate man.

"Please," she managed to whisper, and I could but obey.

By now I had developed such skill at surgery that Wolf Larsen, with a few words of advice, left me to my task with a couple of sailors for assistants. For his task he elected a vengeance on the shark. A heavy swivel-hook, baited with fat salt-pork, was dropped overside; and by the time I had compressed the severed veins and arteries, the sailors were singing and heaving in the offending monster. I did not see it myself, but my assistants, first one and then the other, deserted me for a few moments to run amidships and look at what was going on. The shark, a sixteen-footer, was hoisted up against the main-rigging. Its jaws were pried apart to their greatest extension, and a stout stake, sharpened at both ends, was so inserted that when the pries were removed the spread jaws were fixed upon it. This accomplished, the hook was cut out. The shark dropped back into the sea, helpless, yet with its full strength, doomed to lingering starvation—a living death less meet for it than for the man who devised the punishment.

THE SEA-WOLF

dropped back since he was helpless; yet with his full strength, devoted to fluttering stagnation—a living death-like insurance for Leach, for the man who devised the pursuit itself.

CHAPTER TWENTY-TWO

I KNEW what it was as she came toward me. For ten minutes I had watched her talking earnestly with the engineer, and now, with a sign for silence, I drew her out of earshot of the helmsman. Her face was white and set; her large eyes, larger than usual what of the purpose in them, looked penetratingly into mine. I felt rather timid and apprehensive, for she had come to search Humphrey Van Weyden's soul, and Humphrey Van Weyden had nothing of which to be particularly proud since his advent on the *Ghost*.

We walked to the break of the poop, where she turned and faced me. I glanced around to see that no one was within hearing distance.

"What is it?" I asked gently; but the expression of determination on her face did not relax.

"I can readily understand," she began, "that this morning's affair was largely an accident; but I have been talking with Mr. Haskins. He tells me that the day we were rescued, even while I was in the cabin, two men were drowned, deliberately drowned—murdered."

There was a query in her voice, and she faced me accusingly, as though I were guilty of the deed, or at least a party to it.

"The information is quite correct," I answered. "The two men were murdered."

"And you permitted it!" she cried.

"I was unable to prevent it, is a better way of phrasing it," I replied, still gently.

"But you tried to prevent it?" There was an emphasis on the "tried," and a pleading little note in her voice.

"Oh, but you didn't," she hurried on, divining my

answer. "But why didn't you?"

I shrugged my shoulders. "You must remember, Miss Brewster, that you are a new inhabitant of this little world, and that you do not yet understand the laws which operate within it. You bring with you certain fine conceptions of humanity, manhood, conduct, and such things; but here you will find them misconceptions. I have found it so," I added, with an involuntary sigh.

She shook her head incredulously.

"What would you advise, then?" I asked. "That I should take a knife, or a gun, or an axe, and kill this man?"

She half started back.

"No, not that!"

"Then what should I do? Kill myself?"

"You speak in purely materialistic terms," she objected. "There is such a thing as moral courage, and moral courage is never without effect."

"Ah," I smiled, "you advise me to kill neither him nor myself, but to let him kill me." I held up my hand as she was about to speak. "For moral courage is a worthless asset on this little floating world. Leach, one of the men who were murdered, had moral courage to an unusual degree. So had the other man, Johnson. Not only did it not stand them in good stead, but it destroyed them. And so with me if I should exercise what little moral courage I may possess.

"You must understand, Miss Brewster, and understand clearly, that this man is a monster. He is without conscience. Nothing is sacred to him, nothing is too terrible for him to do. It was due to his whim that I was detained aboard in the first place. It is due to his whim that I am still alive. I do nothing, can do nothing, because I am a slave to this monster, as you are now a slave to him; because I desire to live, as you will desire to live; because I cannot fight and overcome him, just as you will not be able to fight and overcome him."

She waited for me to go on.

"What remains? Mine is the rôle of the weak. I remain silent and suffer ignominy, as you will remain silent and suffer ignominy. And it is well. It is the best we can do if we wish to live. The battle is not always to the strong. We have not the strength with which to fight this man; we must dissimulate, and win, if win we can, by craft. If you will be advised by me, this is what you will do. I know my position is perilous, and I may say frankly that yours is even more perilous. We must stand together, without appearing to do so, in secret alliance. I shall not be able to side with you openly, and, no matter what indignities may be put upon me, you are to remain likewise silent. We must provoke no scenes with this man, nor cross his will. And we must keep smiling faces and be friendly with him no matter how repulsive it may be."

She brushed her hand across her forehead in a puzzled way, saying, "Still I do not understand."

"You must do as I say," I interrupted authoritatively, for I saw Wolf Larsen's gaze wandering toward us from where he paced up and down with Latimer amidships. "Do as I say, and ere long you will find I am right."

"What shall I do, then?" she asked, detecting the anxious glance I had shot at the object of our conversation, and impressed, I flatter myself, with the earnestness of my manner.

"Dispense with all the moral courage you can," I said briskly. "Don't arouse this man's animosity. Be quite friendly with him, talk with him, discuss literature and art with him—he is fond of such things. You will find him an interested listener and no fool. And for your own sake try to avoid witnessing, as much as you can, the brutalities of the ship. It will make it easier for you to act your part."

"I am to lie," she said in steady, rebellious tones, "by speech and action to lie."

Wolf Larsen had separated from Latimer and was coming toward us. I was desperate.

"Please, please understand me," I said hurriedly, lowering my voice. "All your experience of men and things is worthless here. You must begin over again. I know,—I can see it,—you have, among other ways, been used to managing people with your eyes, letting your moral courage speak out through them, as it were. You have already managed me with your eyes, commanded me with them. But don't try it on Wolf Larsen. You could as easily control a lion, while he would make a mock of you. He would—I have always been proud of the fact that I discovered him," I said, turning the conversation as Wolf Larsen stepped on the poop and joined us. "The editors were afraid of him and the publishers would have none of him. But I knew, and his genius and my judgment were vindicated when he made that magnificent hit with his 'Forge'."*

"And it was a newspaper poem," she said glibly.

"It did happen to see the light in a newspaper," I replied, "but not because the magazine editors had been denied a glimpse at it."

"We were talking of Harris," I said to Wolf Larsen.

"Oh, yes," he acknowledged. "I remember the 'Forge.' Filled with pretty sentiments and an almighty faith in human illusions. By the way, Mr. Van Weyden, you'd better look in on Cooky. He's complaining and restless."

Thus was I bluntly dismissed from the poop, only to find Mugridge sleeping soundly from the morphine I had given him. I made no haste to return on deck, and when I did I was gratified to see Miss Brewster in animated conversation with Wolf Larsen. As I say, the sight gratified me. She was following my advice. And yet I was conscious of a slight shock or hurt in that she was able to do the thing I had begged her to do and which she had notably disliked.

CHAPTER TWENTY-THREE

BRAVE winds, blowing fair, swiftly drove the *Ghost* northward into the seal herd. We encountered it well up to the forty-fourth parallel,* in a raw and stormy sea across which the wind harried the fog-banks in eternal flight. For days at a time we could never see the sun nor take an observation; then the wind would sweep the face of the ocean clean, the waves would ripple and flash, and we would learn where we were. A day of clear weather might follow, or three days or four, and then the fog would settle down upon us, seemingly thicker than ever.

The hunting was perilous; yet the boats, lowered day after day, were swallowed up in the gray obscurity, and were seen no more till nightfall, and often not till long after, when they would creep in like sea-wraiths, one by one, out of the gray. Wainwright,—the hunter whom Wolf Larsen had stolen with boat and men,—took advantage of the veiled sea and escaped. He disappeared one morning in the encircling fog with his two men, and we never saw them again, though it was not many days when we learned that they had passed from schooner to schooner until they finally regained their own.

This was the thing I had set my mind upon doing, but the opportunity never offered. It was not in the mate's province to go out in the boats, and though I manoeuvred cunningly for it, Wolf Larsen never granted me the privilege. Had he done so, I should have managed somehow to carry Miss Brewster away with me. As it was, the situation was approaching a stage which I was afraid to consider. I involuntarily shunned the thought of it, and yet the thought continually arose in my mind like a haunting spectre.

I had read sea-romances in my time, wherein figured, as a matter of course, the lone woman in the midst of a shipload of men; but I learned, now, that I had never comprehended the deeper significance of such a situation—the thing the writers harped upon and exploited so thoroughly. And here it was, now, and I was face to face with it. That it should be as vital as possible, it required no more than that the woman should be Maud Brewster, who now charmed me in person as she had long charmed me through her work.

No one more out of environment could be imagined. She was a delicate, ethereal creature, swaying and willowy, light and graceful of movement. It never seemed to me that she walked, or, at least, walked after the ordinary manner of mortals. Hers was an extreme lithesomeness, and she moved with a certain indefinable airiness, approaching one as down might float or as a bird on noiseless wings.

She was like a bit of Dresden china, and I was continually impressed with what I may call her fragility. As at the time I caught her arm when helping her below, so at any time I was quite prepared, should stress or rough handling befall her, to see her crumble away. I have never seen body and spirit in such perfect accord. Describe her verse, as the critics have described it, as sublimated and spiritual, and you have described her body. It seemed to partake of her soul, to have analogous attributes, and to link it to life with the slenderest of chains. Indeed, she trod the earth lightly, and in her constitution there was little of the robust clay.

She was in striking contrast to Wolf Larsen. Each was nothing that the other was, everything that the other was not. I noted them walking the deck together one morning and I likened them to the extreme ends of the human ladder of evolution—the one the culmination of all savagery, the other the finished product of the finest civilization. True, Wolf Larsen possessed intellect to an unusual degree, but it was directed solely to the exercise of his savage instincts and made him but the more formidable a savage. He was splendidly muscled, a heavy man, and though he strode with the certitude and directness of the physical man, there was nothing heavy about his stride. The jungle and the wilderness lurked in the uplift and downput of his feet. He was cat-footed, and lithe, and strong, always strong. I likened him to some great tiger, a beast of prowess and prey. He looked it, and the piercing glitter that arose at times in his eyes was the same piercing glitter I had observed in the eyes of caged leopards and other preying creatures of the wild.

But this day, as I noted them pacing up and down, I saw that it was she who terminated the walk. They came up to where I was standing by the entrance to the companionway. Though she betrayed it by no outward sign, I felt, somehow, that she was greatly perturbed. She made some idle remark, looking at me, and laughed lightly enough; but I saw her eyes return to his, involuntarily, as though fascinated; then they fell, but not swiftly enough to veil the rush of terror that filled them.

It was in his eyes that I saw the cause of her perturbation. Ordinarily gray and cold and harsh, they were now warm and soft and golden, and all adance with tiny lights that dimmed and faded, or welled up till the full orbs were flooded with a glowing radiance. Perhaps it was to this that the golden color was due; but golden his eyes were, enticing and masterful, at the same time luring and compelling, and speaking a demand and clamor of the blood which no woman, much less Maud Brewster, could misunderstand.

Her own terror rushed upon me, and in that moment of fear,—the most terrible fear a man can experience,—I knew that in inexpressible ways she was dear to me. The knowledge that I loved her rushed upon me with the terror, and with both emotions gripping at my heart and causing my blood at the same time to chill and to leap riotously, I felt myself drawn by a power without me and beyond me, and found my eyes returning against my will to gaze into the eyes of Wolf Larsen. But he had recovered himself. The golden color and the dancing lights were gone. Cold and gray and glittering they were as he bowed brusquely and turned away.

"I am afraid," she whispered, with a shiver. "I am so afraid."

I, too, was afraid, and what of my discovery of how much she meant to me my mind was in a turmoil; but I succeeded in answering quite calmly:

"All will come right, Miss Brewster. Trust me, it will come right."

She answered with a grateful little smile that sent my heart pounding, and started to descend the companion-stairs.

For a long while I remained standing where she had left me. There was imperative need to adjust myself, to consider the significance of the changed aspect of things. It had come, at last, love had come, when I least expected it and under the most forbidding conditions. Of course, my philosophy had always recognized the inevitableness of the love-call sooner or later; but long years of bookish silence had made me inattentive and unprepared.

And now it had come! Maud Brewster! My memory flashed back to that first thin little volume on my desk, and I saw before me, as though in the concrete, the row of thin little volumes on my library shelf. How I had welcomed each of them! Each year one had come from the press, and to me each was the advent of the year. They had voiced a kindred intellect and spirit, and as such I had received them into a camaraderie of the mind; but now their place was in my heart.

My heart? A revulsion of feeling came over me. I seemed to stand outside myself and to look at myself incredulously. Maud Brewster! Humphrey Van Weyden, the "cold-blooded fish," the "emotionless monster," the "analytical

demon," of Charley Furuseth's christening, in love! And
then, without rhyme or reason, all sceptical, my mind
flew back to a small biographical note in the red-bound
"Who's Who," and I said to myself, "She was born in
Cambridge, and she is twenty-seven years old." And then
I said, "Twenty-seven years old and still free and fancy
free?" But how did I know she was fancy free? And the
pang of new-born jealousy put all incredulity to flight.
There was no doubt about it. I was jealous; therefore I
loved. And the woman I loved was Maud Brewster.

I, Humphrey Van Weyden, was in love! And again the
doubt assailed me. Not that I was afraid of it, however,
or reluctant to meet it. On the contrary, idealist that I
was to the most pronounced degree, my philosophy had
always recognized and guerdoned love as the greatest thing
in the world, the aim and the summit of being, the most
exquisite pitch of joy and happiness to which life could
thrill, the thing of all things to be hailed and welcomed
and taken into the heart. But now that it had come I
could not believe. I could not be so fortunate. It was too
good, too good to be true. Symons's lines came into my
head:

> "I wandered all these years among
> A world of women, seeking you."*

And then I had ceased seeking. It was not for me, this
greatest thing in the world, I had decided. Furuseth was
right; I was abnormal, an "emotionless monster," a strange
bookish creature, capable of pleasuring in sensations only
of the mind. And though I had been surrounded by women
all my days, my appreciation of them had been aesthetic
and nothing more. I had actually, at times, considered myself outside the pale, a monkish fellow denied the eternal or
the passing passions I saw and understood so well in others.
And now it had come! Undreamed of and unheralded, it

had come. In what could have been no less than an ecstasy, I left my post at the head of the companionway and stated along the deck, murmuring to myself those beautiful lines of Mrs. Browning:

> "I lived with visions for my company
> Instead of men and women years ago,
> And found them gentle mates, nor thought to know
> A sweeter music than they played to me."*

But the sweeter music was playing in my ears, and I was blind and oblivious to all about me. The sharp voice of Wolf Larsen aroused me.

"What the hell are you up to?" he was demanding.

I had strayed forward where the sailors were painting, and I came to myself to find my advancing foot on the verge of overturning a paint-pot.

"Sleep-walking, sunstroke,—what?" he barked.

"No; indigestion," I retorted, and continued my walk as if nothing untoward had occurred.

had come, in what could have been no less than an ecstasy
[I laid] my paw at the hand of the companionway, and stared
along the deck, murmuring to myself those beautiful lines
of Mrs. Br[...]

CHAPTER TWENTY-FOUR

AMONG the most vivid memories of my life are those
of the events on the *Ghost* which occurred during the
forty hours succeeding the discovery of my love for Maud
Brewster. I, who had lived my life in quiet places, only to
enter at the age of thirty-five upon a course of the most
irrational adventure I could have imagined, never had more
incident and excitement crammed into any forty hours of
my experience. Nor can I quite close my ears to a small
voice of pride which tells me I did not do so badly, all
things considered.

To begin with, at the midday dinner, Wolf Larsen informed the hunters that they were to eat thenceforth in
the steerage. It was an unprecedented thing on sealing
schooners, where it is the custom for the hunters to rank
unofficially as officers. He gave no reason, but his motive
was obvious enough. Horner and Smoke had been display-
ing a gallantry toward Maud Brewster, ludicrous in itself
and inoffensive to her, but to him evidently distasteful.

The announcement was received with black silence,
though the other four hunters glanced significantly at the
two who had been the cause of their banishment. Jock
Horner, quiet as was his way, gave no sign; but the blood
surged darkly across Smoke's forehead, and he half opened
his mouth to speak. Wolf Larsen was watching him, waiting for him, the steely glitter in his eyes; but Smoke closed
his mouth again without having said anything.

"Anything to say?" the other demanded aggressively.

It was a challenge, but Smoke refused to accept it.

"About what?" he asked, so innocently that Wolf Larsen
was disconcerted, while the others smiled.

"Oh, nothing," Wolf Larsen said lamely. "I just thought

you might want to register a kick."

"About what?" asked the imperturbable Smoke.

Smoke's mates were now smiling broadly. His captain could have killed him, and I doubt not that blood would have flowed had not Maud Brewster been present. For that matter, it was her presence which enabled Smoke to act as he did. He was too discreet and cautious a man to incur Wolf Larsen's anger at a time when that anger could be expressed in terms stronger than words. I was in fear that a struggle might take place, but a cry from the helmsman made it easy for the situation to save itself.

"Smoke ho!" the cry came down the open companion-way.

"How's it bear?" Wolf Larsen called up.

"Dead astern, sir."

"Maybe it's a Russian," suggested Latimer.

His words brought anxiety into the faces of the other hunters. A Russian could mean but one thing—a cruiser. The hunters, never more than roughly aware of the position of the ship, nevertheless knew that we were close to the boundaries of the forbidden sea,* while Wolf Larsen's record as a poacher was notorious. All eyes centred upon him.

"We're dead safe," he assured them with a laugh. "No salt mines this time, Smoke. But I'll tell you what—I'll lay odds of five to one it's the *Macedonia.*"

No one accepted his offer and he went on. "In which event, I'll lay ten to one there's trouble breezing up."

"No, thank you," Latimer spoke up. "I don't object to losing my money, but I like to get a run for it, anyway. There never was a time when there wasn't trouble when you and that brother of yours got together, and I'll lay twenty to one on that."

A general smile followed, in which Wolf Larsen joined, and the dinner went on smoothly, thanks to me, for he treated me abominably the rest of the meal, sneering at me and patronizing me till I was all a-tremble with suppressed rage. Yet I knew I must control myself for Maud Brewster's sake, and I received my reward when her eyes caught mine for a fleeting second, and they said, as distinctly as if she spoke, "Be brave, be brave."

We left the table to go on deck, for a steamer was a welcome break in the monotony of the sea on which we floated, while the conviction that it was Death Larsen and the *Macedonia* added to the excitement. The stiff breeze and heavy sea which had sprung up the previous afternoon had been moderating all morning, so that it was now possible to lower the boats for an afternoon's hunt. The hunting promised to be profitable. We had sailed since daylight across a sea barren of seals, and were now running into the herd.

The smoke was still miles astern, but overhauling us rapidly, when we lowered our boats. They spread out and struck a northerly course across the ocean. Now and again we saw a sail lower, heard the reports of the shotguns, and saw the sail go up again. The seals were thick, the wind was dying away; everything favored a big catch. As we ran off to get our leeward position of the last lee boat, we found the ocean fairly carpeted with sleeping seals. They were all about us, thicker than I had ever seen them before, in twos and threes and bunches, stretched full length on the surface and sleeping for all the world like so many lazy young dogs.

Under the approaching smoke the hull and upperworks of a steamer were growing larger. It was the *Macedonia*. I read her name through the glasses as she passed by scarcely a mile to starboard. Wolf Larsen looked savagely at the vessel, while Maud Brewster was curious.

"Where is the trouble you were so sure was breezing up, Captain Larsen?" she asked gayly.

He glanced at her, a moment's amusement softening his features.

"What did you expect? That they'd come aboard and cut our throats?"

"Something like that," she confessed. "You understand, seal-hunters are so new and strange to me that I am quite ready to expect anything."

He nodded his head. "Quite right, quite right. Your error is that you failed to expect the worst."

"Why, what can be worse than cutting our throats?" she asked, with pretty naive surprise.

"Cutting our purses," he answered. "Man is so made these days that his capacity for living is determined by the money he possesses."

" 'Who steals my purse steals trash',"* she quoted.

"Who steal my purse steals my right to live," was the reply, "old saws to the contrary. For he steals my bread and meat and bed, and in so doing imperils my life. There are not enough soup-kitchens and bread-lines* to go around, you know, and when men have nothing in their purses they usually die, and die miserably—unless they are able to fill their purses pretty speedily."

"But I fail to see that this steamer has any designs on your purse."

"Wait and you will see," he answered grimly.

We did not have long to wait. Having passed several miles beyond our line of boats, the *Macedonia* proceeded to lower her own. We knew she carried fourteen boats to our five, (we were one short through the desertion of Wainwright), and she began dropping them far to leeward of our last boat, continued dropping them athwart our course, and finished dropping them far to windward of our first weather boat. The hunting, for us, was spoiled. There were no seals behind us, and ahead of us the line of fourteen boats, like a huge broom, swept the herd before it.

Our boats hunted across the two or three miles of water between them and the point where the *Macedonia's* had been dropped, and then headed for home. The wind

had fallen to a whisper, the ocean was growing calmer
and calmer, and this, coupled with the presence of the
great herd, made a perfect hunting day—one of the two
or three days to be encountered in the whole of a lucky
season. An angry lot of men, boat-pullers and steerers
as well as hunters, swarmed over our side. Each man felt
that he had been robbed; and the boats were hoisted in
amid curses, which, if curses had power, would have settled
Death Larsen for all eternity—"Dead and damned for a
dozen iv eternities," commented Louis, his eyes twinkling
up at me as he rested from hauling taut the lashings of his
boat.

"Listen to them, and find if it is hard to discover the
most vital thing in their souls," said Wolf Larsen. "Faith?
and love? and high ideals? the good? the beautiful? the
true?"

"Their innate sense of right has been violated," Maud
Brewster said, joining the conversation.

She was standing a dozen feet away, one hand resting
on the main shrouds and her body swaying gently to the
slight roll of the ship. She had not raised her voice, and yet
I was struck by its clear and bell-like tone. Ah, it was sweet
in my ears! I scarcely dared look at her just then, for the
fear of betraying myself. A boy's cap was perched on her
head, and her hair, light brown and arranged in a loose and
fluffy order that caught the sun, seemed an aureole about
the delicate oval of her face. She was positively bewitching,
and, withal, sweetly spirituelle, if not saintly. All my old-
time marvel at life returned to me at sight of this splendid
incarnation of it, and Wolf Larsen's cold explanation of life
and its meaning was truly ridiculous and laughable.

"A sentimentalist," he sneered, "like Mr. Van Weyden.
Those men are cursing because their desires have been
outraged. That is all. What desires? The desires for the
good grub and soft beds ashore which a handsome pay-
day brings them—the women and the drink, the gorging

and the beastliness which so truly expresses them, the best that is in them, their highest aspirations, their ideals, if you please. The exhibition they make of their feelings is not a touching sight, yet it shows how deeply they have been touched, how deeply their purses have been touched; for to lay hands on their purses is to lay hands on their souls."

"You hardly behave as if your purse had been touched," she said, smilingly.

"Then it so happens that I am behaving differently, for my purse and my soul have both been touched. At the current price of skins in the London market, and based on a fair estimate of what the afternoon's catch would have been had not the *Macedonia* hogged it, the *Ghost* has lost about fifteen hundred dollars' worth of skins."

"You speak so calmly—" she began.

"But I do not feel calm; I could kill the man who robbed me," he interrupted. "Yes, yes, I know, and that man my brother—more sentiment! Bah!"

His face underwent a sudden change. His voice was less harsh and wholly sincere as he said:

"You must be happy, you sentimentalists, really and truly happy at dreaming and finding things good, and, because you find some of them good, feeling good yourself. Now, tell me, you two, do you find me good?"

"You are good to look upon—in a way," I qualified.

"There are in you all powers for good," was Maud Brewster's answer.

"There you are!" he cried at her, half angrily. "Your words are empty to me. There is nothing clear and sharp and definite about the thought you have expressed. You cannot pick it up in your two hands and look at it. In point of fact, it is not a thought. It is a feeling, a sentiment, a something based upon illusion and not a product of the intellect at all."

As he went on his voice again grew soft, and a confiding

note came into it. "Do you know, I sometimes catch myself wishing that I, too, were blind to the facts of life and only knew its fancies and illusions. They're wrong, all wrong, of course, and contrary to reason; but in the face of them my reason tells me, wrong and most wrong, that to dream and live illusions gives greater delight. And after all, delight is the wage for living. Without delight, living is a worthless act. To labor at living and be unpaid is worse than to be dead. He who delights the most lives the most,* and your dreams and unrealities are less disturbing to you and more gratifying than are my facts to me."

He shook his head slowly, pondering.

"I often doubt, I often doubt, the worthwhileness of reason. Dreams must be more substantial and satisfying. Emotional delight is more filling and lasting than intellectual delight; and, besides, you pay for your moments of intellectual delight by having the blues. Emotional delight is followed by no more than jaded senses which speedily recuperate. I envy you, I envy you."

He stopped abruptly, and then on his lips formed one of his strange quizzical smiles, as he added:

"It's from my brain I envy you, take notice, and not from my heart. My reason dictates it. The envy is an intellectual product. I am like a sober man looking upon drunken men, and, greatly weary, wishing he, too, were drunk."

"Or like a wise man looking upon fools and wishing he, too, were a fool," I laughed.

"Quite so," he said. "You are a blessed, bankrupt pair of fools. You have no facts in your pocketbook."

"Yet we spend as freely as you," was Maud Brewster's contribution.

"More freely, because it costs you nothing."

"And because we draw upon eternity," she retorted.

"Whether you do or think you do, it's the same thing. You spend what you haven't got, and in return you get greater value from spending what you haven't got than

I get from spending what I have got, and what I have sweated to get."

"Why don't you change the basis of your coinage, then?" she queried teasingly.

He looked at her quickly, half-hopefully, and then said, all regretfully: "Too late. I'd like to, perhaps, but I can't. My pocketbook is stuffed with the old coinage, and it's a stubborn thing. I can never bring myself to recognize anything else as valid."

He ceased speaking, and his gaze wandered absently past her and became lost in the placid sea. The old primal melancholy was strong upon him. He was quivering to it. He had reasoned himself into a spell of the blues, and within few hours one could look for the devil within him to be up and stirring. I remembered Charley Furuseth, and knew this man's sadness as the penalty which the materialist ever pays for his materialism.

CHAPTER TWENTY-FIVE

YOU'VE been on deck, Mr. Van Weyden," Wolf Larsen said, the following morning at the breakfast table. "How do things look?"

"Clear enough," I answered, glancing at the sunshine which streamed down the open companionway. "Fair westerly breeze, with a promise of stiffening, if Louis predicts correctly."

He nodded his head in a pleased way. "Any signs of fog?"

"Thick banks in the north and northwest."

He nodded his head again, evincing even greater satisfaction than before.

"What of the *Macedonia*?"

"Not sighted," I answered.

I could have sworn his face fell at the intelligence, but why he should be disappointed I could not conceive.

I was soon to learn. "Smoke ho!" came the hail from on deck, and his face brightened.

"Good!" he exclaimed, and left the table at once to go on deck and into the steerage, where the hunters were taking the first breakfast of their exile.

Maud Brewster and I scarcely touched the food before us, gazing, instead, in silent anxiety at each other, and listening to Wolf Larsen's voice, which easily penetrated the cabin through the intervening bulkhead. He spoke at length, and his conclusion was greeted with a wild roar of cheers. The bulkhead was too thick for us to hear what he said; but whatever it was it affected the hunters strongly, for the cheering was followed by loud exclamations and shouts of joy.

From the sounds on deck I knew that the sailors had been routed out and were preparing to lower the boats.

Maud Brewster accompanied me on deck, but I left her at the break of the poop, where she might watch the scene and not be in it. The sailors must have learned whatever project was on hand, and the vim and snap they put into their work attested their enthusiasm. The hunters came trooping on deck with shotguns and ammunition-boxes and, most unusual, their rifles. The latter were rarely taken in the boats, for a seal, shot at long range with a rifle, invariably sank before a boat could reach it. But each hunter this day had his rifle and a large supply of cartridges. I noticed they grinned with satisfaction whenever they looked at the *Macedonia's* smoke, which was rising higher and higher as she approached from the west.

The five boats went over the side with a rush, spread out like the ribs of a fan, and set a northerly course, as on the preceding afternoon, for us to follow. I watched for some time, curiously, but there seemed nothing extraordinary about their behavior. They lowered sails, shot seals, and hoisted sails again, and continued on their way as I had always seen them do. The *Macedonia* repeated her performance of yesterday, "hogging" the sea by dropping her line of boats in advance of ours and across our course. Fourteen boats require a considerable spread of ocean for comfortable hunting, and when she had completely lapped our line she continued steaming into the northeast, dropping more boats as she went.

"What's up?" I asked Wolf Larsen, unable longer to keep my curiosity in check.

"Never mind what's up," he answered gruffly. "You won't be a thousand years in finding out, and in the meantime just pray for plenty of wind."

"Oh, well, I don't mind telling you," he said the next moment. "I'm going to give that brother of mine a taste of his own medicine. In short, I'm going to play the hog myself, and not for one day, but for the rest of the season,— if we're in luck."

"And if we're not?" I queried.

"Not to be considered," he laughed. "We simply must be in luck, or it's all up with us."

He had the wheel at the time, and I went forward to my hospital in the forecastle, where lay the two crippled men, Nilson and Thomas Mugridge. Nilson was as cheerful as could be expected, for his broken leg was knitting nicely; but the Cockney was desperately melancholy, and I was aware of a great sympathy for the unfortunate creature. And the marvel of it was that still he lived and clung to life. The brutal years had reduced his meagre body to splintered wreckage, and yet the spark of life within burned brightly as ever.

"With an artificial foot,—and they make excellent ones,—you will be stumping ships' galleys to the end of time," I assured him jovially.

But his answer was serious, nay, solemn. "I don't know about wot you s'y, Mr. Van Weyden, but I do know I'll never rest 'appy till I see that 'ell-'ound bloody well dead. 'E cawn't live as long as me. 'E's got no right to live, an' as the Good Word puts it, ''E shall shorely die,' an' I s'y, 'Amen, an' damn soon at that.'"

When I returned on deck I found Wolf Larsen steering mainly with one hand, while with the other hand he held the marine glasses and studied the situation of the boats, paying particular attention to the position of the *Macedonia*. The only change noticeable in our boats was that they had hauled close on the wind and were heading several points west of north. Still, I could not see the expediency of the manœuvre, for the free sea was still intercepted by the *Macedonia*'s five weather boats, which, in turn, had hauled close on the wind. Thus they slowly diverged toward the west, drawing farther away from the remainder of the boats in their line. Our boats were rowing as well as sailing. Even the hunters were pulling, and with three pairs of oars in the water they rapidly overhauled what I may appropriately term the enemy.

The smoke of the *Macedonia* had dwindled to a dim blot on the northeastern horizon. Of the steamer herself nothing was to be seen. We had been loafing along, till now, our sails shaking half the time and spilling the wind; and twice, for short periods, we had been hove to. But there was no more loafing. Sheets were trimmed, and Wolf Larsen proceeded to put the *Ghost* through her paces. We ran past our line of boats and bore down upon the first weather boat of the other line.

"Down that flying jib, Mr. Van Weyden," Wolf Larsen commanded. "And stand by to back over the jibs."

I ran forward and had the downhaul of the flying jib all in and fast as we slipped by the boat a hundred feet to leeward. The three men in it gazed at us suspiciously. They had been hogging the sea, and they knew Wolf Larsen, by reputation at any rate. I noted that the hunter, a huge Scandinavian sitting in the bow, held his rifle, ready to hand, across his knees. It should have been in its proper place in the rack. When they came opposite our stern, Wolf Larsen greeted them with a wave of the hand, and cried:

"Come on board and have a 'gam'!"

"To gam," among the sealing schooners, is a substitute for the verbs "to visit," "to gossip." It expresses the garrulity of the sea and is a pleasant break in the monotony of the life.

The *Ghost* swung around into the wind, and I finished my work forward in time to run aft and lend a hand with the main sheet.

"You will please stay on deck, Miss Brewster," Wolf Larsen said, as he started forward to meet his guest. "And you, too, Mr. Van Weyden."

The boat had lowered its sail and run alongside. The hunter, golden-bearded like a sea-king, came over the rail and dropped on deck. But his hugeness could not quite overcome his apprehensiveness. Doubt and distrust showed strongly in his face. It was a transparent face, for all of its hairy shield, and advertised instant relief when he glanced from Wolf Larsen to me, noted that there was only the pair of us, and then glanced over his own two men who had joined him. Surely he had little reason to be afraid. He towered like a Goliath above Wolf Larsen. He must have measured six feet eight or nine inches in stature, and I subsequently learned his weight—240 pounds. And there was no fat about him. It was all bone and muscle.

A return of apprehension was apparent, when, at the top of the companionway, Wolf Larsen invited him below. But he reassured himself with a glance down at his host—a big man himself but dwarfed by the propinquity of the giant. So all hesitancy vanished, and the pair descended into the cabin. In the meantime, his two men, as was the wont of visiting sailors, had gone forward into the forecastle to do some visiting themselves.

Suddenly, from the cabin came a great, choking bellow, followed by all the sounds of a furious struggle. It was the leopard and the lion, and the lion made all the noise. Wolf Larsen was the leopard.

"You see the sacredness of our hospitality," I said bitterly, to Maud Brewster.

She nodded her head that she heard, and I noted in her face the signs of the same sickness at sight or sound of violent struggle from which I had suffered so severely during my first weeks on the *Ghost*.

"Wouldn't it be better if you went forward, say by the companionway, until it is over?" I suggested.

She shook her head and gazed at me pitifully. She was not frightened, but appalled, rather, at the human animality of it.

"You will understand," I took advantage of the opportunity to say, "whatever part I take in what is going on and what is to come, that I am compelled to take it—if you and I are ever to get out of this scrape with our lives."

"It is not nice—for me," I added.

"I understand," she said, in a weak, far-away voice, and her eyes showed me that she did understand.

The sounds from below soon died away. Then Wolf Larsen came alone on deck. There was a slight flush under his bronze, but otherwise he bore no signs of the battle.

"Send those two men aft, Mr. Van Weyden," he said.

I obeyed, and a minute or two later they stood before him.

"Hoist in your boat," he said to them. "Your hunter's decided to stay aboard awhile and doesn't want it pounding alongside."

"Hoist in your boat, I said," he repeated, this time in sharper tones as they hesitated to do his bidding.

"Who knows? you may have to sail with me for a time," he said, quite softly, with a silken threat that belied the softness, as they moved slowly to comply, "and we might as well start with a friendly understanding. Lively now! Death Larsen makes you jump better than that, and you know it!"

Their movements perceptibly quickened under his coaching, and as the boat swung inboard I was sent forward to let go the jibs. Wolf Larsen, at the wheel, directed the *Ghost* after the *Macedonia*'s second weather boat.

Under way, and with nothing for the time being to do, I turned my attention to the situation of the boats. The *Macedonia*'s third weather boat was being attacked by two of ours, the fourth by our remaining three; and the fifth, turn about, was taking a hand in the defence of its nearest mate. The fight had opened at long distance, and the rifles were cracking steadily. A quick, snappy sea was being kicked up by the wind, a condition which prevented fine shooting; and now and again, as we drew closer, we could see the bullets zip-zipping from wave to wave.

The boat we were pursuing had squared away and was

running before the wind to escape us, and, in the course of its flight, to take part in repulsing our general boat attack.

Attending to sheets and tacks now left me little time to see what was taking place, but I happened to be on the poop when Wolf Larsen ordered the two strange sailors forward and into the forecastle. They went sullenly, but they went. He next ordered Miss Brewster below, and smiled at the instant horror that leapt into her eyes.

"You'll find nothing grewsome down there," he said, "only an unhurt man securely made fast to the ring-bolts. Bullets are liable to come aboard, and I don't want you killed, you know."

Even as he spoke, a bullet was deflected by a brass-capped spoke of the wheel between his hands and screeched off through the air to windward.

"You see," he said to her; and then to me, "Mr. Van Weyden, will you take the wheel?"

Maud Brewster had stepped inside the companionway so that only her head was exposed. Wolf Larsen had procured a rifle and was throwing a cartridge into the barrel. I begged her with my eyes to go below, but she smiled and said:

"We may be feeble land-creatures without legs, but we can show Captain Larsen that we are at least as brave as he."

He gave her a quick look of admiration.

"I like you a hundred per cent better for that," he said. "Books, and brains, and bravery. You are well-rounded, a blue-stocking fit to be the wife of a pirate chief. Ahem, we'll discuss that later," he smiled, as a bullet struck solidly into the cabin wall.

I saw his eyes flash golden as he spoke, and I saw the terror mount in her own.

"We are braver," I hastened to say. "At least, speaking for myself, I know I am braver than Captain Larsen."

It was I who was now favored by a quick look. He was

wondering if I were making fun of him. I put three or four
spokes over to counteract a sheer toward the wind on the
part of the *Ghost*, and then steadied her. Wolf Larsen was
still waiting an explanation, and I pointed down to my
knees.

"You will observe there," I said, "a slight trembling.
It is because I am afraid, the flesh is afraid; and I am
afraid in my mind because I do not wish to die. But my
spirit masters the trembling flesh and the qualms of the
mind. I am more than brave. I am courageous. Your flesh
is not afraid. You are not afraid. On the one hand, it
costs you nothing to encounter danger; on the other hand,
it even gives you delight. You enjoy it. You may be unafraid, Mr. Larsen, but you must grant that the bravery is
mine."

"You're right," he acknowledged at once. "I never
thought of it in that way before. But is the opposite
true? If you are braver than I, am I more cowardly than
you?"

We both laughed at the absurdity, and he dropped down
to the deck and rested his rifle across the rail. The bullets
we had received had travelled nearly a mile, but by now
we had cut that distance in half. He fired three careful
shots. The first struck fifty feet to windward of the boat,
the second alongside, and at the third the boat-steerer let
loose his steering-oar and crumpled up in the bottom of
the boat.

"I guess that'll fix them," Wolf Larsen said, rising to his
feet. "I couldn't afford to let the hunter have it, and there
is a chance the boat-puller doesn't know how to steer. In
which case, the hunter cannot steer and shoot at the same
time."

His reasoning was justified, for the boat rushed at once
into the wind and the hunter sprang aft to take the boat-
steerer's place. There was no more shooting, though the
rifles were still cracking merrily from the other boats.

The hunter had managed to get the boat before the wind again, but we ran down upon it, going at least two feet to its one. A hundred yards away, I saw the boat-puller pass a rifle to the hunter. Wolf Larsen went amidships and took the coil of the throat-halyards from its pin. Then he peered over the rail with levelled rifle. Twice I saw the hunter let go the steering-oar with one hand, reach for his rifle, and hesitate. We were now alongside and foaming past.

"Here, you!" Wolf Larsen cried suddenly to the boat-puller. "Take a turn!"

At the same time he flung the coil of rope. It struck fairly, nearly knocking the man over, but he did not obey. Instead, he looked to his hunter for orders. The hunter, in turn, was in a quandary. His rifle was between his knees, but if he let go the steering-oar in order to shoot, the boat would sweep around and collide with the schooner. Also he saw Wolf Larsen's rifle bearing upon him and knew he would be shot ere he could get his rifle into play.

"Take a turn," he said quietly to the man.

The boat-puller obeyed, taking a turn around the little forward thwart and paying the line as it jerked taut. The boat sheered out with a rush, and the hunter steadied it to a parallel course some twenty feet from the side of the *Ghost.*

"Now get that sail down and come alongside!" Wolf Larsen ordered.

He never let go his rifle, even passing down the tackles with one hand. When they were fast, bow and stern, and the two uninjured men prepared to come aboard, the hunter picked up his rifle as if to place it in a secure position.

"Drop it!" Wolf Larsen cried, and the hunter dropped it as though it were hot and had burned him.

Once aboard, the two prisoners hoisted in the boat and under Wolf Larsen's direction carried the wounded boat-steerer down into the forecastle.

"If our five boats do as well as you and I have done, we'll have a pretty full crew," Wolf Larsen said to me.

"The man you shot—he is, I hope—" Maud Brewster quavered.

"In the shoulder," he answered. "Nothing serious. Mr. Van Weyden will pull him around as good as ever in three or four weeks."

"But he won't pull those chaps around, from the look of it," he added, pointing at the *Macedonia's* third boat, for which I had been steering and which was now nearly abreast of us. "That's Horner's and Smoke's work. I told them we wanted live men, not carcasses. But the joy of shooting to hit is a most compelling thing, when once you've learned how to shoot. Ever experienced it, Mr. Van Weyden?"

I shook my head and regarded their work. It had indeed been bloody, for they had drawn off and joined our other three boats in the attack on the remaining two of the enemy. The deserted boat was in the trough of the sea, rolling drunkenly across each comber, its loose spritsail out at right angles to it and fluttering and flapping in the wind. The hunter and boat-puller were both lying awkwardly in the bottom, but the boat-steerer lay across the gunwale, half in and half out, his arms trailing in the water and his head rolling from side to side.

"Don't look, Miss Brewster, please don't look," I had begged of her, and I was glad that she had minded me and been spared the sight.

"Head right into the bunch, Mr. Van Weyden," was Wolf Larsen's command.

As we drew nearer, the firing ceased, and we saw that the fight was over. The remaining two boats had been captured by our five, and the seven were grouped together, waiting to be picked up.

"Look at that!" I cried involuntarily, pointing to the northeast.

The blot of smoke which indicated the *Macedonia*'s position had reappeared.

"Yes, I've been watching it," was Wolf Larsen's calm reply. He measured the distance away to the fog-bank and for an instant paused to feel the weight of the wind on his cheek. "We'll make it, I think; but you can depend upon it that blessed brother of mine has twigged our little game and is just a-humping for us. Ah, look at that!"

The blot of smoke had suddenly grown larger, and it was very black.

"I'll beat you out, though, brother mine," he chuckled. "I'll beat you out, and I hope you no worse than that you rack your old engines into scrap."

When we hove to, a hasty though orderly confusion reigned. The boats came aboard from every side at once. As fast as the prisoners came over the rail they were marshalled forward into the forecastle by our hunters, while our sailors hoisted in the boats, pell-mell, dropping them anywhere upon the deck and not stopping to lash them. We were already under way, all sails set and drawing, and the sheets being slacked off for a wind abeam, as the last boat lifted clear of the water and swung in the tackles.

There was need for haste. The *Macedonia*, belching the blackest of smoke from her funnel, was charging down upon us from out of the northeast. Neglecting the boats that remained to her, she had altered her course so as to anticipate ours. She was not running straight for us, but ahead of us. Our courses were converging like the sides of an angle, the vertex of which was at the edge of the fog-bank. It was there, or not at all, that the *Macedonia* could hope to catch us. The hope for the *Ghost* lay in that she should pass that point before the *Macedonia* arrived at it.

Wolf Larsen was steering, his eyes glistening and snapping as they dwelt upon and leaped from detail to detail of the chase. Now he studied the sea to windward for signs of the wind slackening or freshening, now the *Macedonia*; and again, his eyes roved over every sail, and he gave commands to slack a sheet here a trifle, to come in on one there a trifle, till he was drawing out of the *Ghost* the last bit of speed she possessed. All feuds and grudges were forgotten, and I was surprised at the alacrity with which the men who had so long endured his brutality sprang to execute his orders. Strange to say, the unfortunate Johnson came into my mind as we lifted and surged and heeled along, and I was aware of a regret that he was not alive and present; he had so loved the *Ghost* and delighted in her sailing powers.

"Better get your rifles, you fellows," Wolf Larsen called to our hunters; and the five men lined the lee rail, guns in hand, and waited.

The *Macedonia* was now but a mile away, the black smoke pouring from her funnel at a right angle, so madly she raced, pounding through the sea at a seventeen-knot gait—" 'Sky-hooting through the brine',"* as Wolf Larsen quoted while gazing at her. We were not making more than nine knots, but the fog-bank was very near.

A puff of smoke broke from the *Macedonia*'s deck, we heard a heavy report, and a round hole took form in the stretched canvas of our mainsail. They were shooting at us with one of the small cannon which rumor had said they carried on board. Our men, clustering amidships, waved their hats and raised a derisive cheer. Again there was a puff of smoke and a loud report, this time the cannon-ball striking not more than twenty feet astern and glancing twice from sea to sea to windward ere it sank.

But there was no rifle-firing for the reason that all their hunters were out in the boats or our prisoners. When the two vessels were half a mile apart, a third shot made another hole in our mainsail. Then we entered the fog. It was about us, veiling and hiding us in its dense wet gauze.

The sudden transition was startling. The moment before we had been leaping through the sunshine, the clear sky above us, the sea breaking and rolling wide to the horizon, and a ship, vomiting smoke and fire and iron missiles, rushing madly upon us. And at once, as in an instant's leap, the sun was blotted out, there was no sky, even our mastheads were lost to view, and our horizon was such as tear-blinded eyes may see. The gray mist drove by us like a rain. Every woollen filament of our garments, every hair of our heads and faces, was jewelled with a crystal globule. The shrouds were wet with moisture; it dripped from our rigging overhead; and on the under side of our booms drops of water took shape in long swaying lines, which were detached and flung to the deck in mimic showers at each surge of the schooner. I was aware of a pent, stifled feeling. As the sounds of the ship thrusting herself through the waves were hurled back upon us by the fog, so were one's thoughts. The mind recoiled from contemplation of a world beyond this wet veil which wrapped us around. This was the world, the universe itself, its bounds so near one felt impelled to reach out both arms and push them back. It was impossible that the rest could be beyond these walls of gray. The rest was a dream, no more than the memory of a dream.

It was weird, strangely weird. I looked at Maud Brewster and knew that she was similarly affected. Then I looked at Wolf Larsen, but there was nothing subjective about his state of consciousness. His whole concern was with the immediate, objective present. He still held the wheel, and I felt that he was timing Time, reckoning the passage of the minutes with each forward lunge and leeward roll of the *Ghost*.

"Go for'ard and hard-a-lee without any noise," he said to me in a low voice. "Clew up the topsails first. Set men at all the sheets. Let there be no rattling of blocks, no sound of voices. No noise, understand, no noise."

When all was ready, the word "hard-a-lee" was passed forward to me from man to man; and the *Ghost* heeled about on the port tack with practically no noise at all.

And what little there was,—the slapping of a few reef-points and the creaking of a sheave in a block or two,—was ghostly under the hollow echoing pall in which we were swathed.

We had scarcely filled away, it seemed, when the fog thinned abruptly and we were again in the sunshine, the wide-stretching sea breaking before us to the sky-line. But the ocean was bare. No wrathful *Macedonia* broke its surface nor blackened the sky with her smoke.

Wolf Larsen at once squared away and ran down along the rim of the fog-bank. His trick was obvious. He had entered the fog to windward of the steamer, and while the steamer had blindly driven on into the fog in the chance of catching him he had come about and out of his shelter and was now running down to re-enter to leeward. Successful in this, the old simile of the needle in the haystack would be mild indeed compared with his brother's chance of finding him.

He did not run long. Jibing the fore- and main-sails and setting the topsails again, we headed back into the bank. As we entered I could have sworn I saw a vague bulk emerging to windward. I looked quickly at Wolf Larsen. Already we were ourselves buried in the fog, but he nodded his head. He, too, had seen it—the *Macedonia*, guessing his manoeuvre and failing by a moment in anticipating it. There was no doubt that we had escaped unseen.

"He can't keep this up," Wolf Larsen said. "He'll have to go back for the rest of his boats. Send a man to the wheel, Mr. Van Weyden, keep this course for the present, and you might as well set the watches, for we won't do any lingering to-night."

"I'd give five hundred dollars, though," he added, "just to be aboard the *Macedonia* for five minutes, listening to my brother curse."

"And now, Mr. Van Weyden," he said to me when he had been relieved from the wheel, "we must make these

newcomers welcome. Serve out plenty of whiskey to the
hunters and see that a few bottles slip for'ard. I'll wager
every man Jack of them is over the side to-morrow, hunting
for Wolf Larsen as contentedly as ever they hunted for
Death Larsen."

"But won't they escape as Wainwright did?" I asked.

He laughed shrewdly. "Not as long as our old hunters
have anything to say about it. I'm dividing amongst them
a dollar a skin for all the skins shot by our new hunters.
At least half of their enthusiasm today was due to that.
Oh, no, there won't be any escaping if they have anything
to say about it. And now you'd better get for'ard to your
hospital duties. There must be a full ward waiting for you."

CHAPTER TWENTY-SIX

WOLF LARSEN took the distribution of the whiskey off my hands, and the bottles began to make their appearance while I worked over the fresh batch of wounded men in the forecastle. I had seen whiskey drunk, such as whiskey and soda by the men of the clubs, but never as these men drank it, from pannikins and mugs, and from the bottles— great brimming drinks, each one of which was in itself a debauch. But they did not stop at one or two. They drank and drank, and ever the bottles slipped forward and they drank more.

Everybody drank; the wounded drank; Oofty-Oofty, who helped me, drank. Only Louis refrained, no more than cautiously wetting his lips with the liquor, though he joined in the revels with an abandon equal to that of most of them. It was a saturnalia. In loud voices they shouted over the day's fighting, wrangled about details, or waxed affectionate and made friends with the men whom they had fought. Prisoners and captors hiccoughed on one another's shoulders, and swore mighty oaths of respect and esteem. They wept over the miseries of the past and over the miseries yet to come under the iron rule of Wolf Larsen. And all cursed him and told terrible tales of his brutality.

It was a strange and frightful spectacle—the small, bunk-lined space, the floor and walls leaping and lurching, the dim light, the swaying shadows lengthening and foreshortening monstrously, the thick air heavy with smoke and the smell of bodies and iodoform, and the inflamed faces of the men—half-men, I should call them. I noted Oofty-Oofty, holding the end of a bandage and looking upon the scene, his velvety and luminous eyes glistening in the light like a deer's eyes, and yet I knew the barbaric devil that lurked in his breast and belied all the softness and tenderness, almost womanly, of his face and form. And I noticed the boyish face of Harrison,—a good face once, but now a demon's,—convulsed with passion as he told the newcomers of the hell-ship they were in and shrieked curses upon the head of Wolf Larsen.

Wolf Larsen it was, always Wolf Larsen, enslaver and tormentor of men, a male Circe* and these his swine, suffering brutes that grovelled before him and revolted only in drunkenness and in secrecy. And was I, too, one of his swine? I thought. And Maud Brewster? No! I ground my teeth in my anger and determination till the man I was attending winced under my hand and Oofty-Oofty looked at me with curiosity. I felt endowed with a sudden strength. What of my new-found love, I was a giant. I feared nothing. I would work my will through it all, in spite of Wolf Larsen and of my own thirty-five bookish years. All would be well. I would make it well. And so, exalted, upborne by a sense of power, I turned my back on the howling inferno and climbed to the deck, where the fog drifted ghostly through the night and the air was sweet and pure and quiet.

The steerage, where were two wounded hunters, was a repetition of the forecastle, except that Wolf Larsen was not being cursed; and it was with a great relief that I again emerged on deck and went aft to the cabin. Supper was ready, and Wolf Larsen and Maud were waiting for me.

While all his ship was getting drunk as fast as it could, he remained sober. Not a drop of liquor passed his lips. He did not dare it under the circumstances, for he had only Louis and me to depend upon, and Louis was even now at the wheel. We were sailing on through the fog without a lookout and without lights. That Wolf Larsen had turned the liquor loose among his men surprised me, but he evidently knew their psychology and the best method of cementing in cordiality what had begun in bloodshed.

His victory over Death Larsen seemed to have had a

remarkable effect upon him. The previous evening he had reasoned himself into the blues, and I had been waiting momentarily for one of his characteristic outbursts. Yet nothing had occurred, and he was now in splendid trim. Possibly his success in capturing so many hunters and boats had counteracted the customary reaction. At any rate, the blues were gone, and the blue devils had not put in an appearance. So I thought at the time; but, ah me, little I knew him or knew that even then, perhaps, he was meditating an outbreak more terrible than any I had seen.

As I say, he discovered himself in splendid trim when I entered the cabin. He had had no headaches for weeks, his eyes were clear blue as the sky, his bronze was beautiful with perfect health; life swelled through his veins in full and magnificent flood. While waiting for me he had engaged Maud in animated discussion. Temptation was the topic they had hit upon, and from the few words I heard I made out that he was contending that temptation was temptation only when a man was seduced by it and fell.

"For look you," he was saying, "as I see it, a man does things because of desire. He has many desires. He may desire to escape pain, or to enjoy pleasure. But whatever he does, he does because he desires to do it."

"But suppose he desires to do two opposite things, neither of which will permit him to do the other?" Maud interrupted.

"The very thing I was coming to," he said.

"And between these two desires is just where the soul of the man is manifest," she went on. "If it is a good soul, it will desire and do the good action, and the contrary if it is a bad soul. It is the soul that decides."

"Bosh and nonsense!" he exclaimed impatiently. "It is the desire that decides. Here is a man who wants to, say, get drunk. Also, he doesn't want to get drunk. What does he do? How does he do it? He is a puppet. He is the creature of his desires, and of the two desires he obeys the

strongest one, that is all. His soul hasn't anything to do
with it. How can he be tempted to get drunk and refuse
to get drunk? If the desire to remain sober prevails, it
is because it is the strongest desire. Temptation plays no
part, unless,—" he paused while grasping the new thought
which had come into his mind,—"unless he is tempted to
remain sober."

"Ha! ha!" he laughed. "What do you think of that, Mr.
Van Weyden?"

"That both of you are hair-splitting," I said. "The man's
soul is his desires. Or, if you will, the sum of his desires is
his soul. Therein you are both wrong. You lay the stress
upon the desire apart from the soul, Miss Brewster lays
the stress on the soul apart from the desire, and in point
of fact soul and desire are the same thing.

"However," I continued, "Miss Brewster is right in contending that temptation is temptation whether the man
yield or overcome. Fire is fanned by the wind until it
leaps up fiercely. So is desire like fire. It is fanned, as by a
wind, by sight of the thing desired, or by a new and luring
description or comprehension of the thing desired. There
lies the temptation. It is the wind that fans the desire until
it leaps up to mastery. That's temptation. It may not fan
sufficiently to make the desire overmastering, but in so far
as it fans at all, that far is it temptation. And, as you say,
it may tempt for good as well as for evil."

I felt proud of myself as we sat down to the table. My
words had been decisive. At least they had put an end to
the discussion.

But Wolf Larsen seemed voluble, prone to speech as I
had never seen him before. It was as though he were bursting with pent energy which must find an outlet somehow.
Almost immediately he launched into a discussion on love.
As usual, his was the sheer materialistic side, and Maud's
was the idealistic. For myself, beyond a word or so of
suggestion or correction now and again, I took no part.

He was brilliant, but so was Maud, and for some time I lost the thread of the conversation through studying her face as she talked. It was a face that rarely displayed color, but tonight it was flushed and vivacious. Her wit was playing keenly, and she was enjoying the tilt as much as Wolf Larsen, and he was enjoying it hugely. For some reason, though I know not why, in the argument, so utterly had I lost it in the contemplation of one stray brown lock of Maud's hair, he quoted from Iseult at Tintagel, where she says:

> "Blessed am I beyond women even herein
> That beyond all born women is my sin,
> And perfect my transgression."*

As he had read pessimism into Omar, so now he read triumph, stinging triumph and exultation, into Swinburne's lines. And he read rightly, and he read well. He had hardly ceased reading when Louis put his head into the companionway and whispered down:

"Be easy, will ye? The fog's lifted, an' 'tis the port light iv a steamer that's crossin' our bow this blessed minute."

Wolf Larsen sprang on deck, and so swiftly that by the time we followed him he had pulled the steerage-slide over the drunken clamor and was on his way forward to close the forecastle-scuttle. The fog, though it remained, had lifted high, where it obscured the stars and made the night quite black. Directly ahead of us I could see a bright red light and a white light, and I could hear the pulsing of a steamer's engines. Beyond a doubt it was the *Macedonia*.

Wolf Larsen had returned to the poop, and we stood in a silent group, watching the lights rapidly cross our bow.

"Lucky for me he doesn't carry a searchlight," Wolf Larsen said.

"What if I should cry out loudly?" I queried in a whisper.

"It would be all up," he answered. "But have you thought upon what would immediately happen?"

Before I had time to express any desire to know, he had me by the throat with his gorilla grip, and by a faint quiver of the muscles,—a hint, as it were, he suggested to me the twist that would surely have broken my neck. The next moment he had released me and we were gazing at the *Macedonia's* lights.

"What if I should cry out?" Maud asked.

"I like you too well to hurt you," he said softly—nay, there was a tenderness and a caress in his voice that made me wince. "But don't do it, just the same, for I'd promptly break Mr. Van Weyden's neck."

"Then she has my permission to cry out," I said defiantly.

"I hardly think you'll care to sacrifice the Dean of American Letters the Second," he sneered.

We spoke no more, though we had become too used to one another for the silence to be awkward; and when the red light and the white had disappeared we returned to the cabin to finish the interrupted supper.

Again they fell to quoting, and Maud gave Dowson's "Impenitentia Ultima."* She rendered it beautifully, but I watched not her, but Wolf Larsen. I was fascinated by the fascinated look he bent upon Maud. He was quite out of himself, and I noticed the unconscious movement of his lips as he shaped word for word as fast as she uttered them. He interrupted her when she gave the lines:

"And her eyes should be my light while the sun went
     out behind me,
And the viols in her voice be the last sound in my ear."

"There are viols in your voice," he said bluntly, and his eyes flashed their golden light.

I could have shouted with joy at her control. She finished the concluding stanza without faltering and then slowly guided the conversation into less perilous channels. And all the while I sat in a half-daze, the drunken riot of the steerage breaking through the bulkhead, the man I feared and the woman I loved talking on and on. The table was not cleared. The man who had taken Mugridge's place had evidently joined his comrades in the forecastle.

If ever Wolf Larsen attained the summit of living, he attained it then. From time to time I forsook my own thoughts to follow him, and I followed in amaze, mastered for the moment by his remarkable intellect, under the spell of his passion, for he was preaching the passion of revolt. It was inevitable that Milton's Lucifer should be instanced, and the keenness with which Wolf Larsen analyzed and depicted the character was a revelation of his stifled genius. It reminded me of Taine, yet I knew the man had never heard of that brilliant though dangerous thinker.*

"He led a lost cause, and he was not afraid of God's thunderbolts," Wolf Larsen was saying. "Hurled into hell, he was unbeaten. A third of God's angels he had led with him, and straightway he incited man to rebel against God, and gained for himself and hell the major portion of all the generations of man. Why was he beaten out of heaven? Because he was less brave than God? less proud? less aspiring? No! A thousand times no! God was more powerful, as he said, Whom thunder hath made greater. But Lucifer was a free spirit. To serve was to suffocate. He preferred suffering in freedom to all the happiness of a comfortable servility. He did not care to serve God. He cared to serve nothing. He was no figurehead. He stood on his own legs. He was an individual."

"The first anarchist,"* Maud laughed, rising and preparing to withdraw to her state-room.

"Then it is good to be an anarchist!" he cried. He, too, had risen, and he stood facing her, where she had paused at the door of her room, as he went on:

" 'Here at least
We shall be free; the Almighty hath not built
Here for his envy; will not drive us hence;
Here we may reign secure; and in my choice
To reign is worth ambition, though in hell:
Better to reign in hell than serve in heaven'."*

It was the defiant cry of a mighty spirit. The cabin still rang with his voice, as he stood there, swaying, his bronzed face shining, his head up and dominant, and his eyes, golden and masculine, intensely masculine and insistently soft, flashing upon Maud at the door.

Again the unnamable and unmistakable terror was in her eyes, and she said, almost in a whisper, "You are Lucifer."

The door closed and she was gone. He stood staring after her for a minute, then returned to himself and to me.

"I'll relieve Louis at the wheel," he said shortly, "and call upon you to relieve at midnight. Better turn in now and get some sleep."

He pulled on a pair of mittens, put on his cap, and ascended the companion-stairs, while I followed his suggestion by going to bed. For some unknown reason, prompted mysteriously, I did not undress, but lay down fully clothed. For a time I listened to the clamor in the steerage and marvelled upon the love which had come to me; but my sleep on the *Ghost* had become most healthful and natural, and soon the songs and cries died away, my eyes closed, and my consciousness sank down into the half-death of slumber.

I knew not what had aroused me, but I found myself out of my bunk, on my feet, wide awake, my soul vibrating to the warning of danger as it might have thrilled to a trumpet call. I threw open the door. The cabin light was burning low. I saw Maud, my Maud, straining and struggling and crushed in the embrace of Wolf Larsen's arms. I could see the vain beat and flutter of her as she strove, pressing her face against his breast, to escape from him. All this I saw on the very instant of seeing and as I sprang forward.

I struck him with my fist, on the face, as he raised his head, but it was a puny blow. He roared in a ferocious, animal-like way, and gave me a shove with his hand. It was only a shove, a flirt of the wrist, yet so tremendous was his strength that I was hurled backward as from a catapult. I struck the door of the stateroom which had formerly been Mugridge's, splintering and smashing the panels with the impact of my body. I struggled to my feet, with difficulty dragging myself clear of the wrecked door, unaware of any hurt whatever. I was conscious only of an overmastering rage. I think I, too, cried aloud, as I drew the knife at my hip and sprang forward a second time.

But something had happened. They were reeling apart. I was close upon him, my knife uplifted, but I withheld the blow. I was puzzled by the strangeness of it. Maud was leaning against the wall, one hand out for support; but he was staggering, his left hand pressed against his forehead and covering his eyes, and with the right he was groping about him in a dazed sort of way. It struck against the wall, and his body seemed to express a muscular and physical relief at the contact, as though he had found his bearings, his location in space as well as something against which to lean.

Then I saw red again. All my wrongs and humiliations flashed upon me with a dazzling brightness, all that I had suffered and others had suffered at his hands, all the enormity of the man's very existence. I sprang upon him, blindly, insanely, and drove the knife into his shoulder. I knew, then, that it was no more than a flesh wound,—I had felt the steel grate on his shoulder-blade,—and I raised the knife to strike at a more vital part.

But Maud had seen my first blow, and she cried, "Don't! Please don't!"

I dropped my arm for a moment, and a moment only. Again the knife was raised, and Wolf Larsen would have surely died had she not stepped between. Her arms were around me, her hair was brushing my face. My pulse rushed up in an unwonted manner, yet my rage mounted with it. She looked me bravely in the eyes.

"For my sake," she begged.

"I would kill him for your sake!" I cried, trying to free my arm without hurting her.

"Hush!" she said, and laid her fingers lightly on my lips. I could have kissed them, had I dared, even then, in my rage, the touch of them was so sweet, so very sweet. "Please, please," she pleaded, and she disarmed me by the words, as I was to discover they would ever disarm me.

I stepped back, separating from her, and replaced the knife in its sheath. I looked at Wolf Larsen. He still pressed his left hand against his forehead. It covered his eyes. His head was bowed. He seemed to have grown limp. His body was sagging at the hips, his great shoulders were drooping and shrinking forward.

"Van Weyden!" he called hoarsely, and with a note of fright in his voice. "Oh, Van Weyden! where are you?"

I looked at Maud. She did not speak, but nodded her head.

"Here I am," I answered, stepping to his side. "What is the matter?"

"I am a sick man, a very sick man, Hump," he said, as he left my sustaining grip and sank into a chair.

His head dropped forward on the table and was buried in his hands. From time to time it rocked back and forward as with pain. Once, when he half raised it, I saw the sweat

standing in heavy drops on his forehead about the roots
of his hair.

"I am a sick man, a very sick man," he repeated again,
and yet once again.

"What is the matter?" I asked, resting my hand on his
shoulder. "What can I do for you?"

But he shook my hand off with an irritated movement,
and for a long time I stood by his side in silence. Maud
was looking on, her face awed and frightened. What had
happened to him we could not imagine.

"Hump," he said at last, "I must get into my bunk. Lend
me a hand. I'll be all right in a little while. It's those damn
headaches, I believe. I was afraid of them. I had a feeling—
no, I don't know what I'm talking about. Help me into my
bunk."

But when I got him into his bunk he again buried his
face in his hands, covering his eyes, and as I turned to go I
could hear him murmuring, "I am a sick man, a very sick
man."

Maud looked at me inquiringly as I emerged. I shook my
head, saying:

"Something has happened to him. What, I don't know.
He is helpless, and frightened, I imagine, for the first time
in his life. It must have occurred before he received the
knife-thrust, which made only a superficial wound. You
must have seen what happened."

She shook her head. "I saw nothing. It is just as mysterious to me. He suddenly released me and staggered away.
But what shall we do? What shall I do?"

"If you will wait, please, until I come back," I answered.
I went on deck. Louis was at the wheel.

"You may go for'ard and turn in," I said, taking it from
him.

He was quick to obey, and I found myself alone on the
deck of the *Ghost*. As quietly as was possible, I clewed up
the topsails, lowered the flying jib and staysail, backed the

jib over, and flattened the mainsail. Then I went below
to Maud. I placed my finger on my lips for silence, and
entered Wolf Larsen's room. He was in the same position
in which I had left him, and his head was rocking—almost
writhing—from side to side.

"Anything I can do for you?" I asked.

He made no reply at first, but on my repeating the
question he answered, "No, no; I'm all right. Leave me
alone till morning."

But as I turned to go I noted that his head had resumed
its rocking motion. Maud was waiting patiently for me,
and I took notice, with a thrill of joy, of the queenly poise
of her head and her glorious, calm eyes. Calm and sure
they were as her spirit itself.

"Will you trust yourself to me for a journey of six hundred miles or so?" I asked.

"You mean—?" she asked, and I knew she had guessed
aright.

"Yes, I mean just that," I replied. "There is nothing left
for us but the open boat."

"For me, you mean," she said. "You are certainly as safe
here as you have been."

"No, there is nothing left for us but the open boat," I
iterated stoutly. "Will you please dress as warmly as you
can, at once, and make into a bundle whatever you wish
to bring with you."

"And make all haste," I added, as she turned toward her
state-room.

The lazarette was directly beneath the cabin, and, opening the trap-door in the floor and carrying a candle with
me, I dropped down and began overhauling the ship's
stores. I selected mainly from the canned goods, and by
the time I was ready, willing hands were extended from
above to receive what I passed up.

We worked in silence. I helped myself also to blankets,
mittens, oilskins, caps, and such things, from the slop-

chest. It was no light adventure, this trusting ourselves in a small boat to so raw and stormy a sea, and it was imperative that we should guard ourselves against the cold and wet.

We worked feverishly at carrying our plunder on deck and depositing it amidships, so feverishly that Maud, whose strength was hardly a positive quantity, had to give over, exhausted, and sit on the steps at the break of the poop. This did not serve to recover her, and she lay on her back, on the hard deck, arms stretched out and whole body relaxed. It was a trick I remembered of my sister, and I knew she would soon be herself again. I knew, also, that weapons would not come in amiss, and I re-entered Wolf Larsen's state-room to get his rifle and shotgun. I spoke to him, but he made no answer, though his head was still rocking from side to side and he was not asleep.

"Good-bye, Lucifer," I whispered to myself as I softly closed the door.

Next to obtain was a stock of ammunition,—an easy matter, though I had to enter the steerage companionway to do it. Here the hunters stored the ammunition boxes they carried in the boats, and here, but a few feet from their noisy revels, I took possession of two boxes.

Next, to lower a boat. Not so simple a task for one man. Having cast off the lashings, I hoisted first on the forward tackle, then on the aft, till the boat cleared the rail, when I lowered away, one tackle and then the other, for a couple of feet, till it hung snugly, above the water, against the schooner's side. I made certain that it contained the proper equipment of oars, rowlocks, and sail. Water was a consideration, and I robbed every boat aboard of its breaker. As there were nine boats all told, it meant that we should have plenty of water, and ballast as well, though there was the chance that the boat would be overloaded, what of the generous supply of other things I was taking.

While Maud was passing me the provisions and I was

storing them in the boat, a sailor came on deck from the forecastle. He stood by the weather rail for a time, (we were lowering over the lee rail), and then sauntered slowly amidships, where he again paused and stood facing the wind, with his back toward us. I could hear my heart beating as I crouched low in the boat. Maud had sunk down upon the deck and was, I knew, lying motionless, her body in the shadow of the bulwark. But the man never turned, and, after stretching his arms above his head and yawning audibly, he retraced his steps to the forecastle scuttle and disappeared.

A few minutes sufficed to finish the loading, and I lowered the boat into the water. As I helped Maud over the rail and felt her form close to mine, it was all I could do to keep from crying out, "I love you! I love you!" Truly Humphrey Van Weyden was at last in love, I thought, as her fingers clung to mine while I lowered her down to the boat. I held on to the rail with one hand and supported her weight with the other, and I was proud at the moment of the feat. It was a strength I had not possessed a few months before, on the day I said good-bye to Charley Furuseth and started for San Francisco on the ill-fated *Martinez.*

As the boat ascended on a sea, her feet touched and I released her hands. I cast off the tackles and leaped after her. I had never rowed in my life, but I put out the oars and at the expense of much effort got the boat clear of the *Ghost.* Then I experimented with the sail. I had seen the boat-steerers and hunters set their spritsails many times, yet this was my first attempt. What took them possibly two minutes took me twenty, but in the end I succeeded in setting and trimming it, and with the steering-oar in my hands hauled on the wind.

"There lies Japan," I remarked, "straight before us."

"Humphrey Van Weyden," she said, "you are a brave man."

"Nay," I answered, "it is you who are a brave woman."

We turned our heads, swayed by a common impulse to see the last of the *Ghost*. Her low hull lifted and rolled to windward on a sea; her canvas loomed darkly in the night; her lashed wheel creaked as the rudder kicked; then sight and sound of her faded away and we were alone on the dark sea.

CHAPTER TWENTY-SEVEN

DAY broke, gray and chill. The boat was close-hauled on
a fresh breeze and the compass indicated that we were just
making the course which would bring us to Japan. Though
stoutly mittened, my fingers were cold, and they pained
from the grip on the steering-oar. My feet were stinging
from the bite of the frost, and I hoped fervently that the
sun would shine.

Before me, in the bottom of the boat, lay Maud. She,
at least, was warm, for under her and over her were thick
blankets. The top one I had drawn over her face to shelter
it from the night, so I could see nothing but the vague
shape of her, and her light-brown hair, escaped from the
covering and jewelled with moisture from the air.

Long I looked at her, dwelling upon that one visible
bit of her as only a man would who deemed it the most
precious thing in the world. So insistent was my gaze that
at last she stirred under the blankets, the top fold was
thrown back and she smiled out on me, her eyes yet heavy
with sleep.

"Good morning, Mr. Van Weyden," she said. "Have you
sighted land yet?"

"No," I answered, "but we are approaching it at a rate
of six miles an hour."

She made a *moue* of disappointment.

"But that is equivalent to one hundred and forty-four
miles in twenty-four hours," I added reassuringly.

Her face brightened. "And how far have we to go?"

"Siberia lies off there," I said pointing to the west. "But
to the south-west, some six hundred miles, is Japan. If this
wind should hold, we'll make it in five days."

"And if it storms? The boat could not live?"

She had a way of looking one in the eyes and demanding the truth, and thus she looked at me as she asked the question.

"It would have to storm very hard," I temporized.

"And if it storms very hard?"

I nodded my head. "But we may be picked up any moment by a sealing schooner. They are plentifully distributed over this part of the ocean."

"Why, you are chilled through!" she cried. "Look! You are shivering. Don't deny it; you are. And here I have been lying warm as toast."

"I don't see that it would help matters, if you, too, sat up and were chilled," I laughed.

"It will, though, when I learn to steer, which I certainly shall."

She sat up and began making her simple toilet. She shook down her hair, and it fell about her in a brown cloud, hiding her face and shoulders. Dear, damp brown hair! I wanted to kiss it, to ripple it through my fingers, to bury my face in it. I gazed entranced, till the boat ran into the wind and the flapping sail warned me I was not attending to my duties. Idealist and romanticist that I was and always had been in spite of my analytical nature, yet I had failed till now in grasping much of the physical characteristics of love. The love of man and woman, I had always held, was a sublimated something related to spirit, a spiritual bond that linked and drew their souls together. The bonds of the flesh had little part in my cosmos of love. But I was learning the sweet lesson for myself that the soul transmuted itself, expressed itself, through the flesh; that the sight and sense and touch of the loved one's hair was as much breath and voice and essence of the spirit as the light that shone from the eyes and the thoughts that fell from the lips. After all, pure spirit was unknowable, a thing to be sensed and divined only; nor could it express itself in terms of itself. Jehovah was anthropomorphic because he could address himself to the Jews only in terms of their understanding; so he was conceived as in their own image; as a cloud, a pillar of fire, a tangible, physical something which the mind of the Israelites could grasp.

And so I gazed upon Maud's light-brown hair, and loved it, and learned more of love than all the poets and singers had taught me with all their songs and sonnets. She flung it back with a sudden adroit movement, and her face emerged, smiling.

"Why don't women wear their hair down always?" I asked. "It is so much more beautiful."

"If it didn't tangle so dreadfully," she laughed. "There! I've lost one of my precious hair-pins!"

I neglected the boat and had the sail spilling the wind again and again, such was my delight in following her every movement as she searched through the blankets for the pin. I was surprised, and joyfully, that she was so much the woman, and the display of each trait and mannerism that was characteristically feminine gave me keener joy. For I had been elevating her too highly in my concepts of her, removing her too far from the plane of the human, and too far from me. I had been making of her a creature goddess-like and unapproachable. So I hailed with delight the little traits that proclaimed her only woman after all, such as the toss of the head which flung back the cloud of hair, and the search for the pin. She was woman, my kind, on my plane, and the delightful intimacy of kind, of man and woman, was possible, as well as the reverence and awe in which I knew I should always hold her.

She found the pin with an adorable little cry, and I turned my attention more fully to my steering. I proceeded to experiment, lashing and wedging the steering-oar until the boat held on fairly well by the wind without my assistance. Occasionally it came up too close, or fell off too freely; but it always recovered itself and in the main behaved satisfactorily.

"And now we shall have breakfast," I said. "But first you must be more warmly clad."

I got out a heavy shirt, new from the slop-chest and made from blanket goods. I knew the kind, so thick and so close of texture that it could resist the rain and not be soaked through after hours of wetting. When she had slipped this on over her head, I exchanged the boy's cap she wore for a man's cap, large enough to cover her hair, and, when the flap was turned down, to completely cover her neck and ears. The effect was charming. Her face was of the sort that cannot but look well under all circumstances. Nothing could destroy its exquisite oval, its well-nigh classic lines, its delicately stencilled brows, its large brown eyes, clear-seeing and calm, gloriously calm.

A puff, slightly stronger than usual, struck us just then. The boat was caught as it obliquely crossed the crest of a wave. It went over suddenly, burying its gunwale level with the sea and shipping a bucketful or so of water. I was opening a can of tongue at the moment, and I sprang to the sheet and cast it off just in time. The sail flapped and fluttered, and the boat paid off. A few minutes of regulating sufficed to put it on its course again, when I returned to the preparation of breakfast.

"It does very well, it seems, though I am not versed in things nautical," she said, nodding her head with grave approval at my steering contrivance.

"But it will serve only when we are sailing by the wind," I explained. "When running more freely, with the wind astern, abeam, or on the quarter, it will be necessary for me to steer."

"I must say I don't understand your technicalities," she said, "but I do your conclusion, and I don't like it. You cannot steer night and day and forever. So I shall expect, after breakfast, to receive my first lesson. And then you shall lie down and sleep. We'll stand watches just as they do on ships."

"I don't see how I am to teach you," I made protest.
"I am just learning for myself. You little thought when
you trusted yourself to me that I had had no experience
whatever with small boats. This is the first time I have
ever been in one."

"Then we'll learn together, sir. And since you've had a
night's start you shall teach me what you have learned.
And now, breakfast. My! this air does give one an appetite!"

"No coffee," I said regretfully, passing her buttered sea-
biscuits and a slice of canned tongue. "And there will be
no tea, no soups, nothing hot, till we have made land
somewhere, somehow."

After the simple breakfast, capped with a cup of cold
water, Maud took her lesson in steering. In teaching her
I learned quite a deal myself, though I was applying the
knowledge already acquired by sailing the *Ghost* and by
watching the boat-steerers sail the small boats. She was
an apt pupil, and soon learned to keep the course, to luff
in the puffs and to cast off the sheet in an emergency.

Having grown tired, apparently, of the task, she relinquished the oar to me. I had folded up the blankets, but
she now proceeded to spread them out on the bottom.
When all was arranged snugly, she said:

"Now, sir, to bed. And you shall sleep until luncheon.
Till dinner-time," she corrected, remembering the arrangements on the *Ghost*.

What could I do? She insisted, and said, "Please, please,"
whereupon I turned the oar over to her and obeyed. I
experienced a positive sensuous delight as I crawled into
the bed she had made with her hands. The calm and
control which were so much a part of her seemed to have
been communicated to the blankets, so that I was aware
of a soft dreaminess and content, and of an oval face and
brown eyes framed in a fisherman's cap and tossing against
a background now of gray cloud, now of gray sea, and then

I was aware that I had been asleep.

I looked at my watch. It was one o'clock. I had slept seven hours! And she had been steering seven hours! When I took the steering-oar I had first to unbend her cramped fingers. Her modicum of strength had been exhausted, and she was unable even to move from her position. I was compelled to let go the sheet while I helped her to the nest of blankets and chafed her hands and arms.

"I am so tired," she said, with a quick intake of the breath and a sigh, drooping her head wearily.

But she straightened it the next moment. "Now don't scold, don't you dare scold," she cried with mock defiance.

"I hope my face does not appear angry," I answered seriously; "for I assure you I am not in the least angry."

"N—no," she considered. "It looks only reproachful."

"Then it is an honest face, for it looks what I feel. You were not fair to yourself, nor to me. How can I ever trust you again?"

She looked penitent. "I'll be good," she said, as a naughty child might say it. "I promise—"

"To obey as a sailor would obey his captain?"

"Yes," she answered. "It was stupid of me, I know."

"Then you must promise something else," I ventured.

"Readily."

"That you will not say, 'Please, please,' too often; for when you do you are sure to override my authority."

She laughed with amused appreciation. She, too, had noticed the power of the repeated "please."

"It is a good word—" I began.

"But I must not overwork it," she broke in.

But she laughed weakly, and her head drooped again. I left the oar long enough to tuck the blankets about her feet and to pull a single fold across her face. Alas! she was not strong. I looked with misgiving toward the southwest and thought of the six hundred miles of hardship before us—ay, if it were no worse than hardship. On this sea a storm might blow up at any moment and destroy us. And yet I was unafraid. I was without confidence in the future, extremely doubtful, and yet I felt no underlying fear. It must come right, it must come right, I repeated to myself, over and over again.

The wind freshened in the afternoon, raising a stiffer sea and trying the boat and me severely. But the supply of food and the nine breakers of water enabled the boat to stand up to the sea and wind, and I held on as long as I dared. Then I removed the sprit, tightly hauling down the peak of the sail, and we raced along under what sailors call a leg-of-mutton.

Late in the afternoon I sighted a steamer's smoke on the horizon to leeward, and I knew it either for a Russian cruiser, or, more likely, the *Macedonia* still seeking the *Ghost*. The sun had not shone all day, and it had been bitter cold. As night drew on, the clouds darkened and the wind freshened, so that when Maud and I ate supper it was with our mittens on and with me still steering and eating morsels between puffs.

By the time it was dark, wind and sea had become too strong for the boat, and I reluctantly took in the sail and set about making a drag or sea-anchor. I had learned of the device from the talk of the hunters, and it was a simple thing to manufacture. Furling the sail and lashing it securely about the mast, boom, sprit, and two pairs of spare oars, I threw it overboard. A line connected it with the bow, and as it floated low in the water, practically unexposed to the wind, it drifted less rapidly than the boat. In consequence it held the boat bow on to the sea and wind—the safest position in which to escape being swamped when the sea is breaking into white-caps.

"And now?" Maud asked cheerfully, when the task was accomplished and I pulled on my mittens.

"And now we are no longer travelling toward Japan," I

answered. "Our drift is to the southeast, or south-southeast, at the rate of at least two miles an hour."

"That will be only twenty-four miles," she urged, "if the wind remains high all night."

"Yes, and only one hundred and forty miles if it continues for three days and nights."

"But it won't continue," she said, with easy confidence. "It will turn around and blow fair."

"The sea is the great faithless one."

"But the wind!" she retorted. "I have heard you grow eloquent over the brave trade-wind."

"I wish I had thought to bring Wolf Larsen's chronometer and sextant," I said, still gloomily. "Sailing one direction, drifting another direction, to say nothing of the set of the current in some third direction, makes a resultant which dead reckoning can never calculate. Before long we won't know where we are by five hundred miles."

Then I begged her pardon and promised I should not be disheartened any more. At her solicitation I let her take the watch till midnight,—it was then nine o'clock, but I wrapped her in blankets and put an oilskin about her before I lay down. I slept only cat-naps. The boat was leaping and pounding as it fell over the crests, I could hear the seas rushing past, and spray was continually being thrown aboard. And still, it was not a bad night, I mused—nothing to the nights I had been through on the *Ghost*; nothing, perhaps, to the nights we should go through in this cockle-shell. Its planking was three-quarters of an inch thick. Between us and the bottom of the sea was less than an inch of wood.

And yet, I aver it, and I aver it again, I was unafraid. The death which Wolf Larsen and even Thomas Mugridge had made me fear, I no longer feared. The coming of Maud Brewster into my life seemed to have transformed me. After all, I thought, it is better and finer to love than to be loved, if it makes something in life so worth while that one is not loath to die for it. I forget my own life in the love of another life; and yet, such is the paradox, I never wanted so much to live as right now when I place the least value upon my own life. I never had so much reason for living, was my concluding thought; and after that, until I dozed, I contented myself with trying to pierce the darkness to where I knew Maud crouched low in the stern-sheets, watchful of the foaming sea and ready to call me on an instant's notice.

CHAPTER TWENTY-EIGHT

THERE is no need of going into an extended recital of our suffering in the small boat during the many days we were driven and drifted, here and there, willy-nilly, across the ocean. The high wind blew from the northwest for twenty-four hours, when it fell calm, and in the night sprang up from the southwest. This was dead in our teeth, but I took in the sea-anchor and set sail, hauling a course on the wind which took us in a south-southeasterly direction. It was an even choice between this and the west-northwesterly course which the wind permitted; but the warm airs of the south fanned my desire for a warmer sea and swayed my decision.

In three hours,—it was midnight, I well remember, and as dark as I had ever seen it on the sea,—the wind, still blowing out of the southwest, rose furiously, and once again I was compelled to set the sea-anchor.

Day broke and found me wan-eyed and the ocean lashed white, the boat pitching, almost on end, to its drag. We were in imminent danger of being swamped by the white-caps. As it was, spray and spume came aboard in such quantities that I bailed without cessation. The blankets were soaking. Everything was wet except Maud, and she, in oilskins, rubber boots, and sou'wester, was dry, all but her face and hands and a stray wisp of hair. She relieved me at the bailing-hole from time to time, and bravely she threw out the water and faced the storm. All things are relative. It was no more than a stiff blow, but to us, fighting for life in our frail craft, it was indeed a storm.

Cold and cheerless, the wind beating on our faces, the white seas roaring by, we struggled through the day. Night came, but neither of us slept. Day came, and still the wind beat on our faces and the white seas roared past. By the second night Maud was falling asleep from exhaustion. I covered her with oilskins and a tarpaulin. She was comparatively dry, but she was numb with the cold. I feared greatly that she might die in the night; but day broke, cold and cheerless, with the same clouded sky and beating wind and roaring seas.

I had had no sleep for forty-eight hours. I was wet and chilled to the marrow, till I felt more dead than alive. My body was stiff from exertion as well as from cold, and my aching muscles gave me the severest torture whenever I used them, and I used them continually. And all the time we were being driven off into the northeast, directly away from Japan and toward bleak Bering Sea.

And still we lived, and the boat lived, and the wind blew unabated. In fact, toward nightfall of the third day it increased a trifle and something more. The boat's bow plunged under a crest, and we came through quarter-full of water. I bailed like a madman. The liability of shipping another such sea was enormously increased by the water that weighed the boat down and robbed it of its buoyancy. And another such sea meant the end. When I had the boat empty again I was forced to take away the tarpaulin which covered Maud, in order that I might lash it down across the bow. It was well I did, for it covered the boat fully a third of the way aft, and three times, in the next several hours, it flung off the bulk of the down-rushing water when the bow shoved under the seas.

Maud's condition was pitiable. She sat crouched in the bottom of the boat, her lips blue, her face gray and plainly showing the pain she suffered. But ever her eyes looked bravely at me, and ever her lips uttered brave words.

The worst of the storm must have blown that night, though little I noticed it. I had succumbed and slept where I sat in the stern-sheets. The morning of the fourth day found the wind diminished to a gentle whisper, the sea dying down and the sun shining upon us. Oh, the blessed sun! How we bathed our poor bodies in its delicious warmth, reviving like bugs and crawling things after a storm. We smiled again, said amusing things, and waxed optimistic over our situation. Yet it was, if anything, worse than ever. We were farther from Japan than the night we left the *Ghost.* Nor could I more than roughly guess our latitude and longitude. At a calculation of a two-mile drift per hour, during the seventy and odd hours of the storm, we had been driven at least one hundred and fifty miles to the northeast. But was such calculated drift correct? For all I knew, it might have been four miles per hour instead of two. In which case we were another hundred and fifty miles to the bad.

Where we were I did not know, though there was quite a likelihood that we were in the vicinity of the *Ghost.* There were seals about us, and I was prepared to sight a sealing schooner at any time. We did sight one, in the afternoon, when the northwest breeze had sprung up freshly once more. But the strange schooner lost itself on the sky-line and we alone occupied the circle of the sea.

Came days of fog, when even Maud's spirit drooped and there were no merry words upon her lips; days of calm, when we floated on the lonely immensity of sea, oppressed by its greatness and yet marvelling at the miracle of tiny life, for we still lived and struggled to live; days of sleet and wind and snow-squalls, when nothing could keep us warm; or days of drizzling rain, when we filled our water-breakers from the drip of the wet sail.

And ever I loved Maud with an increasing love. She was so many-sided, so many-mooded—"protean-mooded" I called her. But I called her this, and other and dearer things, in my thoughts only. Though the declaration of my love urged and trembled on my tongue a thousand times, I knew that it was no time for such a declaration. If for no other reason, it was no time, when one was protecting and trying to save a woman, to ask that woman for her love. Delicate as was the situation, not alone in this but in other ways, I flattered myself that I was able to deal delicately with it; and also I flattered myself that by look or sign I gave no advertisement of the love I felt for her. We were like good comrades, and we grew better comrades as the days went by.

One thing about her which surprised me was her lack of timidity and fear. The terrible sea, the frail boat, the storms, the suffering, the strangeness and isolation of the situation,—all that should have frightened a robust woman,—seemed to make no impression upon her who had known life only in its most sheltered and consummately artificial aspects, and who was herself all fire and dew and mist, sublimated spirit, all that was soft and tender and clinging in woman. And yet I am wrong. She *was* timid and afraid, but she possessed courage. The flesh and the qualms of the flesh she was heir to, but the flesh bore heavily only on the flesh. And she was spirit, first and always spirit, etherealized essence of life, calm as her calm eyes, and sure of permanence in the changing order of the universe.

Came days of storm, days and nights of storm, when the ocean menaced us with its roaring whiteness, and the wind smote our struggling boat with a Titan's buffets. And ever we were flung off, farther and farther, to the northeast. It was in such a storm, and the worst that we had experienced, that I cast a weary glance to leeward, not in quest of anything, but more from the weariness of facing the elemental strife, and in mute appeal, almost, to the wrathful powers to cease and let us be. What I saw I could not at first believe. Days and nights of sleeplessness and anxiety had doubtless turned my head. I looked back at Maud, to identify myself, as it were, in time and space. The sight of her dear wet cheeks, her flying hair, and her brave brown eyes convinced me that my vision was still healthy. Again I turned my face to leeward, and again I saw the jutting promontory, black and high and naked, the raging surf that broke about its base and beat its front high up with spouting fountains, the black and forbidding coastline running toward the southeast and fringed with a tremendous scarf of white.

"Maud," I said. "Maud."

She turned her head and beheld the sight.

"It cannot be Alaska!" she cried.

"Alas, no," I answered, and asked, "Can you swim?"

She shook her head.

"Neither can I," I said. "So we must get ashore without swimming, in some opening between the rocks through which we can drive the boat and clamber out. But we must be quick, most quick—and sure."

I spoke with a confidence she knew I did not feel, for she looked at me with that unfaltering gaze of hers and said:

"I have not thanked you yet for all you have done for me, but—"

She hesitated, as if in doubt how best to word her gratitude.

"Well?" I said, brutally, for I was not quite pleased with her thanking me.

"You might help me," she smiled.

"To acknowledge your obligations before you die? Not at all. We are not going to die. We shall land on that island, and we shall be snug and sheltered before day is done."

I spoke stoutly, but I did not believe a word. Nor was I prompted to lie through fear. I felt no fear, though I was sure of death in that boiling surge amongst the rocks which was rapidly growing nearer. It was impossible to hoist sail and claw off that shore. The wind would instantly capsize the boat; the seas would swamp it the moment it fell into the trough; and, besides, the sail, lashed to the spare oars, dragged in the sea ahead of us.

As I say, I was not afraid to meet my own death, there,

a few hundred yards to leeward; but I was appalled at the thought that Maud must die. My cursed imagination saw her beaten and mangled against the rocks, and it was too terrible. I strove to compel myself to think we would make the landing safely, and so I spoke, not what I believed, but what I preferred to believe.

I recoiled before contemplation of that frightful death, and for a moment I entertained the wild idea of seizing Maud in my arms and leaping overboard. Then I resolved to wait, and at the last moment, when we entered on the final stretch, to take her in my arms and proclaim my love, and, with her in my embrace, to make the desperate struggle and die.

Instinctively we drew closer together in the bottom of the boat. I felt her mittened hand come out to mine. And thus, without speech, we waited the end. We were not far off the line the wind made with the western edge of the promontory, and I watched in the hope that some set of the current or send of the sea would drift us past before we reached the surf.

"We shall go clear," I said, with a confidence which I knew deceived neither of us.

"By God, we *will* go clear!" I cried, five minutes later.

The oath left my lips in my excitement—the first, I do believe, in my life, unless "trouble it," an expletive of my youth, be accounted an oath.

"I beg your pardon," I said.

"You have convinced me of your sincerity," she said, with a faint smile. "I do know, now, that we shall go clear."

I had seen a distant headland past the extreme edge of the promontory, and as we looked we could see grow the intervening coast-line of what was evidently a deep cove. At the same time there broke upon our ears a continuous and mighty bellowing. It partook of the magnitude and volume of distant thunder, and it came to us directly from leeward, rising above the crash of the surf and travelling

directly in the teeth of the storm. As we passed the point
the whole cove burst upon our view, a half-moon of white
sandy beach upon which broke a huge surf, and which was
covered with myriads of seals. It was from them that the
great bellowing went up.

"A rookery!" I cried. "Now are we indeed saved. There
must be men and cruisers to protect them from the seal-
hunters. Possibly there is a station ashore."

But as I studied the surf which beat upon the beach,
I said, "Still bad, but not so bad. And now, if the gods
be truly kind, we shall drift by that next headland and
come upon a perfectly sheltered beach, where we may land
without wetting our feet."

And the gods were kind. The first and second headlands
were directly in line with the southwest wind; but once
around the second,—and we went perilously near,—we
picked up the third headland, still in line with the wind
and with the other two. But the cove that intervened! It
penetrated deep into the land, and the tide, setting in,
drifted us under the shelter of the point. Here the sea was
calm, save for a heavy but smooth ground-swell, and I took
in the sea-anchor and began to row. From the point the
shore curved away, more and more to the south and west,
until, at last, it disclosed a cove within the cove, a little
land-locked harbor, the water level as a pond, broken only
by tiny ripples where vagrant breaths and wisps of the
storm hurtled down from over the frowning wall of rock
that backed the beach a hundred feet inshore.

Here were no seals whatever. The boat's stem touched
the hard shingle. I sprang out, extending my hand to
Maud. The next moment she was beside me. As my fingers
released hers, she clutched for my arm hastily. At the same
moment I swayed, as about to fall to the sand. This was
the startling effect of the cessation of motion. We had been
so long upon the moving, rocking sea that the stable land
was a shock to us. We expected the beach to lift up this

way and that, and the rocky walls to swing back and forth like the sides of a ship; and when we braced ourselves, automatically, for these various expected movements, their non-occurrence quite overcame our equilibrium.

"I really must sit down," Maud said, with a nervous laugh and a dizzy gesture, and forthwith she sat down on the sand.

I attended to making the boat secure and joined her. Thus we landed on Endeavor Island,* as we came to it, land-sick from long custom of the sea.

CHAPTER TWENTY-NINE

"FOOL!" I cried aloud in my vexation.

I had unloaded the boat and carried its contents high up on the beach, where I had set about making a camp. There was driftwood, though not much, on the beach, and the sight of a coffee tin I had taken from the *Ghost*'s larder had given me the idea of a fire.

"Blithering idiot!" I was continuing.

But Maud said, "Tut, tut," in gentle reproval, and then asked why I was a blithering idiot.

"No matches," I groaned. "Not a match did I bring. And now we shall have no hot coffee, soup, tea, or anything!"

"Wasn't it—er—Crusoe* who rubbed sticks together?" she drawled.

"But I have read the personal narratives of a score of ship-wrecked men who tried, and tried in vain," I answered. "I remember Winters,* a newspaper fellow with an Alaskan and Siberian reputation. Met him at the Bibelot once, and he was telling us how he attempted to make a fire with a couple of sticks. It was most amusing. He told it inimitably, but it was the story of a failure. I remember his conclusion, his black eyes flashing as he said, 'Gentlemen, the South Sea Islander may do it, the Malay may do it, but take my word it's beyond the white man.'"

"Oh, well, we've managed so far without it," she said cheerfully. "And there's no reason why we cannot still manage without it."

"But think of the coffee!" I cried. "It's good coffee, too. I know. I took it from Larsen's private stores. And look at that good wood."

I confess, I wanted the coffee badly; and I learned, not

long afterward, that the berry was likewise a little weakness of Maud's. Besides, we had been so long on a cold diet that we were numb inside as well as out. Anything warm would have been most gratifying. But I complained no more, and set about making a tent of the sail for Maud.

I had looked upon it as a simple task, what of the oars, mast, boom, and sprit, to say nothing of plenty of lines. But as I was without experience, and as every detail was an experiment and every successful detail an invention, the day was well gone before her shelter was an accomplished fact. And then, that night, it rained, and she was flooded out and driven back into the boat.

The next morning I dug a shallow ditch around the tent, and, an hour later, a sudden gust of wind, whipping over the rocky wall behind us, picked up the tent and smashed it down on the sand thirty yards away.

Maud laughed at my crestfallen expression, and I said, "As soon as the wind abates I intend going in the boat to explore the island. There must be a station somewhere, and men. And ships must visit the station. Some government must protect all these seals. But I wish to have you comfortable before I start."

"I should like to go with you," was all she said.

"It would be better if you remained. You have had enough of hardship. It is a miracle that you have survived. And it won't be comfortable in the boat, rowing and sailing in this rainy weather. What you need it rest, and I should like you to remain and get it."

Something suspiciously akin to moistness dimmed her beautiful eyes before she dropped them and partly turned away her head.

"I should prefer going with you," she said in a low voice, in which there was just a hint of appeal.

"I might be able to help you a—" her voice broke,—"a little. And if anything should happen to you, think of me left here alone."

"Oh, I intend being very careful," I answered. "And I shall not go so far but what I can get back before night. Yes, all said and done, I think it vastly better for you to remain, and sleep, and rest, and do nothing."

She turned and looked me in the eyes. Her gaze was unfaltering, but soft.

"Please, please," she said, oh, so softly.

I stiffened myself to refuse, and shook my head. Still she waited and looked at me. I tried to word my refusal, but wavered. I saw the glad light spring into her eyes and knew that I had lost. It was impossible to say no after that.

The wind died down in the afternoon, and we were prepared to start the following morning. There was no way of penetrating the island from our cove, for the walls rose perpendicularly from the beach, and, on either side of the cove, rose from the deep water.

Morning broke dull and gray, but calm, and I was awake early and had the boat in readiness.

"Fool! Imbecile! Yahoo!" I shouted, when I thought it was meet to arouse Maud; but this time I shouted in merriment as I danced about the beach, bareheaded, in mock despair.

Her head appeared under the flap of the sail.

"What now?" she asked sleepily, and, withal, curiously.

"Coffee!" I cried. "What do you say to a cup of coffee? hot coffee? piping hot?"

"My!" she murmured, "you startled me, and you are cruel. Here I have been composing my soul to do without it, and here you are vexing me with your vain suggestions."

"Watch me," I said.

From under clefts among the rocks I gathered a few dry sticks and chips. These I whittled into shavings or split into kindling. From my note-book I tore out a page, and from the ammunition box took a shotgun shell. Removing the wads from the latter with my knife, I emptied the powder on a flat rock. Next I pried the primer, or cap, from the

shell, and laid it on the rock in the midst of the scattered
powder. All was ready. Maud still watched from the tent.
Holding the paper in my left hand, I smashed down upon
the cap with a rock held in my right. There was a puff of
white smoke, a burst of flame, and the rough edge of the
paper was alight.

Maud clapped her hands gleefully. "Prometheus!" she
cried.

But I was too occupied to acknowledge her delight. The
feeble flame must be cherished tenderly if it were to gather
strength and live. I fed it, shaving by shaving, and sliver
by sliver, till at last it was snapping and crackling as it laid
hold of the smaller chips and sticks. To be cast away on
an island had not entered into my calculations, so we were
without a kettle or cooking utensils of any sort; but I made
shift with the tin used for bailing the boat, and later, as
we consumed our supply of canned goods, we accumulated
quite an imposing array of cooking vessels.

I boiled the water, but it was Maud who made the coffee.
And how good it was! My contribution was canned beef
fried with crumbled sea-biscuit and water. The breakfast
was a success, and we sat about the fire much longer than
enterprising explorers should have done, sipping the hot
black coffee and talking over our situation.

I was confident that we should find a station in some one
of the coves, for I knew that the rookeries of Bering Sea
were thus guarded; but Maud advanced the theory,—to
prepare me for disappointment, I do believe, if disappointment were to come,—that we had discovered an unknown
rookery. She was in very good spirits, however, and made
quite merry in accepting our plight as a grave one.

"If you are right," I said, "then we must prepare to
winter here. Our food will not last, but there are the seals.
They go away in the fall, so I must soon begin to lay in
a supply of meat. Then there will be huts to build and
driftwood to gather. Also, we shall try out seal fat for

lighting purposes. Altogether, we'll have our hands full
if we find the island uninhabited. Which we shall not, I
know."

But she was right. We sailed with a beam wind along
the shore, searching the coves with our glasses and landing
occasionally, without finding a sign of human life. Yet we
learned that we were not the first who had landed on
Endeavor Island. High up on the beach of the second cove
from ours, we discovered the splintered wreck of a boat—a
sealer's boat, for the rowlocks were bound in sennit, a gun-
rack was on the starboard side of the bow, and in white
letters was faintly visible *Gazelle No. 2*. The boat had lain
there for a long time, for it was half filled with sand, and
the splintered wood had that weather-worn appearance
due to long exposure to the elements. In the sternsheets
I found a rusty ten-gauge shotgun and a sailor's sheath-
knife broken short across and so rusted as to be almost
unrecognizable.

"They got away," I said cheerfully; but I felt a sinking
at the heart and seemed to divine the presence of bleached
bones somewhere on that beach.

I did not wish Maud's spirits to be dampened by such a
find, so I turned seaward again with our boat and skirted
the northeastern point of the island. There were no beaches
on the southern shore, and by early afternoon we rounded
the black promontory and completed the circumnavigation
of the island. I estimated its circumference at twenty-five
miles, its width as varying from two to five miles; while
my most conservative calculation placed on its beaches
two hundred thousand seals. The island was highest at
its extreme southwestern point, the headlands and backbone diminishing regularly until the northeastern portion
was only a few feet above the sea. With the exception
of our little cove, the other beaches sloped gently back
for a distance of half a mile or so, into what I might call
rocky meadows, with here and there patches of moss and

tundra grass. Here the seals hauled out, and the old bulls
guarded their harems, while the young bulls hauled out by
themselves.

This brief description is all that Endeavor Island merits.
Damp and soggy where it was not sharp and rocky, buffeted by storm winds and lashed by the sea, with the air
continually a-tremble with the bellowing of two hundred
thousand amphibians, it was a melancholy and miserable
sojourning place. Maud, who had prepared me for disappointment, and who had been sprightly and vivacious all
day, broke down as we landed in our own little cove. She
strove bravely to hide it from me, but while I was kindling
another fire I knew she was stifling her sobs in the blankets
under the sail-tent.

It was my turn to be cheerful, and I played the part to
the best of my ability, and with such success that I brought
the laughter back into her dear eyes and song on her lips;
for she sang to me before she went to an early bed. It
was the first time I had heard her sing, and I lay by the
fire, listening and transported, for she was nothing if not
an artist in everything she did, and her voice, though not
strong, was wonderfully sweet and expressive.

I still slept in the boat, and I lay awake long that night,
gazing up at the first stars I had seen in many nights and
pondering the situation. Responsibility of this sort was a
new thing to me. Wolf Larsen had been quite right. I had
stood on my father's legs. My lawyers and agents had taken
care of my money for me. I had had no responsibilities at
all. Then, on the *Ghost* I had learned to be responsible
for myself. And now, for the first time in my life, I found
myself responsible for some one else. And it was required
of me that this should be the gravest of responsibilities,
for she was the one woman in the world—the one small
woman, as I loved to think of her.

CHAPTER THIRTY

NO wonder we called it Endeavor Island. For two weeks we toiled at building a hut. Maud insisted on helping, and I could have wept over her bruised and bleeding hands. And still, I was proud of her because of it. There was something heroic about this gently bred woman enduring our terrible hardship and with her pittance of strength bending to the tasks of a peasant woman. She gathered many of the stones which I built into the walls of the hut; also, she turned a deaf ear to my entreaties when I begged her to desist. She compromised, however, by taking upon herself the lighter labors of cooking and gathering driftwood and moss for our winter's supply.

The hut's walls rose without difficulty, and everything went smoothly until the problem of the roof confronted me. Of what use the four walls without a roof? And of what could a roof be made? There were the spare oars, very true. They would serve as roof-beams; but with what was I to cover them? Moss would never do. Tundra grass was impracticable. We needed the sail for the boat, and the tarpaulin had begun to leak.

"Winters used walrus skins on his hut," I said.

"There are the seals," she suggested.

So next day the hunting began. I did not know how to shoot, but I proceeded to learn. And when I had expended some thirty shells for three seals, I decided that the ammunition would be exhausted before I acquired the necessary knowledge. I had used eight shells for lighting fires before I hit upon the device of banking the embers with wet moss, and there remained not over a hundred shells in the box.

"We must club the seals," I announced, when convinced

of my poor marksmanship. "I have heard the sealers talk about clubbing them."

"They are so pretty," she objected. "I cannot bear to think of it being done. It is so directly brutal, you know; so different from shooting them."

"That roof must go on," I answered grimly. "Winter is almost here. It is our lives against theirs. It is unfortunate we haven't plenty of ammunition, but I think, anyway, that they suffer less from being clubbed than from being all shot up. Besides, I shall do the clubbing."

"That's just it," she began eagerly, and broke off in sudden confusion.

"Of course," I began. "If you prefer—"

"But what shall I be doing?" she interrupted, with that softness I knew full well to be insistence.

"Gathering firewood and cooking dinner," I answered lightly.

She shook her head. "It is too dangerous for you to attempt alone."

"I know, I know," she waived my protest. "I am only a weak woman, but just my small assistance may enable you to escape disaster."

"But the clubbing?" I suggested.

"Of course, you will do that. I shall probably scream. I'll look away when—"

"The danger is most serious," I laughed.

"I shall use my judgment when to look and when not to look," she replied with a grand air.

The upshot of the affair was that she accompanied me next morning. I rowed into the adjoining cove and up to the edge of the beach. There were seals all about us in the water, and the bellowing thousands on the beach compelled us to shout at each other to make ourselves heard.

"I know men club them," I said, trying to reassure myself and gazing doubtfully at a large bull, not thirty feet away, upreared on his fore-flippers and regarding me intently. "But the question is, how do they club them?"

"Let us gather tundra grass and thatch the roof," Maud said.

She was as frightened as I at the prospect, and we had reason to be, gazing at close range at the gleaming teeth and dog-like mouths.

"I always though they were afraid of men," I said.

"How do I know they are not afraid?" I queried a moment later, after having rowed a few more strokes along the beach.

"Perhaps, if I were to step boldly ashore, they would cut for it, and I could not catch up with one."

And still I hesitated.

"I heard of a man, once, who invaded the nesting grounds of wild geese," Maud said. "They killed him."

"The geese?"

"Yes, the geese. My brother told me about it when I was a little girl."

"But I know men club them," I persisted.

"I think the tundra grass will make just as good a roof," she said.

Far from her intention, her words were maddening me, driving me on. I could not play the coward before her eyes.

"Here goes," I said, backing water with one oar and running the bow ashore.

I stepped out and advanced valiantly upon a long-maned bull in the midst of his wives. I was armed with the regular club with which the boat-pullers killed the wounded seals gaffed aboard by the hunters. It was only a foot and a half long, and in my superb ignorance I never dreamed that the club used ashore when raiding the rookeries measured four to five feet. The cows lumbered out of my way, and the distance between me and the bull decreased. He raised himself on his flippers with an angry movement. We were a dozen feet apart. Still I advanced

steadily, looking for him to turn tail at any moment and
run.

At six feet the panicky thought rushed into my mind,
What if he will not run? Why, then I shall club him,
came the answer. In my fear I had forgotten that I was
there to get the bull instead of to make him run. And just
then he gave a snort and a snarl and rushed at me. His
eyes were blazing, his mouth was wide open; the teeth
gleamed cruelly white. Without shame, I confess that
it was I who turned and footed it. He ran awkwardly,
but he ran well. He was but two paces behind when
I tumbled into the boat, and as I shoved off with an
oar his teeth crunched down upon the blade. The stout
wood was crushed like an egg-shell. Maud and I were
astounded. A moment later he had dived under the boat,
seized the keel in his mouth, and was shaking the boat
violently.

"My!" said Maud. "Let's go back."

I shook my head. "I can do what other men have done,
and I know that other men have clubbed seals. But I think
I'll leave the bulls alone next time."

"I wish you wouldn't," she said.

"Now don't say, 'Please, please,' " I cried, half angrily,
I do believe.

She made no reply, and I knew my tone must have hurt
her.

"I beg your pardon," I said, or shouted, rather, in order
to make myself heard above the roar of the rookery. "If
you say so, I'll turn and go back; but honestly, I'd rather
stay."

"Now don't say that this is what you get for bringing
a woman along," she said. She smiled at me whimsically,
gloriously, and I knew there was no need for forgiveness.

I rowed a couple of hundred feet along the beach so as
to recover my nerves, and then stepped ashore again.

"Do be cautious," she called after me.

I nodded my head and proceeded to make a flank attack on the nearest harem. All went well until I aimed a blow at an outlying cow's head and fell short. She snorted and tried to scramble away. I ran in close and struck another blow, hitting the shoulder instead of the head.

"Watch out!" I heard Maud scream.

In my excitement I had not been taking notice of other things, and I looked up to see the lord of the harem charging down upon me. Again I fled to the boat, hotly pursued; but this time Maud made no suggestion of turning back.

"It would be better, I imagine, if you let harems alone and devoted your attention to lonely and inoffensive-looking seals," was what she said. "I think I have read something about them. Dr. Jordan's book,* I believe. They are the young bulls, not old enough to have harems of their own. He called them the holluschickie,* or something like that. It seems to me if we find where they haul out—"

"It seems to me that your fighting instinct is aroused," I laughed.

She flushed quickly and prettily. "I'll admit I don't like defeat any more than you do, or any more than I like the idea of killing such pretty, inoffensive creatures."

"Pretty!" I sniffed. "I failed to mark anything pre-eminently pretty about those foamy-mouthed beasts that raced me."

"Your point of view," she laughed. "You lacked perspective. Now if you did not have to get so close to the subject—"

"The very thing!" I cried. "What I need is a longer club. And there's that broken oar ready to hand."

"It just comes to me," she said, "that Captain Larsen was telling me how the men raided the rookeries. They drive the seals, in small herds, a short distance inland before they kill them."

"I don't care to undertake the herding of one of those harems," I objected.

"But there are the holluschickie," she said. "The holluschickie haul out by themselves, and Dr. Jordan says that paths are left between the harems, and that as long as the holluschickie keep strictly to the path they are unmolested by the masters of the harem."

"There's one now," I said, pointing to a young bull in the water. "Let's watch him, and follow him if he hauls out."

He swam directly to the beach and clambered out into a small opening between two harems, the masters of which made warning noises but did not attack him. We watched him travel slowly inward, threading about among the harems along what must have been the path.

"Here goes," I said, stepping out; but I confess my heart was in my mouth as I thought of going through the heart of that monstrous herd.

"It would be wise to make the boat fast," Maud said.

She had stepped out beside me, and I regarded her with wonderment.

She nodded her head determinedly. "Yes, I'm going with you, so you may as well secure the boat and arm me with a club."

"Let's go back," I said dejectedly. "I think tundra grass will do, after all."

"You know it won't," was her reply. "Shall I lead?"

With a shrug of the shoulders, but with the warmest admiration and pride at heart for this woman, I equipped her with the broken oar and took another for myself. It was with nervous trepidation that we made the first few rods of the journey. Once Maud screamed in terror as a cow thrust an inquisitive nose toward her foot, and several times I quickened my pace for the same reason. But, beyond warning coughs from either side, there were no signs of hostility. It was a rookery which had never been raided by the hunters, and in consequence the seals were mild-tempered and at the same time unafraid.

In the very heart of the herd the din was terrific. It was almost dizzying in its effect. I paused and smiled reassuringly at Maud, for I had recovered my equanimity sooner than she. I could see that she was still badly frightened. She came close to me and shouted:

"I'm dreadfully afraid!"

And I was not. Though the novelty had not yet worn off, the peaceful comportment of the seals had quieted my alarm. Maud was trembling.

"I'm afraid, and I'm not afraid," she chattered with shaking jaws. "It's my miserable body, not I."

"It's all right, it's all right," I reassured her, my arm passing instinctively and protectingly around her.

I shall never forget, in that moment, how instantly conscious I became of my manhood. The primitive deeps of my nature stirred. I felt myself masculine, the protector of the weak, the fighting male. And, best of all, I felt myself the protector of my loved one. She leaned against me, so light and lily-frail, and as her trembling eased away it seemed as though I became aware of prodigious strength. I felt myself a match for the most ferocious bull in the herd, and I know, had such a bull charged upon me, that I should have met it unflinchingly and quite coolly, and I know that I should have killed it.

"I am all right now," she said, looking up at me gratefully. "Let us go on."

And that the strength in me had quieted her and given her confidence, filled me with an exultant joy. The youth of the race seemed burgeoning in me, over-civilized man that I was, and I lived for myself the old hunting days and forest nights of my remote and forgotten ancestry. I had much for which to thank Wolf Larsen, was my thought as we went along the path between the jostling harems.

A quarter of a mile inland we came upon the holluschickie, sleek young bulls, living out the loneliness of their bachelorhood and gathering strength against the

day when they would fight their way into the ranks of the
benedicts.*

Everything now went smoothly. I seemed to know just
what to do and how to do it. Shouting, making threatening
gestures with my club, and even prodding the lazy ones, I
quickly cut out a score of the young bachelors from their
companions. Whenever one made an attempt to break
back toward the water, I headed it off. Maud took an active
part in the drive, and with her cries and flourishings of
the broken oar was of considerable assistance. I noticed,
though, that whenever one looked tired and lagged, she
let it slip past. But I noticed, also, whenever one, with a
show of fight, tried to break past, that her eyes glinted and
showed bright, and she rapped it smartly with her club.

"My, it's exciting!" she cried, pausing from sheer weakness. "I think I'll sit down."

I drove the little herd (a dozen strong, now, what of the
escapes she had permitted) a hundred yards farther on;
and by the time she joined me I had finished the slaughter
and was beginning to skin. An hour later we went proudly
back along the path between the harems. And twice again
we came down the path burdened with skins, till I thought
we had enough to roof the hut. I set the sail, laid one tack
out of the cove, and on the other tack made our own little
inner cove.

"It's just like home-coming," Maud said, as I ran the
boat ashore.

I heard her words with a responsive thrill, it was all so
dearly intimate and natural, and I said:

"It seems as though I have lived this life always. The
world of books and bookish folk is very vague, more like
a dream memory than an actuality. I surely have hunted
and forayed and fought all the days of my life. And you,
too, seem a part of it. You are—" I was on the verge of
saying, "my woman, my mate,"* but glibly changed it to—
"standing the hardship well."

But her ear had caught the flaw. She recognized a flight that midmost broke. She gave me a quick look.

"Not that. You were saying—?"

"That the American Mrs. Meynell was living the life of a savage and living it quite successfully," I said easily.

"Oh," was all she replied; but I could have sworn there was a note of disappointment in her voice.

But "my woman, my mate" kept ringing in my head for the rest of the day and for many days. Yet never did it ring more loudly than that night, as I watched her draw back the blanket of moss from the coals, blow up the fire, and cook the evening meal. It must have been latent savagery stirring in me, for the old words, so bound up with the roots of the race, to grip me and thrill me. And grip and thrill they did, till I fell asleep, murmuring them to myself over and over again.

CHAPTER THIRTY-ONE

IT will smell," I said, "but it will keep in the heat and keep out the rain and snow."

We were surveying the completed sealskin roof.

"It is clumsy, but it will serve the purpose, and that is the main thing," I went on, yearning for her praise.

And she clapped her hands and declared that she was hugely pleased.

"You might have suggested a window when the walls were going up," I said. "It was for you, and you should have seen the need of a window."

"But I never do see the obvious, you know," she laughed back. "And besides, you can knock a hole in the wall at any time."

"Quite true; I had not thought of it," I replied, wagging my head sagely. "But have you thought of ordering the window-glass? Just call up the firm,—Red, 4451,* I think it is,—and tell them what size and kind of glass you wish."

"That means—" she began.

"No window."

It was a dark and evil-appearing thing, that hut, not fit for aught better than swine in a civilized land; but for us, who had known the misery of the open boat, it was a snug little habitation. Following the housewarming, which was accomplished by means of seal-oil and a wick made from cotton calking, came the hunting for our winter's meat and the building of the second hut. It was a simple affair, now, to go forth in the morning and return by noon with a boat-load of seals. And then, while I worked at building the hut, Maud tried out the oil from the blubber and kept a slow fire under the frames of meat. I had heard of jerking beef on the plains,* and our seal-meat,

cut in thin strips and hung in the smoke, cured excel-
lently.

The second hut was easier to erect, for I built it against
the first, and only three walls were required. But it was
work, hard work, all of it. Maud and I worked from dawn
till dark, to the limit of our strength, so that when night
came we crawled stiffly to bed and slept the animal-like
sleep of exhaustion. And yet Maud declared that she had
never felt better or stronger in her life. I knew this was true
of myself, but hers was such a lily strength that I feared
she would break down. Often and often, her last reserve
force gone, I have seen her stretched flat on her back on
the sand in the way she had of resting and recuperating.
And then she would be up on her feet and toiling hard as
ever. Where she obtained this strength was the marvel to
me.

"Think of the long rest this winter," was her reply to my
remonstrances. "Why, we'll be clamorous for something to
do."

We held a housewarming in my hut the night it was
roofed. It was the end of the third day of a fierce storm
which had swung around the compass from the southeast
to the northwest, and which was then blowing directly in
upon us. The beaches of the outer cove were thundering
with the surf, and even in our land-locked inner cove a
respectable sea was breaking. No high backbone of island
sheltered us from the wind, and it whistled and bellowed
about the hut till at times I feared for the strength of
the walls. The skin roof, stretched tightly as a drum-head
I had thought, sagged and bellied with every gust; and
innumerable interstices in the walls, not so tightly stuffed
with moss as Maud had supposed, disclosed themselves.
Yet the seal-oil burned brightly and we were warm and
comfortable.

It was a pleasant evening indeed, and we voted that
as a social function on Endeavor Island it had not yet

been eclipsed. Our minds were at ease. Not only had we resigned ourselves to the bitter winter, but we were prepared for it. The seals could depart on their mysterious journey into the south* at any time, now, for all we cared; and the storms held no terror for us. Not only were we sure of being dry and warm and sheltered from the wind, but we had the softest and most luxurious mattresses that could be made from moss. This had been Maud's idea, and she had herself jealously gathered all the moss. This was to be my first night on the mattress, and I knew I should sleep the sweeter because she had made it.

As she rose to go she turned to me with the whimsical way she had, and said:

"Something is going to happen—is happening, for that matter. I feel it. Something is coming here, to us. It is coming now. I don't know what, but it is coming."

"Good or bad?" I asked.

She shook her head. "I don't know, but it is there, somewhere."

She pointed in the direction of the sea and wind.

"It's a lee shore," I laughed, "and I am sure I'd rather be here than arriving, a night like this."

"You are not frightened?" I asked, as I stepped to open the door for her.

Her eyes looked bravely into mine.

"And you feel well? perfectly well?"

"Never better," was her answer.

We talked a little longer before she went.

"Good night, Maud," I said.

"Good night, Humphrey," she said.

This use of our given names had come about quite as a matter of course, and was as unpremeditated as it was natural. In that moment I could have put my arms around her and drawn her to me. I should certainly have done so out in that world to which we belonged. As it was, the

situation stopped there in the only way it could; but I was
left alone in my little hut, glowing warmly through and
through with a pleasant satisfaction; and I knew that a
tie, or a tacit something, existed between us which had
not existed before.

CHAPTER THIRTY-TWO

I AWOKE, oppressed by a mysterious sensation. There seemed something missing in my environment. But the mystery and oppressiveness vanished after the first few seconds of waking, when I identified the missing something as the wind. I had fallen asleep in that state of nerve tension with which one meets the continuous shock of sound or movement, and I had awakened, still tense, bracing myself to meet the pressure of something which no longer bore upon me.

It was the first night I had spent under cover in several months, and I lay luxuriously for some minutes under my blankets, (for once not wet with fog or spray), analyzing, first, the effect produced upon me by the cessation of the wind, and next, the joy which was mine from resting on the mattress made by Maud's hands. When I had dressed and opened the door, I heard the waves still lapping on the beach, garrulously attesting the fury of the night. It was a clear day, and the sun was shining. I had slept late, and I stepped outside with sudden energy, bent upon making up lost time as befitted a dweller on Endeavor Island.

And when outside, I stopped short. I believed my eyes without question, and yet I was for the moment stunned by what they disclosed to me. There, on the beach, not fifty feet away, bow on, dismasted, was a black-hulled vessel. Masts and booms, tangled with shrouds, sheets, and rent canvas, were rubbing gently alongside. I could have rubbed my eyes as I looked. There was the home-made galley we had built, the familiar break of the poop, the low yacht-cabin scarcely rising above the rail. It was the *Ghost*.

What freak of fortune had brought it here—here of all spots? what chance of chances? I looked at the bleak, inaccessible wall at my back and knew the profundity of despair. Escape was hopeless, out of the question. I thought of Maud, asleep there in the hut we had reared; I remembered her "Good night, Humphrey"; "my woman, my mate," went ringing through my brain, but now, alas, it was a knell that sounded. Then everything went black before my eyes.

Possibly it was the fraction of a second, but I had no knowledge of how long an interval had lapsed before I was myself again. There lay the *Ghost*, bow on to the beach, her splintered bowsprit projecting over the sand, her tangled spars rubbing against her side to the lift of the crooning waves. Something must be done, must be done.

It came upon me suddenly, as strange, that nothing moved aboard. Wearied from the night of struggle and wreck, all hands were yet asleep, I thought. My next thought was that Maud and I might yet escape. If we could take to the boat and make around the point before any one awoke? I would call her and start. My hand was lifted at her door to knock, when I recollected the smallness of the island. We could never hide ourselves upon it. There was nothing for us but the wide raw ocean. I thought of our snug little huts, our supplies of meat and oil and moss and firewood, and I knew that we could never survive the wintry sea and the great storms which were to come.

So I stood, with hesitant knuckle, without her door. It was impossible, impossible. A wild thought of rushing in and killing her as she slept rose in my mind. And then, in a flash, the better solution came to me. All hands were asleep. Why not creep aboard the *Ghost*,—well, I knew the way to Wolf Larsen's bunk,—and kill him in his sleep? After that—well, we would see. But with him dead there was time and space in which to prepare to do other things; and besides, whatever new situation arose, it could not possibly be worse than the present one.

My knife was at my hip. I returned to my hut for the

shotgun, made sure it was loaded, and went down to the *Ghost*. With some difficulty, and at the expense of a wetting to the waist, I climbed aboard. The forecastle scuttle was open. I paused to listen for the breathing of the men, but there was no breathing. I almost gasped as the thought came to me: What if the *Ghost* is deserted? I listened more closely. There was no sound. I cautiously descended the ladder. The place had the empty and musty feel and smell usual to a dwelling no longer inhabited. Everywhere was a thick litter of discarded and ragged garments, old sea-boots, leaky oilskins—all the worthless forecastle dunnage of a long voyage.

Abandoned hastily was my conclusion as I ascended to the deck. Hope was alive again in my breast, and I looked about me with greater coolness. I noted that the boats were missing. The steerage told the same tale as the forecastle. The hunters had packed their belongings with similar haste. The *Ghost* was deserted. It was Maud's and mine. I thought of the ship's stores and the lazarette beneath the cabin, and the idea came to me of surprising Maud with something nice for breakfast.

The reaction from my fear, and the knowledge that the terrible deed I had come to do was no longer necessary, made me boyish and eager. I went up the steerage companionway two steps at a time, with nothing distinct in my mind except joy and the hope that Maud would sleep on until the surprise breakfast was quite ready for her. As I rounded the galley, a new satisfaction was mine at thought of all the splendid cooking utensils inside. I sprang up the break of the poop, and saw—Wolf Larsen. What of my impetus and the stunning surprise, I clattered three or four steps along the deck before I could stop myself. He was standing in the companionway, only his head and shoulders visible, staring straight at me. His arms were resting on the half-open slide. He made no movement whatever—simply stood there, staring at me.

I began to tremble. The old stomach sickness clutched me. I put one hand on the edge of the house to steady myself. My lips seemed suddenly dry and I moistened them against the need of speech. Nor did I for an instant take my eyes off him. Neither of us spoke. There was something ominous in his silence, his immobility. All my old fear of him returned and by new fear was increased an hundred-fold. And still we stood, the pair of us, staring at each other.

I was aware of the demand for action, and, my old helplessness strong upon me, I was waiting for him to take the initiative. Then, as the moments went by, it came to me that the situation was analogous to the one in which I had approached the long-maned bull, my intention of clubbing obscured by fear until it became a desire to make him run. So it was at last impressed upon me that I was there, not to have Wolf Larsen take the initiative, but to take it myself.

I cocked both barrels and levelled the shotgun at him. Had he moved, attempted to drop down the companionway, I know I would have shot him. But he stood motionless and staring as before. And as I faced him, with levelled gun shaking in my hands, I had time to note the worn and haggard appearance of his face. It was as if some strong anxiety had wasted it. The cheeks were sunken, and there was a wearied, puckered expression on the brow. And it seemed to me that his eyes were strange, not only the expression, but the physical seeming, as though the optic nerves and supporting muscles had suffered strain and slightly twisted the eyeballs.

All this I saw, and my brain now working rapidly, I thought a thousand thoughts; and yet I could not pull the triggers. I lowered the gun and stepped to the corner of the cabin, primarily to relieve the tension on my nerves and to make a new start, and incidentally to be closer.

Again I raised the gun. He was almost at arm's length. There was no hope for him. I was resolved. There was no possible chance of missing him, no matter how poor my marksmanship. And yet I wrestled with myself and could not pull the triggers.

"Well?" he demanded impatiently.

I strove vainly to force my fingers down on the triggers, and vainly I strove to say something.

"Why don't you shoot?" he asked.

I cleared my throat of a huskiness which prevented speech.*

"Hump," he said slowly, "you can't do it. You are not exactly afraid. You are impotent. Your conventional morality is stronger than you. You are the slave to the opinions which have credence among the people you have known and have read about. This code has been drummed into your head from the time you lisped, and in spite of your philosophy, and of what I have taught you, it won't let you kill an unarmed, unresisting man."

"I know it," I said hoarsely.

"And you know that I would kill an unarmed man as readily as I would smoke a cigar," he went on. "You know me for what I am,—my worth in the world by your standard. You have called me snake, tiger, shark, monster, and Caliban. And yet, you little rag puppet, you little echoing mechanism, you are unable to kill me as you would a snake or a shark, because I have hands, feet, and a body shaped somewhat like yours. Bah! I had hoped better things of you, Hump."

He stepped out of the companionway and came up to me.

"Put down the gun. I want to ask you some questions. I haven't had a chance to look around yet. What place is this? How is the *Ghost* lying? How did you get wet? Where's Maud?—I beg your pardon, Miss Brewster—or should I say, 'Mrs. Van Weyden'?"

I had backed away from him, almost weeping at my inability to shoot him, but not fool enough to put down the gun. I hoped, desperately, that he might commit some hostile act, attempt to strike me or choke me; for in such way only I knew I could be stirred to shoot.

"This is Endeavor Island," I said.

"Never heard of it," he broke in.

"At least, that's our name for it," I amended.

"Our?" he queried. "Who's our?"

"Miss Brewster and myself. And the *Ghost* is lying, as you can see for yourself, bow to the beach."

"There are seals here," he said. "They woke me up with their barking, or I'd be sleeping yet. I heard them when I drove in last night. They were the first warning that I was on a lee shore. It's a rookery, the kind of a thing I've hunted for years. Thanks to my brother Death, I've lighted on a fortune. It's a mint. What's its bearings?"

"Haven't the least idea," I said. "But you ought to know quite closely. What were your last observations?"

He smiled inscrutably, but did not answer.

"Well, where's all hands?" I asked. "How does it come that you are alone?"

I was prepared for him again to set aside my question, and was surprised at the readiness of his reply.

"My brother got me inside forty-eight hours, and through no fault of mine. Boarded me in the night with only the watch on deck. Hunters went back on me. He gave them a bigger lay. Heard him offering it. Did it right before me. Of course the crew gave me the go-by. That was to be expected. All hands went over the side, and there I was, marooned on my own vessel. It was Death's turn, and it's all in the family anyway."

"But how did you lose the masts?" I asked.

"Walk over and examine those lanyards," he said, pointing to where the mizzen rigging should have been.

"They have been cut with a knife!" I exclaimed.

"Not quite," he laughed. "It was a neater job. Look again."

I looked. The lanyards had been almost severed, with just enough left to hold the shrouds till some severe strain should be put upon them.

"Cooky did that," he laughed again. "I know, though I didn't spot him at it. Kind of evened up the score a bit."

"Good for Mugridge!" I cried.

"Yes, that's what I thought when everything went over the side. Only I said it on the other side of my mouth."

"But what were you doing while all this was going on?" I asked.

"My best, you may be sure, which wasn't much under the circumstances."

I turned to re-examine Thomas Mugridge's work.

"I guess I'll sit down and take the sunshine," I heard Wolf Larsen saying.

There was a hint, just a slight hint, of physical feebleness in his voice, and it was so strange that I looked quickly at him. His hand was sweeping nervously across his face, as though he were brushing away cobwebs. I was puzzled. The whole thing was so unlike the Wolf Larsen I had known.

"How are your headaches?" I asked.

"They still trouble me," was his answer. "I think I have one coming on now."

He slipped down from his sitting posture till he lay on the deck. Then he rolled over on his side, his head resting on the biceps of the under arm, the forearm shielding his eyes from the sun. I stood regarding him wonderingly.

"Now's your chance, Hump," he said.

"I don't understand," I lied, for I thoroughly understood.

"Oh, nothing," he added softly, as if he were drowsing; "only you've got me where you want me."

"No, I haven't," I retorted; "for I want you a few thousand miles away from here."

He chuckled, and thereafter spoke no more. He did not
stir as I passed by him and went down into the cabin. I
lifted the trap in the floor, but for some moments gazed
dubiously into the darkness of the lazarette beneath. I
hesitated to descend. What if his lying down were a ruse?
Pretty, indeed, to be caught there like a rat. I crept softly
up the companionway and peeped at him. He was lying as
I had left him. Again I went below; but before I dropped
into the lazarette I took the precaution of casting down the
door in advance. At least there would be no lid to the trap.
But it was all needless. I regained the cabin with a store
of jams, sea-biscuits, canned meats, and such things,—all
I could carry,—and replaced the trap-door.

A peep at Wolf Larsen showed me that he had not
moved. A bright thought struck me. I stole into his state-
room and possessed myself of his revolvers. There were
no other weapons, though I thoroughly ransacked the
three remaining state-rooms. To make sure, I returned
and went through the steerage and forecastle, and in
the galley gathered up all the sharp meat and vegetable
knives. Then I bethought me of the great yachtsman's
knife he always carried, and I came to him and spoke
to him, first softly, then loudly. He did not move. I
bent over and took it from his pocket. I breathed more
freely. He had no arms with which to attack me from
a distance; while I, armed, could always forestall him
should he attempt to grapple me with his terrible gorilla
arms.

Filling a coffee-pot and frying-pan with part of my plunder, and taking some chinaware from the cabin pantry, I
left Wolf Larsen lying in the sun and went ashore.

Maud was still asleep. I blew up the embers, (we had not
yet arranged a winter kitchen), and quite feverishly cooked
the breakfast. Toward the end, I heard her moving about
within the hut, making her toilet. Just as all was ready and
the coffee poured, the door opened and she came forth.

"It's not fair of you," was her greeting. "You are usurping one of my prerogatives. You know you agreed that the cooking should be mine, and—"

"But just this once," I pleaded.

"If you promise not to do it again," she smiled. "Unless, of course, you have grown tired of my poor efforts."

To my delight she never once looked toward the beach, and I maintained the banter with such success that all unconsciously she sipped coffee from the china cup, ate fried evaporated potatoes, and spread marmalade on her biscuit. But it could not last. I saw the surprise that came over her. She had discovered the china plate from which she was eating. She looked over the breakfast, noting detail after detail. Then she looked at me, and her face turned slowly toward the beach.

"Humphrey!" she said.

The old unnamable terror mounted in her eyes.

"Is—he—?" she quavered.

I nodded my head.

CHAPTER THIRTY-THREE

WE waited all day for Wolf Larsen to come ashore. It was an intolerable period of anxiety. Each moment one or the other of us cast expectant glances toward the *Ghost*. But he did not come. He did not even appear on deck.

"Perhaps it is his headache," I said. "I left him lying on the poop. He may lie there all night. I think I'll go and see."

Maud looked entreaty at me.

"It is all right," I assured her. "I shall take the revolvers. You know I collected every weapon on board."

"But there are his arms, his hands, his terrible, terrible hands!" she objected. And then she cried, "Oh, Humphrey, I am afraid of him! Don't go—please don't go!"

She rested her hand appealingly on mine, and sent my pulse fluttering. My heart was surely in my eyes for a moment. The dear and lovely woman! And she was so much the woman, clinging and appealing, sunshine and dew to my manhood, rooting it deeper and sending through it the sap of a new strength. I was for putting my arm around her, as when in the midst of the seal herd; but I considered, and refrained.

"I shall not take any risks," I said. "I'll merely peep over the bow and see."

She pressed my hand earnestly and let me go. But the space on deck where I had left him lying was vacant. He had evidently gone below. That night we stood alternate watches, one of us sleeping at a time; for there was no telling what Wolf Larsen might do. He was certainly capable of anything.

The next day we waited, and the next, and still he made no sign.

"These headaches of his, these attacks," Maud said, on the afternoon of the fourth day; "perhaps he is ill, very ill. He may be dead."

"Or dying," was her afterthought, when she had waited some time for me to speak.

"Better so," I answered.

"But think, Humphrey, a fellow-creature in his last lonely hour."

"Perhaps," I suggested.

"Yes, even perhaps," she acknowledged. "But we do not know. It would be terrible if he were. I could never forgive myself. We must do something."

"Perhaps," I suggested again.

I waited, smiling inwardly at the woman of her which compelled a solicitude for Wolf Larsen, of all creatures. Where was her solicitude for me, I thought,—for me whom she had been afraid to have merely peep aboard?

She was too subtle not to follow the trend of my silence. And she was as direct as she was subtle.

"You must go aboard, Humphrey, and find out," she said. "And if you want to laugh at me, you have my consent and forgiveness."

I arose obediently and went down the beach.

"Do be careful," she called after me.

I waved my arm from the forecastle head and dropped down to the deck. Aft I walked to the cabin companion, where I contented myself with hailing below. Wolf Larsen answered, and as he started to ascend the stairs I cocked my revolver. I displayed it openly during our conversation, but he took no notice of it. He appeared the same, physically, as when last I saw him, but he was gloomy and silent. In fact, the few words we spoke could hardly be called a conversation. I did not inquire why he had not been ashore, nor did he ask why I had come aboard. His head was all right again, he said, and so, without further parley, I left him.

Maud received my report with obvious relief, and the sight of smoke which later rose in the galley put her in a more cheerful mood. The next day, and the next, we saw the galley smoke rising, and sometimes we caught glimpses of him on the poop. But that was all. He made no attempt to come ashore. This we knew, for we still maintained our night-watches. We were waiting for him to do something, to show his hand, so to say, and his inaction puzzled and worried us.

A week of this passed by. We had no other interest than Wolf Larsen, and his presence weighed us down with an apprehension which prevented us from doing any of the little things we had planned.

But at the end of the week the smoke ceased rising from the galley, and he no longer showed himself on the poop. I could see Maud's solicitude again growing, though she timidly,—and even proudly, I think,—forebore a repetition of her request. After all, what censure could be put upon her? She was divinely altruistic, and she was a woman. Besides, I was myself aware of hurt at thought of this man whom I had tried to kill, dying alone with his fellow-creatures so near. He was right. The code of my group was stronger than I. The fact that he had hands, feet, and a body shaped somewhat like mine, constituted a claim which I could not ignore.

So I did not wait a second time for Maud to send me. I discovered that we stood in need of condensed milk and marmalade, and announced that I was going aboard. I could see that she wavered. She even went so far as to murmur that they were non-essentials and that my trip after them might be inexpedient. And as she had followed the trend of my silence, she now followed the trend of my speech, and she knew that I was going aboard, not because of condensed milk and marmalade, but because of her and of her anxiety, which she knew she had failed to hide.

I took off my shoes when I gained the forecastle head,

and went noiselessly aft in my stocking feet. Nor did I call
this time from the top of the companionway. Cautiously
descending, I found the cabin deserted. The door to his
state-room was closed. At first I thought of knocking, then
I remembered my ostensible errand and resolved to carry
it out. Carefully avoiding noise, I lifted the trap-door in
the floor and set it to one side. The slop-chest, as well
as the provisions, was stored in the lazarette, and I took
advantage of the opportunity to lay in a stock of under-
clothing.

As I emerged from the lazarette I heard sounds in Wolf
Larsen's state-room. I crouched and listened. The door-
knob rattled. Furtively, instinctively, I slunk back behind
the table and drew and cocked my revolver. The door
swung open and he came forth. Never had I seen so profound a despair as that which I saw on his face,—the face
of Wolf Larsen the fighter, the strong man, the indomitable
one. For all the world like a woman wringing her hands,
he raised his clenched fists and groaned. One fist unclosed,
and the open palm swept across his eyes as though brushing away cobwebs.

"God! God!" he groaned, and the clenched fists were
raised again to the infinite despair with which his throat
vibrated.

It was horrible. I was trembling all over, and I could feel
the shivers running up and down my spine and the sweat
standing out on my forehead. Surely there can be little in
this world more awful than the spectacle of a strong man
in the moment when he is utterly weak and broken.

But Wolf Larsen regained control of himself by an exertion of his remarkable will. And it was exertion. His whole
frame shook with the struggle. He resembled a man on the
verge of a fit. His face strove to compose itself, writhing
and twisting in the effort till he broke down again. Once
more the clenched fists went upward and he groaned. He
caught his breath once or twice and sobbed. Then he was

successful. I could have thought him the old Wolf Larsen, and yet there was in his movements a vague suggestion of weakness and indecision. He started for the companionway, and stepped forward quite as I had been accustomed to see him do; and yet again, in his very walk, there seemed that suggestion of weakness and indecision.

I was now concerned with fear for myself. The open trap lay directly in his path, and his discovery of it would lead instantly to his discovery of me. I was angry with myself for being caught in so cowardly a position, crouching on the floor. There was yet time. I rose swiftly to my feet, and, I know, quite unconsciously assumed a defiant attitude. He took no notice of me. Nor did he notice the open trap. Before I could grasp the situation, or act, he had walked right into the trap. One foot was descending into the opening, while the other foot was just on the verge of beginning the uplift. But when the descending foot missed the solid flooring and felt vacancy beneath, it was the old Wolf Larsen and the tiger muscles that made the falling body spring across the opening, even as it fell, so that he struck on his chest and stomach, with arms outstretched, on the floor of the opposite side. The next instant he had drawn up his legs and rolled clear. But he rolled into my marmalade and underclothes and against the trap-door.

The expression on his face was one of complete comprehension. But before I could guess what he had comprehended, he had dropped the trap-door into place, closing the lazarette. Then I understood. He thought he had me inside. Also, he was blind, blind as a bat. I watched him, breathing carefully so that he should not hear me. He stepped quickly to his state-room. I saw his hand miss the door-knob by an inch, quickly fumble for it, and find it. This was my chance. I tiptoed across the cabin and to the top of the stairs. He came back, dragging a heavy sea-chest, which he deposited on top of the trap. Not content with this, he fetched a second chest and placed it on top of the first. Then he gathered up the marmalade and underclothes and put them on the table. When he started up the companionway, I retreated, silently rolling over on top of the cabin.

He shoved the slide part way back and rested his arms on it, his body still in the companionway. His attitude was of one looking forward the length of the schooner, or staring, rather, for his eyes were fixed and unblinking. I was only five feet away and directly in what should have been his line of vision. It was uncanny. I felt myself a ghost, what of my invisibility. I waved my hand back and forth, of course without effect; but when the moving shadow fell across his face I saw at once that he was susceptible to the impression. His face became more expectant and tense as he tried to analyze and identify the impression. He knew that he had responded to something from without, that his sensibility had been touched by a changing something in his environment; but what it was he could not discover. I ceased waving my hand, so that the shadow remained stationary. He slowly moved his head back and forth under it and turned from side to side, now in the sunshine, now in the shade, feeling the shadow, as it were, testing it by sensation.

I, too, was busy, trying to reason out how he was aware of the existence of intangible a thing as a shadow. If it were his eyeballs only that were affected, or if his optic nerve were not wholly destroyed, the explanation was simple. If otherwise, then the only conclusion I could reach was that the sensitive skin recognized the difference of temperature between shade and sunshine. Or, perhaps,—who can tell?—it was that fabled sixth sense which conveyed to him the loom and feel of an object close at hand.

Giving over his attempt to determine the shadow, he stepped on deck and started forward, walking with a swiftness and confidence which surprised me. And still there was that hint of the feebleness of the blind in his walk. I knew it now for what it was.

To my amused chagrin, he discovered my shoes on the forecastle head and brought them back with him into the galley. I watched him build the fire and set about cooking food for himself; then I stole into the cabin for my marmalade and underclothes, slipped back past the galley, and climbed down to the beach to deliver my barefoot report.

CHAPTER THIRTY-FOUR

IT'S too bad the *Ghost* has lost her masts. Why, we could
sail away in her. Don't you think we could, Humphrey?"

I sprang excitedly to my feet.

"I wonder, I wonder," I repeated, pacing up and down.

Maud's eyes were shining with anticipation as they followed me. She had such faith in me! And the thought of it
was so much added power. I remembered Michelet's "To
man, woman is as the earth was to her legendary son; he
has but to fall down and kiss her breast and he is strong
again."* For the first time I knew the wonderful truth of
his words. Why, I was living them. Maud was all this to
me, an unfailing source of strength and courage. I had but
to look at her, or think of her, and be strong again.

"It can be done, it can be done," I was thinking and
asserting aloud. "What men have done, I can do; and if
they have never done this before, still I can do it."

"What? for goodness sake," Maud demanded. "Do be
merciful. What is it you can do?"

"We can do it," I amended. "Why, nothing else than put
the masts back into the *Ghost* and sail away."

"Humphrey!" she exclaimed.

And I felt as proud of my conception as if it were already
a fact accomplished.

"But how is it possible to be done?" she asked.

"I don't know," was my answer. "I know only that I am
capable of doing anything these days."

I smiled proudly at her—too proudly, for she dropped
her eyes and was for the moment silent.

"But there is Captain Larsen," she objected.

"Blind and helpless," I answered promptly, waving him
aside as a straw.

"But those terrible hands of his! You know how he leaped across the opening of the lazarette."

"And you know also how I crept about and avoided him," I contended gayly.

"And lost your shoes."

"You'd hardly expect them to avoid Wolf Larsen without my feet inside of them."

We both laughed, and then went seriously to work constructing the plan whereby we were to step the masts of the *Ghost* and return to the world. I remembered hazily the physics of my school days, while the last few months had given me practical experience with mechanical purchases. I must say, though, when we walked down to the *Ghost* to inspect more closely the task before us, that the sight of the great masts lying in the water almost disheartened me. Where were we to begin? If there had been one mast standing, something high up to which to fasten blocks and tackles! But there was nothing. It reminded me of the problem of lifting oneself by one's boot-straps. I understood the mechanics of levers; but where was I to get a fulcrum?

There was the mainmast, fifteen inches in diameter at what was now the butt, still sixty-five feet in length, and weighing, I roughly calculated, at least three thousand pounds. And then came the foremast, larger in diameter and weighing surely thirty-five hundred pounds. Where was I to begin? Maud stood silently by my side, while I evolved in my mind the contrivance known among sailors as "shears." But, though known to sailors, I invented it there on Endeavor Island. By crossing and lashing the ends of two spars, and then elevating them in the air like an inverted "V," I could get a point above the deck to which to make fast my hoisting tackle. To this hoisting tackle I could, if necessary, attach a second hoisting tackle. And then there was the windlass!*

Maud saw that I had achieved a solution, and her eyes warmed sympathetically.

"What are you going to do?" she asked.

"Clear that raffle," I answered, pointing to the tangled wreckage overside.

Ah, the decisiveness, the very sound of the words, was good in my ears. "Clear that raffle!" Imagine so salty a phrase on the lips of the Humphrey Van Weyden of a few months gone!

There must have been a touch of the melodramatic in my pose and voice, for Maud smiled. Her appreciation of the ridiculous was keen, and in all things she unerringly saw and felt, where it existed, the touch of sham, the overshading, the overtone. It was this which had given poise and penetration to her own work and made her of worth to the world. The serious critic, with the sense of humor and the power of expression, must inevitably command the world's ear. And so it was that she had commanded. Her sense of humor was really the artist's instinct for proportion.

"I'm sure I've heard it before, somewhere, in books," she murmured gleefully.

I had an instinct for proportion myself, and I collapsed forthwith, descending from the dominant pose of a master of matter to a state of humble confusion which was, to say the least, very miserable.

Her hand leapt out at once to mine.

"I'm so sorry," she said.

"No need to be," I gulped. "It does me good. There's too much of the schoolboy in me. All of which is neither here nor there. What we've got to do is actually and literally to clear that raffle. If you'll come with me in the boat, we'll get to work and straighten things out."

" 'When the topmen clear the raffle with their clasp-knives in their teeth,' " she quoted at me; and for the rest of the afternoon we made merry over our labor.

Her task was to hold the boat in position while I worked at the tangle. And such a tangle—halyards, sheets, guys, downhauls, shrouds, stays, all washed about and back and forth and through, and twined and knotted by the sea. I cut no more than was necessary, and what with passing the long ropes under and around the booms and masts, of unreeving the halyards and sheets, of coiling down in the boat and uncoiling in order to pass through another knot in the bight, I was soon wet to the skin.

The sails did require some cutting, and the canvas, heavy with water, tried my strength severely; but I succeeded before nightfall in getting it all spread out on the beach to dry. We were both very tired when we knocked off for supper, and we had done good work, too, though to the eye it appeared insignificant.

Next morning, with Maud as able assistant, I went into the hold of the *Ghost* to clear the steps of the mast-butts. We had no more than begun work when the sound of my knocking and hammering brought Wolf Larsen.

"Hello below!" he cried down the open hatch.

The sound of his voice made Maud quickly draw close to me, as for protection, and she rested one hand on my arm while we parleyed.

"Hello on deck," I replied. "Good morning to you."

"What are you doing down there?" he demanded. "Trying to scuttle my ship for me?"

"Quite the opposite; I'm repairing her," was my answer.

"But what in thunder are you repairing?" There was puzzlement in his voice.

"Why, I'm getting everything ready for re-stepping the masts," I replied easily, as though it were the simplest project imaginable.

"It seems as though you're standing on your own legs at last, Hump," we heard him say; and then for some time he was silent.

"But I say, Hump," he called down, "you can't do it."

"Oh, yes, I can," I retorted. "I'm doing it now."

"But this is my vessel, my particular property. What if I forbid you?"

"You forget," I replied. "You are no longer the biggest bit of the ferment. You were, once, and able to eat me, as you were pleased to phrase it; but there has been a diminishing, and I am now able to eat you. The yeast has grown stale."

He gave a short, disagreeable laugh. "I see you're working my philosophy back on me for all it is worth. But don't make the mistake of underestimating me. For your own good I warn you."

"Since when have you become a philanthropist?" I queried. "Confess, now, in warning me for my own good, that you are very inconsistent."

He ignored my sarcasm, saying, "Suppose I clap the hatch on, now? You won't fool me as you did in the lazarette."

"Wolf Larsen," I said sternly, for the first time addressing him by this most familiar name, "I am unable to shoot a helpless, unresisting man. You have proved that to my satisfaction as well as yours. But I warn you now, and not so much for your own good as for mine, that I shall shoot you the moment you attempt a hostile act. I can shoot you now, as I stand here; and if you are so minded, just go ahead and try to clap on the hatch."

"Nevertheless, I forbid you, I distinctly forbid your tampering with my ship."

"But, man!" I expostulated, "you advance the fact that it is your ship as though it were a moral right. You have never considered moral rights in your dealings with others. You surely do not dream that I'll consider them in dealing with you?"

I had stepped underneath the open hatchway so that I could see him. The lack of expression on his face, so different from when I had watched him unseen, was enhanced by the unblinking, staring eyes. It was not a pleasant face to look upon.

"And none so poor, not even Hump, to do him reverence,"* he sneered.

The sneer was wholly in his voice. His face remained expressionless as ever.

"How do you do, Miss Brewster," he said suddenly, after a pause.

I started. She had made no noise whatever, had not even moved. Could it be that some glimmer of vision remained to him? or that his vision was coming back?

"How do you do, Captain Larsen," she answered. "Pray, how did you know I was here?"

"Heard you breathing, of course. I say, Hump's improving, don't you think so?"

"I don't know," she answered, smiling at me. "I have never seen him otherwise."

"You should have seen him before, then."

"Wolf Larsen, in large doses," I murmured, "before and after taking."

"I want to tell you again, Hump," he said threateningly, "that you'd better leave things alone."

"But don't you care to escape as well as we?" I asked incredulously.

"No," was his answer. "I intend dying here."

"Well, we don't," I concluded defiantly, beginning again my knocking and hammering.

CHAPTER THIRTY-FIVE

NEXT day, the mast-steps clear and everything in readiness, we started to get the two topmasts aboard. The maintopmast was over thirty feet in length, the foretopmast nearly thirty, and it was of these that I intended making the shears. It was puzzling work. Fastening one end of a heavy tackle to the windlass, and with the other end fast to the butt of the foretopmast, I began to heave. Maud held the turn on the windlass and coiled down the slack.

We were astonished at the ease with which the spar was lifted. It was an improved crank windlass, and the purchase it gave was enormous. Of course, what it gave us in power we paid for in distance; as many times as it doubled my strength, that many times was doubled the length of rope I heaved in. The tackle dragged heavily across the rail, increasing its drag as the spar arose more and more out of the water, and the exertion on the windlass grew severe.

But when the butt of the topmast was level with the rail, everything came to a standstill.

"I might have known it," I said impatiently. "Now we have to do it all over again."

"Why not fasten the tackle part way down the mast?" Maud suggested.

"It's what I should have done at first," I answered, hugely disgusted with myself.

Slipping off a turn, I lowered the mast back into the water and fastened the tackle a third of the way down from the butt. In an hour, what of this and of rests between the heaving, I had hoisted it to the point where I could hoist no more. Eight feet of the butt was above the rail, and I was as far away as ever from getting the spar on board. I sat down and pondered the problem. It did not take long. I sprang jubilantly to my feet.

"Now I have it!" I cried. "I ought to make the tackle fast at the point of balance. And what we learn of this will serve us with everything else we have to hoist aboard."

Once again I undid all my work by lowering the mast into the water. But I miscalculated the point of balance, so that when I heaved the top of the mast came up instead of the butt. Maud looked despair, but I laughed and said it would do just as well.

Instructing her how to hold the turn and be ready to slack away at command, I laid hold of the mast with my hands and tried to balance it inboard across the rail. When I thought I had it I cried to her to slack away; but the spar righted, despite my efforts, and dropped back toward the water. Again I heaved it up to its old position, for I had now another idea. I remembered the watch-tackle,—a small double and single block affair,—and fetched it.

While I was rigging it between the top of the spar and the opposite rail, Wolf Larsen came on the scene. We exchanged nothing more than good mornings, and, though he could not see, he sat on the rail out of the way and followed by the sound all that I did.

Again instructing Maud to slack away at the windlass when I gave the word, I proceeded to heave on the watch-tackle. Slowly the mast swung in until it balanced at right angles across the rail; and then I discovered to my amazement that there was no need for Maud to slack away. In fact, the very opposite was necessary. Making the watch-tackle fast, I hove on the windless and brought in the mast, inch by inch, till its top tilted down to the deck and finally its whole length lay on the deck.

I looked at my watch. It was twelve o'clock. My back was aching sorely, and I felt extremely tired and hungry. And there on the deck was a single stick of timber to show for a whole morning's work. For the first time I

thoroughly realized the extent of the task before us. But
I was learning, I was learning. The afternoon would show
far more accomplished. And it did; for we returned at one
o'clock, rested and strengthened by a hearty dinner.

In less than an hour I had the maintopmast on deck
and was constructing the shears. Lashing the two topmasts
together, and making allowance for their unequal length,
at the point of intersection I attached the double block of
the main throat-halyards. This, with the single block and
the throat-halyards themselves, gave me a hoisting tackle.
To prevent the butts of the masts from slipping on the
deck, I nailed down thick cleats. Everything in readiness,
I made a line fast to the apex of the shears and carried it
directly to the windlass. I was growing to have faith in that
windlass, for it gave me power beyond all expectation. As
usual, Maud held the turn while I heaved. The shears rose
in the air.

Then I discovered I had forgotten guy-ropes. This neces-
sitated my climbing the shears, which I did twice, before I
finished guying it fore and aft and to either side. Twilight
had set in by the time this was accomplished. Wolf Larsen,
who had sat about and listened all afternoon and never
opened his mouth, had taken himself off to the galley and
started his supper. I felt quite stiff across the small of the
back, so much so that I straightened up with an effort and
with pain. I looked proudly at my work. It was beginning
to show. I was wild with desire, like a child with a new toy,
to hoist something with my shears.

"I wish it weren't so late," I said. "I'd like to see how it
works."

"Don't be a glutton, Humphrey," Maud chided me. "Remember, to-morrow is coming, and you're so tired now that
you can hardly stand."

"And you?" I said, with sudden solicitude. "You must
be very tired. You have worked hard and nobly. I am proud
of you, Maud."

"Not half so proud as I am of you, nor with half the reason," she answered, looking me straight in the eyes for a moment with an expression in her own and a dancing, tremulous light which I had not seen before and which gave me a pang of quick delight,—I know not why, for I did not understand it. Then she dropped her eyes, to lift them again, laughing.

"If our friends could see us now," she said. "Look at us. Have you ever paused for a moment to consider our appearance?"

"Yes, I have considered yours, frequently," I answered, puzzling over what I had seen in her eyes and puzzled by her sudden change of subject.

"Mercy!" she cried. "And what do I look like, pray?"

"A scarecrow, I'm afraid," I replied. "Just glance at your draggled skirts, for instance. Look at those three-cornered tears. And such a waist! It would not require a Sherlock Holmes* to deduce that you have been cooking over a campfire, to say nothing of trying out seal-blubber. And to cap it all, that cap! And all that is the woman who wrote 'A Kiss Endured.' "

She made me an elaborate and stately courtesy, and said, "As for you, sir—"

And yet, through the five minutes of banter which followed, there was a serious something underneath the fun which I could not but relate to the strange and fleeting expression I had caught in her eyes. What was it? Could it be that our eyes were speaking beyond the will of our speech? My eyes had spoken, I knew, until I had found the culprits out and silenced them. This had occurred several times. But had she seen the clamor in them and understood? And had her eyes so spoken to me? What else could that expression have meant—that dancing, tremulous light, and a something more which words could not describe? And yet it could not be. It was impossible. Besides, I was not skilled in the speech of eyes. I was only Humphrey Van

Weyden, a bookish fellow who loved. And to love, and to wait and win love, that surely was glorious enough for me. And thus I thought, even as we chaffed each other's appearance, until we arrived ashore and there were other things to think about.

"It's a shame, after working hard all day, that we cannot have an uninterrupted night's sleep," I complained, after supper.

"But there can be no danger now? from a blind man?" she queried.

"I shall never be able to trust him," I averred, "and far less now that he is blind. The liability is that his part helplessness will make him more malignant than ever. I know what I shall do to-morrow, the first thing—run out a light anchor and kedge the schooner off the beach. And each night when we come ashore in the boat, Mr. Wolf Larsen will be left a prisoner on board. So this will be the last night we have to stand watch, and because of that it will go the easier."

We were awake early and just finishing breakfast as daylight came.

"Oh, Humphrey!" I heard Maud cry in dismay and suddenly stop.

I looked at her. She was gazing at the *Ghost*. I followed her gaze, but could see nothing unusual. She looked at me, and I looked inquiry back.

"The shears," she said, and her voice trembled.

I had forgotten their existence. I looked again, but could not see them.

"If he has—" I muttered savagely.

She put her hand sympathetically on mine, and said, "You will have to begin over again."

"Oh, believe me, my anger means nothing; I could not hurt a fly," I smiled back bitterly. "And the worst of it is, he knows it. You are right. If he has destroyed the shears, I shall do nothing except begin over again."

"But I'll stand my watch on board hereafter," I blurted out a moment later. "And if he interferes—"

"But I dare not stay ashore all night alone," Maud was saying when I came back to myself. "It would be so much nicer if he would be friendly with us and help us. We could all live comfortably aboard."

"We will," I asserted, still savagely, for the destruction of my beloved shears had hit me hard. "That is, you and I will live aboard, friendly or not with Wolf Larsen."

"It's childish," I laughed later, "for him to do such things, and for me to grow angry over them, for that matter."

But my heart smote me when we climbed aboard and looked at the havoc he had done. The shears were gone altogether. The guys had been slashed right and left. The throat-halyards which I had rigged were cut across through every part. And he knew I could not splice. A thought struck me. I ran to the windlass. It would not work. He had broken it. We looked at each other in consternation. Then I ran to the side. The masts, booms, and gaffs I had cleared were gone. He had found the lines which held them, and cast them adrift.

Tears were in Maud's eyes, and I do believe they were for me. I could have wept myself. Where now was our project of re-masting the *Ghost*? He had done his work well. I sat down on the hatch-combing and rested my chin on my hands in black despair.

"He deserves to die," I cried out; "and God forgive me, I am not man enough to be his executioner."

But Maud was by my side, passing her hand soothingly through my hair as though I were a child, and saying, "There, there; it will all come right. We are in the right, and it must come right."

I remembered Michelet and leaned my head against her; and truly I became strong again. The blessed woman was an unfailing fount of power to me. What did it matter?

Only a set-back, a delay. The tide could not have carried the masts far to seaward, and there had been no wind. It meant merely more work to find them and tow them back. And besides, it was a lesson. I knew what to expect. He might have waited and destroyed our work more effectually when we had more accomplished.

"Here he comes now," she whispered.

I glanced up. He was strolling leisurely along the poop on the port side.

"Take no notice of him," I whispered. "He's coming to see how we take it. Don't let him know that we know. We can deny him that satisfaction. Take off your shoes,—that's right,—and carry them in your hand."

And then we played hide-and-seek with the blind man. As he came up the port side we slipped past on the starboard; and from the poop we watched him turn and start aft on our track.

He must have known, somehow, that we were on board, for he said, "Good morning," very confidently, and waited for the greeting to be returned. Then he strolled aft, and we slipped forward.

"Oh, I know you're aboard," he called out, and I could see him listen intently after he had spoken.

It reminded me of the great hoot-owl, listening, after its booming cry, for the stir of its frightened prey. But we did not stir, and we moved only when he moved. And so we dodged about the deck, hand in hand, like a couple of children chased by a wicked ogre, till Wolf Larsen, evidently in disgust, left the deck for the cabin. There was glee in our eyes, and suppressed titters in our mouths, as we put on our shoes and clambered over the side into the boat. And as I looked into Maud's clear brown eyes I forgot the evil he had done, and I knew only that I loved her, and that because of her the strength was mine to win our way back to the world.

CHAPTER THIRTY-SIX

FOR two days Maud and I ranged the sea and explored the beaches in search of the missing masts. But it was not till the third day that we found them, all of them, the shears included, and, of all perilous places, in the pounding surf of the grim southwestern promontory. And how we worked! At the dark end of the first day we returned, exhausted, to our little cove, towing the mainmast behind us. And we had been compelled to row, in a dead calm, practically every inch of the way.

Another day of heart-breaking and dangerous toil saw us in camp with the two topmasts to the good. The day following I was desperate, and I rafted together the foremast, the fore and main booms, and the fore and main gaffs. The wind was favorable, and I had thought to tow them back under sail; but the wind baffled, then died away, and our progress with the oars was a snail's pace. And it was such dispiriting effort. To throw one's whole strength and weight on the oars, and to feel the boat checked in its forward lunge by the heavy drag behind, was not exactly exhilarating.

Night began to fall, and to make matters worse, the wind sprang up ahead. Not only did all forward motion cease, but we began to drift back and out to sea. I struggled at the oars till I was played out. Poor Maud, whom I could never prevent from working to the limit of her strength, lay weakly back in the stern-sheets. I could row no more. My bruised and swollen hands could no longer close on the oar handles. My wrists and arms ached intolerably, and, though I had eaten heartily of a twelve o'clock lunch, I had worked so hard that I was faint from hunger.

I pulled in the oars and bent forward to the line which

held the tow. But Maud's hand leaped out restrainingly to mine.

"What are you going to do?" she asked in a strained, tense voice.

"Cast it off," I answered, slipping a turn of the rope. But her fingers closed on mine.

"Please don't," she begged.

"It is useless," I answered. "Here is night, and the wind blowing us off the land."

"But think, Humphrey. If we cannot sail away on the *Ghost*, we may remain for years on the island—for life even. If it has never been discovered all these years, it may never be discovered."

"You forget the boat we found on the beach," I reminded her.

"It was a seal-hunting boat," she replied, "and you know perfectly well that if the men had escaped they would have been back to make their fortunes from the rookery. You know they never escaped."

I remained silent, undecided.

"Besides," she added haltingly, "it's your idea, and I want to see you succeed."

Now I could harden my heart. As soon as she put it on a flattering personal basis, generosity compelled me to deny her.

"Better years on the island than to die to-night, or to-morrow, or the next day, in the open boat. We are not prepared to brave the sea. We have no food, no water, no blankets, nothing. Why, you'd not survive the night without blankets. I know how strong you are. You are shivering now."

"It is only nervousness," she answered. "I am afraid you will cast off the masts in spite of me."

"Oh, please, please, Humphrey, don't!" she burst out, a moment later.

And so it ended, with the phrase she knew had all power

over me. We shivered miserably throughout the night. Now and again I fitfully slept, but the pain of the cold always aroused me. How Maud could stand it was beyond me. I was too tired to thrash my arms about and warm myself, but I found strength time and again to chafe her hands and feet to restore the circulation. And still she pleaded with me not to cast off the masts. About three in the morning she was caught by a cold cramp, and after I had rubbed her out of that she became quite numb. I was frightened. I got out the oars and made her row, though she was so weak I thought she would faint at every stroke.

Morning broke, and we looked long in the growing light for our island. At last it showed, small and black, on the horizon, fully fifteen miles away. I scanned the sea with my glasses. Far away in the southwest I could see a dark line on the water, which grew even as I looked at it.

"Fair wind!" I cried in a husky voice I did not recognize as my own.

Maud tried to reply, but could not speak. Her lips were blue with cold, and she was hollow-eyed—but oh, how bravely her brown eyes looked at me! How piteously brave!

Again I fell to chafing her hands, and to moving her arms up and down and about until she could thrash them herself. Then I compelled her to stand up, and though she would have fallen had I not supported her, I forced her to walk back and forth the several steps between the thwart and the stern-sheets, and finally to spring up and down.

"Oh, you brave, brave woman," I said, when I saw the life coming back into her face. "Did you know that you were brave?"

"I never used to be," she answered. "I was never brave till I knew you. It is you who have made me brave."

"Nor I, until I knew you," I answered.

She gave me a quick look, and again I caught that dancing, tremulous light and something more in her eyes. But it was only for the moment. Then she smiled.

"It must have been the conditions," she said; but I knew she was wrong, and I wondered if she likewise knew.

Then the wind came, fair and fresh, and the boat was soon laboring through a heavy sea toward the island. At half-past three in the afternoon we passed the southwestern promontory. Not only were we hungry, but we were now suffering from thirst. Our lips were dry and cracked, nor could we longer moisten them with our tongues. Then the wind slowly died down. By night it was dead calm and I was toiling once more at the oars—but weakly, most weakly. At two in the morning the boat's bow touched the beach of our own inner cove, and I staggered out to make the painter fast. Maud could not stand, nor had I strength to carry her. I fell in the sand with her, and, when I had recovered, contented myself with putting my hands under her shoulders and dragging her up the beach to the hut.

The next day we did no work. In fact, we slept till three in the afternoon, or at least I did, for I awoke to find Maud cooking dinner. Her power of recuperation was wonderful. There was something tenacious about that lily-frail body of hers, a clutch on existence which one could not reconcile with its patent weakness.

"You know I was travelling to Japan for my health," she said, as we lingered at the fire after dinner and delighted in the movelessness of loafing. "I was not very strong. I never was. The doctors recommended a sea voyage, and I chose the longest."

"You little knew what you were choosing," I laughed.

"But I shall be a different woman for the experience, as well as a stronger woman," she answered; "and, I hope, a better woman. At least I shall understand a great deal more of life."

Then, as the short day waned, we fell to discussing Wolf Larsen's blindness. It was inexplicable. And that it was grave, I instanced his statement that he intended to stay and die on Endeavor Island. When he, strong man that he was, loving life as he did, accepted his death, it was plain that he was troubled by something more than mere blindness. There had been his terrific headaches, and we were agreed that it was some sort of brain breakdown, and that in his attacks he endured pain beyond our comprehension.

I noticed, as we talked over his condition, that Maud's sympathy went out to him more and more; yet I could not but love her for it, so sweetly womanly was it. Besides, there was no false sentiment about her feeling. She was agreed that the most rigorous treatment was necessary if we were to escape, though she recoiled at the suggestion that I might sometime be compelled to take his life to save my own—"our own," she put it.

In the morning we had breakfast and were at work by daylight. I found a light kedge anchor in the fore hold, where such things were kept, and with a deal of exertion got it on deck and into the boat. With a long running-line coiled down in the stern, I rowed well out into our little cove and dropped the anchor into the water. There was no wind, the tide was high, and the schooner floated. Casting off the shore lines, I kedged her out by main strength, (the windlass being broken), till she rode nearly up and down to the small anchor—too small to hold her in any breeze. So I lowered the big starboard anchor, giving plenty of slack; and by afternoon I was at work on the windlass.

Three days I worked on that windlass. Least of all things was I a mechanic, and in that time I accomplished what an ordinary machinist would have done in as many hours. I had to learn my tools to begin with, and every simple mechanical principle which such a man would have at his finger ends I had likewise to learn. And at the end of three days I had a windlass which worked clumsily. It never gave the satisfaction the old windlass had given, but it worked and made my work possible.

In half a day I got the two topmasts aboard and the shears rigged and guyed as before. And that night I slept on board and on deck beside my work. Maud, who refused to stay alone ashore, slept in the forecastle. Wolf Larsen had sat about, listening to my repairing the windlass and talking with Maud and me upon indifferent subjects. No reference was made on either side to the destruction of the shears; nor did he say anything further about my leaving his ship alone. But still I had feared him, blind and helpless and listening, always listening, and I never let his strong arms get within reach of me while I worked.

On this night, sleeping under my beloved shears, I was aroused by his footsteps on the deck. It was a starlight night, and I could see the bulk of him dimly as he moved about. I rolled out of my blankets and crept noiselessly after him in my stocking feet. He had armed himself with a draw-knife from the tool locker, and with this he prepared to cut across the throat-halyards I had again rigged to the shears. He felt the halyards with his hands and discovered that I had not made them fast. This would not do for a draw-knife, so he laid hold of the running part, hove taut, and made fast. Then he prepared to saw across with the draw-knife.

"I wouldn't, if I were you," I said quietly.

He heard the click of my pistol and laughed.

"Hello, Hump," he said. "I knew you were here all the time. You can't fool my ears."

"That's a lie, Wolf Larsen," I said, just as quietly as before. "However, I am aching for a chance to kill you, so go ahead and cut."

"You have the chance always," he sneered.

"Go ahead and cut," I threatened ominously.

"I'd rather disappoint you," he laughed, and turned on his heel and went aft.

"Something must be done, Humphrey," Maud said, next morning, when I had told her of the night's occurrence. "If he has liberty, he may do anything. He may sink the vessel, or set fire to it. There is no telling what he may do. We must make him a prisoner."

"But how?" I asked, with a helpless shrug. "I dare not come within reach of his arms, and he knows that so long as his resistance is passive I cannot shoot him."

"There must be some way," she contended. "Let me think."

"There is one way," I said grimly.

She waited.

I picked up a seal-club.

"It won't kill him," I said. "And before he could recover I'd have him bound hard and fast."

She shook her head with a shudder. "No, not that. There must be some less brutal way. Let us wait."

But we did not have to wait long, and the problem solved itself. In the morning, after several trials, I found the point of balance in the foremast and attached my hoisting tackle a few feet above it. Maud held the turn on the windlass and coiled down while I heaved. Had the windlass been in order it would not have been so difficult; as it was, I was compelled to apply all my weight and strength to every inch of the heaving. I had to rest frequently. In truth, my spells of resting were longer than those of working. Maud even contrived, at times when all my efforts could not budge the windlass, to hold the turn with one hand and with the other to throw the weight of her slim body to my assistance.

At the end of an hour the single and double blocks came together at the top of the shears. I could hoist no more. And yet the mast was not swung entirely inboard. The butt rested against the outside of the port rail, while the top of the mast overhung the water far beyond the starboard rail. My shears were too short. All my work had been for nothing. But I no longer despaired in the old way. I was acquiring more confidence in myself and more confidence in the possibilities of windlasses, shears, and hoisting tackles.

There was a way in which it could be done, and it remained for me to find that way.

While I was considering the problem, Wolf Larsen came on deck. We noticed something strange about him at once. The indecisiveness, or feebleness, of his movements was more pronounced. His walk was actually tottery as he came down the port side of the cabin. At the break of the poop he reeled, raised one hand to his eyes with the familiar brushing gesture, and fell down the steps—still on his feet—to the main deck, across which he staggered, falling and flinging out his arms for support. He regained his balance by the steerage companionway and stood there dizzily for a space, when he suddenly crumpled up and collapsed, his legs bending under him as he sank to the deck.

"One of his attacks," I whispered to Maud.

She nodded her head; and I could see sympathy warm in her eyes.

We went up to him, but he seemed unconscious, breathing spasmodically. She took charge of him, lifting his head to keep the blood out of it and despatching me to the cabin for a pillow. I took his pulse. It beat steadily and strong, and was quite normal. This puzzled me. I became suspicious.

"What if he should be feigning this?" I asked, still holding his wrist.

Maud shook her head, and there was reproof in her eyes. But just then the wrist I held leaped from my hand, and the hand clasped like a steel trap about my wrist. I cried aloud in awful fear, a wild inarticulate cry; and I caught one glimpse of his face, malignant and triumphant, as his other hand compassed my body and I was drawn down to him in a terrible grip.

My wrist was released, but his other arm, passed around my back, held both my arms so that I could not move. His free hand went to my throat, and in that moment I knew the bitterest foretaste of death earned by one's own idiocy. Why had I trusted myself within reach of those terrible arms? I could feel other hands at my throat. They were Maud's hands, striving vainly to tear loose the hand that was throttling me. She gave it up, and I heard her scream in a way that cut me to the soul, for it was a woman's scream of fear and heart-breaking despair. I had heard it before, during the sinking of the *Martinez.*

My face was against his chest and I could not see, but I heard Maud turn and run swiftly away along the deck. Everything was happening quickly. I had not yet had a glimmering of unconsciousness, and it seemed that an interminable period of time was lapsing before I heard her feet flying back. And just then I felt the whole man sink under me. The breath was leaving his lungs and his chest was collapsing under my weight. Whether it was merely the expelled breath, or his consciousness of his growing impotence, I know not, but his throat vibrated with a deep groan. The hand at my throat relaxed. I breathed. It fluttered and tightened again. But even his tremendous will could not overcome the dissolution that assailed it. That will of his was breaking down. He was fainting.

Maud's footsteps were very near as his hand fluttered for the last time and my throat was released. I rolled off and over to the deck on my back, gasping and blinking in the sunshine. Maud was pale but composed,—my eyes had gone instantly to her face,—and she was looking at me with mingled alarm and relief. A heavy seal-club in her hand caught my eyes, and at that moment she followed my gaze down to it. The club dropped from her hand as though it had suddenly stung her, and at the same moment my heart surged with a great joy. Truly she was my woman, my mate-woman, fighting with me and for me as the mate of a caveman would have fought, all the primitive in her aroused, forgetful of her culture, hard

under the softening civilization of the only life she had
ever known.

"Dear woman!" I cried, scrambling to my feet.

The next moment she was in my arms, weeping convulsively on my shoulder while I clasped her close. I looked
down at the brown glory of her hair, glinting gems in
the sunshine far more precious to me than those in the
treasure-chests of kings. And I bent my head and kissed
her hair softly, so softly that she did not know.

Then sober thought came to me. After all, she was only
a woman, crying her relief, now that the danger was past,
in the arms of her protector or of the one who had been
endangered. Had I been father or brother, the situation
would have been in no wise different. Besides, time and
place were not meet, and I wished to earn a better right
to declare my love. So once again I softly kissed her hair
as I felt her receding from my clasp.

"It was a real attack this time," I said; "another shock
like the one that made him blind. He feigned at first, and
in doing so brought it on."

Maud was already rearranging his pillow.

"No," I said, "not yet. Now that I have him helpless,
helpless he shall remain. From this day we live in the cabin.
Wolf Larsen shall live in the steerage."

I caught him under the shoulders and dragged him to
the companionway. At my direction Maud fetched a rope.
Placing this under his shoulders, I balanced him across the
threshold and lowered him down the steps to the floor. I
could not lift him directly into a bunk, but with Maud's
help I lifted first his shoulders and head, then his body,
balanced him across the edge, and rolled him into a lower
bunk.

But this was not to be all. I recollected the handcuffs in
his stateroom, which he preferred to use on sailors instead
of the ancient and clumsy ship irons. So, when we left
him, he lay handcuffed hand and foot. For the first time

in many days I breathed freely. I felt strangely light as I
came on deck, as though a weight had been lifted from my
shoulders. I felt, also, that Maud and I had drawn more
closely together. And I wondered if she, too, felt it, as we
walked along the deck side by side to where the stalled
foremast hung in the shears.

CHAPTER THIRTY-SEVEN

AT once we moved aboard the *Ghost*, occupying our old state-rooms and cooking in the galley. The imprisonment of Wolf Larsen had happened most opportunely, for what must have been the Indian summer of this high latitude was gone and drizzling stormy weather had set in. We were very comfortable, and the inadequate shears, with the foremast suspended from them, gave a businesslike air to the schooner and a promise of departure.

And now that we had Wolf Larsen in irons, how little did we need it! Like his first attack, his second had been accompanied by serious disablement. Maud made the discovery in the afternoon while trying to give him nourishment. He had shown signs of consciousness, and she had spoken to him, eliciting no response. He was lying on his left side at the time, and in evident pain. With a restless movement he rolled his head around, clearing his left ear from the pillow against which it had been pressed. At once he heard and answered her, and at once she came to me.

Pressing the pillow against his left ear, I asked him if he heard me, but he gave no sign. Removing the pillow and repeating the question, he answered promptly that he did.

"Yes," he answered in a low, strong voice, "and worse than that. My whole right side is affected. It seems asleep. I cannot move arm or leg."

"Feigning again?" I demanded angrily.

He shook his head, his stern mouth shaping the strangest, twisted smile. It was indeed a twisted smile, for it was on the left side only, the facial muscles of the right side moving not at all.

"That was the last play of the Wolf," he said. "I am paralyzed. I shall never walk again. Oh, only on the other side," he added, as though divining the suspicious glance I flung at his left leg, the knee of which had just then drawn up and elevated the blankets.

"It's unfortunate," he continued. "I'd liked to have done for you first, Hump. And I thought I had that much left in me."

"But why?" I asked, partly in horror, partly out of curiosity.

Again his stern mouth framed the twisted smile, as he said:

"Oh, just to be alive, to be living and doing, to be the biggest bit of the ferment to the end, to eat you. But to die this way—"

He shrugged his shoulders, or attempted to shrug them, rather, for the left shoulder alone moved. Like the smile, the shrug was twisted.

"But how can you account for it?" I asked. "Where is the seat of your trouble?"

"The brain," he said at once. "It was those cursed headaches brought it on."

"Symptoms," I said.

He nodded his head. "There is no accounting for it. I was never sick in my life. Something's gone wrong with my brain. A cancer, a tumor, or something of that nature,—a thing that devours and destroys. It's attacking my nerve-centres, eating them up, bit by bit, cell by cell—from the pain."

"The motor-centres, too," I suggested.

"So it would seem; and the curse of it is that I must lie here, conscious, mentally unimpaired, knowing that the lines are going down, breaking bit by bit communication with the world. I cannot see, hearing and feeling are leaving me, at this rate I shall soon cease to speak; yet all the time I shall be here, alive, active, and powerless."

"When you say *you* are here, I'd suggest the likelihood of the soul," I said.

"Bosh!" was his retort. "It simply means that in the attack on my brain the higher psychical centres are untouched. I can remember, I can think and reason. When that goes, I go. I am not. The soul?"

He broke out in mocking laughter, then turned his left ear to the pillow as a sign that he wished no further conversation.

Maud and I went about our work oppressed by the fearful fate which had overtaken him,—how fearful we were yet fully to realize. There was the awfulness of retribution about it. Our thoughts were deep and solemn, and we spoke to each other scarcely above whispers.

"You might remove the handcuffs," he said that night, as we stood in consultation over him. "It's dead safe. I'm a paralytic now. The next thing to watch out for is bed sores."

He smiled his twisted smile, and Maud, her eyes wide with horror, was compelled to turn away her head.

"Do you know that your smile is crooked?" I asked him; for I knew that she must attend him, and I wished to save her as much as possible.

"Then I shall smile no more," he said calmly. "I thought something was wrong. My right cheek has been numb all day. Yes, and I've had warnings of this for the last three days; by spells, my right side seemed going to sleep, sometimes arm or hand, sometimes leg or foot."

"So my smile is crooked?" he queried a short while after. "Well, consider henceforth that I smile internally, with my soul, if you please, my soul. Consider that I am smiling now."

And for the space of several minutes he lay there, quiet, indulging his grotesque fancy.

The man of him was not changed. It was the old, indomitable, terrible Wolf Larsen, imprisoned somewhere within that flesh which had once been so invincible and splendid. Now it bound him with insentient fetters, walling his soul in darkness and silence, blocking it from the world which to him had been a riot of action. No more would he conjugate the verb "to do" in every mood and tense. "To be" was all that remained to him—to be, as he had defined death, without movement; to will, but not to execute; to think and reason and in the spirit of him to be as alive as ever, but in the flesh to be dead, quite dead.

And yet, though I even removed the handcuffs, we could not adjust ourselves to his condition. Our minds revolted. To us he was full of potentiality. We knew not what to expect of him next, what fearful thing, rising above the flesh, he might break out and do. Our experience warranted this state of mind, and we went about our work with anxiety always upon us.

I had solved the problem which had arisen through the shortness of the shears. By means of the watch-tackle, (I had made a new one), I heaved the butt of the foremast across the rail and then lowered it to the deck. Next, by means of the shears, I hoisted the main boom on board. Its forty feet of length would supply the height necessary properly to swing the mast. By means of a secondary tackle I had attached to the shears, I swung the boom to a nearly perpendicular position, then lowered the butt to the deck, where, to prevent slipping, I spiked great cleats around it. The single block of my original shears-tackle I had attached to the end of the boom. Thus, by carrying this tackle to the windlass, I could raise and lower the end of the boom at will, the butt always remaining stationary, and, by means of guys, I could swing the boom from side to side. To the end of the boom I had likewise rigged a hoisting tackle; and when the whole arrangement was completed I could not but be startled by the power and latitude it gave me.

Of course, two days' work was required for the accomplishment of this part of my task, and it was not till the morning of the third day that I swung the foremast from the deck and proceeded to square its butt to fit the step.

Here I was especially awkward. I sawed and chopped and chiselled the weathered wood till it had the appearance of having been gnawed by some gigantic mouse. But it fitted.

"It will work, I know it will work," I cried.

"Do you know Dr. Jordan's final test of truth?" Maud asked.

I shook my head and paused in the act of dislodging the shavings which had drifted down my neck.

" 'Can we make it work? Can we trust our lives to it?' is the test."*

"He is a favorite of yours," I said.

"When I dismantled my old Pantheon and cast out Napoleon and Caesar and their fellows, I straightway erected a new Pantheon," she answered gravely, "and the first I installed was Dr. Jordan."

"A modern hero."*

"And a greater because modern," she added. "How can the Old World heroes compare with ours!"

I shook my head. We were too much alike in many things for argument. Our points of view and outlook on life at least were very like.

"For a pair of critics we agree famously," I laughed.

"And as shipwright and able assistant," she laughed back.

But there was little time for laughter in those days, what of our heavy work and the awfulness of Wolf Larsen's living death.

He had received another stroke. He had lost his voice, or he was losing it. He had only intermittent use of it. As he phrased it, the wires were like the stock market, now up, now down. Occasionally the wires were up and he spoke as well as ever, though slowly and heavily. Then speech would suddenly desert him, in the middle of a sentence perhaps, and for hours, sometimes, we would wait for the connection to be re-established. He complained of great pain in his head, and it was during this period that he arranged a system of communication against the time when speech should leave him altogether—one pressure of the hand for "yes," two for "no." It was well that it was arranged, for by evening his voice had gone from him. By hand pressures, after that, he answered our questions, and when he wished to speak he scrawled his thoughts with his left hand, quite legibly, on a sheet of paper.

The fierce winter had now descended upon us. Gale followed gale, with snow and sleet and rain. The seals had started on their great southern migration, and the rookery was practically deserted. I worked feverishly. In spite of the bad weather, and of the wind which especially hindered me, I was on deck from daylight till dark and making substantial progress.

I profited by my lesson learned through raising the shears and then climbing them to attach the guys. To the top of the foremast, which was just lifted conveniently from the deck, I attached the rigging, stays, and throat and peak halyards. As usual, I had underrated the amount of work involved in this portion of the task, and two long days were necessary to complete it. And there was so much yet to be done—the sails, for instance, which practically had to be made over.

While I toiled at rigging the foremast, Maud sewed on canvas, ready always to drop everything and come to my assistance when more hands than two were required. The canvas was heavy and hard, and she sewed with the regular sailor's palm and three-cornered sail-needle. Her hands were soon sadly blistered, but she struggled bravely on, and in addition doing the cooking and taking care of the sick man.

"A fig for superstition," I said on Friday morning. "That mast goes in today."*

Everything was ready for the attempt. Carrying the boom-tackle to the windlass, I hoisted the mast nearly clear of the deck. Making this tackle fast, I took to the windlass the shears-tackle, (which was connected with the end of the boom), and with a few turns had the mast perpendicular and clear.

Maud clapped her hands the instant she was relieved from holding the turn, crying:

"It works! It works! We'll trust our lives to it!"

Then she assumed a rueful expression.

"It's not over the hole," she said. "Will you have to begin all over?"

I smiled in superior fashion, and, slacking off on one of the boom-guys and taking in on the other, swung the mast perfectly in the centre of the deck. Still it was not over the hole. Again the rueful expression came on her face, and again I smiled in a superior way. Slacking away on the boom-tackle and hoisting an equivalent amount on the shears-tackle, I brought the butt of the mast into position directly over the hole in the deck. Then I gave Maud careful instructions for lowering away and went into the hold to the step on the schooner's bottom.

I called to her, and the mast moved easily and accurately. Straight toward the square hole of the step the square butt descended; but as it descended it slowly twisted so that square would not fit into square. But I had not even a moment's indecision. Calling to Maud to cease lowering, I went on deck and made the watch-tackle fast to the mast with a rolling hitch. I left Maud to pull on it while I went below. By the light of the lantern I saw the butt twist slowly around till its sides coincided with the sides of the step. Maud made fast and returned to the windlass. Slowly the butt descended the several intervening inches, at the same time slightly twisting again. Again Maud rectified the twist with the watch-tackle, and again she lowered away from the windlass. Square fitted into square. The mast was stepped.

I raised a shout, and she ran down to see. In the yellow lantern light we peered at what we had accomplished. We

looked at each other, and our hands felt their way and
clasped. The eyes of both us, I think, were moist with the
joy of success.

"It was done so easily after all," I remarked. "All the
work was in the preparation."

"And all the wonder in the completion," Maud added.

"I can scarcely bring myself to realize that that great
mast is really up and in; that you have lifted it from the
water, swung it through the air, and deposited it here
where it belongs. It is a Titan's task."

"And they made themselves many inventions," I began
merrily, then paused to sniff the air.

I looked hastily at the lantern. It was not smoking. Again
I sniffed.

"Something is burning," Maud said, with sudden conviction.

We sprang together for the ladder, but I raced past her
to the deck. A dense volume of smoke was pouring out of
the steerage companionway.

"The Wolf is not yet dead," I muttered to myself as I
sprang down through the smoke.

It was so thick in the confined space that I was compelled
to feel my way; and so potent was the spell of Wolf Larsen
of my imagination, I was quite prepared for the helpless
giant to grip my neck in a strangle hold. I hesitated, the
desire to race back and up the steps to the deck almost
overpowering me. Then I recollected Maud. The vision
of her, as I had last seen her, in the lantern light of the
schooner's hold, her brown eyes warm and moist with joy,
flashed before me, and I knew that I could not go back.

I was choking and suffocating by the time I reached
Wolf Larsen's bunk. I reached my hand and felt for his.
He was lying motionless, but moved slightly at the touch
of my hand. I felt over and under his blankets. There was
no warmth, no sign of fire. Yet that smoke which blinded
me and made me cough and gasp must have a source. I

lost my head temporarily and dashed frantically about the
steerage. A collision with the table partially knocked the
wind from my body and brought me to myself. I reasoned
that a helpless man could start a fire only near to where
he lay.

I returned to Wolf Larsen's bunk. There I encountered
Maud. How long she had been there in that suffocating
atmosphere I could not guess.

"Go up on deck!" I commanded peremptorily.

"But, Humphrey—" she began to protest in a queer,
husky voice.

"Please! Please!" I shouted at her harshly.

She drew away obediently, and then I thought, What if
she cannot find the steps? I started after her, to stop at
the foot of the companionway. Perhaps she had gone up.
As I stood there, hesitant, I heard her cry softly:—

"Oh, Humphrey, I am lost."

I found her fumbling at the wall of the after bulkhead,
and, half leading her, half carrying her, I took her up the
companionway. The pure air was like nectar. Maud was
only faint and dizzy, and I left her lying on the deck when
I took my second plunge below.

The source of the smoke must be very close to Wolf
Larsen—my mind was made up to this, and I went straight
to his bunk. As I felt about among his blankets, something
hot fell on the back of my hand. It burned me, and I
jerked my hand away. Then I understood. Through the
cracks in the bottom of the upper bunk he had set fire
to the mattress. He still retained sufficient use of his left
arm to do this. The damp straw of the mattress, fired
from beneath and denied air, had been smouldering all
the while.

As I dragged the mattress out of the bunk it seemed
to disintegrate in mid-air, at the same time bursting into
flames. I beat out the burning remnants of straw in the
bunk, then made a dash for the deck for fresh air.

Several buckets of water sufficed to put out the burning mattress in the middle of the steerage floor; and ten minutes later, when the smoke had fairly cleared, I allowed Maud to come below. Wolf Larsen was unconscious, but it was a matter of minutes for the fresh air to restore him. We were working over him, however, when he signed for paper and pencil.

"Pray do not interrupt me," he wrote. "I am smiling."

"I am still a bit of the ferment, you see," he wrote a little later.

"I am glad you are as small a bit as you are," I said.

"Thank you," he wrote. "But just think of how much smaller I shall be before I die."

"And yet I am all here, Hump," he wrote with a final flourish. "I can think more clearly than ever in my life before. Nothing to disturb me. Concentration is perfect. I am all here and more than here."

It was like a message from the night of the grave; for this man's body had become his mausoleum. And there, in so strange sepulture, his spirit fluttered and lived. It would flutter and live till the last line of communication was broken, and after that who was to say how much longer it might continue to flutter and live?

CHAPTER THIRTY-EIGHT

"I THINK my left side is going," Wolf Larsen wrote, the morning after his attempt to fire the ship. "The numbness is growing. I can hardly move my hand. You will have to speak louder. The last lines are going down."

"Are you in pain?" I asked.

I was compelled to repeat my question loudly before he answered.

"Not all the time."

The left hand stumbled slowly and painfully across the paper, and it was with extreme difficulty that we deciphered the scrawl. It as like a "spirit message," such as are delivered at séances of spiritualists for a dollar admission.

"But I am still here, all here," the hand scrawled more slowly and painfully than ever.

The pencil dropped, and we had to replace it in the hand.

"When there is no pain I have perfect peace and quiet. I have never thought so clearly. I can ponder life and death like a Hindoo sage."

"And immortality?" Maud queried loudly in the ear.

Three times the hand essayed to write but fumbled hopelessly. The pencil fell. In vain we tried to replace it. The fingers could not close on it. Then Maud pressed and held the fingers about the pencils with her own hand, and the hand wrote, in large letters, and so slowly that the minutes ticked off to each letter:

"B–O–S–H."

It was Wolf Larsen's last word, "bosh," sceptical and invincible to the end. The arm and hand relaxed. The trunk of the body moved slightly. Then there was no movement.

Maud released the hand. The fingers spread slightly, falling apart of their own weight, and the pencil rolled away.

"Do you still hear?" I shouted, holding the fingers and waiting for the single pressure which would signify "Yes." There was no response. The hand was dead.

"I noticed the lips slightly move," Maud said.

I repeated the question. The lips moved. She placed the tips of her fingers on them. Again I repeated the question. "Yes," Maud announced. We looked at each other expectantly.

"What good is it?" I asked. "What can we say now?"

"Oh, ask him—"

She hesitated.

"Ask him something that requires 'no' for an answer," I suggested. "Then we will know with certainty."

"Are you hungry?" she cried.

The lips moved under her fingers, and she answered, "Yes."

"Will you have some beef?" was her next query.

"No," she announced.

"Beef-tea?"

"Yes, he will have some beef-tea," she said quietly, looking up at me. "Until his hearing goes we shall be able to communicate with him. And after that—"

She looked at me queerly. I saw her lips trembling and the tears swimming up in her eyes. She swayed toward me and I caught her in my arms.

"Oh, Humphrey," she sobbed, "when will it all end? I am so tired, so tired."

She buried her head on my shoulder, her frail form shaken with a storm of weeping. She was like a feather in my arms, so slender, so ethereal. "She has broken down at last," I thought. "What can I do without her help?"

But I soothed and comforted her, till she pulled herself bravely together and recuperated mentally as quickly as she was wont to do physically.

"I ought to be ashamed of myself," she said. Then added, with the whimsical smile I adored, "but I am only one small woman."

That phrase, the "one small woman," startled me like an electric shock. It was my own phrase, my pet, secret phrase, my love phrase for her.*

"Where did you get that phrase?" I demanded, with an abruptness that in turn startled her.

"What phrase?" she asked.

"One small woman."

"Is it yours?" she asked.

"Yes," I answered, "mine. I made it."

"Then you must have talked in your sleep," she smiled.

The dancing, tremulous light was in her eyes. Mine, I knew, were speaking beyond the will of my speech. I leaned toward her. Without volition I leaned toward her, as a tree is swayed by the wind. Ah, we were very close together in that moment. But she shook her head, as one might shake off sleep or a dream, saying:

"I have known it all my life. It was my father's name for my mother."

"It is my phrase, too," I said stubbornly.

"For your mother?"

"No," I answered, and she questioned no further, though I could have sworn her eyes retained for some time a mocking, teasing expression.

With the foremast in, the work now went on apace. Almost before I knew it, and without one serious hitch, I had the mainmast stepped. A derrick-boom, rigged to the foremast, had accomplished this; and several days more found all stays and shrouds in place, and everything set up taut. Topsails would be a nuisance and a danger for a crew of two, so I heaved the topmasts on deck and lashed them fast.

Several more days were consumed in finishing the sails and putting them on. There were only three—the jib, foresail, and mainsail; and, patched, shortened, and distorted, they were a ridiculously ill-fitting suit for so trim a craft as the *Ghost*.

"But they'll work!" Maud cried jubilantly, "We'll make them work, and trust our lives to them!"

Certainly, among my many new trades, I shone least as a sail-maker. I could sail them better than make them, and I had no doubt of my power to bring the schooner to some northern port of Japan. In fact, I had crammed navigation form text-books aboard; and besides, there was Wolf Larsen's star-scale, so simple a device that a child could work it.

As for its inventor, beyond an increasing deafness and the movement of the lips growing fainter and fainter, there had been little change in his condition for a week. But on the day we finished bending the schooner's sails, he heard his last, and the last movement of his lips died away—but not before I had asked him, "Are you all there?" and the lips had answered, "Yes."

The last line was down. Somewhere within that tomb of the flesh still dwelt the soul of the man. Walled by the living clay, that fierce intelligence we had known burned on; but it burned on in silence and darkness. And it was disembodied. To that intelligence there could be no objective knowledge of a body. It knew no body. The very world was not. It knew only itself and the vastness and profundity of the quiet and the dark.

CHAPTER THIRTY-NINE

THE day came for our departure. There was no longer anything to detain us on Endeavor Island. The *Ghost*'s stumpy masts were in place, her crazy sails bent. All my handiwork was strong, none of it beautiful; but I knew that it would work, and I felt myself a man of power as I looked at it.

"I did it! I did it! With my own hands I did it!" I wanted to cry aloud.

But Maud and I had a way of voicing each other's thoughts, and she said, as we prepared to hoist the mainsail:

"To think, Humphrey, you did it all with your own hands!"

"But there were two other hands," I answered. "Two small hands, and don't say that was a phrase, also, of your father."

She laughed and shook her head, and held her hands up for inspection.

"I can never get them clean again," she wailed, "nor soften the weather-beat."

"Then dirt and weather-beat shall be your guerdon of honor," I said, holding them in mine; and, spite of my resolutions, I would have kissed the two dear hands had she not swiftly withdrawn them.

Our comradeship was becoming tremulous. I had mastered my love long and well, but now it was mastering me. Wilfully had it disobeyed and won my eyes to speech, and now it was winning my tongue—ay, and my lips, for they were mad this moment to kiss the two small hands which had toiled so faithfully and hard. And I, too, was mad. There was a cry in my being like bugles calling me to her.

And there was a wind blowing upon me which I could not resist, swaying the very body of me till I leaned toward her, all unconscious that I leaned. And she knew it. She could not but know it as she swiftly drew away her hands, and yet could not forbear one quick, searching look before she turned away her eyes.

By means of deck-tackles I had arranged to carry the halyards forward to the windlass; and now I hoisted the mainsail, peak and throat, at the same time. It was a clumsy way, but it did not take long, and soon the foresail as well was up and fluttering.

"We can never get that anchor up in this narrow place, once it has left the bottom," I said. "We should be on the rocks first."

"What can you do?" she asked.

"Slip it," was my answer. "And when I do, you must do your first work on the windlass. I shall have to run at once to the wheel, and at the same time you must be hoisting the jib."

This manoeuvre of getting under way I had studied and worked out a score of times; and, with the jib-halyard to the windlass, I knew Maud was capable of hoisting that most necessary sail. A brisk wind was blowing into the cove, and though the water was calm, rapid work was required to get us safely out.

When I knocked the shackle-bolt loose, the chain roared out through the hawse-hole and into the sea. I raced aft, putting the wheel up. The *Ghost* seemed to start into life as she heeled to the first fill of her sails. The jib was rising. As it filled, the *Ghost*'s bow swung off and I had to put the wheel down a few spokes and steady her.

I had devised an automatic jib-sheet which passed the jib across of itself, so there was no need for Maud to attend to that; but she was still hoisting the jib when I put the wheel hard down. It was a moment of anxiety, for the *Ghost* was rushing directly upon the beach, a stone's throw distant. But she swung obediently on her heel into the wind. There was a great fluttering and flapping of canvas and reef-points, most welcome to my ears, then she filled away on the other tack.

Maud had finished her task and come aft, where she stood beside me, a small cap perched on her wind-blown hair, her cheeks flushed from exertion, her eyes wide and bright with the excitement, her nostrils quivering to the rush and bite of the fresh salt air. Her brown eyes were like a startled deer's. There was a wild, keen look in them I had never seen before, and her lips parted and her breath suspended as the *Ghost*, charging upon the wall of rock at the entrance to the inner cove, swept into the wind and filled away into safe water.

My first mate's berth on the sealing grounds stood me in good stead, and I cleared the inner cove and laid a long tack along the shore of the outer cove. Once again about, and the *Ghost* headed out to open sea. She had now caught the bosom-breathing of the ocean, and was herself a-breath with the rhythm of it as she smoothly mounted and slipped down each broad-backed wave. The day had been dull and overcast, but the sun now burst through the clouds, a welcome omen, and shone upon the curving beach where together we had dared the lords of the harem and slain the holluschickie. All Endeavor Island brightened under the sun. Even the grim southwestern promontory showed less grim, and here and there, where the sea-spray wet its surface, high lights flashed and dazzled in the sun.

"I shall always think of it with pride," I said to Maud.

She threw her head back in a queenly way, but said, "Dear, dear Endeavor Island! I shall always love it."

"And I," I said quickly.

It seemed our eyes must meet in a great understanding, and yet, loath, they struggled away and did not meet.

There was a silence I might almost call awkward, till I broke it, saying:

"See those black clouds to windward. You remember, I told you last night the barometer was falling."

"And the sun is gone," she said, her eyes still fixed upon our island, where we had proved our mastery over matter and attained to the truest comradeship that may fall to man and woman.

"And it's slack off the sheets for Japan!" I cried gayly. "A fair wind and a flowing sheet,* you know, or however it goes."

Lashing the wheel, I ran forward, eased the fore and main sheets, took in on the boom-tackles, and trimmed everything for the quartering breeze which was ours. It was a fresh breeze, very fresh, but I resolved to run as long as I dared. Unfortunately, when running free, it is impossible to lash the wheel, so I faced an all-night watch. Maud insisted on relieving me, but proved that she had not the strength to steer in a heavy sea, even if she could have gained the wisdom on such short notice. She appeared quite heart-broken over the discovery, but recovered her spirits by coiling down tackles and halyards and all stray ropes. Then there were meals to be cooked in the galley, beds to make, Wolf Larsen to be attended upon, and she finished the day with a grand house-cleaning attack upon the cabin and steerage.

All night I steered, without relief, the wind slowly and steadily increasing and the sea rising. At five in the morning Maud brought me hot coffee and biscuits she had baked, and at seven a substantial and piping hot breakfast put new life into me.

Throughout the day, and as slowly and steadily as ever, the wind increased. It impressed one with its sullen determination to blow, and blow harder, and keep on blowing. And still the *Ghost* foamed along, racing off the miles till I was certain she was making at least eleven knots. It was too good to lose, but by nightfall I was exhausted. Though in splendid physical trim, a thirty-six-hour trick at the wheel was the limit of my endurance. Besides, Maud begged me to heave to, and I knew, if the wind and sea increased at the same rate during the night, that it would soon be impossible to heave to. So, as twilight deepened, gladly and at the same time reluctantly, I brought the *Ghost* up on the wind.

But I had not reckoned upon the colossal task the reefing of three sails meant for one man. While running away from the wind I had not appreciated its force, but when we ceased to run I learned to my sorrow, and well-nigh to my despair, how fiercely it was really blowing. The wind balked my every effort, ripping the canvas out of my hands and in an instant undoing what I had gained by ten minutes of severest struggle. At eight o'clock I had succeeded only in putting the second reef into the foresail. At eleven o'clock I was no farther along. Blood dripped from every finger end, while the nails were broken to the quick. From pain and sheer exhaustion I wept in the darkness, secretly, so that Maud should not know.

Then, in desperation, I abandoned the attempt to reef the mainsail and resolved to try the experiment of heaving to under the close-reefed foresail. Three hours more were required to gasket the mainsail and jib, and at two in the morning, nearly dead, the life almost buffeted and worked out of me, I had barely sufficient consciousness to know the experiment was a success. The close-reefed foresail worked. The *Ghost* clung on close to the wind and betrayed no inclination to fall off broadside to the trough.

I was famished, but Maud tried vainly to get me to eat. I dozed with my mouth full of food. I would fall asleep in the act of carrying food to my mouth and waken in torment to find the act yet uncompleted. So sleepily helpless was I that she was compelled to hold me in my chair to prevent my being flung to the floor by the violent pitching of the schooner.

Of the passage from the galley to the cabin I knew nothing. It was a sleep-walker Maud guided and supported. In fact, I was aware of nothing till I awoke, how long after I could not imagine, in my bunk with my boots off. It was dark. I was stiff and lame, and cried out with pain when the bed-clothes touched my poor finger-ends.

Morning had evidently not come, so I closed my eyes and went to asleep again. I did not know it, but I had slept the clock around and it was night again.

Once more I woke, troubled because I could sleep no better. I struck a match and looked at my watch. It marked midnight. And I had not left the deck until three! I should have been puzzled had I not guessed the solution. No wonder I was sleeping brokenly. I had slept twenty-one hours. I listened for a while to the behavior of the *Ghost*, to the pounding of the seas and the muffled roar of the wind on deck, and then turned over on my side and slept peacefully until morning.

When I arose at seven I saw no sign of Maud and concluded she was in the galley preparing breakfast. On deck I found the *Ghost* doing splendidly under her patch of canvas. But in the galley, though a fire was burning and water boiling, I found no Maud.

I discovered her in the steerage, by Wolf Larsen's bunk. I looked at him, the man who had been hurled down from the topmost pitch of life to be buried alive and be worse than dead. There seemed a relaxation of his expressionless face which was new. Maud looked at me and I understood.

"His life flickered out in the storm," I said.

"But he still lives," she answered, infinite faith in her voice.

"He had too great strength."

"Yes," she said, "but now it no longer shackles him. He is a free spirit."

"He is a free spirit surely," I answered; and, taking her hand, I led her on deck.

The storm broke that night, which is to say that it diminished as slowly as it had arisen. After breakfast next morning, when I had hoisted Wolf Larsen's body on deck ready for burial, it was still blowing heavily and a large sea was running. The deck was continually awash with the sea which came inboard over the rail and through the scuppers. The wind smote the schooner with a sudden gust, and she heeled over till her lee rail was buried, the roar in her rigging rising in pitch to a shriek. We stood in the water to our knees as I bared my head.

"I remember only one part of the service," I said, "and that is, 'And the body shall be cast into the sea.'"

Maud looked at me, surprised and shocked; but the spirit of something I had seen before was strong upon me, impelling me to give service to Wolf Larsen as Wolf Larsen had once given service to another man. I lifted the end of the hatch cover, and the canvas-shrouded body slipped feet first into the sea. The weight of iron dragged it down. It was gone.

"Good-by, Lucifer, proud spirit," Maud whispered, so low that it was drowned by the shouting of the wind; but I saw the movement of her lips and knew.

As we clung to the lee rail and worked our way aft, I happened to glance to leeward. The *Ghost*, at the moment, was uptossed on a sea, and I caught a clear view of a small steamship two or three miles away, rolling and pitching, head on to the sea, as it steamed toward us. It was painted black, and from the talk of the hunters of their poaching exploits I recognized it as a United States revenue cutter. I pointed it out to Maud and hurriedly led her aft to the safety of the poop.

I started to rush below to the flag-locker, then remembered that in rigging the *Ghost* I had forgotten to make provision for a flag-halyard.

"We need no distress signal," Maud said. "They have only to see us."

"We are saved," I said, soberly and solemnly. And then, in an exuberance of joy, "I hardly know whether to be glad or not."

I looked at her. Our eyes were not loath to meet. We leaned toward each other, and before I knew it my arms were about her.

"Need I?" I asked.

And she answered, "There is no need, though the telling of it would be sweet, so sweet."

Her lips met the press of mine, and, by what strange trick of the imagination I know not, the scene in the cabin of the *Ghost* flashed upon me, when she had pressed her fingers lightly on my lips and said, "Hush, hush."

"My woman, my one small woman," I said, my free hand petting her shoulder in the way all lovers know though never learn in school.

"My man," she said, looking at me for an instant with tremulous lids which fluttered down and veiled her eyes as she snuggled her head against my breast with a happy little sigh.

I looked toward the cutter. It was very close. A boat was being lowered.

"One kiss, dear love," I whispered. "One kiss more before they come."

"And rescue us from ourselves," she completed, with a most adorable smile, whimsical as I had never seen it, for it was whimsical with love.

APPENDIX 1

JACK LONDON AND THE *SOPHIA SUTHERLAND*

IT is easy to forget that *The Sea-Wolf* is a novel about the pelagic sealing industry; more so as that industry has long since ceased to exist. Like the extermination of the American bison, or the clearing of the Amazonian rain-forests, the history of pelagic sealing chronicles an ecological disaster born of commercial greed and inadequate regulation. The northern Pacific fur seal herd was millions strong in the 1860s. By 1893, when Jack London went to sea in the *Sophia Sutherland* (sometimes called the *Sophie Sutherland*) the seal population was still large, but had been reduced to three migratory groups. By 1910, only 140,000 seal were estimated to survive and the industry was no longer financially viable.

Three world powers had a direct interest in preventing the destruction of this resource—America, Russia, and Britain (through her colony, Canada). Their attempts to regulate the industry were frustrated by the unusual habits of the north Pacific fur seal (*Callorhinus ursinus*) and the unprotected status of animal life beyond the three-mile territorial limit. The fur seal swims every year to its breeding grounds ("rookeries") on the Pribilof Islands—a small archipelago off the coast of Alaska, in the Bering Sea, about 160 miles from the nearest land. The older bulls arrive first, in late April or early May, followed by the younger males. These breeding males have spent the winter feeding off fish around the nearby Aleutian Islands, south of the Pribilofs. The gravid females and immature males segregate themselves for most of the year. In early spring they make a much longer journey—in some cases as long as 6,000 miles—from feeding grounds as far south as San Francisco, or Japan. They arrive for their annual rendezvous two months after the males, in June and July. By this time, some eighty per cent of the species is clustered on these small lumps of rock in the Bering Sea. Smaller rookeries on the Asiatic, or Russian, side of the ocean, account for the other twenty per cent (mainly in the

Commander Islands, which London calls the "Copper" islands in *The Sea-Wolf*).

On arrival at the Pribilof islands, the gravid females give birth to a single pup. Almost immediately, they are impregnated again by some dominant bull, a "benedict" who has won his "harem" by combat with other bulls. The females remain until October, feeding the newborn pups until they are weaned. Some of the herd then swim down the Asiatic coast to Japan, others down the North American coast to California. The males go off to their own feeding grounds. These groups, or "sub-herds", will reunite again next summer at the Pribilofs, following their respective migrations.

There were two ways in which the seals could be killed in large enough numbers to make hunting a commercial proposition: at sea as they swam in their tightly-bunched herds, or on land, in their rookeries where they were sitting targets. Killing them on land was more efficient. The discovery by Russian fur traders of the breeding grounds in the Pribilofs in 1786 led to an orgy of indiscriminate slaughter, and near extermination of the species. This ecological vandalism was regulated when the Pribilofs became the exclusive preserve of the Russian-American company, in 1799. Control of the islands then passed into American hands with the Alaska purchase in 1867. But the Russians retained the smaller rookeries off their Siberian coast. In 1893, the year in which *The Sea-Wolf* is set, the Russian authorities were imposing savage punishments and confiscations on any Wolf Larsens they apprehended.

Although the rookeries in the Pribilofs were regarded as preserves, to be harvested judiciously, no such control was possible while the seals were on their great oceanic migrations. At sea, the seal was anyone's to kill. Their gregarious habits, sedate pace of surface swimming, and unvarying travel routes made them easy prey. In 1883 the American schooner *City of San Diego* sailed to the Bering Sea, and came back with a huge haul. The techniques used for catching the seal at sea were adapted from what the coastal Indians had used from time immemorial. Hunters in small boats, or dories, would be dropped from the mother ship and would enter the swimming herds, shooting or harpooning single animals at will with long-handled spears. As London points out in *The Sea-Wolf*, it was advantageous to disable the seal with a shotgun since a rifle bullet would cause the beast to die and sink before it could be dragged aboard. As many as fifty animals might be taken by a hunter

and his two-man crew in one day. On board the mother ship
the pelts were salted and stored. At the end of the season, they
would be landed at Yokohama, Vancouver, or San Francisco for
auction and transport to London and other cities in Europe,
where demand for the fur was greatest. Jack London insists that
"woman's vanity" was the driving force behind the industry. It
is true that seal skin was fashionable for women's muffs and
trimming on dress. But the great attraction of the fur was that
men also wore it, without any imputation of femininity. There
was a fashion in the early 1900s, for instance, for sealskin mo-
toring coats. (Early automobiles tended to expose the motorist
to the elements.) Such a coat would require as many as five
pelts to make—at a cost of $16 per-skin in 1903, when Jack
London wrote *The Sea-Wolf.* Male vanity played its part in
decimating the north Pacific seal population.

By the late 1880s, two full-time pelagic seal fleets were established: one Canadian, sailing from Victoria, the other American, sailing principally from San Francisco. The American vessels were largely privately owned, many—like the *Ghost*—by
their masters. The absence of company (or government) control, the prospect of quick profits, and fierce competition—
all led to a spirit of freebooting in the sealing fleet. It was
also extraordinarily dangerous work. Between 1886 and 1900,
sixteen vessels were lost (Jack London notes that Pete Holt, the
hunter who persuaded him to sign on the *Sophia Sutherland,*
was lost when his ship went down with all hands in 1894. Had
he stayed with his ship-mate, as he was tempted to do, the
world would never have had *The Sea-Wolf.*)

The average weight of sealing schooners was seventy tons,
and they were usually sail- rather than steam-driven. Crews
and hunters were recruited on a per-voyage basis (so sometimes
were captains where the ships were not master-owned, like the
Ghost). The sailors were paid on a monthly basis. In 1893,
the year of the *Ghost*'s voyage, a first mate would get $45
per month, a cook $40, a cabin boy $10, pullers and steerers
$30. The seamen would be obliged to buy items of working
equipment (heavy duty clothing, for instance) from the vessel's
stores. Food and drink was provided. Hunters were not salaried.
They would be paid on their "lay", $2 per skin taken. Hunters
were not required to work on board ship, but did stand watch—
for which they were not paid. On the average schooner working
crewmen would be quite small in number. With twelve sailors,
the *Ghost* was carrying two or three more than many sealers.

Most of the sealers could make do with just one officer, other than the captain. Schooners smaller than the *Ghost* might have a member of the crew double as cook and would dispense with a cabin boy. But 1890–2 had been boom years for the trade, and it is likely that Larsen was—temporarily at least—very prosperous and could afford to crew his vessel lavishly.

The sealing fleets adopted a pattern that paralleled the migrations of the herd they hunted. Before 1891 the schooners would leave port in early spring and follow the seal northward, killing as they went. On their return to their home ports in summer, they would unload their cargoes, restock and sail again for the Bering sea where they would slaughter the seal again as close to the rookeries as current regulations permitted them to go. The number of dories carried by any one mother ship varied from five to twenty. Often the Canadian vessels had Indian hunters; the American ships tended to have American hunters. The fleets found the gravid cows—large and slow beasts—a particularly convenient catch. But killing such seals clearly threatened the long-term viability of the herds. Since mother seals bear only one pup a year, a large maternal population is required for the survival of the species.

The speed with which pelagic hunting depleted the herds soon alarmed the authorities. The Alaska Commercial Company, who held the exclusive lease on harvesting the Pribilofs, regarded the pelagic sealers from the first as "pirates". In 1886, only three years after the *City of San Diego*'s pioneering voyage, the US authorities began arresting Canadian sealing vessels in the Bering Sea, on the grounds that it was a *mare clausum*. The legal grounds for doing this were dubious. By 1890, there was a full-blown stand-off between America and Britain (who felt their Canadian subjects were being denied the freedom of the waves). Intervention by the Royal Navy was threatened. Tempers cooled, however, and the so-called "modus vivendi" was put into effect in June 1891. This limited the United States kill, and put the Bering Sea out of bounds to all pelagic sealers, of whatever nation. In late 1893 (just after Jack London returned from his voyage) an international Tribunal of Arbitration recommended a close season in the Bering Sea, a *cordon sanitaire* of sixty mile radius around the Pribilofs, and a ban on the use of firearms in hunting seals in the Bering Sea. Effectively this quarantined the rookery area.

It was all to no avail. When they were barred from the Bering Sea, the sealing fleets promptly turned their attention

to the Asiatic coast and would skirt Russian territorial waters
as closely as they dared. They could still legitimately intercept
the herds on the open sea. Wolf Larsen's voyage on the *Ghost*
takes place in 1893, and closely reflects the tactics necessary for
the resourceful, freebooting captain-owner in that year, with
the closure of the Bering Sea to hunting in 1891. On its first
leg the *Ghost* leaves San Francisco in January, making a fast
south-west voyage with the trade winds, skirting just north
of Hawaii, over to the Bonin Islands to the south of Japan,
where the schooner will take on fresh provisions, and await the
herd as it swims its leisurely way north. Then it will follow
its prey along the northern Japanese Islands, off the coast of
Siberia, veering away from the Copper Islands, coming as close
to the "forbidden [Bering] sea" as Larsen dares. At the end of
the half-season, in summer, the *Ghost* will off-load its cargo
in Yokohama. It will then beat as fast a journey back to San
Francisco as it can, where the crew will be paid off.

Given the extra leg on this typical 1893 voyage, only one trip
is taken by a boat like the *Ghost*. Instead of leaving in early
spring (as in the years before 1891), Larsen sails in January.
With luck, he will get back in late summer. The *Ghost* will
have a longer period idle at the end of the year than in previous
two-trip seasons. But since the catches are high at this period,
Larsen will still come out well ahead and not suffer unduly from
the meddling of the authorities in closing off the Bering Sea.

Early on, Wolf Larsen is forced to make some changes to
this schedule. Because of the mutinous condition of his men
Larsen does not dare to touch the populated Bonin islands as
he had evidently done in 1892. (See Louis' conversation with
Humphrey in Chapter 6.) He is obliged to stop off at a deserted
bay, to get fresh water. It seems likely that had it completed its
voyage the *Ghost* would have run short of fresh food at some
point. The only gross improbability in Jack London's depiction
of the 1893 voyage of the *Ghost*, and its wreck, is the invention
of Endeavor Island. This is supposedly a hitherto undiscovered
rookery which is outside the Bering Sea area of United States
government control, or Russian territorial waters. As such, it
can be plundered at will by whoever first comes across it. One of
the unanswered questions at the end of *The Sea-Wolf* is—what
will Humphrey do with this valuable knowledge? Wolf Larsen's
starscale has accurately fixed the location of Endeavor Island.
If Humphrey has learned anything at all from Wolf he will go
to Yokohama, refit the *Ghost* (which will be his by the laws

of marine salvage) crew it with American sailors and return to
the island next spring. One good harvest, and the sale of the
Ghost on his return to San Francisco, will make him a rich man
for life. Or will Humphrey revert to his "bookworm" character,
take first-class passage back to California on a steamer, forget
about Endeavor Island, and live happily ever after with Maud
as the "Dean of American Letters the Second"? My guess is
that Humphrey will go for the money.

The years 1890–3 were a boom time for the sealers. By 1894
the combined American and Canadian fleets numbered some
111. Many of the newer schooners were large and specially built
as factory vessels. By 1897, it was clear that the survival of
the seal was in jeopardy. There was too much fleet chasing
too few seals too efficiently. In that year the United States
prohibited all its citizens from pelagic seal hunting. But after
a brief respite the slaughter continued. It was driven partly
by the high price the fur fetched at auction. By 1904 it had
risen to $20 per-skin (in 1893, it was $12.50). By 1909, it was a
sky-high $31. The schooners were forced into ever fiercer rivalry
with each other for the dwindling herd. While Jack London was
writing *The Sea-Wolf*, in 1902–3, the piratical exploits of the
McLean brothers were making headlines in the San Francisco
newspapers. The McLeans had begun sealing in separate vessels
as early as 1885, when they were perfectly respectable business-
men. By 1893, they had made a reputation for themselves as
the hard men of the trade. And by 1902, they were thought
of as no better than buccaneers. Their ruthlessness, however,
was probably more the consequence of sharper rivalry in the
industry than natural vice. (See below for the influence of the
McLean brothers on Jack London's conception of the Larsen
brothers.)

A census in 1909 reckoned the herd size had shrunk to under
150,000. In 1911, far too late, Britain, the United States, Japan,
and Russia signed the North Pacific Fur Seal treaty, banning
all pelagic sealing. The treaty is still in force. By 1911, as
D. G. Paterson, notes, the great sealing fleets had become "a
historical curiosity" and with them sailors like Wolf Larsen.
Eighty years later, the seals are now harvested with strict international supervision and are protected at sea. Their population
has recovered to some 1.6 million.

Jack London's involvement with the fur seal industry
began when he signed on as a crewman and boat-puller on the
Sophia Sutherland in January 1893. The *Sophia Sutherland* was

"a three-topmast schooner of eighty tons, Captain Sutherland commanding." The description of the *Ghost* at the beginning of Chapter 6 of *The Sea-Wolf* is almost certainly drawn from Jack London's memory of the *Sophia Sutherland*. Like the *Ghost*, the *Sophia Sutherland* had previously been a private yacht. It was converted in the rush to cash in on the sealing boom in the late 1880s. According to London's biographer, Richard O'Connor, Captain Sutherland's schooner had also once been "a pirate craft" and had sailed under at least three other names. She was known by her crew to have once sailed on "black-birding" raids—that is, snatching natives from Pacific islands for forced labour.

London gave a number of accounts of his seven months aboard the *Sophia Sutherland*. The most factual is in *John Barleycorn*, his "alcoholic memoirs" (1913). In late 1892, he tells us, he realized that he was "getting into a bad way of living." The sealing fleet was wintering in San Francisco Bay, and he met a seal-hunter, Pete Holt. Over drinks, he agreed to sail with Holt as his boat-puller. Eight days after his seventeenth birthday, on 20 January 1893, he signed before the shipping commissioners the articles of the *Sophia Sutherland*, bound for the coast of Japan.

The *Sophia Sutherland* had a crew of twenty-three. The *Ghost* has twenty-two (Jack presumably absented himself). In the novel, they break down as: two officers (Larsen, and a mate—the first dies, the second, Johansen, is promoted and killed; the third is Humphrey); twelve crew, boat-steerers and pullers; six hunters; one cook; one cabin boy. In *John Barleycorn*, London describes various members of the *Sophia Sutherland*'s crew, who approximate to the characters in *The Sea-Wolf*. In the forecastle "the oldest man, fat and fifty, was Louis. He was a broken skipper." He reappears as Louis in *The Sea-Wolf*. London records himself as having two particularly close friends on the *Sophia Sutherland*, "Victor and Axel [Gunderson], a Swede and a Norwegian". They presumably contributed something to the most amiable of the crew members on the *Ghost*, Johnson ("Yonson", as Larsen sneeringly calls him). There was another Scandinavian whom Jack London mentions in *John Barleycorn*, "Red John" (elsewhere called "Big Red"). From other accounts, one gathers that this Swede was the bully of the forecastle, and Jack was obliged to fight and nearly strangle him. Perhaps he became the unpleasant and overbearing Johansen and the fight became

Humphrey's battle with Mugridge. The *Sophia Sutherland* was nominally under the command of Captain Sutherland, but he was nearly 80 years old and delegated his master's authority to his son, who served as mate. Effective command was wielded by the vessel's very competent sailing master, an officer called Scott.

Obviously neither the owners nor Mr Scott were models for Wolf Larsen. In June 1905, London wrote to the editor of the *San Francisco Examiner* to say that "I based my Sea Wolf character" on the pirate Alexander McLean. McLean, who was constantly falling foul of the law for poaching seal in the early 1900s, was captain of the *Carmencita*. He was drowned in January 1906. McLean had a "big record", as London recalled in an obituary article, "as a rough character and was known as the worst man, so far as physical violence was concerned, among the seal hunters. He also had a brother, Dan McLean, who was almost as rough a customer as Alex." On 12 December 1914 Jack London wrote to Emma McLean that "I never personally laid eyes on Captain Alex. McLean in my life but I was seal hunting off the coast of Japan and crossed the trail of his schooner many times in 1893. At that time, on the Steamer *Alexandria*, another seal hunter, was his brother Captain Dan McLean." It will be remembered that Death Larsen's steamer is called *Macedonia*—which seems a clear echo of *Alexandria*.

Just a week before Jack took to sea in the *Sophia Sutherland* there was a report in the American papers about Daniel McLean which must surely have excited the young sailor. I quote from the 15 January 1893 issue of *New York Times* (which has a slightly different spelling of the name of McLean's vessel). The article is headed "Captain McLean's Bold Exploit":

San Francisco, Jan. 14—The steamer *Alexander*, which flies the Hawaiian flag, is fitting out here for a raid on the Russian seal rookeries on Copper Island. The *Alexander* was formerly the *Lewis*, but was caught last year by a Russian cruiser thirty miles away from the Siberian coast. She was taken to Petropaulovski and rechristened the *Alexander*. Captain McLean was finally allowed to recover his vessel, but he was forced to keep aloft the Russian flag. When he reached here he set about a scheme of revenge. He ascertained that Copper Island was guarded by only twenty men, most of whom are natives. He decided to raid the rookeries with a strong force. He has engaged sixty men, and they are all armed. The *Alexander* can make fourteen knots, and there is no Russian cruiser on the Siberian coast that can overhaul her. The scheme is, in company with the schooner *Edward F. Webster*, to make a descent on the Copper Island rookeries, clean out the garrison, and slaughter the seals.

McLean's bloody scheme evidently came to nothing. But it must surely have laid some seeds of *The Sea-Wolf* when London came to write the novel ten years later.

The *Sophia Sutherland* left San Francisco on 23 January, and followed the "southern passage in the northeast trades to the Bonin Islands", tiny points of land south of Japan. The *Sophia Sutherland* reached these in early summer, after 51 days at sea. Jack London recalls a monumental debauch while the vessel reprovisioned. The *Sophia Sutherland* then raced north from the Bonin Islands to pick up the seal herd, and hunted it for a hundred days moving upwards "into frosty, wintry weather and into and through vast fogs which hid the sun from us for a week at a time." The vessel was by now off the Siberian coast (or Jack London claimed it was; Franklin Walker in his 1964 edition of *The Sea-Wolf* guesses that the *Sophia Sutherland* probably did not go "further north than Cape Erimo on the southern coast of the most northerly Japanese Island, Hokkaido"). But it could not venture into the "forbidden" Bering Sea—where the seals were protected. And Captain Sutherland would have kept a wary eye about blundering into Russian waters and being apprehended like McLean. With a "big catch of skins in our salt" the *Sophia Sutherland* then sailed to Yokohama. They lay in the harbour for two drunken weeks while the cargo was unloaded. Then the *Sophia Sutherland* beat its way back to its home port. It arrived at San Francisco in August, when Jack and the rest of the crew were paid off.

In *John Barleycorn*, London records that "one of our number had been dropped overboard, with a sack of coal at his feet, between two snow squalls in a driving gale off Cape Jerimo" (i.e. Cape Erimo). Jack London worked this episode up for his first published piece of work, "Story of a Typhoon off the Coast of Japan". It was written—at his mother's encouragement—for a contest run by the *San Francisco Morning Call* for writers under twenty-two (Jack qualified by a full five years). Jack's "Story" won the first prize of $25 and was published in the paper on 12 November 1893.

There are some differences in the 1893 account of the typhoon and the version which Jack London wrote later in Chapter 17 of *The Sea-Wolf*. In the earlier essay, the typhoon blows

up on 10 April, as the *Sophia Sutherland* is sailing off the
Japan coast, near Cape Jerimo. All the six hunting boats are
out, with eighteen of the crew in them. The author is himself
in one of the boats. When they have landed a dozen seals,
they see the recall flag on the schooner's mizzen. They reach
the schooner as the sea begins to turn really dangerous. The
other five boats have already returned. The *Sophia Sutherland*
rides out the subsequent typhoon, while below decks "our green
hand, the 'Bricklayer', [was] dying of consumption." During the
storm, while the crew slept below, Jack—like Hump—steered
the *Sophia Sutherland* for an hour. By ten the next day the
typhoon (luridly described by the young London) had blown
itself out and "below, a couple of men were sewing the Bricklayer's body in canvas preparatory to the sea burial. And so
with the storm passed away the Bricklayer's soul."[1]

Jack London filled in the sad history of the Bricklayer in a
late autobiographical piece called "That Dead Men Rise Up
Never", published posthumously in *The Human Drift* (1917).
London again recreates life on the *Sophia Sutherland* in some
detail. There are twelve crewmen in the forecastle, ten of whom
(all Scandinavians) are "hardened, tarry-thumbed sailors". The
other two—the young Jack and the Bricklayer, a Missourian—
are novices who have never been to sea before. Jack proves
himself by always being eager to work beyond what is asked
of him and by standing up for himself (although he fights only
when he has to). He quickly picks up the skills of seamanship.
The Bricklayer, by contrast, is hopelessly inept: "no man less
fitted for the sea ever embarked on it." Forty years old (to Jack
London's seventeen) he is too old a dog to learn new tricks. He
is mercilessly bullied by the captain and mates. They force him
aloft into the rigging, where he freezes with terror, and has to be
brought down by two other sailors. His character is loathsome,
"vicious, malignant, dirty, and without common decency". He
fights with everyone. His shipmates detest the Bricklayer, and
treat him "like a beast". Looking back, London can see "how
heartless we were to him"—more so as the Bricklayer was at
the time a dying man. "We wanted him to die", London recalls,
"and he died hating us and hated by us."

When he finally died the Bricklayer's corpse was sewn up in

---

[1] London's essay can be read in *Jack London: Short Stories*,
edited by Earle Labor, Robert C. Leitz III, and I. Milo Shepard,
New York: Macmillan, 1990.

his soiled blankets instead of a canvas shroud. A gunnysack full of galley coal was fastened to his feet to add to the indignity of the ceremony. Captain Sutherland stumbled over the burial at sea service, and his son impatiently jerked the text away from his father's hands and rushed through the form of words. The phrase "And the body shall be cast into the sea" stuck indelibly in the young London's mind. Jack took over the Bricklayer's bunk, and later—while on solitary watch at night—saw what he took to be the ghost of his departed, and unloved, shipmate. As Franklin Walker notes: "The Bricklayer's experiences suggested more than one episode in *The Sea-Wolf.*"[2]

[2]   In this appendix I have drawn on D. G. Paterson and J. Wilen, "Depletion and Diplomacy: The North Pacific Seal Hunt, 1886–1910", *Research in Economic History*, Vol. 2, 1977, 81–139; D. G. Paterson, "The North Pacific Seal Hunt, 1886–1910: Rights and Regulations", *Explorations in Economic History*, Vol. 14, 1977, 97–119; Franklin Walker, "Afterword", *The Sea-Wolf*, (New York: NAL, 1981), pp. 337–48.

APPENDIX 2

FILM VERSIONS OF *THE SEA-WOLF*

JACK London assigned the dramatic rights of *The Sea-Wolf* to his then friend, Joseph Noel, shortly after the novel's publication. According to Noel it was he who had suggested the character of Larsen and the author was grateful. The two men later fell out. Noel meanwhile had sold the performance rights to a Broadway producer. There were other pirated, or semi-pirated stage and short film versions. When it was proposed to London that an authorized film be made of *The Sea-Wolf*, the dramatic rights had to be bought back in February 1914 at a cost of $3,835. Among other things, the dispute was a factor in the setting up of the Authors' League of America. Complex legal ties meant that Jack London never, while living, profited as he should have done from film or stage versions of *The Sea-Wolf* although it has always been his most successfully adapted work.

It was Hobart Bosworth, a pioneer of early Hollywood cinema, who proposed an authorized eight-reel film of *The Sea-Wolf* in summer 1913. (It was eventually cut back to seven reels—still very long by the standards of the time.) Jack London would receive 50 per cent of profits; Bosworth would play Larsen; $6,000 would be spent in production costs; London himself would play the supporting part of a seaman. (There was also an opening shot of Jack London, writer, at his desk in California.) The female lead—Maud Brewster—would be played by Viola Barry. To London's surprise the ensuing film was very faithful to the original, although the *dramatis personae* was reduced. Because of legal difficulties, release of Bosworth's *The Sea-Wolf* was held back until December 1913, and the film seems not to have been a great success financially. It ran against a rival unauthorized version (*Hellship*) made by the Balboa Amusement Company which—thanks to a legal loophole—could use London's story but not his title.

The Sea-Wolf was remade by Famous Players-Lasky Corporation in 1920. Another seven-reeler, this version was directed by George Melford and starred Noah Beery as Larsen. Some liberties were taken with the opening part of the story. Humphrey and Maud are romantically attached before the film starts—although she will not marry him because she thinks him a weakling. They are both on the ferry which is rammed and sinks. Larsen is attracted to Maud, and refuses to let the couple go after he has saved them from drowning. Thereafter the story more or less follows London's version. Wolf is stricken blind by one of his "headaches" while attempting to rape Maud. The lovers escape from the *Ghost* and drift to Endeavor Island. The *Ghost*, with only a blind Larsen on board, also drifts ashore. With his last energy, Larsen attempts to kill Humphrey, but dies in the attempt. Maud finally realises that Humphrey is worthy of her. They are rescued by a cruiser.

Another *Sea-Wolf* was made by the Ralph W. Ince Corporation in 1926. Also a seven-reeler, this production was a showcase for Ince, who directed and played Larsen. Claire Adams played Maud, Theodore von Eltz played Humphrey, and Snitz Edwards played Mugridge. Ince took gross liberties with London's story. Again both Humphrey and Maud are initially found on board the fateful ferry in San Francisco Bay. He is a novelist, and she has just been to a fancy dress party dressed in man's clothes. On being rescued, her sex is not apparent and she is forced to become a cabin boy. When Mugridge realises she is a woman, he tries to rape her. She is rescued by Larsen, who intends to rape her legally by marrying her—a ceremony which, as captain, he can perform himself. As the ceremony begins, the crew mutinies, and simultaneously Larsen is stricken blind. The boat is set on fire. Maud and Humphrey escape on a passing steamer, but Larsen chooses to go down with the burning *Ghost*, like the Viking warrior he is.

The 1930 *Sea-Wolf* ran to a massive ten reels and was the first "talkie" version of the novel. Produced by Fox Film Corporation, it was directed by Alfred Santell. Milton Sills played Larsen. The part of Humphrey was dispensed with altogether. Maud in this travestied version becomes "Lorna Marsh", a prostitute who catches Larsen's fancy in a Japanese port. She is lured on board the hell-ship *Ghost* when Allen Rand, a man with whom she is in love, is shanghaied. Rand, a landlubber, is made assistant to the cook, Mugridge. Later Rand is promoted to first mate when he saves Larsen's life in a mutiny. After a large catch of seals, Larsen attempts to rape Maud, but he is foiled when the *Ghost* is boarded by his brother "Death"

Larsen. Lorna and Rand escape in a sealing boat, and Mugridge blinds Wolf with a red-hot poker. "Death" ravages the *Ghost.* Eventually, the lovers' boat drifts back to the mother-ship, a floating wreck under the command of a blind captain. Knowing that he is dying, Wolf makes amends by giving Lorna and Rand provisions and directing them to the nearest shore.

The 1940 version of *The Sea-Wolf* is the most famous, and is most frequently re-run on television and in revival movie houses. It was produced by Warner Brothers and Hal B. Wallis, directed by Michael Curtiz, and had a screenplay by Robert Rossen. The cast was star-studded. Warner's had recently invested in a huge new tank (for scenes at sea) and a fog machine. Both were used in the gloomily atmospheric opening on the ferry (the setting is given specifically as "San Francisco, 1900"). Van Weyden, a novelist, was played by Alexander Knox. A Canadian, Knox was fresh from the London West End stage, and projected a desiccated, patrician image of his character. On the ferry, he is approached by an escaped convict, "Ruth Webster" (i.e. Maud Brewster, played by Ida Lupino) who is trying to hide from two detectives, who are also on board. Van Weyden declines to aid the girl, but at this point the ferry is rammed by the *Ghost* and sinks. Wolf Larsen (played by Edward G. Robinson) rescues the couple, but refuses to let them go ashore. Humphrey is made assistant to the cook (played by the Irish character actor, Barry Fitzgerald). Larsen has shanghaied a mysterious young sailor—in fact another escaped convict—George Leach (played by John Garfield). Ruth and Leach fall in love.

The middle parts of Curtiz's *The Sea-Wolf* more or less follow London's—with the role of Humphrey (lover and bookworm) split between the glamorous Garfield and the rather stuffy Knox. The climax, however, is strikingly changed. Leach is imprisoned on the sinking *Ghost* by the blind and vengeful Larsen (played with exuberant malevolence by Robinson). Knox engages in a battle of wills and wits with Robinson, allowing Lupino and Garfield to escape to a nearby island. Knox, who has been shot, goes down with Robinson and the *Ghost.* This version of the film is well worth seeing and despite its departures from London's narrative is a very worthy adaptation.

One of the odder episodes in the history of *The Sea-Wolf* was its transposition to a Western cowboy setting in *Barricade* (1950), directed by Peter Godfrey and starring Raymond Massey and Robert Douglas. The hell-ship *Ghost* becomes a

mining camp in this quite entertaining exercise. A more pedes-
trian version of *The Sea-Wolf*, retitled *Wolf Larsen*, was made
by Allied Artists in 1958. The film was directed by Harmon
Jones and showcased Barry Sullivan as the anti-hero of the title.
Around 1890, Wolf Larsen rescues a young man called "Van
Weyden" (no "Humphrey") who has been shipwrecked at sea.
He is pressed into service as a member of the crew. A mutiny is
put down, much as described in London's narrative. Meanwhile,
another group of shipwreck survivors is picked up, including a
beautiful girl, "Kristina" (played by Gita Hall). Later, during the seal-hunting, Larsen attempts to rape Kristina, but is
stricken with blindness. The crew put him in chains, and later
kill him. Van Weyden and Kristina have meanwhile fallen in
love. The film was shot entirely at sea on board a schooner
owned by Sterling Hayden. Reviewers found the movie "old
hat" and ponderously melodramatic.

In 1975, *The Sea-Wolf* was remade as *Wolf Larsen* (also
known as *Legend of the Seven Seas* and *Larsen, Wolf of the
Seven Seas*) by an Italian company. This version, which is a
very free adaptation, is primarily a showcase for the American
action star Chuck Connors. Directed by Giuseppi Vari, this
inferior film sometimes surfaces on American television and
video versions have been released. Admirers of London's novel
should avoid it.

EXPLANATORY NOTES

In a number of places I gratefully acknowledge the assistance of Donald Pizer's notes in the "Library of America" edition of *The Sea-Wolf* (1982). Frequent reference is made to *The Letters of Jack London* (1988), edited by Earle Labor, Robert C. Leitz III, and I. Milo Shepard.

1 *Mill Valley:* a city in Marin County, across the Golden Gate straits. Mill Valley is north-west of San Francisco, at the base of Mount Tamalpais (at 2,604 feet, the highest mountain on the west side of the Bay). At the period of *The Sea-Wolf* Mill Valley was a summer settlement. It became a year-round community when San Franciscans moved away from the city centre after the 1906 earthquake. "Furuseth" is a somewhat perverse choice of name for Van Weyden's decadent friend. For first readers of *The Sea-Wolf* it would inevitably recall the Norwegian-born labour leader Andrew Furuseth (1854–1938) a well known San Franciscan figure. Furuseth was a sailor who settled in California in 1891 and thereafter devoted himself to improving working conditions for men at sea. He was the President of the International Seaman's Union from 1908 to 1938, for which he accepted only the pay of an able-bodied seaman.

Nietzsche and Schopenhauer: Friedrich Nietzsche (1844–1900) and Arthur Schopenhauer (1788–1860), German philosophers. London disliked Schopenhauer's misogyny, to which he had recently exposed himself (see his letter of 28 May 1899 to Cloudesley Johns, in which he writes "Have been reading Schopenhauer's terrific arraignment of women [i.e. 'On Women', in *Studies in Pessimism*], or rather his phillipic against them. . . . Don't believe that I endorse them in toto." *Letters*, I, 80). In a much later letter to Mary Austin (5 November 1915, see *Letters*, III, 1513) London claimed that *The Sea-Wolf* was an attack on "Nietzsche and his super-man idea." But the biographer Andrew Sinclair argues that although Jack had been introduced to the philosopher by a fellow tramp in 1894, he did not seriously read Nietzsche's works until summer 1904, after writing *The Sea-Wolf*. Some critics have reconciled the contradiction by pointing out that Nietzsche's ideas were "in the air" in 1903, when London was writing the novel, and that he could have known them from conversations with the "Crowd"—the literary–bohemian set he had been mixing with for a couple of years (here personified by Charley Furuseth).

1 *this particular January Monday morning:* this is presumably the morning of 23 January 1893, when Jack London sailed out of San Francisco Bay on the *Sophia Sutherland.*

between Sausalito and San Francisco: Sausalito is the water-front town in Marin County where the main ferry docked. The Golden Gate Bridge was not built until 1936. In 1893, and in 1903 when London was writing, the San Francisco Bay was criss-crossed by thousands of miles of ferry routes, regarded as one of the transport wonders of the world. At this period the San Francisco population was about a third of a million and the city was the ninth largest in the United States. Since 1869 it had had a transcontinental railway link with the East Coast, but still retained much of its rough frontier character. Physically it was very different from the post-1906 earthquake San Francisco on which the present city is founded.

2 *in the current* Atlantic: the *Atlantic Magazine* was founded in 1857 in Boston and at this period—1893—retained a "Brahmin," East-Coast, character (like Humphrey himself). From 1890 to 1898 its editor was H. E. Scudder. There is nothing in current 1892–3 issues which resembles Humphrey's article. But it has been suggested that London may have been thinking of his own essay on "The Terrible and Tragic in Fiction" which was published in the June 1903 issue of the *Critic.*

"The Necessity for Freedom: A Plea for the Artist": this is

apparently a cue to the influence of Oscar Wilde on Van
Weyden. See Jack London's remark in a letter to Cloudesley
Johns, 7 June 1899, "I think I have the very thing for you,
The Soul of Man under Socialism, by Oscar Wilde. I have
not had a chance to read it myself, yet, but as soon as I do
I will forward it to you" (*Letters*, I, 82).

3 *the Heads:* a cluster of islands, just beyond the Golden Gate.

5 *rending of timber:* early readers of *The Sea-Wolf* would associate this accident at sea with the sinking of the ferry
San Rafael, which collided in fog with its sister ferry the
Sausalito, on 30 November 1901. Three lives were lost when
the *San Rafael* sank.

10 *my tremendous flight:* this passage looks forward to Jack
London's later story *The Star Rover* (1915) in which the
hero has the power of willing the death of his body in order
to wander the stars, living previous incarnations of himself.

11 *Bow Bells with his mother's milk:* the classic definition of a
cockney is a Londoner who has been born within the sound
of St Mary le Bow's church bells. In 1902 Jack spent six
weeks in the underworld of London, researching his book
The People of the Abyss. One of the byproducts was the
character of Mugridge in *The Sea-Wolf*. The reference to
Mugridge's "slim hips" in the next sentence is one of several
hints that the *Ghost*'s cook is homosexual. In conversation
with Joseph Noel (who is not entirely reliable) in 1912 London recalled "the foc'stle lovers he had encountered [on the
Sophia Sutherland]. It was frank, brutal, disgusting." Jack,
Noel adds, "despised homosexuals" (See Joseph Noel, *Footloose in Arcadia*, 1940, p. 224).

12 *the Farallones:* a group of islands about thirty miles west of
San Francisco Bay. Humphrey has been unconscious for a
long time.

seal-hunting to Japan: see Appendix 1 for the need in 1893
to hunt the seal off the coast of northern Japan rather than
sailing directly to their breeding grounds in the Bering Sea.

12 *sling yer 'ook:* i.e., "sling your hook", cockney slang for scurry off—usually furtively.

13 *brogans:* i.e. brogues, coarse shoes of untanned leather.

14 *Thomas Mugridge:* the author had actually met a 71-year-old Londoner (rather more sympathetic than the cook of the *Ghost*) of this name in 1902, and commemorated him in Chapter 15 of *The People of the Abyss*.

19 *a very superior breed to common sailor-folk:* for the superior status of the hunters, see Appendix 1.

your palm: i.e., a canvas pad with which to press the sewing needle through coarse fabric.

24 *the captain snapped sharply:* there is some mystery here. Later it emerges that "Leach" is indeed called McCarthy (see p. 139). Why he is on the run, we never find out. This mystery was built on to make a starring part for John Garfield in the 1940 film version of *The Sea-Wolf* (see Appendix 2).

Telegraph Hill: a district in north-eastern San Francisco named for the semaphore erected there in 1850. It would signal the arrival of ships in the Bay. Overlooking the North Beach and the "Barbary Coast" areas of the city, Telegraph Hill was a notoriously rough part of town.

Who shipped you, anyway?: i.e. what brokers did you sign with? They would take a commission for matching a sailor with an appropriate vessel. In Leach's case, since he is on the run, they squeezed him dry.

25 *You'll never see eighteen again:* Leach has lied about his age so as not to fit any police description of him that may have been circulated among the captains in the port.

26 *pilot-boats:* as Donald Pizer explains, boats would cruise some miles outside the Bay Area, and provide a pilot for any incoming vessel requiring one. When all its pilots were gone the boat, like the *Lady Mine* here, would return to the port to pick up another group of them.

27 *'Frisco tanglefoot:* a slang phrase current from the early nineteenth century onwards. It denotes cheap liquor, especially whisky, and is so-called because large quantities make the imbiber stumble.

29 *this burial at any rate:* for the origins of this episode in Jack London's own experience on the *Sophia Sutherland* see Appendix 1.

33 *pain from my hurt knee was agonizing:* Jack London had had an accident with a horse and carriage in December 1902, just before beginning to write *The Sea-Wolf*, in which one of his knees was badly injured.

34 *Gawd blime me:* i.e., "Gorblimey". The author must have heard this cockney semi-profanity many times in London and guessed at a wrong etymology—i.e. "God blame me." In fact it is a corruption of "God blind me".

38 *the University Club and the Bibelot:* as Donald Pizer notes, "the University Club, on Powell Street, was for men with a college background." The "Bibelot" is apparently London's pseudonym for the Bohemian Club, which he frequented at this period. "Bibelot" is French for trinket.

40 *Bill Sykes must have routed out his dog:* Bill Sikes, the murderer in Dickens's *Oliver Twist*, has a dog called Bull's eye. When we are introduced to Sikes in Chapter 15 he is in the act of kicking his dog and threatening to cut its throat for "winking" at him.

41 *gold and paper:* gold coins were legal tender in the United States until 1933.

43 *as Shakespeare, Tennyson, Poe, and De Quincey:* Literary giants: William Shakespeare (1564–1616), Alfred Tennyson (1809–92), Edgar Allan Poe (1809–49), Thomas De Quincey (1785–1859).

men such as Tyndall . . . a copy of "The Dean's English": John Tyndall (1820–93), professor of natural history at the Royal Institution from 1853; Richard A. Proctor (1837–88), astronomer; Charles Darwin (1809–92), author of *The Origin of Species* (1859). Thomas Bulfinch (1796–1867) compiled various popular studies of fable and mythology. Pizer identifies "Shaw" as Thomas B. Shaw (1813–62), author of *A Complete Manual of English Literature, with a Sketch of American Literature* (1865). "Johnson's 'Natural History' " Pizer guesses might be *Johnson's New General Encyclopedia* (1885). Robert C. and Thomas Metcalf published their *English Grammar for Common Schools* in 1894. Alonzo Reed and Brainerd Kellogg published their *Higher Lessons in English* in 1878. "The Dean's English", as Pizer notes, alludes to George W. Moon's *The Dean's English: A Criticism on the Dean of Canterbury's Essays on the Queen's English* (1864).

43 *"In a Balcony":* a poetic drama by Robert Browning. It opens with Norbert describing a violent headache to Constance, which may be prophetic here. Jack London was very interested in the Brownings at this period of his life, and saw resemblances in their "forbidden" relationship and his own affair with Charmian Kittredge (see *Letters*, I, 391–2). The plot of "In a Balcony" may be read as an allegory of the Jack, Charmian, and Bess triangle. In Browning's drama, Norbert, the Queen's favourite, must doom himself by confessing to her that he (treacherously) loves Constance.

45 *immortality in your eyes:* an echo, apparently, of Cleopatra's boast in *Antony and Cleopatra* that "eternity was in our lips and eyes".

my idealism: in the strict philosophical sense, in opposition to Larsen's materialism. Humphrey is, apparently, a disciple of the leading American idealist philosopher of the period, Josiah Royce (1855–1916).

46 *so does the jellyfish move:* Larsen's ruthlessly materialistic "monism" is derived (anachronistically) from Ernest Haeckel's *The Riddle of the Universe* (*Welträthsel*, 1899). London read Haeckel's treatise shortly before writing *The Sea-Wolf*, and in his darker moods he was strongly attracted to the philosopher's theories. In March 1900, he wrote

to Cloudesley Johns that "Haeckel's position is as yet unassailable" (*Letters*, I, 164). On 6 January 1902, he told the same correspondent: "But after all, what squirming, anywhere, damned or otherwise, means anything? That's the question I am always prone to put: What's this chemical ferment called life all about? . . . I have at last discovered what I am. I am a materialistic monist." Haeckel's *Riddle* took the form of an answer to a series of "enigmas" about life and the universe—much as outlined in the philosophical dialogues between Larsen and Van Weyden. Haeckel's solution to the riddle, "Monism", assumed that all life derived from, and remained forever connected with, the most basic protozoic, unicellular forms. "Man is separated from other animals only by quantitative, not qualitative, differences", he asserted. All life was connected in a genealogical "tree" with "monera" (Larsen's "yeasts") at its root. Haeckel's most quoted observation was that "ontogeny recapitulates phylogeny". In his/her life cycle, the individual replays the entire evolutionary drama, from the most simple functions of the monera up. It is his (or Haeckel's) monism that justifies Larsen's provocative equation between the immensely sophisticated operation of a human being like himself and "yeast". Haeckel's scepticism about traditional religion and ethics (and some of his racial theories) are also reproduced by Larsen.

46 *like a frigate bird:* according to the *OED*, "a large, swift, tropical bird of prey."

49 *the San Francisco and Victoria fleets:* the two principal sealing fleets were headquartered in these two ports. See Appendix 1.

50 *on Bering Sea:* for the reason why the *Ghost* cannot venture into the Bering Sea this year (1893) see Appendix 1.

and a very sociable fellow: Louis is based on an actual shipmate of Jack London's on the *Sophia Sutherland.* He gives a description of him in Chapter 16 of *John Barleycorn:* "In the forecastle, the oldest man, fat and fifty, was Louis. He

was a broken skipper. John Barleycorn had thrown him, and
he was winding up his career where he had begun it, in the
forecastle."

51 *Hakodate:* port on the northern island of Japan, Hokkaido.

Kura Island: Pizer guesses this to be "Kurish, one of Japan's
Kuril Islands, north of Hokkaido Island".

the great big beast mentioned iv in Revelation: i.e. the "First
Wild Beast" in Revelation 13 who comes "out of the sea".

52 *which is a Roosian preserve:* Copper Island is the English
name for Medny Island in the south-west Bering Sea. The
seal rookery there was under strict Russian control (see Appendix 1). There was in 1893 considerable resentment in
America at Russian naval action against foreign sealers, the
confiscation of their ships and imprisonment of their crews.
This was partly the inspiration of Kipling's narrative poem
"The Rhyme of the Three Sealers" (1893), which also seems
to have been a source for *The Sea-Wolf.* The poem concerns
three American sealers, the *Baltic,* the *Northern Light,* and
the *Stralsund.* It begins: "Now this is the law of the Mus-
covite, that he proves with shot and steel / When you come
by his isles in the Smoky Sea you may not take the seal." The
Northern Light nevertheless goes into the Smoky Sea (i.e.
the Bering Sea, in Russian territorial waters) with a stove
pipe stuck from her starboard port, to resemble a cannon.
Thus disguised as a Russian cruiser (complete with flag) she
comes on the *Baltic,* frightens her into flight, and pirates her
cargo of (poached) seal. The *Baltic*'s crew are terrified of
being captured by the Russian excisemen, "For life it is that
is worse than death, by force of Russian law / To work in
the mines of mercury that loose the teeth in your jaw." An
epic battle ensues between Tom Hall, master of the *Northern
Light* and the *Stralsund*'s Reuben Paine.

54 *humming coster songs:* i.e. London street songs. The term
costermonger (apple-seller) has come to denote all cockneys.

55 *But it is a revelation, on the other hand:* between chapters 6

and 14, London experiments with breaking into the present
tense from time to time. When *The Sea-Wolf* was serialized in the *Century*, the editors regularized these present
tense changes (in addition to removing much of what they
considered to be foul-mouthed in London's text). It must
have been familiar to the author. When in 1893 he wrote his
first published piece of writing—a description of weathering
a typhoon on board the *Sophia Sutherland*—the editors of
the *San Francisco Morning Call* insisted that he change his
present tense narration to past tense.

55 *sodgerin'*: see Eric Partridge's *Dictionary of Slang and Un-
conventional English*, "soger, sojer; sodger—a soldier (col-
loquial and dialect). If applied to a sailor it constitutes a
a grave, damaging pejorative, for it connotes shirking and
malingering."

making his first voyage: Harrison is apparently based on the
character called the "Bricklayer" on the *Sophia Sutherland*.
See Appendix 1.

62 *she sows a thousand lives:* there seems to be an echo of
Tennyson's *In Memoriam* (1850), stanza 46, in which "Nature", contemplating evolution, declares "A thousand types
are gone / I care for nothing, all shall go."

dockers fighting like wild beasts for a chance to work: London
had come to know London dockers well in his research for
The People of the Abyss. He describes at length the hardship
of their lives in a number of places, but not this particular
phenomenon.

65 *and a wild delight:* misquoted, as Pizer points out, from
Robert Browning's *The Ring and the Book*, Book 1, 1391–2.
It should be "a wild desire".

66 *the trail that is always new:* from Rudyard Kipling's poem
"The Long Trail" (1892). In Kipling's version "Her plates are
scarred" reads "Her plates are flaked". The poem is a hymn
to the irresistible call of the ocean.

67 *Song of the Trade Wind:* David Mike Hamilton records that
in his library copy of A. B. Lubbock's *Round the Horn before
the Mast* (1902) London noted, on p. 116, a shanty "song of
the tradewind".

68 *this culminating century of civilization:* i.e., the 1890s. See
also note to page 117.

   the cruel hand of a vivisectionist: a resonant word at the
time. Vivisection was relatively little used in American med-
ical research although it was a favourite tool of physiolo-
gists and other scientists in Britain. The law relating to
vivisection in Britain had been regulated by the Cruelty to
Animals Act of 1876 which decreed that only experiments
necessary for the "advancement of physiological knowledge"
were permissible. It became known as the "Scientist's Bill."
Every two years from 1897 bills were introduced in the American Congress banning animal experimentation. None was
passed. Works of fiction which anthropomorphized animals,
like Anna Sewell's *Black Beauty* (1877) and Jack London's
The Call of the Wild, were regarded as useful to the anti-
vivisectionist cause.

69 *Nap:* or "Napoleon", a variety of two- or four-handed euchre
particularly popular in England. The player is given five
cards and must predict the tricks he will win.

   a remittance man: i.e. a black sheep of some well-off family
who pay him a regular pension to keep out of England.

72 *altruism:* the term was invented by the French sociologist
Auguste Comte and popularized in England by his disciple Herbert Spencer (1820–1903). Although a Darwinian,
Spencer argued that altruism (as opposed to purely selfish
egoism) tended ultimately to the survival of the fittest, as
society moved beyond inefficient individualism to efficient
collectivist forms of organisation.

73 *his 'Data of Ethics':* the works of Spencer alluded to in
this paragraph are his *First Principles* (1862), *Principles of
Biology* (1864–7), *Principles of Psychology* (1870–2), *Data*

of Ethics (1879). Spencer was probably the largest single intellectual influence on Jack London. In the autobiographical novel *Martin Eden* (1909) the hero is described as idly picking up *First Principles* one afternoon and reading it, without break (even for food or sleep), for thirty-six hours. The intellectual impact is equivalent to that of rebirth: "here was the man Spencer, organizing all knowledge for him, reducing everything to unity, elaborating ultimate realities, and presenting to his startled gaze a universe so concrete of realization that it was like the model of a ship such as sailors make and put into glass bottles."

73 *the benefit of his race:* the relevant passage in Chapter 3, section 8 of the *Data* reads: "Moreover, just as we [earlier] saw that evolution becomes the highest possible when the conduct simultaneously achieves the greatest totality of life in self, in offspring, and in fellow-men; so here we see that the conduct called good rises to the conduct conceived as best, when it fulfills all three classes of ends at the same time."

74 *what is a hedonist?:* in the *Data* Spencer divides hedonism into two kinds: "egotistic and universalistic, according as the happiness sought is that of the actor himself or is that of all."

a Caliban who has pondered Setebos: a reference to Browning's *Caliban upon Setebos; or Natural Theology in the Island* (1864; the island reference may be prophetic here). A dramatic monologue. Caliban, the monster of Shakespeare's *Tempest,* meditates upon Setebos's (i.e. God's) purposes as he wallows on his desert island, before the arrival of Prospero. The particular passage alluded to here seems to be that in which Caliban observes a line of crabs marching to the sea and decides, god-like, to "let twenty pass, and stone the twenty-first / Loving not, hating not, just choosing so."

79 *Telegraph Hill billingsgate:* for Telegraph Hill, see the note to p. 24. "Billingsgate" means "swearing"; the term alludes to the proverbially foul-mouthed porters in the London fish market of the name.

82 *two years in Reading:* i.e. Reading Gaol. Possibly put in

London's mind by Wilde's *Ballad of Reading Gaol* (1898).

82 *a tu-penny gaff:* a fun-fair charging twopence for entry.

86 *Tomlinsonian ghosts:* an allusion to the hero of Rudyard
    Kipling's "Tomlinson" in *Barrack-Room Ballads* (1892).
    Tomlinson, a bookish aesthete, dies in his house in Berkeley
    Square. He is taken by a spirit to heaven and to hell. St
    Peter and Lucifer both bar him entrance, on the grounds
    that he has not really lived.

    Mrs. Grundy: symbol of rigid and ridiculous respectabil-
    ity. The character was invented by the now entirely forgot-
    ten playwright Thomas Morton (1764?–1838) in his comedy
    Speed the Plough (1798). At the time of writing *The Sea-
    Wolf* London applied the term to the generic reader of the
    Century magazine, in which the novel was serialized.

88 *the ship's precise location!:* in Jack London's library was
    a marked-up copy of John E. Davis's *Sun's True Bearing
    or Azimuth Tables* (1900). David Mike Hamilton describes
    the marginalia London made, presumably about the time
    of writing *The Sea-Wolf:* "London wanted to know how to
    use Sumner's method of finding the position of a ship at sea,
    and marked the latitude table . . . The flyleaves of the book
    were used as a scratch pad for navigational arithmetic."

    footprints on the sands of time: a quotation from H. W.
    Longfellow's poem *Resignation:* "Lives of great men all re-
    mind us / We can make our lives sublime / And, departing,
    leave behind us, / Footprints on the sands of time."

90 *and choked them:* see Christ's parable, Matthew 13.

91 *I am a Dane:* Romsdal Fiord is about 100 miles south of
    Trondheim in Norway. Larsen's family presumably migrated
    because more work was available there for poor fishermen
    and sailors.

92 *The Corsican:* i.e. Napoleon Bonaparte.

94 *black-birding:* abducting natives to work as slaves.

96 *under the sun:* Ecclesiastes 9. Jack London originally forgot that earlier in the novel, in Chapter 3 (see p. 20), he had specifically written that there was no Bible on board the *Ghost.* It was Cloudesley Johns (who read the manuscript for London) who pointed the error out in March 1904. The necessary correction was made about the Bible being found in the dead mate's gear at this late stage. (See *Letters,* I, 421.)

97 *the memory of that insolence!:* from the fourth (1879) edition of Edward Fitzgerald's translation of the *Rubáiyát of Omar Khayyám.* This melancholy poem (which contains much praise of drink) by the twelfth-century Persian was a favourite of Jack London's. (See *Letters,* I, 59).

112 *tommy:* cockney slang for "food", more particularly bread. Mugridge's complaints here repeat points made in Chapter 25 "The Hunger Wail", in Jack London's *The People of the Abyss.*

113 *Aspinwall:* i.e. Colón, the second largest city in Panama. The name was changed in 1890.

Unalaska: an island on the Aleutian chain, off the coast of Alaska. Mugridge is thinking of the hottest and coldest places to which his work has taken him.

117 *Yes, eighty-three. Ten years ago:* noteworthy as fixing the primary date of *The Sea-Wolf*'s action as 1893—something confirmed by Larsen's tortuous voyage to hunt the seal. But as will be clear, many of the literary allusions in the text are to works of later date.

121 *a story out of Boccaccio:* as Pizer points out, the allusion is to the second story of the third day of the *Decameron* where a king tries to detect the identity of his wife's lover by feeling the pulses of suspects while they (perhaps supposedly) sleep.

a Kanaka: i.e. a native Hawaiian or South Sea islander.

thruppenny bits . . . sixpence: the old pre-copper British threepenny pieces (or bits) were of silver, like sixpences ("tanners") and could easily be mistaken by a foreigner.

122 *what a pony is I don't know:* it is cockney for twenty-five pounds sterling.

127 *gazabas:* more usually "gazabos", turn-of-the-century slang from the Spanish *gazapo*—a shrewd fellow. (Here used ironically.)

136 *Say nothin' but saw wood:* i.e., snore, pretend you are asleep.

Wainwright Island: Wainwright is on the northern tip of Alaska—far further north than the *Ghost* now is (i.e., somewhere below the 30th parallel). Perhaps one of the Bonin Islands (now called Ogasawara-Jima) is intended. See, for instance, Chapter 16 of *John Barleycorn*, describing the *Sophia Sutherland*'s calling at one of these islands to take on fresh water.

139 *He's my old man:* see note to p. 29. On their first meeting Larsen mysteriously knew Leach's real name.

156 *at-biscuit toss:* nautical variant of "within a stone's throw".

157 *the trans-Pacific steamships:* plying the 3,500 miles between San Francisco and Yokohama. See Humphrey's remark to Leach below.

159 *ulster:* a long loose rough overcoat, usually with a waist belt.

176 *is called vagrancy:* Jack London was himself arrested for vagrancy in late June 1894 and spent thirty days in Erie County Penitentiary. See *The Road* (1907).

178 *Lang . . . the English language?:* the reference is to the British man of letters Andrew Lang (1844–1912). Presumably it is in his *Letters on Literature* (1889) that he is supposed to have made this judgment on Miss Brewster.

the American Mrs Meynell!: a reference to the English poet Alice Meynell (1847–1922), whose verse was famously delicate and fine-drawn. If this is 1893 the reference is slightly

anachronistic since Meynell's reputation was established by
her *Poems* published in that year.

179 *the Dean of American Letters, the Second:* the first was
William Dean Howells (1837–1920).

189 *that magnificent hit with his 'Forge':* Pizer plausibly suggests
that this is an allusion to Edward Markham's radical poem
"The Man with the Hoe", first published in the *San Francisco Examiner*, 15 January 1899. The poem was a favourite
of London's. "Written after seeing Millet's World-Famous
Painting" on its being displayed in San Francisco the poem
was promoted by Jack London and by other members of the
"Crowd". It became itself world-famous. The reference is, of
course, anachronistic if this is 1893.

190 *the forty-fourth parallel:* the *Ghost* is now some 600 miles
north of Yokohama, and three-quarters up the length of
Hokkaido. This is probably farther north than Jack London
himself went in the *Sophia Sutherland* in 1893.

194 *seeking you:* from Arthur Symons's poem "Magnificat", 1895.
Maud Brewster was created by Jack London at the height of
his early infatuation with Charmian Kittredge. In a letter of
September 1903 (around the time that he was writing this
passage) Jack quoted to Charmian two rather less decent
lines from "Magnificat": "God made our bodies each for each,
and put your hand into my hand" (see *Letters*, I, 382).

195 *they played to me:* from Sonnet 26 of Elizabeth Barrett
Browning's *Sonnets from the Portuguese* (1850). About
the period he was writing this section of *The Sea-Wolf* Jack
London wrote to Charmian Kittredge: "I always held, always
I say, that there were rare loves, such as the Browning love,
once in a generation of folks. But I little dreamed that
such a love would be my love affair" (28 September 1903,
Letters, I, 391). He and Charmian steeped themselves in the
Brownings' love poetry at this period of their affair.

197 *the forbidden sea:* for the reasons that hunting in the Bering
Sea was forbidden in 1893, see Appendix 1.

199 *Who steals my purse steals trash:* Iago to Othello (III.iii.151); usually quoted, as here, without allusion to Iago's brazen cynicism.

soup-kitchens and bread-lines: 1893 was a period of severe trade depression. In April 1894, seven months after signing off the *Sophia Sutherland*, Jack London joined Kelly's "Army of the Unemployed" on its march on Washington. (See *The Road*, 1907.)

202 *He who delights the most lives the most:* Larsen has evidently been reading *Festus* (1889), P. J. Bailey's poetical rewriting of *Faust*. Here he echoes Festus's declaration "We live in deeds not years; in thoughts not breaths; / In feelings, not in figures on a dial. / We should count time in heart throbs. He most lives / Who thinks most—feels the noblest—acts the best."

215 *Sky-hooting through the brine:* this looks as if it ought to be Kipling, but I have been unable to locate it. "Sky-hooting" means "scooting", or "scudding".

220 *a male Circe:* Humphrey is thinking of the episode in the *Odyssey* in which Circe enchants the shipmates of Ulysses, and transforms them into swine.

223 *perfect my transgression:* quoted from Part V of *Tristram of Lyonesse* (1882) by Swinburne. This is the passage in which Iseult realizes that she loves Tristram more than God. It is likely that the poem, like others quoted in *The Sea-Wolf*, had a private significance for Jack London and Charmian Kittredge, who were—like Tristram and Iseult—secret, adulterous, lovers.

224 *Dowson's "Impenitentia Ultima":* the title of one of the poems in Ernest Dowson's *Verses* (1896). Wolf Larsen and Maud Brewster are continuing the theme of atheistic rebellion and the world well lost. Dowson's poem (the title means "final impenitence") is a monologue in which the speaker imagines himself at the judgement seat. There he exchanges an eternity of bliss for a last glimpse of his earthly love, and

an hour with her: "Before the ruining waters fall and my life
be carried under / And Thine anger cleave me through as
child cuts down a flower / I will praise Thee, Lord, in Hell,
while my limbs are racked asunder / For the last sad sight
of her face and the little grace of an hour."

225 *that brilliant though dangerous thinker:* Hippolyte Taine
(1828–93), French literary critic and author of *A History
of English Literature* (1863). Humphrey thinks Taine is
"dangerous" because of his materialist line of analysis, and
such widely quoted remarks as "le vice et la vertu sont des
produits comme le vitriol et le sucre." Taine promoted
novelists like Zola who would have been anathema to
Humphrey Van Weyden, although they might well have
appealed to the materialistic monist Wolf Larsen.

The first anarchist: in the context of 1903–4 a loaded term.
On 6 September 1901 the anarchist Leon Czolgosz shot President McKinley in Buffalo. The President died eight days
later. At his trial Czolgosz claimed that he was converted to
anarchism by the writings of Emma Goldman. There was a
huge popular revulsion against anarchist doctrines. London
was sympathetic to Czolgosz, commenting "he is the fruit
of society, and for society he suffers" (to Elwyn Hoffman,
18 September 1901, *Letters*, I, 252). London had met Emma
Goldman (1869–1939) through the Strunsky sisters "probably in 1899" (see *Letters*, I, 269).

226 *than serve in heaven:* Satan's boast in *Paradise Lost*, Book
1, 257–63.

250 *Endeavor Island:* initially (see the remark on p. 249 about
"a station") Humphrey assumes that the island is one of the
Russian preserves or the American controlled Pribilofs. But
we are to assume that Endeavor Island is in fact outside the
territorial control of either of the great powers, presumably
a hitherto undiscovered rookery south of the Bering Sea.

251 *Crusoe:* in Defoe's novel (1719). In fact Robinson Crusoe
salvages fire-making materials from his wrecked vessel.

251 *I remember Winters:* Winters, the "newspaper fellow with an
     Alaskan and Siberian reputation" is evidently supposed to be
     Jack London himself. See the author's best-known story "To
     Build a Fire" (1908).

261 *Dr. Jordan's book:* as Pizer points out, Maud refers to David
     Starr Jordan (1851–1931), naturalist, social reformer, and
     (from 1891–1913) first president of Stanford University.
     Specifically, Maud recalls (somewhat improbably) the fourth
     volume of Jordan's *The Fur Seals and the Fur-Seal Islands
     of the North Pacific Ocean* (1898–9).

     holluschickie: from the Russian, meaning "young bachelors".

264 *benedicts:* i.e., newly coupled bulls (named after the sworn
     bachelor Benedick who finally succumbs to marriage in
     Shakespeare's *Much Ado about Nothing*).

     my woman, my mate: the use of this term marked a notable
     point in the Jack–Charmian relationship. See his letter to
     her of 12 October 1903 (about the time he was writing this
     passage of *The Sea-Wolf*): "God! You do love me! I never
     needed any proof of it, yet each new proof is sweet, so sweet.
     And this last proof is not alone sweet; it is heroic. You *are*
     brave, my own brave mate woman" (*Letters*, I, 394–5).

266 *Red, 4451:* this must be a San Francisco exchange and (hy-
     pothetical) telephone number, I think.

     jerking beef on the plains: i.e. beef which has been cut into
     narrow strips and cured in the sun. Much loved by cowboys.

268 *their mysterious journey into the south:* for the annual mi-
     grations of the seals, see Appendix 1.

274 *which prevented speech:* some commentators wonder if Wolf is
     really blind or not. But probably he detects Hump's identity
     by the unusual fact that he does not spit after coughing.

286 *and he is strong again:* Jules Michelet (1798–1874), historian.
     In later life, Michelet wrote *L'Amour* (1858) and *La Femme*

(1859). According to Pizer this remark "appears to be a loose paraphrase of one of many such remarks" in these books.

287 *an inverted "V" . . . And then there was the windlass!:* Jack London gave a great deal of thought to the business of stepping the *Ghost*'s masts. He took specialist advice, and experimented on his sloop the *Spray*. On 20 December 1903 he wrote the following letter on the subject to Robert Johnson: "Dear Mr. Johnson:—By the time you take the topmast off the foremast, and further reduce the butt by the dismasting, you will have a 65 or 70-foot spar, say 15 inches in diameter at the butt and weighing somewhere around 3500 pounds. Rig a sheers out of the fore and main-topmasts thus [London draws a large inverted "V"]. Put a hoisting tackle at apex of sheers. Carry this tackle to an improved crank windlass capable of lifting 3 tons (one man heaving), and something's bound to happen. If I couldn't step—not one mast, but both masts,—single-handed, it would be because I didn't have somebody to "hold the turn". Van Weyden has Maud to hold the turn, and he is going to put in both masts. . . . Seriously, though, the thing can be done. And I consulted, in rigging my schooner at the very start, the shipyard men. They gave me the figures, length, weights, powers of windlasses, etc. I am just in the thick of stepping the masts now—and it proves up" (*Letters*, I, 400-1).

291 *none so poor . . . to do him reverence:* from Antony's funeral oration in *Julius Caesar*, where he recalls "the word of Caesar might / Have stood against the world; now lies he there, / And none so poor to do him reverence".

295 *would not require a Sherlock Holmes:* topical. Conan Doyle's detective was introduced to the reading world with *A Study in Scarlet* (1887).

314 *Can we trust our lives to it?' is the test:* Pizer identifies this as a statement by David Starr Jordan in "The Stability of Truth", an article in *Popular Science Monthly*, 50 (March 1897): "The final test of scientific truth is this: Can we make it work? Can we trust our lives to it?"

314 *A modern hero:* London met Jordan as early as 1892. In a
letter to Cloudesley Johns of 29 July 1899 he wrote that
Jordan was "to a certain extent, a hero of mine" (*Letters*,
I, 99). But in later life, long after writing *The Sea-Wolf*,
London fell out with Jordan. He rejected Jordan as bourgeois
and publicly quarreled with him. He went so far as to claim
in August 1916 that "I have been all my life an intellectual
opponent to David Starr Jordan" (see *Letters*, III, 1567).

315 *A fig for superstition. . . . That mast goes in today:* an
allusion to the nautical superstition about starting tasks, or
leaving ports, on Friday, the unlucky day of the week.

322 *one small woman . . . my love phrase for her:* see Jack
London's letter to Charmian, 27(?) October 1903, where he
addresses her as "the one small woman who means all the
world to me, who is all the world and upon whom I base my
hope of Paradise" (*Letters*, I, 397).

327 *a fair wind and a flowing sheet:* loosely quoted from Allan
Cunningham's (1784–1842) ballad "A wet Sheet and a flowing Sea".

GLOSSARY

The Sea-Wolf—particularly in its later chapters—is liberally laced with nautical terminology. Often these terms are baffling, even when definitions are supplied. For those who, like myself, are not expert the following glossary may be helpful. I have drawn on *The Concise Oxford Dictionary* (revised edition, 1946), Gershom Bradford's *The Mariner's Dictionary* (published by Weathervane Books, 1952), and the very useful "Glossary of Nautical Terms" appended to Thomas Philbrick's "Penguin Classics" edition of R. H. Dana's *Two Years before the Mast* (1981). For those interested in the nautical aspects of London's novel Professor Philbrick's annotated edition is an invaluable companion. In using this glossary it should be remembered that the *Ghost* is a fore-and-aft rigged schooner. Illustrations of the layout of such vessels can be found in standard encyclopædias and dictionaries such as *Webster*'s.

Abeam on a line at right angles to the ship's length.

Aft the back part (stern) of the vessel, as in "come aft" (come back).

After-mast mast nearest stern.

Astern behind the ship.

Athwart across, or at right angles to the fore and aft line of the ship.

Back to back a sail (or "back it over") is to throw it aback (i.e. the situation of the sails when the wind presses their surface against the mast, forcing the vessel astern). This can happen accidentally, or be a deliberate manœuvre.

Beam a ship's breadth.

Beam-ends a vessel is on beam ends when it is turned over so that its beams (i.e. cross pieces of timber, or joists supporting the deck) are almost or entirely perpendicular.

Belay a command, meaning "make the rope fast".

Bitts pieces of timber or iron going perpendicularly through the deck, to which ropes, etc., may be attached.

Blanket impede another vessel by passing between it and the wind.

Block a piece of wood, or pulley, with sheaves, or wheels, in it to allow a rope to run. Blocks with ropes running through them form a tackle.

Boat-tackles the windlass, or other mechanism for lifting a boat on board or out of the water.

Bomb gun gun used to indicate a ship's presence in fog, or at night.

Bow fore-end of boat or ship from where it begins to arch inwards; often used as a plural as in "the bows of the ship." "Bow on" is head-on.

Bowline simple but secure knot which forms a hole, or "eye" in the rope.

Bowsprit-spar spar running out from ship's stem to which forestays are fastened. Sometimes shortened to "Bowsprit".

Break as in "break of the poop", that part of the deck when it rises or falls suddenly.

Bulkhead upright partition, dividing ship's cabins or water-tight compartments.

Butt the end of a mast, where it joins the deck.

Cable strong rope or chain, to which the anchor is attached.

Calking material (usually oakum or cotton) used for water- or weather-proofing the seams of the deck or the vessel's side planks.

Capstan a revolving barrel, worked by men walking round and pushing horizontal levers or bars for winding cable so as to hoist heavy sails. In men-of-war anchors are hoisted by capstan, in merchant ships by windlass.

Careen cause a vessel to heel over or "list".

Cleats pieces of wood or metal with two horns used to belay ropes (i.e. make them fast). Wedges.

Clew up to haul up the clew (i.e. back corner) of a sail.

Close-hauled with sails lined up as tight as possible to long (fore and aft) axis of the vessel in order to sail as directly into the wind (on a tack) as possible.

Close-reefed with the last reefs of the topsails, or other sails, taken in so reducing area exposed to the wind.

Companionway covered staircase to a cabin.

Crosstrees two horizontal, comparatively light, cross timbers bolted to the head of the lower mast to support the mast above.

Derrick-boom boom rigged to act as a crane; usually set at the foot of a mast.

Dingey or "dinghy"; ship's small boat propelled either by sail or oars.

Dog-watch dog watches are half watches from 4 to 6, and from 6 to 8 in the evening.

Downhauls ropes or tackle for lowering sail.

Drag sea-anchor in the form of a spar with a weighted sail attached, or a large canvas bag.

Dunnage loose wood, or mats, or rope stowed under or among cargo in the holds to prevent moisture and rubbing.

Eight-bells the half hours of the four-hour watches are measured in one to eight bells.

Even-keel the trim of the vessel when it is perfectly upright in the water.

Eyes the very forward part of the ship.

Flag-halyard rope on which to haul up signal flags.

Flensing-knives to "flense" (or "flinch") is to strip the blubber blanket from a whale or seal; loosely, to skin it.

Flying-jib light sail set before the jib on a flying jib-boom.

Fo'c'sle or forecastle, the forward part of the vessel, under the deck, where the crew lives in merchant ships.

Fore-sheets inner part of bows of boat, with gratings for the bowman.

Foreboom tackle the ropes used to control the spar used to extend the sail at the front of the vessel.

Forecastle-head the area at the bow of the vessel.

Forefoot foremost part of the keel on the ship; the point at which the stem joins the keel.

Foremast the forward mast.

Foresail principal sail on the foremast.

Gaff spar extending top of fore-and-aft sail behind the mast supporting a trapezoid (rather than a triangular) sail.

Gaff-topsail a light sail set over a gaff, the foot, or lower end of the sail, being spread by it.

Galley ship's kitchen.

Gunwale upper edge or rail of ship's or boat's side.

Guy a rope attached to anything to steady a spar (usually) in a horizontal or inclined position. A "stay" is used to support a mast in its upright position.

Halyards ropes or tackles used for hoisting and lowering yards and sails.

Hands ship's crew.

Hardtack ship's bread or biscuit made with hard, dark flour so as to survive climatic changes.

Hatch any opening in a ship's deck; also applied to the covers that close the openings.

Hatch-combing hatch top.

Haul a term with many meanings other than "pull" or "heave". A vessel "hauls her wind" when she comes up close upon the wind. The wind "hauls" when it changes direction.

Hawse-hole the hole in the bows through which the cable or anchor chain runs.

Head lying "head to" means the vessel is directly facing towards some specified direction or point of the compass.

Head-sails general name given to all sails that set forward of the foremast, the jibs, and the fore stay-sail.

Headway forward motion.

Heave to to put a vessel in the position of lying to (i.e. stopped in the water). To heave to in bad weather means to lay a ship where she takes the seas most comfortably.

Heel as a verb, when the vessel lies over on one side; as a noun, the after (or rear) part of the keel.

Hold interior compartment of vessel, where cargo is stowed.

House cabin housing; any structure on deck.

Jib triangular sail set forward of the foremast.

Jib-boom (or "jibboom") spar run out from end of bowsprit; steadied at the side by jib-boom guys.

Jibe or "gybe"; when the wind is from the stern (i.e., the vessel is running before the wind) with the boom out wide to one side,

GLOSSARY 371

jibing involves swinging the boom all the way over to the other
side, even in a slight change of the vessel's general direction.

Kedge to kedge a vessel is to move it (or "warp" it) from one
place to another by means of a kedge—a light anchor.

Keel lowest longitudinal timber (or backbone) of a vessel, on
which the framework of the whole is built up.

Knot a measure of speed—that in which a nautical mile is
covered. "Ten knots" means a speed of ten nautical miles an
hour.

Lay to be paid "on lay" means according to the amount (of
seals) caught.

Lazarette compartment in stern or after part of ship's hold
used for stores. Originally the hospital area of the ship (from
Italian *lazzaretto*) where patients could be quarantined.

Lee the side of the ship opposite to that from which the wind
is blowing.

Lee-boat dingey farthest away from the direction in which
the wind is blowing.

Lee rail rail on the sheltered side of the ship, away from the
direction of the wind.

Lee-shore shore sheltered from the wind.

Leeward (pronounced "luard" or "looward") the side opposite to that from which the wind is blowing.

Leeway what a vessel loses by drifting leeward with the wind.

Leg run made on a single tack.

Lift as in jib-boom-lift, a rope or tackle, going to the mast
head, to support the boom.

Log-line line to which the patent-log is attached, as it is towed
behind the vessel.

Luff to put the helm so as to bring the bow of the ship nearer
to the direction of the wind.

Mainmast the second mast from the bow (in line, foremast,
mainmast, mizzen).

Mainsail large sail set on after part of mainmast.

Maintopmast see topmast.

Marlinspike an iron pin, sharpened at one end to make
splices, and with a hole at the other end for a lanyard (or rope
made fast to something to secure it).

Mast-head upper end, or top of a mast.

Mate officer under the master, or captain on merchant vessels.

Men forward the working men whose living quarters are in the forecastle, or forward section of the ship.

Mizzen aftermost mast on the ship.

Patent-log or "taffrail log". A device towed by the vessel for gauging speed and distance covered.

Pay off when a vessel's head swings off from the wind.

Pay out slack off on a cable and let it run out.

Peak upper and after corner of sail; the end of the gaff.

Poop stern of a ship; area behind the mizzen.

Port or larboard, left hand side of a vessel, looking forward.

Quarter a vessel has the wind on its quarter when it blows from behind in a line between that of the keel and the beam.

Quarter-deck part of upper deck, usually between the gangway and the mizzen.

Raffle rubbish.

Ratline or rattlins, lines running across the shrouds, horizontally, like the rungs of a ladder; used in climbing rigging.

Reef one of three or four strips across the bottom of a fore-and-aft sail that can be taken in or rolled up to reduce the sail's surface; as a verb, to take in or roll up the area of a sail exposed to the wind.

Reef-points short pieces of cord at lower edge of sail for tying up of a reef.

Reeve pass the end of a rope through a block or hole.

Rigging the general term for all the ropes of a ship.

Ring-bolt an eye-bolt, with a ring through the eye for fastening rope.

Rowlocks swivelling pins in the shape of jaws which hold oars in place when rowing.

Scuppers drains cut along the side of the deck for water to run away.

Scuttle a small hatchway. As a verb, deliberately to hole and sink a ship.

Sea-anchor or "drag anchor", floating frame on a cable to slow the progress of the vessel and allow it to sail more safely in heavy seas.

Send the motion of a vessel as it goes down the incline of a wave, opposite of "lift".

Sennit or "sinnet", braided cordage, in flat, round, or square form.

Shackle-bolt bolt that goes through a link in a chain.

Shears or "sheers"; hoisting apparatus or derrick formed by two or three poles standing upright lashed together near top and separated near bottom in the form of an inverted "V".

Sheave the wheel or roller in a block through which rope runs.

Sheer a sheer is a sudden deviation from course.

Sheet rope used in setting or controlling a sail.

Ship oars to bring oars out of the rowlocks and lay them inside the boat.

Shrouds set of strong ropes reaching from the mast-heads to the vessel's sides, to support the masts.

Signal book a manual containing standard signalling conventions and semaphore codes with lamps and flags.

Slop-chest store or compartment where seamen's spare gear is kept from which it can be sold to them as needed.

Sou'wester oilskin hat for heavy weather, projecting considerably more to the rear than the front.

Spar general term for masts, yards, booms, gaffs, etc.

Spill the sail is spilled of wind when it is tautened, so that its belly empties.

Splice to join two ropes together by interweaving their strands.

Spoke movements of the ship's steering wheel (whose spokes extend beyond the rim) by the helmsman are measured by spokes (e.g. the command "a spoke down" from the captain would mean the helmsman moving the wheel by that much).

Spritsail sail extended by a sprit, or light spar reaching diagonally from mast to upper outer corner of sail.

Stanchion upright posts of wood or iron, placed along the sides of a vessel, to support the bulwarks and rail. Any fixed, upright, support.

Starboard the right side of a vessel, looking forward.

State-room private sleeping apartment.

Stay large ropes used to support masts.

Stay-sail a triangular sail which hoists upon a stay.

Steerage that part of the between-decks forward of the cabins. Where passengers would go on a passenger ship; on the *Ghost* where the hunters are lodged—inferior to the captain and mates in their state-rooms, but superior to the crew in the forecastle.

Stem a piece of timber, reaching from the forward end of the keel, coming up to the bowsprit. The foremost timber or steel bar in a vessel.

Step to step a mast is to raise it, and to "unstep" a mast to lower it.

Stern the rear, or after end of the vessel.

Sticks masts.

Swab mop made of old rope, used for cleaning and drying decks.

Tack a word with a number of meanings on board ship. As a verb (intransitive) it means to come about so as to bring the bow of the boat through the direction of the wind involving a sharp change of course. The word is also used as a noun. A vessel may "change its tack", so as to come on to either a "starboard tack" or a "port tack".

Tackle see "block".

Tail-on a command (also "tally on") meaning "get hold of the rope and pull".

Throat-halyard halyard close to the mast Throat halyards are used to raise gaffs.

Thwart seat going across a boat, upon which the oarsman sits.

Topmast the second mast above the deck; next above the lower mast.

Topsails second sails above the deck.

Trade winds or "trades" winds blowing continually towards thermal equator within parallels thirty degrees north and south in the Atlantic and Pacific and deflected to the west by the rotation of the earth.

Trim to arrange yards, or sails, to suit the peculiar condition of the wind.

Truck a circular piece of wood, at the head of the highest mast. It has small holes for signal halyards to pass through.

Turn to take a turn is to pass a rope once round a pin, so shortening its length.

Unreeve see "Reeve".

Waist that part of the upper deck between the quarter-deck and the forecastle.

Watch-tackle a small tackle comprising a single and double block. Used for general lifting purposes around deck.

Watches divisions of time on board ship, and by extension the men who keep watch. There are seven watches a day, five of four hours and two two-hour watches called "dog watches".

Water-breakers kegs of water.

Weather-boat dingey closest to the direction from which the wind is blowing.

Weather-poop that part of the poop facing the wind.

Windjammer nautical slang for merchant sailing ship.

Windlass the machine used in merchant vessels to weigh (or raise) anchor. Humphrey Van Weyden uses a crank windlass to raise the masts of the wrecked *Ghost*.

Windward weather side, from which the wind is coming. Opposite to "leeward".

Wing and wing sail of a fore-and-aft vessel running before the wind with her booms on opposite sides.

Yard a spar crossing a mast horizontally from which a square sail is set.

Truck, a circular piece of wood, at the head of the highest mast. It has small holes for signal halyards to pass through.

Turn, to take a turn is to pass a rope once round a pin, so shortening its length.

Unreeve, see "Reeve."

Waist, that part of the upper deck between the quarter-deck and the forecastle.

Watch-tackle, a small tackle comprising a single and double block. Used for general lifting purposes around deck.

Watches, divisions of time on board ship, and by extension the men who keep watch. There are seven watches a day, five of four hours and two two-hour watches called "dog watches."

Water-breakers, kegs of water

Weather-beam, danger closest to the direction from which the wind is blowing.

Weather-poop, that part of the poop facing the wind.

Windjammer, nautical slang for merchant sailing ship.

Windlass, the machine used in merchant vessels to weigh (or raise) anchor. Humphrey Van Weyden uses a crank windlass to raise the masts of the wrecked Ghost.

Windward, weather side, from which the wind is coming. Opposite to "leeward."

Wing and wing, sail of a fore-and-aft vessel running before the wind with her booms on opposite sides.

Yard, a spar crossing a mast horizontally from which a square sail is set.

THE WORLD'S CLASSICS

A Select List

HANS ANDERSEN: Fairy Tales
Translated by L. W. Kingsland
Introduction by Naomi Lewis
Illustrated by Vilhelm Pedersen and Lorenz Frølich

ARTHUR J. ARBERRY (Transl.): The Koran

LUDOVICO ARIOSTO: Orlando Furioso
Translated by Guido Waldman

ARISTOTLE: The Nicomachean Ethics
Translated by David Ross

JANE AUSTEN: Emma
Edited by James Kinsley and David Lodge

Mansfield Park
Edited by James Kinsley and John Lucas

**Northanger Abbey, Lady Susan, The Watsons,
and Sanditon**
Edited by John Davie

HONORÉ DE BALZAC: Père Goriot
Translated and Edited by A. J. Krailsheimer

CHARLES BAUDELAIRE: The Flowers of Evil
Translated by James McGowan
Introduction by Jonathan Culler

WILLIAM BECKFORD: Vathek
Edited by Roger Lonsdale

R. D. BLACKMORE: Lorna Doone
Edited by Sally Shuttleworth

KEITH BOSLEY (Transl.): The Kalevala

ORIENTAL TALES
Edited by Robert L. Mack

OVID: Metamorphoses
Translated by A. D. Melville
Introduction and Notes by E. J. Kenney

FRANCESCO PETRARCH:
Selections from the Canzoniere and Other Works
Translated by Mark Musa

EDGAR ALLAN POE: Selected Tales
Edited by Julian Symons

JEAN RACINE: Britannicus, Phaedra, Athaliah
Translated by C. H. Sisson

ANN RADCLIFFE: The Italian
Edited by Frederick Garber

The Mysteries of Udolpho
Edited by Bonamy Dobrée

The Romance of the Forest
Edited by Chloe Chard

THE MARQUIS DE SADE:
The Misfortune of Virtue and Other Early Tales
Translated and Edited by David Coward

PAUL SALZMAN (Ed.):
An Anthology of Elizabethan Prose Fiction

OLIVE SCHREINER: The Story of an African Farm
Edited by Joseph Bristow

SIR WALTER SCOTT: The Heart of Midlothian
Edited by Claire Lamont

Waverley
Edited by Claire Lamont